Praise for Paul Almond's

D1129178

"This memoir provides a fascinating journey of a young artist as he achieves success in early Canadian television and film. A prolific writer ... Paul's *Inheritor* is a must read for all those interested in Canadian Culture."
– **Norman Jewison**

"Eons ago, I had a dear friend named Paul Almond. Our careers went in different paths and I lost touch with him. The Alford Saga reminds me of the beauty and the creative energy and the turmoil that existed in Canada during the time I spent in Canada with Paul. This is a book that should be read by everybody, not just hot-blooded Canadians."
– **William Shatner**

"Paul Almond is on my list of great Canadians."
– **Senator Colin Kenny**

"I've always admired Paul's productions, so I'm quite sure that dancers and balletomanes everywhere will enjoy reading Paul's personal take on the early years of our National Ballet when he was married to one of our principal dancers, Angela Leigh."
– **Karen Kain, CC, past Chair of the Canada Council, Artist Director of the National Ballet**

"The Alford Saga scores! If the author's careful and captivating treatment of our military and chaplaincy history can be the measure, then his recounting of the explosion of Canadian culture is certainly sure to satisfy."
– **Brigadier General Fletcher, Chaplain General of the Canadian Military**

"Paul Almond, one of the leading lights of Canadian film in the sixties and seventies, draws on his own experiences in this mesmerizing story of twists and turns, highs and lows, love and heartbreak."
– **Piers Handling, Executive Director of TIFF**

"I love it when you start reading a book and you just can't put it down... And this is just what happened to me. When I started reading *The Deserter*, the first book of the Alford Saga by Paul Almond, I fell under the spell: The writing, the story telling, the characters... everything is so captivating! And the best of it all? The emotions and the charm can be found in all the books of the series. Paul Almond is a words magician and I hope he'll continue to write and entertain us for a long time."
– **Carolle Brabant, Head of Telefilm Canada**

Also by Paul Almond

THE ALFORD SAGA

The Deserter: book one

The Survivor: book two

The Pioneer: book three

The Pilgram: book four

The Chaplain: book five

The Gunner: book six

The Hero: book seven

THE
INHERITOR

Paul Almond

Red Deer Press

Published in Canada by Red Deer Press, 195 Allstate Parkway, Markham,
Ontario L3R 4T8
Published in the United States by Red Deer Press, 311 Washington Street,
Brighton, Massachusetts 02135

10 9 8 7 6 5 4 3 2 1

Red Deer Press acknowledges with thanks the Canada Council for the Arts,
and the Ontario Arts Council for their support of our publishing program. We
acknowledge the financial support of the Government of Canada through the
Canada Book Fund (CBF) for our publishing activities.

Library and Archives Canada Cataloguing in Publication
Almond, Paul, 1931-, author
The inheritor / Paul Almond.
(The Alford saga ; bk. 8)
ISBN 978-0-88995-526-4 (pbk.)
Data available on file

Publisher Cataloging-in-Publication Data (U.S.)
ISBN 978-0-88995-526-4
Data available on file

Design by Daniel Choi
Cover image courtesy of ?
Frontispiece image courtesy of Getty images

Printed in Canada by Friesens Corporation

DEDICATION

How very sad, and yet tender, is the thought of so many richly enchanted people described herein who have now left this earth. I sometimes wonder why I, rather than they, have been chosen to tell their story. How I wish I could bring them all back!

I write that they may live again, if only in our imaginations.

One of the privileges accruing to us who remain is that we are able to recount such glorious times, so frequently forgotten. To these "hale dead and deathless" as Dylan Thomas said — their lives once flaming across Canada's cultural landscape — I dedicate this book.

PREAMBLE 1952-53

"Eric dead. Please come home," the telegram said. Eric, the father he had never known, a Gunner, a veteran from the Canadian Field Artillery, locked up for years in Ste. Anne de Bellevue Military Hospital with shell shock. So Paul Alford, having spent three years at Balliol College in the University of Oxford, a few months playing hockey in Italy, and another year in England, came back on a steamship to Montreal.

At the Old Homestead in Shigawake on the shores of Quebec's Gaspe Coast, he was pecking away with two fingers on the battered Underwood portable typewriter his mother had given him as a child, working at a novel, *The Farmer*. He'd sell it (he hoped) to support his one — some said hopeless — overwhelming desire to become a poet.

Arriving back in Montreal with no money or prospects, Paul had decided to return to the Old Homestead, built by his great-grandfather one hundred and fifty years before. His Uncle Earle, the farmer, had recently passed away; only his Aunts, Wyn and Lilian, remained. Lonely? Oh yes. The life at Balliol had been ever so full:

he had directed Ronald Duncan's *This Way to the Tomb*, and later gone on to act in productions of the University's two dramatic societies, the OUDS and directing, writing, becoming president of the O.U. Poetry Society, and then, miracle of miracles, being appointed editor of *The Isis*, the university magazine. Winters playing hockey with the combined Oxford and Cambridge team all over the Continent, summers travelling in Ireland and elsewhere with his friend Michael Ballantyne. But now, after those flurries of activity, the life of a lonely poet with two elderly aunts in Shigawake.

"Auntie Wyn," Paul asked, "why did Mummy never take me out to see my father? Every weekend she went by train."

Auntie Wyn, a distinguished nurse and thus a harsh disciplinarian as they were in those days, had taken care of several Governors-General. Now retired, with piercing black eyes, a craggy face, wispy white hair, and a big heart, she'd come back to live at the Old Homestead with her sister Lillian. She avoided his eyes. "Eric wasn't well, you see. We thought it best you didn't see him in that... state."

"But Dad and I had started to write each other, my last year in Balliol," Paul insisted. "His letters were quite sane and sensible."

"I don't know, dear." Auntie Wyn's eyes misted over. He had been the baby of the Alford family and her favourite brother. "He was a very handsome man, your father."

By his wood stove in the Old Homestead, Paul opened one of the letters he'd written to Harry Boyd from Ronald Duncan's farm in Devonshire. Harry, former Captain of Toronto Varsity, had encouraged Paul to play professional hockey in the chic Dolomite resort of Cortina d'Ampezzo. They had cemented their friendship then, for Harry had been a disciple of Northrop Frye, and both hockey players loved poetry.

"Welcombe sits on the border between Devon and Cornwall, on the coast of the Bristol Channel. To the south lies Bodmin Moor, the bleakest moor in England, and to the east Dartmoor... The land, the grass, the people, are tough, weathered like the hedges. The sun almost never shines, though it has today!

"We are twenty miles from the nearest railway station; Welcombe itself is just four or five farm houses; a combe is a local term for a valley (Wel-combe). One feels the power of nature here very strongly. So we are, as you can see, gloriously cut off. Thus I spend all my time reading and writing, and I'm determined to translate La Divina Commedia *for CBC to earn good money."*

Read no more, he told himself and sat back, warming his hands. Hard times in Devon, really. He'd been lucky to get a room in an old Victorian mansion run by two wispy spinsters, the Misses Oke. Having settled in, Paul had worked under Bailiff Bob, when at last the Duncan's invitation to dinner arrived, drawing him down to their low, thatch-roofed farmhouse, dated 1629. The playwright and poet Ronald Duncan, small, with thick black hair combed straight back, had a swarthy skin that suggested his Celtic ancestry.

Stepping down into the low ceilinged room with its peat fire, Paul caught a welcome sight — Antonia, wild brown hair, big, rawboned, in a man's loose farmer's trousers and a rough blue shirt. A real farm girl, he supposed, but soon he realized she was a great deal more.

She gathered her things and unwound her six feet. "Ronnie, I'll be back tomorrow afternoon with the letters typed." Ah, so she's his secretary? "It's going to be such an exciting festival this summer."

Paul pricked up his ears. "What festival?"

"The Taw and Torridge, of course. Ronnie started it last summer, with Queen Mary's son, Lord Harewood, and Ben Britten. Surely you read about it?"

"I'm afraid I was off touring with my company," Paul answered meekly. "I didn't have much time to look at the papers." The company he had formed, The Oxford and Cambridge Players, now the Elizabethan Theatre Company, was still touring England; they'd like to know of such a festival where they might play. "What's being planned for next summer?"

"Ronnie wants Martin Brown, the great director, to do productions of Tom Eliot's *The Cocktail Party* and his own play, *The Death of Satan.* We're trying to involve Oscar Lowenstein —"

"The London impresario?"

Antonia nodded. "We're founding a new company for the Royal Court Theatre, too. We're going to call it the English Stage Company."

She sure is taking credit for herself, thought Paul. "I'd love to be here for all that! Might I meet some of these guys when they come, Ronnie?"

Ronnie looked up and half smiled at the show of enthusiasm. Not many boisterous hockey players in North Devon, that's for sure.

"See you tomorrow, Ronnie." Antonia came by close, very close, as she went out, and Paul felt his heart flip flop. Was she aware of this as she passed?

Ronnie indicated a seat opposite him by the fire, and began to unsheathe Paul's few poems, but Rose Marie called them to dinner. Mrs. Duncan was more vivacious than he remembered from his earlier trips to discuss *This Way to the Tomb.* Her shock of wild blonde hair topped a lined, lived-in face with broad features and bold, protruding blue eyes sending out a strong "come-hither." Paul found her full of *double entendres,* quick wit and fun.

"I'd forgotten what he looked like," Rose Marie remarked as her husband ushered Paul to a chair. "Thank you, Ronnie, for bring-ing this delicious hockey-playing Canuck to the wilds of Devon."

Ronnie hardly acknowledged her; he sat at the head of the ta-ble and began to serve the vegetables and carve the mutton Rose Marie had roasted.

"Now," Ronnie began, "I told you about the warp and the woof of a poem." He handed the plate of meat, mashed potatoes, car-rots and turnips to Paul.

"I don't think so, Ronnie." Paul quickened. Just what he'd come for!

"A poem is like cloth: strands like words run in both directions, sometimes at cross purposes, but that's how they strengthen the verse, just as the threads run perpendicular in cloth, giving it strength."

Rose Marie leaned across and gave Paul's hand a squeeze. "You can't learn from a better master!" Her warm, glistening eyes fas-tened on him.

Ronnie paid no attention. "Sprung rhythm, that's the key. Like Hopkins, one of my masters."

Well, if I want to learn about writing, thought Paul, I've come to the right place. Farm work mornings on the windy moors, and af-ternoons by my little fire writing, with hope of catching that wild and wonderful Antonia.

Wonderful? All too soon, Paul found that Antonia had eyes only for Ronnie. No room for any newly-hatched Oxford graduate.

Then the inevitable moment arrived as the Misses Oke laid out his evening's dinner at one end of their long oak table. Old por-traits on the wall seemed to frown — did they know what was to come? "I'm sorry, Mr. Alford," one Miss Oke lit his lamp, "but in June the visitors start arriving. They did book a year ago. So I'm afraid you'll have to leave..."

Thrown out. Well, what now?

Look on the bright side... A new beginning, perhaps? But heavens, how long could a young poet keep pretending to himself?

In desperation, Paul wrote to his best friend Tom Espie in the London suburb of Croydon. Stocky, with a poor complexion, rigidly combed hair in the manner of the day, Tom had been a student playwright while studying PPE, too. So Paul set off on his motorbike, a dear old war surplus Royal Enfield (top speed 45 mph) and got to Tom's in Croydon around midnight, waking everyone, though Mr. and Mrs. Espie seemed glad to see him.

Monday afternoon, he and Tom went up to London to find it already crowded with people settling in for the night. The next day, June 2, 1953, was the Coronation of Queen Elizabeth. Edmund Hillary had just climbed Mount Everest the week before.

They got together with their best friend from Balliol, Stanley Myers, who – unlike Paul and Tom — had achieved first class honours in Modern Greats (Philosophy Politics and Economics, or PPE.) Stanley was a pianist and composer, having written many of the Oxford musical reviews. That night they repaired to Stanley's flat, a tiny servants' quarters on the sixth floor of a once-elegant town house in Mayfair, so convenient for the coming events. Unfortunately, Stanley's landlady had warned she would charge any guest five pounds for that pre-coronation night. As Paul had paid only three pounds fifteen for a full week's board and lodging in Devon, they found this outrageous. But still, they sneaked upstairs, tiptoed past the landlady's flat and fell asleep on the floor.

Stanley set his alarm for six and they sneaked out. The lift was noisy, so they started walking down the six flights of stairs. But they heard above them the lift gate clang shut. They raced down, round and round, and just escaped out the door and around the corner before the landlady appeared. They had made it!

At this hour, Oxford Street was already full of spectators, three deep. But Tom with amazing foresight had arranged a temp job teaching at some fly-by-night academy whose second floor premises overlooked the very route of the procession. From ten that morning, Tom, now a staff member, and his two guests sat snacking and drinking, and then went out onto the balcony with other teachers to watch the grand and colourful parade pass by.

After the procession had passed, they watched on TV as the Queen and the Duke of Edinburgh came out on the Buckingham Palace balcony. Paul was delighted to be a part of this momentous celebration, having arrived in London almost by accident. On they went to Shirley Catlin's (later Baroness Williams) flat in Whitehall Court on the embankment to enjoy the fireworks across the river, and listen to the Queen and Winston Churchill. At Oxford, Paul had been keen on Shirley and was hoping to meet her mother, the famous Vera Brittain, author of *Testament of Youth*, the definitive memoire on WWI, but she wasn't home.

After Stanley left, Tom and Paul continued drinking till they caught the last train back to Croydon. But falling dead asleep, they snored four stations past Croydon.

Off they got and faced a rather sobering ten-mile walk — at three in the morning.

The next day, hanging around the Mall, they got a curbside view of the Queen and the Duke passing on their first carriage ride around the city. Golly, thought Paul, he sure is good looking and the Queen, too, she's beautiful.

But he could not stay in Croydon indefinitely. So again, Paul had to face another move. Don't be downhearted — buoy yourself up! He thought. And fortunately, Tom had offered their tiny family cottage in North Wales: unfurnished, but it might do as a place to write.

Off Paul went again, motoring along the Conwy River with Great Orme on his right, through Betws-y-Coed, a lovely green valley, and stopped for an evening pint to get directions to the small market town centred on Conwy Castle, whose red crumbling walls enclosed grassy courtyards. He was directed to Tom's isolated cottage: a table, two chairs, a bed (thank heaven) and a stove that worked on gas from a tank behind. No electricity. Oh well, all a future poet needed, he told himself.

Not long afterwards, Tom Espie came up by train. Later, over a simple meal, Tom asked how it was all going.

"I keep spending what money I have on sending out stories. They need return postage, too, damn it."

"And they're being returned?"

Paul nodded meekly. "Every one. But off to Canada they go again: Montreal's *Weekend Magazine, Liberty, Family Herald, Macleans...* I even tried the top in America — *The Saturday Evening Post.*" He caught Tom's look. "Once you crack that, a real Niagara of cash will flow. I've written thirty-eight stories so far. Enough to keep me for ages."

"Once they sell?"

"Yeah, once they sell. But you, Tom, are you planning another play? You were the best playwright at Oxford."

Tom made a face. "Mum and Dad don't like the idea. They wanted their boy to earn a good weekly wage." He went on to confess: "Did I tell you? I got laid off in April. But Dad still insists I leave on the 8.10 every morning. I go to a library — well, where else? I do get a lot of reading done. Then back I come on the same commuter train in the evening. The neighbours never guess."

"Oh my heavens!" Paul shook his head. "At least my mum lets me do whatever I want. And that is... to be a poet."

Which is how Paul Alford ended up that winter at the Old Homestead on the Gaspe Coast, banging away on his trusty typewriter.

* * *

But now, Paul wondered, was this writing a novel in Shigawake actually getting him anywhere? Would anyone publish it? In fact, were there any Canadian publishers? All he knew was a branch office of the British Macmillans run by John Gray, the Ryerson Press, headed by Lorne Pierce, and McClelland & Stewart, now under a young Jack McClelland. That seemed to be all. So, why not put his learning into something profitable! Recitals? Yes, farmers — they loved poetry, didn't they? Packed halls, applause, money flowing...

Before he knew it, Paul was standing nervously behind the stage curtain in nearby Port Daniel's Community Hall. Having donned his dinner jacket, he adjusted his black tie. He had helped cousin Elton arrange the chairs beforehand and now imagined the applause when he would step out on stage. Hearing chairs scrape and the conversation drop, he realized his time had come.

He strode to the lectern in front of his audience. Oh dear, not even a dozen!

The first part seemed to go well enough. The novelty of it, perhaps? But when he began Robert Browning's dramatic monologue, *My Last Duchess*:

That's my last Duchess painted on the wall,
Looking as if she were alive. I call
That piece a wonder, now: Frà Pandolf's hands
Worked busily a day, and there she stands.
Will 't please you sit and look at her...

He hesitated. Several had left their seats and were moving to the exit. Cousin Elton, craggy, bold, tough as barbed wire, had been selling tickets. Quickly he pushed the table against the door and stood against it, arms crossed. No one dared challenge him. They returned to their seats.

Afterwards, Elton said reassuringly, "Me son, ya did terble!" Which meant, in Gaspesian, he'd been a hit. But thinking of the next few recitals he'd give to half a dozen people in large village halls, admissions not even covering his modest costs, Paul wished the whole process over.

Back in the Old Homestead, Aunt Lil popped in, braided hair crowning her head like a tiara, her face harrowed from harsh farm life. "Elton's mother brought this round. An article on you!"

Amazing! He'd actually made a Montreal newspaper! Eagerly, he sat down and read every word, his first mention in the big time.

Shigawake Boy Entertains Gaspesians with Recitals.

Paul Alford, a Shigawake boy and graduate of Oxford University, has returned to give recitals along the Gaspe coast. For farmers and others it is a return to Tennyson and Shakespeare — and The Shooting of Dan McGrew. *Wearing a dinner jacket for the classics, then changing into a black sweater and yellow scarf for* The Shooting, *Mr. Alford acts out some sections. Particularly appreciative was the mayor of Shigawake. He was in fact a relative of the young poet's.*

"You're a smart fellow," one farmer explained. "You will never have to work for a living." That day, the poet had rehearsed all morning, copied by hand six posters for the next town, visited the Mayor, had a quick lunch, carried chairs and benches from another hall for the evening performance, returned to his lodgings to work on a story, stoked the fire in the hall, dressed, gave the recital, and was about to return all the benches and chairs when the farmer spoke. "Maybe not with a pitchfork," the poet replied, "but I sure work, never doubt it."

Now, time to take up his next challenge: a big city.

PART ONE — ANGELA

Angela Leigh with Family

CHAPTER ONE
DEC 1953 — JAN 1954

In his tiny cottage near Montreal, Paul came out onto the landing, and stared down. There, on the heating grate in a teal blue overcoat stood a tall, blonde, blue-eyed, and quite striking woman with flawless features, who glanced up. They both froze. The moment stretched on and on, "like a patient etherised upon a table..."

She was among the dozen merrymakers downing rough cider and attacking bread, cold meats, lettuce and tomatoes arranged by his pretty friend, Gloria. An almost doll-like blonde, Gloria's slim figure gave no hint of the powerful determination that had gotten her a job sewing costumes for the nascent National Ballet of Canada. "Paul, they're coming to Her Majesty's Theatre? Why don't we give them a party after the performance?" Why not? Life out on Mont Saint-Hilaire was actually rather dull, with Gloria visiting only on weekends. She now worked at the CBC weekdays, where Paul had met her.

Twenty-five miles outside Montreal on the slopes of Mont Saint-

Hilaire, two miles from the nearest market, Paul's mother's cottage had once been a shed to store apples, the area being covered with orchards. Somewhat bowed rafters spanned the low ceiling between walls of rough boards painted a perky yellow. Against the low partition for the open kitchen sat an old sofa draped with Maori shawls from Australia and New Zealand, where his mother and Aunt Hilda had taught dancing. Just the sort of ivory tower a poet needed, Paul had told himself. Here, he could finish his novel and if need be, drive his Aunt's old Austin in to the CBC or even to Montreal theatres. But his short stories kept coming back, one after another.

Gloria knew that dancers were starving after performances. Of course, none had been warned that his cottage lay forty-five minutes away on a freezing winter night. Now, with music on the radio, their superb bodies lounged happily in front of the flaming fireplace having just danced *Coppelia* and *Dark of the Moon*. Myrna Aaron, an exotic-looking dancer with eyebrows that streaked across her brow like Cupid's arrows was holding forth on the sofa, keeping others in gales of laughter, when Colleen Kenney, a trim dancer with wild and abundant black hair intercepted Paul. "Lovely cottage you have."

"Was it a terrible drive getting here?"

Colleen hesitated. "Gloria didn't tell us it was so far out of town. But once we saw this..." She shrugged. "I think it's cozy." She eyed him.

"Oh, thanks." My, she's pretty! Paul thought. "Tomorrow can you sleep in, maybe?"

She shook her head. "We have class every morning."

"Philosophy and calculus?" Paul grinned, but thought, how stupid! He still longed to talk to the blonde on the heating grate.

Colleen finished her sandwich. "Every day we have to do class — and you know very well it's not reading and writing. First we do a barre, mostly leg exercises..."

"Then?"

"Then we move into the centre and do *enchaînments* — sequences of steps that the ballet mistress gives. Limbers up our bodies for the evening performance. Tomorrow I think class is late, eleven o'clock."

"So every day, you have to do a class, as well as perform?"

Colleen nodded. "Hour and a half, six days a week." She gave him a sweet smile. "And no alternate casts or understudies when we're performing. If you're dying, you go on anyway!"

Rigorous life, Paul thought. Terrific of Gloria to have gotten so many of them to come.

A scholarly-looking dancer came up, smoking a pipe. Colleen introduced him: "Grant Strate is now doing choreography. He's one of our character dancers." Grant began chatting to him as Colleen excused herself to fetch more food. Paul couldn't keep his eyes from straying to the stunning blonde who had by now moved off the heating grate to crouch by the fireplace. Another dancer, he noticed, had made her a sandwich. As she began to eat, she had the bearing of someone a little older, perhaps more experienced.

"Angela Leigh, from England," Grant explained. "One of our principal dancers."

"She's the lead?"

"No, Lois Smith and Irene Apiné, they're the ballerinas who lead the company. Then comes principal dancers, soloists, then corps de ballet. I'm corps." Grant smiled and relit his pipe.

"But Colleen said you'd begun choreographing?"

"We'll see."

As soon as he could, Paul went over to Angela by her fire. "Still cold?"

"I'm just getting used to your Canadian winters."

"So why on earth come?"

"I got carried away by a uniform. My ex-husband, he was in the Royal Canadian Air Force, so handsome then. He's from Orillia, not far from Toronto." She paused. "Very dashing back in the Old Country. But in Orillia, I found that a wife's place is in the home..."

"You are still dancing..."

She shrugged. "I couldn't give it up. So we separated."

"Oh?" Paul absorbed that, and then went on, "My mother used to be a dancer. A woman should have her own career. At Oxford, none of the girls I've known ever intended to be relegated to a kitchen. In fact, I doubt any even knew how to cook!"

Angela smiled. "So you were at Oxford?"

"I guess so. But I sure didn't learn anything. PPE. You know, those female students did nothing to catch a man — even a comb might have helped!" She smiled. "Every one of them so focussed on brain work..." Now, with all these gorgeous creatures sur-rounding him, accomplished, attractive, pursuing careers that involved bodies, not minds, Paul felt on top of the world.

"So what do you do now?" Angela asked.

"I'm a writer." Then Paul realized he had absolutely no basis for saying that. "Well, I'm trying," he added. "In fact, I'm getting no-where." An admission he was not used to making. But somehow, he knew Angela's sharp mind would puncture any bravado. His innate confidence had momentarily deserted him.

"You'll have to come and watch us dance," she said. "Saturday matinee, I'm taking over Black Swan in Swan Lake because Lois Smith is dancing the role that night."

"I'd love to!" Oh yes, would he not! If his mother got them tick-ets, he and Gloria would go. But he didn't say that — his modesty didn't go quite that far.

* * *

Sunday, Paul drove Angela Leigh out in his Aunt's little Austin. Imagine! Taking a principal dancer of Canada's National Ballet for Sunday lunch at his cottage and a walk on the slopes of Mont Saint-Hilaire.

"Wonderful performance at yesterday's matinee, Angela. Mother couldn't stop talking about it. She and Auntie Hilda made Gloria and me a nice little dinner afterwards at her apartment on Chomedey Street near the Forum."

"So where is Gloria this afternoon?"

Paul turned to glance at her. She was watching the snow-covered farms of Mont St. Bruno on their way to Beloeil, and thence to Mont Saint-Hilaire. "Friends invited her for skiing up in the Laurentians, so she left early. But she loved your performance."

"Your mother mentioned that she had been a dancer, but I had no idea that she ran her own school in Australia. She's even danced with the great Pavlova. She gave me useful tips."

Paul glowed with delight. He had been mesmerized at the matinee. So proud of his new friend! And of her extraordinary physique, trained over the years to be effortlessly graceful. "You're a terrific actress in your dancing, Angela. We were all impressed."

"Thanks, old bean." She flashed a smile.

"We didn't have enough time to talk at the party," Paul said. "Grant told me you'd trained at Sadler's Wells?

"Under Ninette de Valois, yes. When I came here with Buzz, my husband, I even opened a small school of dancing in Orillia, where we lived. But I didn't like teaching."

"You're older than most of the corps?" Paul asked

She looked quickly at him. "Yes. Does it matter?"

"No, of course not. And you've been married. So much more mature than the others. I find that rather compelling."

Angela said nothing.

"I have some beans soaking, so we can whip up a bit of a chili. I bought some ground beef." He didn't say that it was the cheapest meat he could find.

"I meant to ask you last night," Angela persisted, "why do I hear a bit of an English accent? Surely it's not just Oxford. Your British mother, perhaps? Or were you over there for a longer time?"

"Well, I was at Balliol for three years. Then I stayed in Europe. I played professional hockey." Why had he said that, dummy? Hoping to impress her? But he noticed her eyes flash with momentary admiration. "And then, well, I worked on a farm and things..."

"Oxford scholar AND athlete?" She seemed duly impressed.

"Hardly. But anyway, when my father passed on, Mother wanted me home. I'm just as glad. So many opportunities here. Though when I arrived, I found no professional theatre in Montreal, hardly much of anything, actually." What could he add? That he wanted to get work but found none? That he wanted to be a poet, a writer, but every story rejected? On he went, regardless: "I've heard that last July a pretty good theatre opened in Stratford, Ontario, with *Richard III* and *All's Well That Ends Well*."

"Oh yes, Tony Guthrie started it — he's a terrific director. Scottish."

Paul nodded. "Yes, I've seen his productions in the West End. I used to go down to London every couple of weeks. I loved the Sadler's Wells, and I went to the Edinburgh Festival every year and watched ballets there." Why hadn't he added that he'd brought his own theatre company there himself, twice? For some reason, he wasn't able to blow his own horn in her presence.

She looked at him. "An accomplished young man!"

Paul shrugged. "No, no... I just keep trying."

They arrived at the little cottage and Angela, cold as usual, headed for the fireplace, which Paul hastily lit. He poured them both a sherry, then went round into the kitchen. Angela came beside. "Let me help."

"Help? You're a principal dancer."

"Paul! I'm also a woman... I hope."

He let that sit. As Uncle Earle would say: "Some woman, fer shore!"

They prepared a simple lunch and, with Paul's prodding, Angela talked more about herself. "I was born, in Kampala, Uganda, where my father was a British bank manager."

"Ah, that's why you're always cold!"

"I was lucky in my childhood, with black nurses and cooks. Mother loved being a white settler's wife. But when I was six, back we came to England."

"And you always wanted to dance?"

"Oh yes. We had a water tower at the foot of the garden, and I believed that fairies lived up there. One used to come down to our garden and lead me in dance steps . 'Hightop' I called her. We'd dance all afternoon together, me on the tips of my toes trying to get up into the sky with Hightop."

"Have you been back since?"

"Oh no. But I'd love to one day..." If he got going somehow, he'd take her. That would be a coup!

They sat opposite each other at the rustic table with its two benches. Paul was growing more and more attracted to this rather imperious, but at the same time curiously vulnerable, British dancer with her tiny hands, tall sapling-like body, magnificent legs he hadn't failed to notice, and her dry wit.

For his part, he told her about the poets he'd known, and eventually the poetry he was writing, and his beloved Shigawake where he'd just been giving recitals, careful of course, not to be too specific about the numbers attending.

"And now you're here in Montreal?" she asked. "To stay?"

"Well, maybe, but there doesn't seem to be a lot of work." That's putting it mildly, he thought. "I'm wondering about New York.

From what I've heard, that's where I might have a chance."

"No, Toronto first!" Angela announced. "We need new young writers and creators like you."

Paul looked up.

"Ten hours by bus. Not expensive." Was that the hint of an invitation?

He suggested a walk on the mountain. "It's not too cold today."

Angela agreed, and they both set off through the orchard on a track Paul had beaten down during his daily forays into wolf country — local papers spoke of a wolf pack down from the north. With lots of small animals, even a muskrat or two in the lake, they seemed to be staying. But he didn't mention that.

The whole mountain had been bought by Brig. Hamilton Gault, founder of the Princess Patricia's Light Infantry Regiment. He had equipped his regiment with uniforms and rifles for WWI, when the Canadian Armed Forces were developing as a separate entity from the British. Paul had first gone with his mother to tea with Mrs. Gault, a striking white-haired lady who loved poetry. Hammy, as he was known, was an old school gentleman, tremendously polite, hale and hearty despite having lost a leg in the war. Paul often dropped in, and they'd discuss the most famous French-Canadian artist, Ozias Leduc, who lived by the Richelieu River in Saint Hilaire, as did his renowned pupil, Paul-Emile Borduas. But much as Paul wanted to impress Hammy with this new ballet friend, he thought it a bit early to do that.

"This mountain is an untouched haven: they've found fauna from the ice age," Paul began, as they entered the mountain road between stone pillars. "I've seen lots of tracks here, snowshoe hares, fox and even porcupine. I saw one the other day."

Angela seemed suitably impressed. "Go on..."

"Well, it emerged from a melting ice sheet some twelve thousand or more years ago. It was once an island in the Champlain

Sea. This road I live on was built around 1770."

"Do you have nice neighbours?"

Paul assented. "Back there across the orchard, the Guerins live in an old stone house, once the seigneurial mill of Hertel de Rouville. Two lovely daughters."

Angela glanced sharply at him, and he realized he'd forgotten himself. Did that mean she was getting interested?

During the walk, which ended at the mountain lake in front of the Gault house, they talked on and on, becoming closer.

Finally, back to warm themselves by the fire, Paul realized he had to take Angela back to a Montreal reception before the troupe left on tour: eighteen cities and sixty-four performances, all over the United States and Canada. Angela made him promise to write. He quickly agreed. Was he actually falling in love?

* * *

On with the writing. On with the dreaming. On with forays into Montreal to meet the important radio producer Rupert Caplan, who had given occasional roles to Paul's mother.

Before too long, he heard that Guthrie's new Stratford Theatre begun by Tom Patterson was holding auditions. Full of excitement, Paul decided to go. Perhaps he'd play Hamlet, or some other major role — the whole summer taken care of! On weekends he could come from Stratford to see Angela in Toronto. Yes, a great idea.

He made his way to the suite in the Queen Elizabeth Hotel — only to find it packed with a dozen other would-be actors, sprawled about.

When Guthrie's assistant arrived, everyone quickened. From his clipboard, he read out their names and went around, making a pretense, Paul saw, of talking to each one. Nonetheless, Paul still did his best, outlining the many things he had done at Oxford. But the assistant spent most of his time talking to another young actor Paul had known at McGill: Bill Shatner. In fact, he spent more time on Bill than on everyone else. When it was over, Paul headed in his little Austin back to the lonely cottage, reflecting that if they chose anyone, it would not be him. It would be William Shatner.

And choose William they did.

CHAPTER TWO
SPRING SUMMER 1954

The phone call announced: "W.H. Auden arrives tonight." The McGill University student went on to say, "We've been delegated to pick him up after breakfast tomorrow morning and we don't know what to do. Peter Scott claims you knew him. Do you? If so, shall we bring him out to your cottage?"

"Splendid idea," Paul had replied. "I do, and you can."

Late the next morning, the great poet arrived in a car with Peter Dale Scott and Ian Clark, an editor of Forge, McGill's literary magazine that had published both Peter and Paul.

"Awfully good of you to receive us!" Wystan Hugh Auden shook Paul's hand, and they all took off their coats and got closer to the fireplace. The group was animated, for the great poet was a major celebrity and no one had met him before, except Paul. The poet's face was exactly as he remembered it from Balliol: battered and lined, wise, and genuinely warm. Paul asked him about John Bryson, the English tutor at Balliol who had introduced them.

"We corresponded about six weeks ago, and he seems very

well, thank you."

Paul dished out soup he'd made the previous night, with bread, butter and a block of cheese. He apologized: all he had was rough cider, and they shared a glass.

"Made locally?" Auden asked. "And sold at your Liquor Commission?"

"Oh no, we get this illegally just up the road at M. Auclair's. If you'd like to see his basement, it's packed with barrels; we can go after lunch."

The poet agreed and they trooped up the gentle slope to the corner where M. Auclair had his cellar of large round casks burping rhythmically like noisy frogs.

What a time they had of it! M. Auclair spoke no English, so Paul explained in French who their distinguished visitor was, and how much he loved the cider. They tasted various stocks of the aging powerful liquid and, by the time they chose which to buy, they were soused. Paul bought a gallon and Auden graciously bought another, two dollars and fifty cents each.

Back at the cottage they continued drinking, discussing the poetry scene in England.

"And what's happening with my old friend, John Lehmann?" Paul asked about the premier literary publisher in all England.

"He's just begun his autobiography, *Whispering Gallery*," Auden told them. "Should prove an interesting read."

In the midst of the revelry, Wystan turned to Paul. "You and Peter must take my villa on Ischia. I've been looking for a couple of writers to rent it for the summer. Ten dollars a month, complete with maid service."

Paul and Peter looked at each other. The chance of a lifetime!.

They thanked the great man profusely, and promised to get back to him in the morning at his hotel before he left. But in the end Peter said no, claiming he was not yet a good enough poet to throw up working on his Ph.D. at McGill. Paul had no such qualms, never one to allow verdicts on his writing to ruin his plans. But the cost of a flight to Italy made it impossible. Anyway, the invitation had been made and was often recalled in future conversations.

The next day, Gloria called. "I don't know what you fellows did with your guest yesterday, but Auden could hardly stand at the lectern. His reading was superb, but I watched him sway, waiting for him to topple over at any minute."

"Oh dear," replied Paul. "I did send him back with a fair amount of cider... But Gloria, you know, Peter told me his father has invited us to his weekly salon tomorrow night. Can you make it?"

"Of course!" Peter's father, F.R., was the son of the famous chaplain Frederick George Scott, whose book *The Great War as I Knew It* had been widely read. Frank would become justly known as the great constitutional lawyer who represented Frank Roncarelli, a wealthy owner of Quaff's Café and a practising Jehovah's Witness, who kept bailing out other Witnesses whom Duplessis persecuted. The Premier of Quebec was an ardent, though politically convenient, Catholic. So he'd had Roncarelli's liquor licence revoked — in perpetuity. Frank would take the case all the way to the Supreme Court of Canada and in 1958 would win, as he would on five other occasions. Duplessis died in 1959 shortly after the verdict.

But Frank really preferred to be known as a poet; he would gather salons of young poetesses at his home at 451 Clarke Avenue, just at the bottom of the steep hill. He gracefully introduced Paul and Gloria when they arrived. Aside from having had Auden as a guest, Paul had published four poems in Canada's foremost literary journal, *Northern Review*, edited by John Sutherland.

"This is Irving Layton..." Frank began. "And Louis Dudek." — an important local poet, teaching at McGill. And on Frank went:

Phyllis Webb, more Paul's age, and British-born P.K. Page, as well as many younger poetesses.

Wine flowed as they sat around at the feet of Frank, who took the great armchair. Irving sat on another and on a third, Louis, as befitting their pecking order. A young Leonard Cohen also turned up a few times later on. The words that fell from published poets' lips were ingested as would openmouthed chicks accept delicious worms. Paul became somewhat of a regular but, as his relationship with Gloria disintegrated, she came less and less.

On one occasion, Paul found himself in intense discussion with an attractive, round-faced psychologist Stephanie Zuperko, an expert in the Rorschach ink-blots, a means of testing patients. She offered Paul a test for free. Overhearing her make that offer, several other poets laughed. "She's done all of us."

"No kidding? Why, Stephanie?" Paul asked.

"I'm doing a paper on the M factor, which tests the imagination. I ask poets, artists, writers; I don't charge them for the testing and they don't charge me for being my subjects. It's all confidential, of course. But I'm hoping to find parallels that will contrast them with the businesspeople I test."

Paul invited her to Apple Barrel, where she dutifully gave him a Rorschach test. All he got out of her was that he had rather too vivid an imagination. After an extended tea and then dinner, Stephanie actually went so far as to suggest he come to New York, where she had an apartment. Recently separated, she was making a go as a psychiatrist south of the border.

Well, it didn't take Paul long to solicit a bus ticket from his mother and head south. At last, he would make a name for himself in the most important theatre city in America.

* * *

Paul hardly slept that first night on Stephanie's uncomfortable sofa, his second time in New York. He had visited briefly with Zeke Cleveland in 1949, when they drove across the country to find Christopher Isherwood, a top British writer who had come before the war to live in America. That time, he had stayed at the Zete house at New York University. But here he was, on West 22<u>nd</u> Street in Chelsea, and ready to take on the world. After all, an Oxford acquaintance, Roger Bannister, had just broken the four minute mile in May, why wouldn't Paul conquer the Great White Way?

The first play they went to see the next evening was an all-black version *Of Mice and Men,* presented off-Broadway in cabaret style. Nothing in England compared, he realized, so theatre here must be thriving. Next, the two of them went off to see Chekhov's *The Seagull* at the Phoenix Theatre, Stephanie again paying for the tickets. As a psycho-diagnostician, she earned good money, and Paul felt quite at ease with this, for was he not a poet? — and as such he expected to be looked after. He'd soon make a go of it, no doubt. And before too long was moved from the sofa to Stephanie's more comfortable double bed.

The next morning at breakfast, Stephanie went to a bookshelf and handed him a copy of Reich's *The Function of the Orgasm.*

Oh dear!

She waxed on about Wilhelm Reich and his "orgone energy accumulator" in which patients sat and absorbed the energy circling the earth being thrust into their bodies. But now, what was being expected of him? The more he looked into Reich's book, the more nervous he became. What on earth would they do that night?

Stephanie, whose parents hailed from a central European country, was slightly plump with a round cheerful face and motherly eyes. As part of her research, she soon planned to visit

Ezra Pound, incarcerated in Queen Elizabeth Hospital for his anti-American broadcasts during WWII.

"Ezra Pound! But he's the most famous poet in America!"

"Apart from Dylan Thomas," Stephanie prompted, "when he's here on tour."

"May I come?"

"Of course." She looked down. "If you're... still here."

Oh-oh. What was she saying? More pressure. Should he read that book again? Focus? Goodness! Paul was growing more nervous by the minute. But he'd do almost anything to meet the author of *The Cantos*, and the poet Eliot named in *The Waste Land* as *"il miglior fabbro"*, the better tailor.

That afternoon an important interview helped divert his mind. Norris Houghton ran the Phoenix Theater, a leading off-Broadway group he had founded with Edward Hamilton. Excited at getting an impromptu meeting, Paul hurried off to have tea with "Norrie" and used every trick he'd learned in the hallowed halls of Oxford to make sure they hit it off.

But the night ahead loomed larger and larger. How could he perform up to the exacting standards of Prof. Reich? For the first time in his life, he dreaded what might come. He drank rather too much wine at dinner and, as feared, the night was not a success.

But she forgave him and they agreed that he would try harder next time.

Another diversion ahead, thank heaven! He went to see the director of the well-known Players Theater. The lead actor in their next play had left for three weeks to do television in Denmark. Paul read for the part and delivered a couple of Shakespeare monologues he knew by heart, and lo! They offered him the lead. His first New York job! He was so excited that he managed a slightly better night with Stephanie.

Then off again to meet a businessman who wanted to mount

Romeo and Juliet at the Cherry Lane Theater later in the autumn. Paul had developed an extensive knowledge of Shakespeare and the Elizabethan theatre, as well as Jacobean tragedies. At Oxford, most of the twenty-nine colleges put on plays and usually chose the most récherché of historical dramas. What American university could mount so many different classics every year? And Paul had made sure to see even more plays on his frequent forays to London and the Edinburgh Festival. So having learned during Oxford tutorials how to use — when knowledge failed (as it usually did) — a good supply of bullshit, he ended up being chosen as director.

His fortunes gradually improved, as did nights with Stephanie. He met the directors of the prestigious Theatre Guild, and was offered small upstate engagements with a well-known actress at the Westport Repertory Theater in Connecticut, and at four different schools, always unpaid, of course.

Oddly enough, in spite of these improvements, Stephanie gave him to understand that his summer idyll could not last for ever. But find an apartment in New York, with off-Broadway rehearsal rates of five dollars a week? Twenty-five during the play's run? No hope. So no acting with the Players Theater. No visit to Ezra Pound. No more New York.

Thrown out again!

However, the memories of the lithe and beautiful Angela Leigh, now back from tour, kept haunting him. Get to Angela, oh yes, but how? With no money for bus fare? Hitch-hike? Rob a bank? Luckily at an audition, another actor told him that Lynn Riggs, a playwright, was in hospital with stomach cancer and needed transfusions. He was paying fifteen dollars a pint.

Paul had a horror of blood. But Toronto was his only option now. Eyes clenched, teeth gritted, off he went to be bled for bus fare.

At a barely functional donor clinic, he was ordered into an unoccupied room. A nurse came in with a needle — which immediately threw Paul into a fit. Hold yourself steady, he demanded of his quaking body. As he lay on the unadorned bed, she plunged the needle into his arm. He managed to stifle the wild cry that threatened to wake the entire clinic. Finally, when he did open his eyes, Paul saw that she had gone. But the tube in his arm now led to a bottle on the floor beside him.

What if she forgot to come back? My blood, he gasped, it will just keep running into the bottle. And then, overflow... They'll find a white, bloodless corpse, my life spread all over the linoleum.

Wild images sprang into his mind — how would they tell his mother? What about Angela? Aah, but the headlines would be superb:

Canadian Poet of Great Promise Expires
while giving life's blood
to save a playwright

CHAPTER THREE
AUG 1954

Late in the evening after Paul's bus arrived in Toronto, he carried his suitcase over to Bathurst Street to catch a streetcar up the hill, better and shorter, he thought, than by the brand new subway on Yonge Street. Angela was expecting him. He'd given blood, said goodbye to dear Stephanie, and paid the bus fare. And now, this new challenge, a city he did not know: Toronto.

As Paul headed toward Vaughan Road, he thought back to a conversation that wonderful Sunday afternoon on the mountain behind Apple Barrel. He had noticed that Angela seemed tense. Finally, she had broached the subject: "I told you I was married, didn't I?"

"Oh yes, to an airman who was farming. But now you said he's moving into real estate?"

"Yes, but what I didn't tell you..." She stared ahead, and then went on, "is we have a daughter." She turned anxiously.

"A daughter! How old? Does she live with you?"

"Of course. When we separated, Buzz moved out and left us the apartment — which he still pays for. Stephanie has her own bed-room. She's five now and going to nursery school."

Angela had looked at him, anxiously. Was she nervous about having a child? No, of course not; they'd only just met. But for Paul, this relationship had become pretty intense. Could it be that way for her, too? Or was she, as a principal dancer, simply out of his league?

"Gosh," he said, "that's terrific. I'd love to see her sometime. Will she want to be a dancer, too?"

"I hope not. It's a pretty hard life, old bean."

"How many in the company now?"

"About twenty-nine. We know each other so well — being to-gether for months at a time. This last winter after I left, we played eighteen cities, nineteen including Toronto, travelling every day by bus, out to Victoria, B.C., and through the United States: end-less bus rides, hard classes, then a performance, six days a week." Paul shook his head. Exhausting, he thought.

"What did you do with Stephanie?"

"She stays with her grandmother in Orillia. The family life is so good for her." She paused. "But once she starts school, I'll have to find some other arrangement."

Paul crossed St. Clair Avenue and continued up Vaughan Road. The night was warm and, in his Harris Tweed jacket and raincoat, he was hot and sweaty. He found number 163, the dry cleaner above which Angela lived, and rang the bell.

Through the glass door, he watched a blonde, slender dancer in a pale jacket and loose slacks swoop down and open the door. She gave him a rather intense kiss on his lips.

"Well, I'm sure glad to be here at last, Angela!" Paul followed her up, along a narrow hallway, past her bedroom into the living room, where he took off his coat and loosened his tie.

"How was the trip?"

"I'm not really a fan of bus travel," he said. "I prefer trains, but they're so expensive." She offered him a glass of wine, and he told her how he'd literally given his blood to buy the ticket. But as soon as the story came out, he wondered if he'd revealed rather too much about his financial state. "So Angela, where is this daughter of yours?"

She led him back down the corridor, opened Stephanie's door and in they went. Paul studied the sleeping face, the blonde braided hair, the tiny mouth; she looked to him like a pretty doll. He took Angela's hand and squeezed; then they tiptoed out.

"I have a babysitter every morning; she stays till lunch so that after the morning class I can get my errands done. But now that you're here, you can help carry the groceries up from the corner store." She smiled.

Over more wine, they dwelt on their backgrounds, Paul's at Oxford and playing on the Oxford and Cambridge hockey team, mainly in Germany and Austria, but also against the *Racing Club de Paris.* "We used to sing songs and party with *Glühwein*, you know, hot mulled wine... But I want to know about you, Angela. How did you get started?"

"When we moved from East Africa to London, I went right on to study with Lydia Kyasht." Paul frowned. "She danced with the Bolshoi and the Diaghilev, what a divine teacher! Encouraging, warm, just a wonderful woman. I remember the audition I did for her — in a studio with balconies at either end. I had always danced on my toes. After my little dance, she told mother, 'We'll have to take her off her toes!'

"After a while she started giving me extra classes: I must have had something... Another great inspiration was Margot Fonteyn, who used to take Saturday classes with Kyasht." Paul's eyes widened. "She was about 16 at the time and I will always remember standing behind her at the barre."

"How exciting!"

"Yes. But first, my parents had sent me to boarding school in southern England. That lasted until I was 14." Paul was shocked. A new country, and then off to a strange school. But that's how it was done in those days. "When I got back to London, I auditioned at Sadler's Wells, the present Royal Ballet School. We had to carry gas masks to classes because we often had to hide in air raid shelters. Nikolai Sergeyev, Vera Volkova, and sometimes even Ninette de Valois, would give classes — between bombs."

Paul drank it all in. His first contact with a ballet dancer — and star, it seemed. "At the school, the Sadler's Wells company would come in and rehearse, dancers like June Brae, Michael Soames, Robert Helpmann, very exciting!"

"I bet! But how did you get to our National Ballet?"

Angela shrugged. "Buzz hoped I'd be the little wife with an apron! I still wanted to dance but," she paused, "nothing much was doing. When we moved to Orillia, I started a ballet school. And another in Barrie. Then in 1949, Stephanie was born."

Paul nodded. Such a sweet little thing, sound asleep next door.

"In 1951, Celia Franca, whom I knew of in England, had come over and was teaching Sundays at Boris Volkoff's studio. So I drove down from Orillia. I even remember at the end of my first class going up and saying, 'I would like to join your company, Celia.' I don't think she was quite ready for that one!"

"Damn good, Angela."

"Yes, but I hadn't danced for several years! She did accept me, though."

"Good for you!"

"So as soon as the National Ballet Company was formed in September, I got Buzz to move here to Toronto."

"You were in it from the beginning?"

Angela leaned back against the sofa, sipping her wine. "I remember that first public performance, a really rainy night, November 12th, three years ago, 1951, the Eaton Auditorium. We started out, just a small bunch of us: Myrna Aaron, whom I room with on tour, Judie Colpman, Colleen you've met, Nat Butko, Grant and Earl (Kraul) and of course David and Lois. Two dozen, I think. We did *Les Sylphides*, a few *pas de deux* and Borodin's *Polovtsian Dances*."

"Lois Smith, the ballerina, she's married to her partner, David Adams, isn't she?"

Angela nodded; they both led the Company. But, Paul thought, Angela's still a principal dancer. Finally, she made him a bed on the sofa and he fell asleep, feeling at peace and yes, even at home.

* * *

Within a few days Angela brought news from the St. Lawrence Hall, where they took class and rehearsed, that a businessman connected with the Ballet Guild had offered a few dancers a job for three weeks. "I asked him if I could bring a friend, and he said yes."

Paul was delighted. Money at last! He was further buoyed up by the news that one of his stories, *A Sheaf of Wheat*, had been accepted by *The Family Herald and Weekly Star*, only a farm newspaper, but at last the big start to his surely bountiful career.

On the appointed day, he and Angela set off by streetcar down Bathurst to sell programs for the Coronation Robes of Queen Elizabeth I at the Ex, the Canadian National Exhibition, on a large fairground near Lake Ontario.

"You'll be selling programs at the door," their employer had told them, "but between ourselves, the Ex is not allowed to charge. So try and make it appear that they gotta buy a program to get in."

Rather hard to swallow, Paul thought, and traded looks with Angela. But what choice did they have? They needed the money. Angela and the company lived all summer off Unemployment Insurance, supplemented in Angela's case by child support from her husband. But Paul was still penniless. "We'll do our best, sir."

"Good. Because you'll be working on commission. No sales, no money! But several hundred should turn up daily, making you a small fortune. And if you do, I will, too. So let's just hope for the best."

But the best did not always happen, as Paul had been discovering — over and over again! What with the other CNE exhibits: the fat lady, the shooting galleries, the tattooed man, the jugglers, the food booths, not too many visitors wanted to see the Royal Robes. And those that did were smart enough to ask, "Do we *have* to buy a program?"

And the answer had to be, "Well no, but you can't really get the full benefit without one." Most of the visitors opted for less benefit.

At the end of the first day, Paul and Angela sat glumly as the streetcar rumbled its way up towards St Clair. "Look, it's a start," Paul said brightly. But his principal dancer did not reply.

Later, they sat down to eat dinner with Stephanie, so well behaved, Paul thought, but perhaps a bit withdrawn. She handled her knife and fork beautifully for her age, and chatted happily about her day. When she had gone to bed, Angela asked if she would like Paul to read her a story. "Is he staying here again?" Stephanie asked.

"Yes darling, he sleeps on the sofa while he looks for an apartment. He's just new in Toronto. We're lucky to have him as a guest for a few days."

"No, I want *you* to read to me, Mummy," Stephanie said firmly. That "sweet little girl" was not overly pleased with this interloper, Paul noted. Her mother was away too much. What did that presage?

* * *

They sold so few programs that the job soon ended. But Paul had managed to get an interview as an actor with a new professional theatre, the Crest, up on Mount Pleasant Road. The recent Royal Commission on National Development in the Arts, Letters and Sciences (chaired by Vincent Massey), which examined Canada's cultural sovereignty, had recommended the creation of cultural institutions such as the National Library of Canada, the Canada Council and other grant-giving government agencies. Paul wondered if that had given impetus to the Crest.

That night at dinner he told Angela about it. "It's run by the Davis Brothers, Murray and Donald; I met Donald, actually. His sister, Barbara Chilcott, is involved, but she's just back from England where she'd been appearing on stage. Donald was awfully nice, and even liked what I told him about my background."

"They started the Straw Hat Players, didn't they?"

"Yes, 1947 in Muskoka, Donald told me. Finally, they got this lease on the Crest, which used to be a vaudeville house and then a movie theatre. They have to build their sets out in the east end, and make their costumes in a store they rented just south of the theatre. A new play every two weeks. Imagine! Last January they opened with *Richard of Bordeaux*."

"After the tour last spring," Angela told him, "I went with a friend to see *Haste to the Wedding,* by Tyrone Guthrie. Patrick Macnee was in it, I remember, and your friend Donald Davis. I think Barbara Chilcott, too."

"They plan on presenting Graham Greene's *The Living Room*. Nothing for me in that, but afterwards, they're doing *Charlie's*

Aunt and maybe I could land something there. Later, they're doing Eliot's *Confidential Clerk,* all terrific plays, Angela."

"Where do they get their money?"

"Some must be their own," Paul surmised. "And they raise it. Their family's in leather tanning, believe it or not. You know, tanning leather has been around since the dawn of mankind! Just think, cavemen, they wore skins, in other words, leather. Early civilizations all dressed in leather. It's a big business, even today. Donald told me they had the biggest tanning factory in all Ontario."

"Sounds as if he liked you, Paul." Angela was eating hungrily.

"Donald's acted in England," Paul went on. "He worked with Peter Potter over there, after he did Eliot's *Cocktail Party* here at the Straw Hat. He's also appeared with the Glasgow Citizens."

"So Murray and Donald are both managers? As well as actors?"

"It's a great tradition, actor managers — goes back to James Burbridge, David Garrick, and the great Henry Irving. And Donald Wolfit — I saw him at His Majesty's in *Tamburlaine*. Wonderful old ham."

Certainly this was the life, Paul thought, no rent, fed by a beautiful dancer, and talking shop. But watch out, he told himself.

"So who did you go to the Crest with?" Paul asked casually, to disguise his jealousy. "I guess nice young beaus often ask you out?"

She smiled, seeing through him at once. "Not many 'nice young beaus' around, Paul. We're such a tightknit group, the company, we tend to just go out with each other." She looked down, and focussed on the last bit of her pork chop. "And I don't 'go out' with just any Tom Dick and Harry... unless they are making at least one hundred dollars a week!"

Paul coughed. So, this was his target price? "Poets don't count though, do they?"

Angela raised her eyes and looked across the table. "Poets do count. From what I hear, poets write in the evenings or when they have time, but they take other jobs."

What a traitorous thought, Paul decided. Yes, she's a traitor! I never thought she would be. "So you think being a poet is just a spare time occupation? Like dancing, I suppose?" Tense, he threw this out as a clear challenge.

Angela went on eating. "You know very well what I mean."

Paul should have let it go. But no one had challenged him quite so brazenly. "Angela, let me tell you, being a poet is just as full-time as dancing. I don't *ever* intend to get a job behind a desk. You had better realize that right here and now." Throw caution to the winds! If that's how she thought, he'd better move out in the morning!

He gulped a large mouthful of wine. Be careful, he told himself, but he was still seething at her betrayal. Still, where else could he go? Back to Mont Saint-Hilaire? Why, oh why, had he blurted that out?

Angela looked pained. After a time, she spoke. "You know very well, Paul, that you don't intend to spend the rest of your life sitting on sofas writing poems. You know that as well as I do. Let's not get ourselves all fussed over a few remarks. I know you're having a hard time. Don't let that get between us. I think we have..." she paused, and looked up, almost anxiously, "so much going for us, don't you?"

Dammit, he had been such an idiot. Wasn't she wonderful, making it easy for him to back down? He reached out across the table and took her hand. "Angela, I'm sorry. I make a fool of myself sometimes. It's just... I guess I really am scared. I hate admitting it. But you see, I've got nothing..." He looked back at his plate and continued eating in silence. "Nothing at all, if the truth were known."

"Don't be ridiculous, Paul. You have a great deal. And something will come along, don't worry."

But worry he did...

CHAPTER FOUR
SEPT 1954

And worry he should. The next Sunday, after she got back from class and errands, Angela poured Paul a glass of wine and began, for it must have been much on her mind, "You know Buzz picked up Stephanie yesterday..." Paul nodded. "Well, he phoned this morning. Apparently she told him that you're staying here. He was not pleased."

Paul made a face. "None of his business, is it?"

"No, but it's ours. He pays alimony. If I live with someone else, he could cut me off." Angela let the sentence hang in the air.

Paul thought for a moment. "Not too good." Angela said nothing. "Amazing he has that control over you."

Angela shrugged. "Well, at the end of every month, the money keeps coming. We need that."

Paul nodded. "I see." He started to object, then thought better of it, and changed the subject. "Isn't it fantastic about Marilyn Bell?"

Angela nodded. "Thousands of people went down to the shore to meet her, I heard at class. But I didn't have time to look in the papers."

"Front page news, of course." Paul went on, "Do you know, when she swam across, it's over thirty miles, the Lake Ontario waves were sometimes fifteen feet high. I read that she got so annoyed that the CNE would offer money to an American, Florence Chadwick, she decided to do it herself. Who cares if Flo was more famous? What's wrong with a Canadian?"

"Yes, but Marilyn — she's only is sixteen!"

"Chadwick had to give up — vomiting and stomach pains. But Angela, that poor Marilyn — over twenty hours straight swimming — and she made it! Around eight last night. They'd better give her the ten thousand dollars prize money."

He lapsed into silence, and then said, "So I should find a room somewhere?" Only chivalrous, he thought. But where? And how? With what money?

Angela was silent, then responded, "Perhaps, for the time being, it might be best." She went on quickly, "We can keep on seeing each other. It's just that officially, you wouldn't be living here."

He nodded. Thrown out again!

He should be used to it by now. But frankly, he found it rather hard. Back to Montreal? The end of the idyll? Start over? He tried to make himself happy, but this last defeat he found a hard one to take.

* * *

Paul pushed back his chair, wiped his mouth, and put the napkin down on the table. "Wonderful dinner, Cay. Thank you very much." On waking that morning, he had remembered that his hockey friend, Harry Boyd, lived in Toronto. He rang and Harry's wife Cay invited him to dinner.

"You and Harry go sit over on the sofa while I clean up." Cay, an athletic pretty blonde with blue eyes, had a sharp face that matched her razor-like mind.

"No, no, I'll help," Paul said.

"I'm used to doing it all myself, thanks, don't worry."

During dinner, the two old friends had ranged over their exploits. Harry had used his salary playing for the English Hockey League to pay his way through Cambridge. Then for Cortina d'Ampezzo, Harry had played centre and Paul left wing, the two being a mainstay of the team. "But how about teaching history, Harry? Not boring after that adulation? Remember, those Italian kids? They'd follow you home after a game, yelling 'Arryboyg, arryboyg.'"

Harry, still athletic, with close-cropped dark hair and a rather wise face, shook his head. "Teaching boring? Not at all." He was hardly the picture of a hockey player as he leaned back on the sofa and yawned. "I love it. I just joined Leaside High School, and I even found a way to teach them Norrie Frye." The great Northrop Frye had been his mentor at Victoria College. "And I'm coaching kids in hockey and track and field. I used to be a track star, remember."

Paul did and grinned. Harry had often spoken about his athletic prowess as they lay on their twin beds in the Bellevue Hotel, reminiscing far into the night, Paul about his poetry, Harry about *Fearful Symmetry*, Frye's ground-breaking book on Blake. But now, how should he bring up the real reason he had phoned: to find a place to stay.

Harry saved him. "So where are you staying? Have you moved to Toronto?"

"Well, I was at Angela's, she's pretty terrific, as I told you. But her ex-husband might stop paying the rent if I stayed. So I... have to move out."

Paul heard Cay's sharp voice from the kitchen, "I heard that,

Paul, and we've got no room here. I have two kids — Harry doesn't lift a finger — and I teach too, and do all the washing, ironing, get the meals, wash up, and we don't have a spare bedroom."

Harry looked nervously in her direction. "Now Cay, you don't need to be quite so harsh."

"I know you, Harry, you'd agree to anything," she shouted back.

Well, that's that, Paul thought to himself. Back to Montreal...

But he needed bus fare. Try to think positively: Mont Saint-Hilaire in autumn would be lovely. Yes, those red maple leaves! But didn't one need money, as well? So ask Mother for help again? Could he? Heavens, the life of a lonely poet... A bit brutal at times.

Harry's new house, one of four amid fields on Goulding Avenue, was a long way north, and the last bus left early. So they'd agreed that Paul should stay the night. Perhaps over breakfast, he could borrow his Montreal bus fare.

Later, Paul lay wide awake. One setback after another. He prayed again, harder than ever, for the good Lord to intervene in earthly affairs and bring him just one touch of good news. A few days before, Hurricane Hazel had wreaked its havoc on Toronto, with eighty-one people killed. What was going on?

The next day, the Lord obliged. Arriving at Angela's to collect his belongings to take to the bus station, he found her already home from class. "There's a message," Angela told him cheerily. "The CBC phoned back to say you have an appointment with the casting director at two o'clock."

"Wonderful!" A job as an extra? He'd be able to pay Harry back for the bus fare. But where would he stay if he got the job?

* * *

Dressed properly in his Harris Tweed jacket and tie, Paul took a streetcar to the CBC on the once elegant Jarvis Street, now gone somewhat to seed. He passed through the parking lot with its broadcasting tower, over eight hundred feet high and built in 1952. On his left, red brick buildings built in 1898, once Havergal Ladies' College, housed the radio building, and on his right, the smaller "Kremlin" used by CBC executives. Straight into the new four-story television building he went, and up the lift to Eva Langbord's office, to clutch at yet another straw.

He met a stylishly dressed, dark-red-haired lady in her early forties, with a gamine figure, large brown eyes and sensuous mouth. A former actress, she had played the ingenue in *Winterset* on Broadway. "So tell me about yourself," Eva began. "I have your résumé here, and it looks like you've done a lot."

That's nice, thought Paul, so give her the works — it's now or never. "Before I went over to England, I acted in a couple of plays at the MRT in Montreal — have you heard of it?"

"Of course, Paul! The main amateur theatre in Montreal — and it's not disparaging to say 'amateur'. Standards can be high. Look at our Dominion Drama Festival in Ottawa run by Amelia Hall. Some fine actors every year. I always go." He saw her watching him with appreciative eyes. That's all he needed.

"Well, Miss Langbord —"

"You can call me Eva, everyone does."

"Thank you. Well, at Balliol — thought of now as the best college in Oxford — in my second term I directed the college play — usually one does that only in third year. I chose *This Way to the Tomb*, by Ronald Duncan, and went down to meet him in Devon on the back of a friend's motorcycle, Mitchell Raper. Ronnie gave me the rights, and the production went well. Then... oh, I guess you only want the highlights..."

Eva nodded.

"Well, I acted in two big OUDS productions directed by Tony Richardson: *Peer Gynt* with John Schlesinger as the Troll King, such a fun chap, and *The Duchess of Malfi*. Tony's a wonderful director. Oh, and I directed short plays for the ETC, the Experimental Theatre Company, and the OUDS, the Oxford University Dramatic Society, a proper old organization. I wrote an original one-act play for one of their competitions, and you know Eva," he leaned forward, "I actually won: *The Legend of Lionus*, directed by a don, Rev. Roy Porter." He paused. Enough is enough, perhaps? "So now, I was wondering if you might get me some kind of extra job, maybe..." He was tempted to add: to pay back my bus fare to Montreal — but something told him to stop.

"Good," said Eva, still eyeing him. What should she make of all this, she must have been thinking.

"Yes, and I actually won an acting competition in a Saroyan play: *Hello Out There*. So I've won both acting and play writing competitions, and directed quite a few others. And I was President of the Oxford University Poetry Society and, by some miracle, got appointed editor of *Isis*, the University Magazine, and —" he stopped. She'd held up her hand. Oh Lord, have I talked too much? No job? No bus fare?

Eva leaned back. "Paul, you'd better go see Bob Allen. He's supervising producer of drama. I'll make an appointment for you for tomorrow. And don't talk about working as an extra!"

* * *

The next day at three o'clock, Paul found himself outside the office of Robert Allen. He had only recently taken over from John Barnes, who succeeded Mavor Moore, CBC television's first executive in charge of production. The offices were functional rather than impressive, but Paul noticed an energy wherever he went, secretaries and director/producers, all with an air of creating something new and exciting.

Ushered into the office, Paul saw a young Robert Allen come around his desk and extend a warm handshake. Not tall, slightly chunky with curly brown hair, twinkling eyes, and a warm face with none of the harried look Paul was used to seeing on New York executives. Bob indicated a chair and Paul sat, ready to give his full spiel. But instead, Bob simply chatted about what they were doing. "You know, this season we're producing a half-hour drama every week, it's called *On Camera*. Have you seen any?"

Oh damn, thought Paul, that's torn it! Needless to say, Angela didn't have a TV set and, in fact, he'd never even seen a TV show... So what should he reply? He shifted uncomfortably. "Well you see, Mr. Allen — "

"Call me Bob."

"Well, Bob, I'm fortunate enough to be staying with a principal dancer of the National Ballet, and she doesn't have a television."

"Oh yes? Who?"

"Angela Leigh."

"Really!" Bob seemed impressed. "I went to see her dance twice last winter. Just beautiful on stage. At one reception, I actually met her. What a sense of humour! She doesn't brook fools gladly. So you're a friend of hers?"

Paul shrugged. "I suppose so."

"Eva Langbord's been telling me about your experiences at Oxford." He tapped the résumé, and went on. "So, as I was saying, we also do a one-hour television anthology drama, *General Motors Presents*. We have another half-hour in the works, so we're looking for producers right now – that's what we call our directors, as they do function as both. Sydney Newman runs the drama department, you should meet him. He would be your supervising producer when you start."

When I start? Paul asked himself: What's that supposed to mean?

"I think, though, if I'm to do my job properly, I'd better ask for some sort of evidence of your background." Bob grinned. "I'm sure it's all legitimate, but you know... Is there anyone who could write something?"

Paul thought fast. He quickly rejected his poet friends, however well known. But what about his acting and directing? No undergrad would count, he knew. Aah! What about Neville Coghill? He'd accepted Paul's offer to be on the board of the Oxford and Cambridge Players, and Paul had started a new weekly series in *The Isis* that featured Oxford dons, called *Guardian Angels*. He had chosen Neville as one of them. "Have you heard of Neville Coghill?

"Professor Coghill!" Bob Allen leaned forward over his desk. "You actually know him? But could you get him to... ?"

"May I have a go?"

A few days later, Paul tore up Angela's stairs with the mail he'd found inside the door. He still came to dinner every day before taking the streetcar back along St Clair to Yonge and getting the subway down to Rosedale where he'd walk over to Grant and Earl's nicely bizarre attic apartment with its angles and nooks, where Angela had arranged for him to stay temporarily.

"Angela! Come quick!" He hurried down the hall.

"What's wrong?" Back from class, Angela was waiting for the babysitter to bring Stephanie home.

"Look!" Paul handed her the letter that bore an English postmark. "From Neville Coghill. Ever heard of him? He's a Don at Oxford, and quite famous."

Angela took the letter and read it:

Exeter College Oxford

12th of August, 1954

I had the pleasure of knowing Mr. Paul Alford well while he was at Balliol College Oxford, and have kept up with him since. As an undergraduate he quickly became prominent for his charm, his energy and the diversity of his interests and talents. Apart from his athletic interests, he was active in the dramatic work of the University and in the Poetry Club, of which I happen to be the Senior Member in control. So I came much in contact with him and was always impressed by his sincerity intelligence and reliability. I do not know anyone in whom I would more readily or wholly trust; he is also a man of vitality and ideas. It was he who with one other founded the Oxford and Cambridge Players (now renamed the Elizabethan Theatre Company), a professional company, to be chiefly composed of young university graduates, to tour England and elsewhere with Shakespearean plays. This company is now operating in England and enjoys a high prestige. Its existence is due in large measure to Mr. Alford, to his vision, energy, and resource.

As I've already said, Mr. Alford is a man of great personal charm and easy to get on with. In talking to him one feels one is talking to someone of great promise and all round humanity

Neville Coghill

Fellow and Tutor at Exeter College, Oxford

Senior Member of the Oxford University Dramatic Society

and of the Oxford University Poetry Society.

She looked up in admiration and gave him a big kiss. "I'm sure this will do the trick."

CHAPTER FIVE

OCT-DEC 1954

"Sydney is just a terrific guy, Angela. Salt of the earth type, no pretensions. He says he gets along with all his crazy producers because he never *orders* them, just tries to see their point of view."

"What does Mr. Newman look like?" She sipped a glass of wine before getting up to make dinner.

"A bit heavy set, young, you know, late thirties, black moustache and bushy eyebrows — he's from the National Film Board, not intellectual at all, but a good administrator, it seems. Claims he's not artistic, but I think he must be. After all, he's head of CBC drama."

Stephanie was in her bedroom happily drawing pictures. During the conversation she would run in with another page of her drawings. Angela looked after her anxiously and then turned to Paul. "So now you'll be getting a salary?"

"Darn right! Three seventy-five a month. Not one hundred a week yet..." Paul laughed. "Yesterday, Sydney introduced me to

David Greene, he's the top director here. And to his script assistant, Billie Powell, who looks tough; she's Welsh, but awfully nice and helpful. Spent the afternoon filling me in on stuff I should know."

Each producer had a script assistant, a kind of a secretary factotum, even a soul mate. "You'll find you completely rely on us," Billie went on, "and on the Studio Director, who's with you for rehearsals. On the studio floor he relays your orders to the crew and cast. I guess, with Eva Langbord, that makes up our entire drama department — we turn out two dramas every week, one half hour and one hour."

"You've never even seen a TV show — and you're going to direct at the CBC? Across all Canada?" Angela could not stop her incredulity from showing.

"No no, not right away, I'm apprenticing first to David. He just finished on Tuesday *Deadlier Than The Male,* for *General Motors Theatre*. We'll have to get a television set." She looked up sharply. "I mean, I will..."

"Good. You know I can't afford that."

* * *

The first day of rehearsing *The Picture of Dorian Gray*! What would it be like, going out on the national television network — funded by the government? Acts of parliament, no expense spared. Paul was beside himself with excitement.

But arriving at the decrepit old warehouse in the downtrodden east end of Toronto, Paul had to think again. The River Street building had been a customs warehouse for liquor around the turn of the century, with nothing much done to it since then. Now, its ground floor held paint and carpenter shops, the second floor rehearsal rooms. Up the creaky stairs he went, down a dusty walkway between partitions into a low-ceilinged room lit by high, factory-style, cobwebbed windows.

David Greene was taller and more imposing than Paul's skinny self; he'd been an actor in England and had come across the Atlantic, as had many others, when they heard CBC television was starting. David's preferences were for classics and well-written thrillers, often British in background, just what Paul liked. A good match.

Soon the rest of the cast, headed by the ultimately handsome Lloyd Bochner, wandered in and gathered around the table for the first reading of the play.

David sat at the head of the long fold-up table with his script assistant Billie Powell on his left, and introduced Paul. Then he talked about his ideas for the production to be telecast live in ten days on Tuesday October 26th at 9.30 pm. Next, the great Russian designer, Nikolai Soloviov, rose to talk, sketches in hand. Nik had designed motion pictures in the thirties for the legendary Russian director, Sergei Eisenstein. The Design Department staffed all dramas, variety shows, Public Affairs and News departments, and had assigned Nik to David for this, and most of his shows. Nikolai commanded attention, being imposing and heavy with a fierce peaked face, receding hairline and tiny black pencil moustache. Stagehands were afraid of him, especially during the chaos of a studio day, when he could become a towering thunderstorm. But with a heart as big as a teddy bear, he was also well loved.

Nikolai showed his designs, sketched with charcoal on illustration boards and then sprayed with fixative. Then he and David walked around, pointing out for the actors the lines taped on the large worn floor boards to represent the walls of the sets. Nikolai described the "set dressing": pictures on the walls, sideboards, chairs put side by side for sofas, and so on. Their first day in the studio, everything would be put in place by the night crew; one-hour dramas were given two days with cameras before going out live across the nation in black and white. Amazing, Paul thought: everyone well paid and loving their jobs; theatres he'd worked in so far had been far less lucky.

First the actors read the script out loud, some trying for performances and others mumbling, feeling for character — the latter being the more experienced.

The rehearsal broke up promptly on time, for each show had a union steward. Several actors stayed behind to chat to David as Paul watched respectfully. After the last cast had left, Paul gathered up his things and headed out with David and Billie. "Great cast, David."

"One of my best shows, I think. Now, Kate wants you to come home to dinner one night. Would you like to?"

"Would I ever!" Kate Blake, David's wife, was a leading actress. But for the time being, following the great David Greene through every phase of a show was just the cat's meow.

* * *

But change was in the offing. Towards the end of rehearsals, before they went into studio, Sydney called Paul into his office.

Uh-oh, thought Paul. With my luck, it's all over.

"Shut the door." Sydney indicated the chair. "Look, I don't think you can finish these rehearsals."

Paul's heart sank. He knew it. All too good to be true. Well, he'd enjoyed every minute. Now, back to looking for work. Awful — what could he do? Try for an extra job again? Head back to Montreal? No more Angela. No more CBC. How could he absorb this abject failure after such excitement? Preparing for the worst, he said a special fierce prayer to his Lord.

"I've got a studio free in ten days. Just enough time to do a half-hour show." Paul frowned and looked up. Had he heard right? A show? "What did you say, Sydney?"

"Studio One is free. Wednesday, the week after David's show. I have a script here that Mel Breen wrote. Not good enough for *On Camera*, but not bad: one set, four characters in a dorm room, not hard to cast. If you start right away, you should be able to do it."

Again, Paul found himself speechless. He just looked at Sydney.

Sydney must have misinterpreted. "Oh don't worry, it won't go out live. It's what we call a kinescope. We put it on 16mm film, shitty quality, but then we watch it afterwards." Sydney looked at him. Paul still said nothing. "You'll have the same camera crew as *On Camera*; I've arranged that. So it will be just as if you're doing a live show. Think you can handle it?"

Paul nodded dumbly.

"I mentioned it to David, and he thought it was much too early, as did everyone else. You've only just arrived, after all. I even heard you'd never even seen television before..."

Paul shrugged. What could he say?

Sydney paused, then grinned. "But kid, I think you can do it."

Finally, Paul found his tongue. "Damn right!" He got up. "But I can't leave David's show. I've been helping him some, fixing dialogue, et cetera. David and I get on so well together. I think he even... likes me being there. So I can't think about anything until after *The Picture of Dorian Gray*."

"But that's Tuesday night. General Motors goes out live, as you know. If you don't start till the Wednesday morning, that gives you just one week. We always allot two weeks for half-hour dramas. Even ten days is too short."

"Well, you said I can do it. I know I can." Paul grinned. The old dynamism was returning. "Just give me that script of Mel's..."

Sydney handed him the purple mimeographed script, and as he left called, "You know, we're spending a couple of thousand on this."

Paul reacted in horror, as Sydney had expected.

"Aah forget it, kid!" Sydney grinned. "We figure you're worth it."

Paul had seen Melwyn Breen around. A bit chunky with owl-like glasses, Mel proved to be gentle, friendly, a real writer. He'd been one of the four dozen applicants for Studio Director, a stepping stone to Producer, into which Paul had leapt right away.

"I'll get Mel assigned to you," Sydney said. "He'll be a great help; he wants his play to be as good as possible. I've checked with him."

And so on the Wednesday morning after David's show, Paul plunged in. With Mel's help, and a script assistant who had been assigned to him, he threw together *Night Watch*, the story of students in a dorm.

* * *

"I'm so glad everyone thought you did well." Angela was frying up steaks for the three of them. Paul had taken this Friday off after his show, and had laid the table. "I go off on tour in January, remember." She called out, " Stephanie!" Her daughter came trotting down from her room. "Wash your hands, please."

The plates were placed on the table and then Angela began again to unload her many tribulations. "Celia hasn't given me anything more this autumn, either. I'm working so damn hard, and I'm dancing well, too."

"I'm sure you are. But what do you —"

"*Lilac Garden*. The Tudor ballet. I really want the lead and she keeps saying I'm not ready."

"Oh come on, I bet you are."

"Thanks, old bean." She went right on; Paul listened but had learned not to say anything during these nightly rants.

"Well," Angela said, "tomorrow is Saturday, so we'll have the weekend to relax. Let's go to the botanical gardens. Or perhaps over to the Island. I haven't been for ages. It's nice to walk around there."

Once again, it was not to be. Sydney phoned to ask if Paul could come into the office. Oh Lord, thought Paul, what next? He's finally found me out. Sure: "Paul, just enjoy your Christmas holidays, you're free to go." Yeah, with no jobs, no money, no future. And no cheque. Maybe back to Apple Barrel? That would at least please his mother and Aunt Hilda. His mind whirled on and on.

Dutifully, Paul made his way down to the CBC as though to the guillotine. No one was in the department, so he didn't shut the door. He sank into a chair and put on a brave smile. "Working Saturdays, Sydney?"

"Yeah. Now look, kid, I got the same studio again next Wednesday."

Paul frowned. What was he saying?

"In four days. Don't know if we can get anything together in time. Last night John Barnes told me: it's just not possible." John was above Sydney and head of all TV production. "He didn't even want to let me have the studio! But I said, John, it's there; it's free; the crew is idle. So come on, let me give Paul Alford another shot. You see, when we had our big meeting in the autumn, we agreed that new producers could have two dry runs before they went on the air. It only made sense."

While Sydney was talking, Paul felt his creative juices begin to flow.

"I got a little stinker here, a detective story." He reached under a pile of scripts, pulled one out and handed it to Paul. "Piece of shit, but it'll do. Easy task, one set, maybe you can make something of it."

Paul just looked at him. "Sydney, this is not going out on air, is it?"

"No, I told ya, it's a dry run. But who knows? If you made something out of it, we could rewrite and next season, we might do it."

"Not good enough, Sydney!" Paul even surprised himself. "Look, if it's not going out, I want to pick something myself."

Sydney raised his eyebrows. "Yeah?" He sat back to look at Paul.

"Yes! What about T.S. Eliot's, *Sweeney Agonistes?*"

"What?"

"Sydney, I was reading it again last week. Such a nice little half-hour."

Silence fell in the room while Sydney thought for a while. "I don't even know... What the hell is it, a chunk of dumb poetry?"

"All right, all right, I know it's not for the masses, but you said it's not going out. Why not do something worthwhile? Yes, Sydney, that's what I want," Paul concluded.

"Well, I've heard of TS Eliot. But what the hell are you trying to foist on me?"

"Sydney, it's a Fragment of an Agon." He threw that out as if any fool should know.

Sydney reacted just as Paul expected. "What the hell's that supposed to mean?"

"An Agon, Sydney, an Agon — everyone knows what an Agon is."

"Don't be such a smart ass."

Paul burst out laughing. He'd got him! "Look, it's sort of a play, it's written with characters, yeah, it's got characters talking."

"I thought it was poetry."

"Well, it is, sort of."

"Whaddya mean, sort of?"

"Look Sydney, it's got real characters."

"Real characters?"

"Yes, Sydney, two sexy girls. And a wise guy — maybe I could get Barry Morse."

"Barry Morse? In a dry run? Never."

"Sydney, Barry loves the classics. It's a prestige item. It's TS Eliot. I bet I can get him."

Sydney looked at Paul with a mixture of admiration and exasperation. Then he shook his head and leaned forward. "I don't know what to do with you guys. I really don't." He shook his head. "Okay kid, go ahead, do whatever you want."

With a whoop of delight, Paul leapt up and tore out of the room.

Sydney yelled, "They all said it's impossible. Now don't let me down!"

Paul poked his head back in the door. "Count on me, Sydney."

* * *

Sweeney Agonistes. What a challenge! Paul had better pull out all the stops. When he met with his technical producer from the On *Camera* series, he asked about every optical trick a cameraman could produce: prisms, upside-down lenses, anything never tried on air. Mystified, the TP — after Paul's sales pitch – agreed. Bill Davis, excellent, efficient, was assigned as studio director. Then Paul called Barry Morse, who as predicted, agreed to play Sweeney.

Together they cooked up that, Sweeney, as a kind of seer, should have a glass eye. A half-blind seer. Great idea! Then Paul talked to Grant Strate and got him to join the cast and to choreograph a dance for Howard (Hi) Meadows and another male dancer. They would dance, not to music, but to the rhythm of Eliot's words.

So much fun, thought Paul – even if Sydney will hate it! Why not go out in a blaze of glory? I haven't even been paid yet...

So into Studio One they went.

Song by wauchope and horsfall
Under the bamboo
Bamboo bamboo
Under the bamboo tree
Two live as one
One live as two
Two live as three
Under the bam
Under the boo
Under the bamboo tree...

One of the actors played the spoons, another used a wooden la-
dle on a selection of pots and pans as timpani, and they set up a
rhythm to accompany the metre of the poem.

Tell me in what part of the wood
Do you want to flirt with me?
Under the breadfruit, banyan, palmleaf
Or under the bamboo tree?
Any old tree will do for me
Any old wood is just as good...

They rehearsed for just a couple of days. Chaos! But Paul had an
idea, although no one else did, how it should all end up, and he
persevered.

Studio One had never seen anything like it. Like a madman
Paul rushed up and down the metal stairs from the control room
to the studio, adjusting shots, coaching actors, leaping back up to
the booth again, shirt-tails flapping, a veritable whirlwind.

During Grant's dance, Barry decided that Sweeney would take
out his glass eye, and tap it on the telephone! An eye on a phone:
"So symbolic," Paul shouted at his cameramen, no one under-

standing whatsoever, as he bounded back up the stairs to ready the cameras for the dress rehearsal.

During the dance, one cameraman put on a prism and turned it, so that six images of the dance rotated, Barry tapping in rhythm to the poem — oh so seriously with his glass eye — the dancers gyrating to Grant's special choreography. Oddly enough, the production even seemed polished when they finally put it on kine. As they say in the classics, a good time was had by all.

Paul was so focussed on cutting from camera to camera, cueing actors, calling instructions to his crew over the mic into their headphones, he never looked behind. Had he done so, he'd have seen several producers and, indeed, even a few executives, dropping in to watch.

They observed, whispered together, and one after another went out. Who was this crazy new director? they apparently asked. "Having a lot of fun," one of them commented, somewhat enviously, as reported to Paul by Angela who had come to sit discreetly but prettily at the back on a stool — herself an object of admiration for all and sundry.

A few days after the fun had subsided, Sydney called Paul into his office again. Paul sensed that his brief tenure was finally at an end. But he had sure enjoyed himself. Well, Christmas was coming. Maybe it was a good time to go back home. He might even get Angela to come. They'd have a lovely holiday before she went off on tour, and he'd begin all over again, hunting for work in Montreal.

Paul sat down, trying not to look too downcast. "I know, Sydney, I'm sorry. But look, we had so much fun..." He saw Sydney frown as he sat back in his chair, hands across his stomach. Paul went on a bit breathlessly, "You could see that, couldn't you? The actors, too. The cameramen got new ideas about their equipment. So... so maybe if I come back one day, we could still have lunch, maybe?"

"Lunch? What are you telling me, kid? You're going full time on Procter & Gamble's *On Camera*," he scolded, "with Leo Orenstein and Murray Cherkover alternating. You'll do every second show."

"What?"

"You heard me."

"No. You mean every two weeks, I do a half-hour?"

Sydney nodded. "No one's seen anything like that damn Eliot you did. You'll have a busy goddam winter."

CHAPTER SIX
JANUARY 1956

Soon after seven o'clock, Paul presented himself at David Greene's door. The great director ushered him in to meet Katherine Blake, David's wife, a British actress of striking demeanour: Spanish-looking with a mane of rich auburn hair, dark eyes and bold features — like no one else in Toronto, that was certain! In spite of her rather awesome looks, she turned out to be warm and welcoming.

David poured Paul a gin and tonic, everyone's drink of choice. "We've invited an old friend, Patrick Macnee — you should meet him. Wonderful actor, though a bit of a Don Juan — wise enough to draw the line at Kate, because he knows I'm his great supporter."

"Oh yes, I've heard of him, of course." So here he was, mingling with the top actors in Toronto. He felt like pinching himself. Was it all a dream? "Who's directing *Studio One* tonight?" he asked David. The directors often gathered to watch the American dramas out of New York, such as *Philco Goodyear Playhouse*, and later on in the week on Thursday, the hour and a half *Playhouse Ninety*, run by Martin Manulis.

"Sydney Lumet, I think."

Being Monday, Westinghouse Studio One started at ten. Paul had been mumbling about getting a TV set just as soon as he got paid. "I should be getting a cheque, I think."

"You haven't yet? And you've done two shows?"

"Two Kines and a Christmas show, *Miracle at the Windsor*." Paul shook his head. "Funny thing you know, rehearsing *Miracle*, I saw someone handing around envelopes and I wondered." He grinned. "Imagine getting paid for having so much fun!"

"I'm shocked." David handed Paul his drink.

"I did go in to see Sydney," Paul continued. "He sent me right over to the employment office."

"You went to see the fearsome Margery Hand?" David asked with a grin.

Paul nodded. She had been at her desk, queen of all she surveyed. Short red hair, a slight sprinkling of freckles that did nothing to tone down her ill-natured demeanour, pale white skin common to redheads, and prim lips, usually pressed together in disapproval.

"Boy, was she angry! How had I slipped through the cracks? No one, she told me seriously, no one can get into the CBC without seeing her. Well, I said, there's always a first!" They both laughed, and Kate came out of the kitchen to see what was causing the merriment; David brought her up to date.

David told Katherine, "You should've seen Paul in the control room. I tried to stay and watch, but he even frightened me!" He chuckled as he went on, "No one's seen anything like my pupil!"

The doorbell rang, and in came Pat Macnee. No doubt about it, he turned out to be, as predicted, so very personable. Tremendously good-looking, tall, well-built, but with a gentle side. An alarmingly long list of young actresses had been drawn to him. But Patrick was intrigued by Paul's background. "You actually started a theatre company?"

Kate hadn't heard this either, so Paul filled them in: "Well, I borrowed money to buy an old furniture van. No brakes, really, a pantechnicon with a compartment above the hood, you know? We all travelled in that, fourteen of us including the cook, who helped with the costumes and props, but mainly served food right on the theatre stage with a Bunsen burner and some little camp stools. I bought second hand beds at an army surplus for the actors to sleep on in the halls, and a few flats, and I borrowed costumes from OUDS. I kind of organized the booking of town halls."

"Playing villages just like the travelling players in Shakespeare's time?" Kate asked.

"Exactly. Others did it for the Festival of Britain, not quite like us, of course, but that was our idea. Living communally. You know, I chose a pretty talented lot —some have already started to make a name for themselves. I bet even one red-haired scallywag of seventeen, Maggie Smith, had so much talent, she'll have a bit of a career, too." Paul went on with the exploits of the company, and then how he had gotten unceremoniously dumped by the Cambridge University graduate, Toby Robertson, whom he had brought on. "He took it over and it's still doing well as the Elizabethan Theatre Company."

They all sat down to a delicious dinner, and got into drama department gossip, who was sleeping with whom, who had a crush on whom, and confirming such amorous adventures as Paul had only guessed at.

After dinner, Paul broached the subject of his next play. "*August Heat*, it's a kind of thriller, but with a twist." Paul looked across at Pat. "Only two characters; not bad. Want to be in it?"

"Sure! Got a script?"

As easy as that? This was going to be fun! "I'll send it round. Simple play, all set in an artists' studio – you're the artist — and in a tombstone maker's yard. Supposed to be dreadfully hot, hence the title. I like this one, actually."

So now he'd cast half of the play, had a good dinner, and it was time to walk to Grant and Earle's apartment on the top floor of the old Rosedale house. Once he got that cheque, he'd rent a room.

* * *

No one was prouder than Paul when he brought Angela to the fourth floor of the television building, and into the drama department: eight offices, four to a side, arranged around a central pool of desks. Sydney Newman's ample office occupied one corner.

"Who sits at those desks outside each office?" asked Angela.

"Script assistants. And in the centre, studio directors copy scripts, write cues, and so on. Come."

"It open to anyone, I notice. So any actor can just wander in?"

"Why not? We're public servants, paid by Canadian taxes. We should be open to anybody who wants to see us."

Paul first introduced Angela to Silvio Narizzano. "One of our best directors and a terrific actor! I saw Silvio at the MRT a couple of years ago as the Gentleman Caller in *The Glass Menagerie*. He was just so poetic and romantic." Silvio was indeed handsome, Latin-looking with short black hair and a gentle manner. "Mother had suggested I ring him for a job as an extra. And now, here we are, companions in crime!"

Silvio laughed. "So Angela, you came to see where we do all our messy business?"

"That's the idea."

"Silvio," Paul explained, "is one of the three directors, with David and Hank Kaplan, who do the one-hour *General Motors The-*

atre. I'm only on half-hours, *On Camera*, with Leo Orenstein, Art Hiller, and Murray Chercover."

Paul then took Angela to Leo's office, who leapt up when he recognized her. "Well, hello!"

"Leo, this is Angela Leigh, she's —"

"Don't tell me you've got her in your next show!" Leo chuckled.

"No actually, well, we're..."

"We're together," Angela volunteered, not at all daunted.

"Oh, I hadn't heard. Honoured to meet you, Angela, I've seen you on stage, and you were so charismatic." His gracious old-world manners appealed to them both.

After they came back to Paul's own bare but functional office, Angela looked around and commented, "I'll have to do something about this... if you'd like me to."

"Oh, don't bother. I'll stick up a couple of pictures of you dancing and that'll be it."

Then who should appear in the doorway but Hank Kaplan. "I hear we have a ballerina in the office today."

"Hello, Hank," Angela said cheerily.

"You know each other!"

"Paul, you don't think we'd have a fledgling ballet company and I wouldn't go?" Hank was nothing if not flamboyant, with a bright-coloured waistcoat and hands that moved like swallows. He would clearly fit any ballet company, Paul reflected, except he was a bit heavy, almost florid. His reputation for swearing did not prevent him from getting a lot out of his cast on *General Motors Theatre*.

"You two are shacking up, I hear," said Hank.

"Jealous?" Paul grinned.

"I don't bend that way," Hank whispered, waving his fingers at Angela, who laughed. "And what are you dancing these days, Angela? I'm expecting to see you in *Lilac Garden* any time soon."

"Bloody Celia won't let me. But I have my eye on the role, don't worry."

Before they left to go out for a sandwich, Paul took Angela across the room to meet Arthur Hiller, from Alberta, mild, charming, almost bureaucratic, a complete contrast to Hank. The next summer, Art would hightail it for Hollywood and *Matinee Theater*.

"Well, that's our Drama Department. And I hear we're getting another weekly drama half hour: *Ford Theatre*."

"Very exciting, Paul. And even more so when you get your cheque!"

* * *

Paul, covered in splashes of paint, heard his doorbell ring and trotted down the old staircase with its ornate bannisters. The cheque had finally arrived. He threw open the door and, after giving Angela a big hug, led her up to his newfound lodging. "I'm dying to know what you'll think." She stepped in.

The walls glowed a hot pinkish yellow, the carved wood frames purple. Being in an old residence due for destruction, the aged room had high ceilings; a double bed stood against the left wall, and three tall bay windows shed southern light. To their right, a kind of "kitchen" contained a circular hot plate on a wobbly table and a frying pan. Against the far wall, Paul had stuffed his defunct fireplace with newspapers to keep soot from falling. "And just a few blocks down, a five minute walk, is the CBC."

Eighty-eight Charles Street East was not in one of the finer residential areas. Close by, on Jarvis Street, night-ladies trolled for pickups, and earned their nightly wages just below College Street in seedy hotels. But that was the last thing Paul cared about. He'd just painted his own space and felt all set.

Angela gulped. Being a rather good decorator, she must have

decided to squash her impulses: "It... it looks fine, Paul."

Out they went for a sandwich on nearby Yonge Street. "Mother said she is coming through Toronto for a conference in Windsor, the head office of Beauty Counsellors: it's a make-up and skin protection organisation."

"Yes, you told me that's what she's doing."

"Moving up in the world all right. More money for her than teaching dancing. She seems terrific at selling beauty products. But listen, a couple she knows are going back to England and want to sell their TV set, so she's bringing it on her way through."

The next week, Paul got his television set, a large heavy square box with a tiny round porthole about six inches across. He also got another present. The previous summer, two pretty sisters, Alice and Carol Guerin, had found a litter of baby skunks who had lost their mother. Alice had brought one over to Paul, and he had adopted it. When he'd left for Toronto, his mother had kept it and now was dropping it off. He'd had it descented, and named it Alice after one of the sisters. Now he had not only a home and a television set but also a pet skunk. What more could anyone want?

* * *

After the excitement of his first kinescopes, Paul found the regular On Camera plays rather a snap: *Deadlock*, *The Woman of Bally Bunyan* with Kate Blake, and then *The Liar*, all two weeks apart. Exhilarating, but not without moments of peril. Every decision made in that control room was seen by viewers from Newfoundland to Vancouver Island. But that never crossed his mind. Well, perhaps it did when phone calls would come in afterwards, directed to the control room by hard-working CBC switchboard operators.

The morning after *The Liar*, Paul swallowed scrambled eggs

and walked down Jarvis to his office, tired after the week of rehearsal and a tough day in the studio. He went in to see Sydney to get his next script.

He never looked forward to these meetings. Sydney was so charming, so persuasive, and would counter Paul's every argument with disarming honesty. "All right, all right, Paul, I know it's a piece of shit. But it's the best piece of shit we've got. I wouldn't lie to you. If you think this is bad, you should see what I gave the other directors. I saved this especially for you, because it's the best."

Usually Paul would reach out and, with sinking heart, take the purple-inked mimeographed script of some twenty-five pages, and sigh. How could you say no to such a charming rascal? Probably with a bit of patching and twisting and pepping up, he'd make it work. But this morning was different.

Sitting back in his chair, Sydney looked as pleased as if he'd just shaken hands with the devil. "I've finally got something you'd like."

"Yeah yeah, I know, Sydney, it's the best piece of shit —"

Sydney interrupted. "No, no, this... is a classic!"

Paul opened his eyes wide. "A classic? What kind of a classic fits into twenty-four minutes?"

"It's called *The Queen's Ring*. About the first Queen Elizabeth. Lots of that old-fashioned stuff you love."

"Aha!" Paul leaned over the desk and grabbed the script. "Merry Olde England! At last!"

"You can cast those English actors you like so much. Go to it."

Paul tore straight over to his office. His script assistant, Olwyn Millington, was at home in bed after the hard day in the studio, having typed shot lists most of the night before. He put his feet up on his desk and began to read.

Pretty awful, no doubt. But, with a bit of panache, it might work.

Little did Paul know what he was in for.

He rang his mother, who was full of the news of the Montreal riots. Maurice "The Rocket" Richard had been suspended by Clarence Campbell, president of the NHL, after a game with the Detroit Red Wings. All around the forum, rioting crowds had surged and smashed, so she and her sister, Hilda, had stayed indoors.

Paul wanted someone special for Elizabeth and asked about an elderly actress he remembered that his mother knew. "I think her name was Stuart or something." He listened. "Yes, that's it, Eleanor Stuart. You know how to reach her?" He jotted down the number.

The next day he knocked on Sydney's door and went in. "Sydney, we need to bring Eleanor Stuart from Montreal."

"Who?"

"She's Canadian, Sydney, but she's worked in the West End, yeah, in the 20s, and she's a top elocution teacher —"

"Dammit, Paul, more of that theatre stuff?"

"No no, Sydney, look, she's even taught Chris Plummer, John Colicos, I'll make her believable, don't worry. I've met her once or twice, she's regal, imperious even —"

"Don't start using those long words on me!"

"Sorry, Sydney. What I mean is, she's perfect for Queen Elizabeth. You brought in some actor from Montreal three weeks ago. Can't we try again?"

Sydney shook his head. "I don't know what to do with you guys, honest I don't." He reached for the phone. Paul watched as John Barnes, head of all programming, gave Sydney approval for a return train fare. Grinning, Paul tore around the desk, hugged Sydney, and rushed out.

Next, the most famous actress in all Toronto — Frances Hyland! Heart beating wildly, Paul waited in his office, door closed. Soon, the dark-haired and elegant Olwyn Millington looked in. "Frances Hyland here to see you, Paul." Olwyn always kept her little doggie in a basket by her side, a big bow round his neck.

"Ah good. Ask her in."

Paul felt anything but sure of himself. Here was the very star he had seen in that famous 1951 Peter Brook production of Shakespeare's *Winter's Tale*, playing opposite John Gielgud, at the Phoenix Theatre. So this precocious ingenue had actually come back to Canada. Imagine! Him going from a student gaping at a gorgeous actress in London to meeting her in person, and possibly even directing her. Well, don't look a gift horse in the mouth! And try to appear calm.

In she came, casual trousers and jacket. Not at all the big star, thought Paul, as they sat down to chat. He began by apologizing for the small size of the role, then told her how he had been so entranced by her Perdita. "What was it like working with John Gielgud?"

"He's such a gentleman," Frances began, and they chatted about the production, quite unaware that Paul was doing his best to hide his awe at being in her presence.

"Have you ever worked with Eleanor Stuart?"

"No," Frances replied, "but she has an excellent reputation. I thought about studying elocution under her before I went over to RADA. It will be fun to work with her."

Paul breathed a sigh of relief. So that was that: she was accepting the tiny role.

To complete the cast, Paul was especially pleased that Douglas Campbell, a Scottish actor of vast experience, agreed to play another small part. And Pat Macnee said he was happy to be cast as a confidante of the Queen.

Next, Paul drew up a rehearsal schedule. First, his script assistant phoned actors for their previous commitments: *On Camera* usually rehearsed from 10 till 1 and 2.30 to 5.30 in the old River

Street warehouse. Actors were paid by the hour and Paul juggled scenes to keep the hours at a minimum. The CBC, being a public corporation supported by Canadian taxpayers, was always strapped for money. For the last rehearsal day, Paul scheduled a final run-through which Olwyn would follow, stopwatch in hand, to check the timing. On Camera dramas had to run exactly 24.30, not the full half hour. The "credit roll" at the end was speeded up or slowed down to help with the timing on air.

At this final run-through, the technical producer, responsible for three cameramen and two mic-boom operators, and the designer with his props and set dresser, also showed up. So the performers gave their best for this tiny audience.

Most important, Sydney Newman always gave notes afterwards, which producers could agree with, or not, as they felt. Supervising Producers were there to help — not lay down laws.

During the run-through, Paul, a bundle of energy, took camera positions, bending low to show the technical producer the angles, sometimes snapping fingers to indicate camera changes, and a few times framing a shot with forefingers and thumbs. This rarely disturbed actors' concentration, just helped them know whether they were in a close-up or in the background.

Paul was disconcerted to see that Eleanor gave her all, whether in close-up or longshot, her magnificent voice booming out. Occasionally Paul glanced over at Sydney, standing with folded paper and pencil, scribbled furiously, making faces when she'd launch out.

After the run-through, Paul gave the actors a break and sat with Sydney. Olwyn put on her winter coat to go out across River Street to the small café run by a Japanese named George, to bring back coffees for them; no canteen in their warehouse building.

Sydney lambasted Eleanor's acting, and even Franny Hyland's, both more familiar with theatre. Frances, having the hang of it, would be easier to adjust. But Eleanor was another piece of work.

The technical producer pointed out some low angles that might shoot off set, but Paul reassured him. After the impromptu production meeting, the cast came back from their break. Paul, with Olwyn beside him, gave them his own notes, incorporating those of Sydney's that he agreed with.

He ended up by congratulating them on a wonderful performance. "Now, remember, we only want the best performances when we go out live, and not before!" Paul was saying this to everyone to save Eleanor's embarrassment, as she had apparently not done much television before. "In the morning, it will be chaos. Expect that. Don't panic. When you get there, it will look awful: the day painters won't have done touch-ups, the cameramen will have had a hard day before, so will seem half-asleep. You'll all wonder, how the hell can our director pull this off?"

Pat Macnee nodded. "Well said, Paullie, I always hate it when I arrive." Pat could be counted on to support him.

"Okay," Paul went on, "so first thing in the morning, after some sorting out, we walk through — just for the benefit of the boom guys and cameramen. So say your lines loudly and show the boom guys which direction you'll be facing. The cameramen follow on their shot lists which dear Olwyn will spend most of tonight typing." He wondered if this got through to Eleanor, who looked increasingly nervous.

"Then, before lunch, I'll try to put something on camera. That first go through on camera can be really unnerving. You'll say your favourite lines and the studio director will yell cut! And then he'll talk to me in his mic and the cameramen will discuss their concerns, and you'll wonder what the hell's going on." A couple of the cast grinned. They knew, of course. "That's when we're just sorting out problems. And having fun!

"After we muddle through as best we can, we break for lunch, and after we come back, we finish that run-through. Then we do it again, slowly, interrupting it all the time.

"Next, after tea, we stage what we call the Rough Dress Rehearsal. That's when we begin to see some kind of semblance of the play. But for Pete's sake, don't give a performance. Just say the lines loud and clear. We'll still have to stop occasionally. Then, we break for supper.

"After supper, you'll get into makeup and have costumes adjusted, though most of you will be wearing them throughout. Eleanor, you're an old hand at wearing that stuff, and so is Frances. We'll even see what Pat looks like in tights!" Grins all around.

"Anyway, after supper, around seven o'clock, we have the Dress Rehearsal. Now in that dress rehearsal, even with problems we do not stop, no matter what. Because it should be like the show itself. That's when Olwyn gets a good timing, so that's important.

"During the actual show, you'll see the studio director doing this —" Paul motioned to Johnson Ashley, who pulled his hands apart in the sign for stretching, and then by whirling his finger for speeding up — "because performances change on air, which means the show will either be running fast or slow, so we have to adjust as we go along. We always do."

Eleanor gave a loud sigh, and Paul suppressed a grin. "Don't worry, it makes for excitement. And frankly, Eleanor, you're such an old hand, once you get the knack... But you've got to expect a speed-up, or a slowdown.

"In conclusion, why I'm boring you all with this is: when we go live across the nation at nine o'clock tomorrow night, just relax and give your best performance. A great one during the Dress Rehearsal won't help. The only time to shine is On Air when everyone in Canada will be watching — we hope!

"The joy of working in our little studio is that nothing will disturb us, as happens in the theatre, when coughs abound or an idiot in the front row talks. The last thing is, I might move the camera in closer than previously, or back it off, so don't worry if the cameras don't move precisely as before. We have to give and take a bit as the show goes out.

"Anyway, good luck tomorrow. The main idea is, just enjoy yourselves. And tomorrow night at 9.30, it will all be over. You're invited back to my dreadful little room in a boarding house up on Charles Street, if you need a drink. Because I certainly will."

CHAPTER SEVEN
1955-56

The next day, his show having been a success in spite of any misgivings, Paul was working on a script when the office phone rang. Angela sounded tense. "Paul? Can you come down to the Market right away? I went in to talk to Celia before class, and when I came out Stephanie had disappeared. I can't find her."

"I'll grab a street car down Church and be there in ten minutes." Paul left quickly, wearing his raincoat for the spring day was cold and tending to rain.

Getting off the streetcar, he strode quickly along King Street toward the old St. Lawrence Market where the company took classes and rehearsed once the homeless left. Beforehand, they would rehearse at the Pape Street space. Above the Market's impressive centre entranceway, free-standing Corinthian columns rose to a Mansard roof – an historic building, compared by critics to fine Gothic churches and even Osgoode Hall. A splendid showcase in 1850s for its architect, William Thomas, now the building had clearly seen better days.

Paul began to worry. What could have happened? Had Steph fallen down stairs? An image of her lying twisted at the bottom rose, but he brushed it off. He hurried in the shabby entrance and up the worn wood staircases. On the first floor, he passed a make-shift counter for bygone ticket sales and tore up to the third floor where a corridor led to the large, grubby rehearsal room, once described as the Great Hall. Down one wall above ancient radiators, dusty uncleaned windows shed light; unused beds from the homeless still lay stacked opposite.

Angela broke out of class, her pink tights covered by hockey stockings, a rough grey woollen sweater over her black leotard, blonde hair bound in a scarf, sweat glistening. "I've looked every-where!"

"The little scallywag," Paul said soothingly, "I bet she's hiding in some cupboard, just to spite us. I'll search from top to bottom, then I'll do a walk-around. You go on with class. No use both of us worrying."

Angela flashed him a half-hearted smile and went back into class, given that day by Celia Franca. The founder of the National was petite, as befits a dancer, and still dancing major dramatic roles in *Coppelia* and Tudor's *Lilac Garden*. Black hair, piercing eyes, and a prominent nose made her seem even more of a martinet. The company both loved and hated her. The dancers were still doing their barre, Lois and David among them, with Jury Gotshalks, but no Irene Apiné, his partner. Paul waved to Myrna Aaron and Colleen Kenney, who waved back.

He climbed onto the hall's barren and dusty stage to check the wing spaces, then crossed to look in a cupboard. No one. His nerves jangled. Where was she?

A trapdoor caught his eyes — aha! Was she down there? He lifted it and flicked a switch. Noisy scamperings spoke of rats racing to hide. He shivered. Fortunately, no Stephanie. Those rats, Paul knew, found lots to eat from the market stalls behind the hall. Had Steph gone there to look at the produce? The next day, Saturday, was market day.

He hurried back along a corridor towards the stairs and stopped at the first door with a hastily scrawled sign: "boys dressing room". A dancer on scholarship was cleaning. He motioned to the wet floor he'd been swabbing. "Late start this morning. Had to wait till everyone got dressed for class."

"Do they always wear hockey stockings?"

The dancer nodded. "When it's cold, like today... We always try to get a barre position near the radiators."

Paul checked the handwritten tour schedule behind the door. Just as Angela claimed: a different city every day, late to bed, up again for a rushed breakfast. He remembered Myrna, Angela's roommate on tour, telling him: "Every morning we'd come down, half asleep, and line up to check out of the hotel. After a long wait at the reception, we'd grab breakfast in the cafeteria. So listen — I would line up, check Angela out, go to the cafeteria and get her breakfast, and then down would swan Angela, eat, and waft onto the bus!" They both chuckled.

Paul went down to the second floor to try other locked doors. At the girls' dressing room, he listened carefully and went in. Simple green curtains hung across the toilet cubicles — not much privacy there. Down the centre, a long metal trough served for the dancers to wash. He wondered when they'd get decent basins, as had the boys. Still no Stephanie.

Against the back of the door he saw a notice signed by Celia warning against the chewing of gum and a dire warning for any dancer who missed class. He kept calling Steph's name, but no answer.

Back to the central staircase he came. Heaven's, what a smell!

Urine and stale tobacco from the winter. What now? He was beginning to panic. Go outside and tour the building? Then he thought about the cupola. Check that out first?

He went up this last unused set of stairs filled with dirt and cobwebs. Had Stephanie really climbed here?

He reached the door to the bell tower. Unlocked. In he went. Stephanie! Perky as ever.

He didn't know whether to be angry or happy. "Well, hello!"

"Could you lift me up?" Paul did so, and they both stared out at Lake Ontario and then back north over the city. "I thought I could get a nice view. But look." She pointed. Spiders were busy on intricate webs. "I've been watching them," she said. "Isn't that fun?"

Paul nodded. "Amazing how they spin. Well now, why don't we pop downstairs and watch a bit of class?" He had work to do, but thought he'd better pay her some attention. As they started downstairs, he asked casually, "Were you hiding?"

"No need to hide," she exclaimed brightly as she trotted down beside him. "Nobody sees me, even when I'm right in front of them. I hide in full sight."

"Good for you, Stephanie." When they got into the hall, the dancers had put away the barre and were doing *enchaînments*. Angela broke into a big smile and waved to her daughter. Little Stephanie waved back.

* * *

As they walked down the wooden steps for some lunch, Angela asked, "By the way, I never asked what you saw in New York this winter? A lot of plays, I gather."

Paul had managed another trip, staying with his psychologist friend. "A play every night. Remember the first time I went, I met Norris Houghton? So the first thing I did was go and see his *Mas-*

ter Builder at the Phoenix. Then the new Menotti opera, *The Saint of Bleeker Street.* Boy, was that exciting!" Paul pulled open the heavy door and out they went onto King Street.

"Neil McCallum was there — remember him in my production of *Julie the Jink*? He took me to see his girlfriend, Julie Andrews, in *The Boyfriend,* a musical takeoff on the 20s. We all hung out afterwards. The next day I took Neil to *Bus Stop,* a new William Inge play. About a bunch of people gathered in a restaurant. Only so-so."

"You were busy."

"The best I think was *Tea and Sympathy*, by Robert Anderson. Deborah Kerr was in it — directed by Vincente Minnelli." They held Stephanie's hand as they crossed King Street. "... and *The Three Sisters* in a little theatre off-Broadway. Made me yearn for the stage again; so well produced, very enjoyable. Oh yes, and *Juno and the Paycock*, off-Broadway, with all the vigour of those off Broadway shows. I once asked Sean O'Casey to the University Poetry Society when I was president. He wrote me a nice letter, but couldn't get away from Ireland. Oh, and I also went to *Teahouse of the August Moon.* Bored me to tears, though it's the longest running show on Broadway: a bunch of Yank soldiers on a Pacific island, full of American wit which I do not admire."

"Neither do I."

"*The Flowering Peach,* the new Clifford Odets play, was kind of interesting, but poorly acted by some old Yiddish actor, a comedian who hammed it up. But a delightful idea, a contemporary handling of the flood legend."

"There I was, dancing like mad and there you were, enjoying yourself."

"I have to. Part of my job. I should hit Broadway every year." They went into the greasy spoon. "So how many cities did you do on that tour? Twenty-eight or something?

"Apart from Toronto and Montreal, we did ten cities, mostly one night stands. Fifty-one performances." A note of pride sounded. "We were exhausted, but then, so much camaraderie; we laughed a lot. That's what saved us. And in June, we're off to Washington, nine or ten performances."

They sat down in the greasy spoon, and Angela read Stephanie the menu. "It was fun watching that rehearsal, Angela," Paul commented. "I really enjoyed myself."

"Thanks. You know, Celia is beginning to rely on Grant as her assistant. And so she should."

"Will she let Grant choreograph a ballet?"

"She takes a while, Celia does. I've been waiting and waiting for her to give me that role in *Lilac Garden*. And I want Queen of the Wilis too, in *Giselle*.

Paul nodded. "I like Grant and Earl a lot. So talented, both of them. Earl is just a great dancer."

"And a great partner. And they're so comfortable together. I envy them."

"What do you mean? Aren't we comfortable?"

Angela gave him a look, which said everything. I guess not, thought Paul. Their relationship, he had to admit, was too often stormy. "They sure were nice keeping Alice until I got my room in that boarding house."

"I think they enjoyed having her. She's friendly."

"I like her a lot," piped up Steph.

"Oh yes. And now that it's spring, she seems to be more lively. Oh! Let me tell you. A couple of nights ago, Barry Morse came over for a drink. I thought he'd like to be in my next production —"

"Which is?"

"The *Return of Don Juan*, Ronnie Duncan's play. And suddenly, Barry jumped up and backed against the wall!"

Angela looked surprised. "Why?"

"Well," Paul drew it out, "he was looking across the room, and..."

"And?" Stephanie insisted.

"And... in the fireplace, stuffed with newspapers, appeared a little black nose..."

"Alice!" shrieked Stephanie, laughing.

"You got it, Steph. Alice came and stood in front of the fireplace, tail up!"

Stephanie was chuckling delightedly. "He's never seen a skunk?"

"Not in a living room... When I take her out for a walk on a leash at night, passers-by often get a fright, too." They all joined in Steph's delight.

The waitress put down their salads. Steph had a small plate of spaghetti.

"But I've been thinking... I'm out a lot, and we all want to go to Montreal... so I might put an ad in the paper. To sell her."

"Oh no!" Stephanie was disappointed.

Three weeks later, after an ad had run in the Toronto papers, Paul answered a knock at his door.

When it opened, there stood a pianist Paul knew: Glenn Gould. "You have a skunk for sale?"

"Hi, Glenn. Yes. I'm Paul Almond, I'm a director at CBC."

Glenn nodded. "So I've heard. A fair-haired boy, apparently."

"Come in, come in, Glenn. Can I get you something?" Paul reached out his hand to shake Glenn's but Glenn shook his head. "No, thank you."

Paul noticed that, although it was not a particularly cold spring day, Glenn had gloves on with the ends of the fingers cut off. He wore a grey overcoat with a dark blue scarf around his neck, and a navy-blue peaked cap. "May I see your skunk?"

"Alice? Oh sure." Paul went over to the fireplace and started to pull out the paper. "She might be a bit sooty." She dropped down, half awake. "I read somewhere you're going to New York to record the Goldberg Variations for CBS?"

"I will, but I have someone who can look after Alice. They're only releasing it next winter, they told me." Glenn was often seen around the radio building these days. He was building a reputation as a fine pianist.

Paul brought Alice over, brushing off the soot, and handed her to Glenn. He stepped back, but Paul thrust her forward, giving him no option. He took Alice in his arms and began to stroke her. She started to snuggle up and climb into his scarf, still sleepy.

"She sleeps all day," Paul warned him. "I'm afraid at night she gets a bit lively."

"That's to be expected," said Glenn. "Well, how much do you want for her?"

"How about twenty-five dollars?"

"I have a twenty here..." Glenn countered.

"Fine." Paul took the proffered twenty and went about getting the cat food he fed Alice, and her various dishes, putting them all in a shopping bag.

With Alice round his neck, Glenn took the shopping bag and, saying goodbye, went out and closed the door.

Whew, thought Paul, she'll have a nice master now. Listening to his piano all day. What could be better?

* * *

"Where are we going?" asked Angela.

"You sound like Stephanie. 'When will we get there?' Ask me no questions and I'll tell you no lies!" Paul was in full good humour as he drove northwards in the little Austin that he'd managed to buy. Beside him, Angela looked stunning in a light frock she had made. All her dresses came from patterns: stylish, perfect fits, saving money. But it meant she spent long hours at the sewing machine when not rehearsing. Stephanie sat in the back with a colouring book.

"You seem in a good mood!" Angela remarked.

"Why wouldn't I be? Now that I'm definitely getting my first full one-hour show. All in verse — I don't know how Sydney let me do it. But I told him it had sex, well, with a name like *The Return of Don Juan*. It's written by Ronnie Duncan. After I got Pat Macnee and Toby Robins, his eyes lit up. I don't think he even bothered to read it — at least I hope not."

Paul slowed down and turned the car into a wooded lane. Stephanie put aside her colouring book and leaned on the front seat, looking.

Paul pulled up a few yards from a dilapidated cabin. On stilts, it jutted out over a steep hillside that led down to a small lake.

"Are we here for a picnic?" Angela asked.

"Oh goody, a picnic!" Stephanie exclaimed.

"Not really."

"Are we going for a swim?" Angela frowned. "But I didn't bring a bathing suit."

Paul said nothing and opened Stephanie's door. "Come on, everyone out."

"I still don't see why you brought us here," Angela said.

"Because..." Paul paused for emphasis, gestured to the lake and then to the flimsy cottage. "I rented it! Heart Lake. Owned by a nice old guy. He's selling it all. But we can have this for a year or two..."

Angela turned and stared. Then she threw her arms round his neck and gave him a big kiss. "Oh, that's wonderful. Stephanie and I will love this."

Stephanie clapped her hands, delighted. Paul got out a key, opened the door and they went in.

During the winter, colonies of mice had thrived under cobwebs spread by armies of spiders. The three of them surveyed the room. "I guess we have our work cut out for us..." Paul looked a bit bleak.

Angela walked around. "Don't worry, I'll soon make it bright, just some paint, and I'll make curtains..." — probably remembering Paul's decorating job — "I see exactly what to do."

"I bet." Paul felt lucky to be with such a talented designer. Though being two such creative people, they found it hard to keep a balance sometimes; this new life did occasionally get a bit rough.

* * *

After his first one hour-long drama, Paul made an important contact with the smart, fair and freckled Rev. Brian Freeland. He ran the Religious Department of the CBC, which he made unusually active, often through devious means. Their first task, Brian explained, was to devise a play on the biblical Ruth, about whom Keats had written: "When sick for home, she stood in tears amid the alien corn". They commissioned the American writer now in Toronto, Charles E. Israel, rather shy (as befitting a writer) and the son of a well-known American rabbi. Paul, being the son of a clergyman, rather hit it off with "Chuck".

Paul found a gorgeous young actress, Sharon Acker, long brown hair framing perfect features with liquid and innocent brown eyes — delectable and just right for *Ruth*. And he'd been given a new script assistant, Eileen Jack. Attractive, with red hair and freckles, but very slight, almost stick-like, she was a bit stand-offish as befitted one from the educated classes of Old Scotland.

After their morning's work, Paul suggested, "How about a bite of lunch? We should get to know each other…"

Off they went to Old Angelo's on Elm Street where directors sometimes ate, often as not with script assistants as a prelude to some budding romance — but this was not that.

Paul talked about *On Camera* switching Studios, as they walked over to Bay and then down to Elm. "Four is much bigger than Studio One, so I'm really looking forward to that. Better dressing rooms, more space for sets, and that wonderful crane camera. At last we can do top shots and splendid swooping movements…"

Eileen kept up with his long strides, listening.

"For my next play, *The Walking Stick*, I've found a new actor, Charles Jarrott, he's staying with David Greene. Awfully nice. Very British, he'll play the lead. I think you'll like it. We're getting better scripts this year."

They went into an interior appropriately darkened to conceal the many trysts: producers out to seduce script assistants and businessmen their secretaries. The place seethed with adventures about to happen. The head waiter showed Paul to a discreet corner. "He thinks that we're here to begin an affair. So unusual to have just a business lunch." Paul laughed. Eileen did not.

After they had given their order, Eileen chatted about her background: her degree from Edinburgh University pleased Paul. "Now, Paul, tell me what else might be in the wind."

"The rumour is that the great Esse W. Ljungh and Andrew Allen are coming over from radio to do television. Have you heard of them?"

"Yes, everyone has. But tell me…"

"Andrew Allen ran a series of radio dramas on Sunday nights, *The Stage Series*: *Stage 48*, *Stage 49* and so on." Paul leaned forward, and sipped his wine. "The thing is, I'm helping Esse do his first show, *Hedda Gabler*. You and me both."

"How will that work?"

"Esse is Swedish, so he's an expert on Ibsen. We should learn a lot!"

"Very exciting!" Eileen beamed. "Just the reason I wanted to get into the CBC."

"It seems Esse would direct the actors, and I would put it on camera. He wants Barbara Chilcott as Hedda. There's Indian blood somewhere, so she has fantastic features."

"And... are you married?" she asked, matter-of-factly, though with concern.

"No, but I live with Angela Leigh. She's got a tiny apartment on Church Street, just behind the television building. I live out at Heart Lake."

Reassured, Eileen went on, "After we do *Hedda Gabler*, what then?

"Probably another religious play at Christmas, *Our Lady's Tumbler*, by Ronald Duncan. I worked on his farm in North Devon, you know. From a story by Anatole France, in turn based on a 13th-century medieval legend. Very touching."

Eileen was gratified. "So both *Ruth* and this are religious?"

"Sort of. Brian and I are kind of sneaking them on. He works on Sydney from his end, and I do from mine. I always try to get some kind of message, or thought, into my productions."

"Good for you, Paul." Eileen started into her plate of spaghetti and salad. "I'm going to enjoy working with you."

CHAPTER EIGHT
JAN - MARCH 1956

The Hill

The Rev. Brian turned up one day at River Street while Paul was rehearsing Anna Cameron and John Sullivan for *The Guests,* due out January. Anna was shortly to become the hostess of Open House, replacing Corinne Conley. "I need to talk to you," Brian announced, looking like the proverbial cat who'd swallowed a canary.

Curious, Paul thought. He's coming to discuss the Wilbert Coffin hanging coming soon, February 10th in fact. They all knew how the right-wing Quebec Premier Maurice Duplessis, catering to US interests, got the court to condemn a poor backwoodsman from the Gaspe for the killing of two American hunters. It was only too obvious that he would never have done it.

But Brian had not come for that. "I've managed to squeeze

from management a one-hour drama on Good Friday." He looked pleased.

"Terrific, Brian. What have you got planned?"

Brian had a twinkle in his eyes. "That's just the point. Nothing."

"Oh dear. Well, maybe one of Eliot's plays? *Murder in the Cathedral*?"

Brian shook his head. "I'd like something contemporary, but squarely about the crucifixion."

Paul absorbed that. "About the crucifixion..."

Eileen in her overcoat brought Paul a cup of coffee and went back for a cup of tea for Brian.

Brian went on, "I've gotten Sydney to let you off after your next show, so we have five weeks."

"Are you asking me to write something?" Paul felt a growing excitement.

"Well, writing or adapting. If we think about it, we might come up with something."

And come up with something they did.

But first, Paul wanted to meet the new designer he'd been assigned: Rudi Dorn, an Austrian, apparently quite a handful. But just oh so creative. He looked like Beethoven: big head, heavy features, squat body; you'd never believe any brilliance lay inside. But watch out!

Paul collared Rudi one day in the drama department. "Hi Rudi. It's me. We're doing a show together."

"Ach Gott, not another show! I chust finished one."

"No, this might be fun." Paul let that hang in the air.

"Fun? What you think? Better at home drinking a beer."

Good beginning? Oh well, persevere, Paul thought. "Listen. I might write a religious play for Good Friday."

Rudi moaned. "Not more religious stuff!" He pulled his hand down across his face, stretching his features like a mournful gargoyle. "I can't face all dat rubbish!" he cried. "People in pyjamas mumbling old Bible words."

Paul had to laugh. "No Rudi, I'm writing it. You think I'm going to write stuff for people in pyjamas? It's contemporary. I've decided to do something about the ascent up the hill of Golgotha. Where they crucified Christ. At the top. You know, a one-word title. Golgotha, or something."

"Golgotha!" Rudi complained. "I can chust see the sets switching off!"

"Okay okay, not Golgotha, I'll find something, don't worry."

Rudi shrugged. "Give it to Soloviov, he likes dat rubbish."

"No, Rudi, you're going to do it. I mean, what will we do for sets?"

"You want me to build some old mud houses out of canvas flats? I can chust see it." He chuckled. "Takes my breath away..." He kept laughing.

Paul had to laugh, too, in spite of himself. "Well, that's what they do in religious films. People accept shitty-looking buildings, if they have decent actors to follow."

"What we need sets for, anyway?" Rudi asked, enigmatically.

Hmm... "Rudi, I'm trying to figure out how I'm going to picture Christ. I mean, do we build him a special set? Up in the corner? Cut to him from time to time, or what? But they beat him, they made him carry this heavy cross most of the way up the hill, and then, he gets crucified — I'm just trying to figure all that out."

"And you're going to have that chew, Lloyd Bochner, playing Christ?" Rudi grinned again.

"No, you're right, it's impossible to cast. Who could look like Jesus anyway?"

Rudi gave another exclamation of disgust. "Fake beards!" He moaned again. "Glue coming off, beards hanging, stage hands sneaking under the camera to fix dem — I know, you're writing a comedy!"

"Ah come on, Rudi, be of some use."

"I don't put up sets." He shook his head, thinking, and started to scribble ideas. "Hmmm.... Dey have new cyc [-lorama, a clear blue curtain]. Goes most round the studio. I could get it joined together. Then we have sky all around."

"What? So I have to shoot everything low-low angle so we don't see the tops of the buildings?"

"No," growled Rudi. "What do you see on television? You chust watch actors. Who cares about buildings! Actors. Actors!" Rudi started to scribble again on the floor plans.

Paul began to think hard. "Yeah... Yeah Rudi. Listen, when I left Oxford I thought up this theatre company — "

"What? Now you gonna tell me your life's story?" Rudi said mischievously.

"No, no, no — listen, I made a company, I formed it, I bought a furniture van, I took them round, and we played all sorts of places, town halls. But we had no sets or anything, so you know what we did?"

"I don't want to hear!" Rudi shouted as he scribbled designs furiously onto a blank sheet, thinking hard.

"So, the first play we did was Hank Cinq!"

Rudi looked up, curious.

"Henry Five!" Paul explained. "Listen."

"On your imaginary forces work.

Think when we talk of horses that you see them

Printing their proud hoofs i' the receiving earth;

for ' tis your thoughts that now must deck our kings..."

"See? We had no sets. The Chorus, he said it all: Use your bloody imaginations!" Even now Paul remembered tall, long-necked Toby Robertson in front of audiences in town halls, speaking so beautifully those opening lines of Henry V. "Maybe we can do that here — is that what you're saying?"

"What? More big Shakespeare words no one understands? Now more sets switch off!"

"No no no, I'd write stuff like:

"You see this bunch of actors?" Paul started improvising.

"This is just a television studio.

So let us act out something for you.

Forget we're just actors,

*and try watching...*That sort of thing." Paul saw Rudi grimace which, he was to learn, meant he was thinking. Fearful! "Then we kind of see the story in their eyes."

"Their eyes..." Rudi nodded, far away. "Television. Eyes..."

"Yeah, television," repeated Paul. "Good thinking, Rudi. Faces of actors. That's all the damn little screen is good for. Faces."

"So I give you cyclorama, I give you rostra, they walk up and down, the ground is rough over dere, and you got your set. I go home and drink beer."

They both laughed.

"Okay okay okay," Paul said, "that's given me ideas. I'll go away and write the damn thing."

"I'm sick of all this talk." Rudi picked up his floor plans and turned to go.

"Rudi, no more talk; I'm going back to write. A television one hour. Okay?"

"All television is boring." And with that, Rudi left.

* * *

George Crum, the National Ballet's conductor had left town, and Angela had asked him to lend them his apartment. Paul holed himself up there, undisturbed, to write his drama. Angela was performing at the Royal Alex, eighteen performances, prior to leaving for tour. They would visit seventeen cities, thirty-eight performances in two months.

Fourteen Stations of the Cross: that gave some kind of shape. And indeed, it did encompass the whole story — in one hour. Some characters were set: the Centurion at the foot of the cross, Pontius Pilate, John and Peter, and other followers. But what about the conflict? He decided to write for actors he'd want to work with: John Drainie, Jill Foster, Jimmy Doohan, pretty little Welsh Sarah Davies — she had been wonderful in *The Walking Stick,* perfect for Veronica who wiped the face of Christ. Jill would make a terrific dumb blonde, a friendly housewife, contemporary. Then the Virgin Mary, and Mary Magdalene — Kate Blake, with her wild dark red mane of hair and soothing brown eyes, when they weren't flashing. So he started writing the television play, *The Hill.*

What, he wondered, would most of them be thinking? In those days, with no television, no radio, and no Roman circuses, a crucifixion might well be one of the few enjoyable outings. So Jill, she'd bring sandwiches and sit with Veronica to have a picnic while they waited for the chaps on the cross to die. Jimmy Doohan's character emerged as a weirdo who revelled in torture. Slowly, snatches of dialogue emerged.

What about the actual words of Christ? Brian had suggested different versions of the Bible. The one that Paul liked most was E.V. Rieu's Penguin translation of the *Four Gospels.* So he went through, underlining bits he might want:

Let not your heart be troubled,
have faith in God, have faith also in me
in your father's house are many mansions.
If it were not so I would have told you.
I go to prepare a place for you,

so that where I am, there you may be also.

Another thing troubling him: how to involve his audience. He needed to represent the mass of people. And as he daydreamed, he remembered his mother and aunt, in the 1930s, with their choral speaking. The ladies of Westmount would come and speak choruses from Greek plays, Rene conducting them in unison — probably the only elocutionist doing that in Montreal. He could hear them, upstairs at 37 Chesterfield Avenue, AAAEEEIIIOOUU. So why not a CHORUS of actors? Never seen or heard before on television. Write that in verse. Yes. A Chorus who commented throughout on the action. What would they say? He could just see Sydney's hair rise. But Brian was behind him...

Angela would arrive, worn out from performing. A glorious time. Paul could write with his Angela nearby. When at night he got out of bed to jot something down, she'd awaken and call him back into her arms. He'd stand looking down at her white, oh-so-white, body in its thin, soft nightdress, amazed that she was all his. That glorious creature on stage who kept hundreds entranced with her grace, the perfection of her arabesques and her superbly sculptured body. How lucky he felt. And then he'd come and lie beside her, cover them both with sheets and hold her tightly.

* * *

When Paul entered the drama department offices, Sydney's secretary spotted him and waved him over. "They're waiting for you."

"They?" Paul stood and looked.

"Sydney has Brian with him."

Paul wondered if that was a good or a bad thing. He glanced across at Eileen, where she sat outside his office door. She smiled. "I read it this morning, Paul. Don't change a word. They're bound to like it."

Paul wasn't so sure. He hesitated.

Sydney's secretary motioned him again and he walked over, knocked, and went in. Behind his desk, Sydney just sat, saying nothing, and looked at him — at a loss, it seemed, for words.

"Well," Paul asked cheerily, "how did you like it Sydney?" The best defence was to appear more confident than he actually felt.

"What the hell do you think our viewers are going to say when they see that on the screen?"

"Sydney, it's not my job to imagine what they're going to say. I just wrote the Crucifixion in today's terms."

Brian nodded.

"All right, listen to this," Sydney went on:

"The soldier kneels with a mallet, starts hammering a spike through the hand of the prisoner.

"Mrs L, I can't stand it."

"Aaw, don't watch it. Come over here and have a sandwich. I always do this when they start their hammering. Lovely view from up here on a fine day...

I don't think I could eat. But I'll sit down with you.

Oh come on, try this cold mutton. Ever so nice."

Sydney looked up from the manuscript: "What will the public say if we broadcast this?"

Paul leapt to defend his script. "Look, what about when Mary Magdalene sees them nailing that spike through her Lord's feet?

Mary, weeping: "The feet I kissed. They bleed..."

(Fade up Jesus voice over) She watered my feet with her tears, and dried them with her hair. So I wish you to know that her sins, her many sins, have been forgiven, because she loved much... And I tell you...

Cross fade audio

MARY *... in all truth that wherever in the whole world the Gospel is preached, the thing this woman did will be spoken of, so that she* *shall not be forgotten.*

"I find that very moving." Brian said emphatically and put down his copy, eyes watering.

Sydney nodded to himself.

"Sydney, you said IF we broadcast this." Paul pressed. "There's no if. It's going out on Good Friday. That's the plan. Isn't it, Brian?"

"That's our intention," Bryan said enigmatically.

"And you're going to want me," Sydney snorted, "to take the flak?"

Brian spoke up. "Sydney, we want flak. Shock them into knowing what it was like. I'll take it. It's my bailiwick, after all. Religious programs. And there may be less flak than you think."

Whoopee, thought Paul. Good old Brian.

Sydney then tried another tack. "And what's this Chorus you've got written here. You want to hire a dozen speaking parts just to say a bunch of verse? They won't be extras, you know."

Paul attacked. "Choral speaking, it's a great tradition, Sydney. Look at Oedipus. Stratford next year."

"Who's going to train them? You'll have your hands full trying to get this crap on in just two weeks."

"I'll train them. But Sydney, I meant to ask, we'll need three days in the studio."

"That's one thing you definitely won't have. It's two days or nothing."

"But the way we're doing it, Sydney, we won't even have to build sets. Rudi's going to stretch a cyc around the studio and all we need is a couple of stock rostra. Think of the money we'll save there."

"Are you crazy? No sets? What are you going to use?"

"Sydney, Sydney, didn't you read the opening paragraph? We see everything — the countryside, the conflicts — in the eyes, on the faces, the whole story will be told by our actors' expressions."

Sydney shook his head again in shock.

Brian grinned.

Two days, thought Paul, that's going to be tough. Well, just let the Supervising Producer get it all off his chest. But had he not he heard Sydney say, two days or nothing? So, it would be going out!

Pleased, Paul came out of Sydney's office to find a slim, elegant costume designer in a tasteful get-up with his sketchbook and biblical references. Horst Dantz, German, talented, was the best costume designer around. Horst began to show a couple of designs: "You see, I make zese just like zis history book here. And — "

"Horst, Horst, no historical accuracy shit. The costumes must be out of time. Stylised. That's how we'll do the production. Have you seen Rudi's sets?"

"No, I'm sorry, no time to speak wiz Rudi."

"Horst, listen, there are no sets, just a cyc."

"No sets? Mein Gott, what are you doing?"

And so it went, Paul persuading first the props department, the technical producer, and then the actors. For Christ himself, well, only one — Douglas Rain — could play that. But where? Ah, in the little-used announce booth. A stand-in, never seen on camera, would make Christ's moves for the eyelines of the followers. Men and women of the Chorus? Put them in another studio connected by earphones. All so unheard of. But gradually, an enthusiasm began to build.

But who knew what it would be like when this show went out LIVE across the nation?

* * *

"Ten minutes to air!" Eileen Jack's electric announcement over the loudspeaker cut through the rising excitement and organized chaos. Good Friday March 30th. 1956: the clock showed 8:50.

Paul Alford was going over some last-minute notes in the music booth with Bill McClelland. His tiny room contained three turntables with 78s of music and the various paraphernalia from radio: latches, windows to open, a pad on which to make footsteps, and so on. In front of him in a homemade rack stood records that he had selected from the Music Library in the adjacent Radio Building. "So if you back-time that music to end where it did, Bill, I might bring it in a bit sooner, so just be ready."

"Do my best; may not be perfect." Bill was a genius, every director knew that. He handled so much in that booth of his: all the sound effects, all the background music, chosen somehow during the first day's walk-through.

Paul hurried through the control room, past Brian and Sydney, who wished Paul luck as he grabbed his notes, tore out along the catwalk, clanged down the winding metal staircase onto the studio floor and over to an elderly, grey-haired actor reviewing his lines from a folded script. Earl Grey had been on stage in England and first appeared on film in 1934. Slightly wizened but statuesque, with a British accent and short, neat grey hair, he was a perfect Pontius Pilate.

"Earl, I forgot to mention, when you do the hand washing, please hold them a bit higher to get them on camera, because I'll go in pretty close."

Paul paused just long enough to make sure Earl had absorbed it, then hurried over to where Katherine Blake, Mary Magdalene, sat at the edge of the cyclorama, composing herself. "Katherine, you were perfect in the dress rehearsal. Saving yourself, damn good. So now you can go at it. John (the studio director) got you a handkerchief, so if you cry, he'll hand it to you off camera."

Kate smiled up at him. "Don't worry, I have one. Horst was clever enough to put pockets in our robes."

Consulting his notes, he went to Davie Dron, a heavier and older cameraman, having begun at the BBC in the legendary days of "Ally Pally" (Alexandra Palace, the first television broadcast anywhere). He was studying his shot list and sweating as he always did, due to the hot studio. "Davie, I forgot to mention, be extra careful on that low angle of Jill at the cross, you might shoot off set."

Dave nodded. Of course he knew.

For the procession up the hill of Golgotha, the actors wound round the sides of the studio in front of the pale blue cyc, with the cameras following. After passing in front of the camera, actors had to tear around behind it to their next positions on another camera, making it seem as if the procession never stopped, except when Christ fell or Veronica wiped His face with her handkerchief.

Paul hurried to George Clements getting onto his seat on the crane. "Fabulous what you guys have been doing. Good luck, eh?" He also waved to sturdy Ron Manson, the third cameraman.

The crane required a superb team of three men to operate: one assistant at the rear on the electric controls for motion and direction; another beside the boom arm to move it fluidly up, down or sideways, and of course, the cameraman. Paul loved it because the crane shot down from a height of twelve feet, and, at its lowest, from a foot below the pedestal camera.

Earlier Paul had given the cameramen their notes, after first talking to his cast and releasing them for touch-ups or costumes, or to concentrate before their performances. He crossed to the two disciples, John and Peter. The latter, John Drainie, acknowledged to be the finest radio actor in the world, was now making his way into television. He wore a fisherman's beard as befitting Saint Peter, while Jeremy Wilkin, as the Beloved Disciple, looked younger with blonde hair and complexion, an excellent contrast.

Jeremy had played the lead in *Our Lady's Tumbler*. "You guys are terrific. John, could you turn a little bit more on those two profile views at the beginning?"

John nodded, and Paul trotted over to the two thieves crucified with Jesus. Arranging these crosses had taken quite a time on the first studio day. Paul could not shoot up at a cross because the studio cyc was only fifteen feet high. So how would they ever solve that one? Rudi, the genius, laid the crosses flat with their tops on a rostrum, so the camera shot them against the cyc as if it were looking up into the sky. The stagehands were now tying the arms of the British actor, Donald Ewer as the Good Thief, onto his cross.

"You don't need to do that now. It's an hour away from the ending..." Paul began, concerned.

"I don't mind," said Don. "Better for me to be in position now, than trying to do this during the show. We'd make noise and so on."

"Wonderful!"

"FIVE minutes to air!" Eileen's voice crackled over the loudspeaker, sending everyone into a quickened sense of anticipation. Paul looked up.

"Good luck, everyone," he called and tore again up the winding metal staircase, shirt-tails flying. He came through the door to fling himself down in front of the bank of monitors, above a glass window that gave onto the studio. Cec Johns, the technical producer, spoke a terse message into the loudspeaker. The cameramen put on their earphones and guided their cameras into position.

To Paul's right sat the switcher, who pressed buttons on his console that cut from camera to camera. Cec took his place on a stool behind. Close to Paul on his left, sat Eileen Jack, twirling one of her red curls, right hand with the pencil following shots throughout the show. Between them on a stool sat Rudi Dorn, not yet here, of course, off talking. His assistant, Bob Hackburn, would stay on the studio floor for any emergency.

Further to the left on the long counter sat the audio engineer, who spoke through a separate mic to his boom and mic operators. On this show with its two mic booms, one man stood behind each large boom to reposition it, and on its platform, the operator, one hand on a small crank, pushed the mic out or in, his other hand controlling the direction.

Paul turned to Don, the switcher. "Open the mic to the announce booth, please." There, Douglas Rain, the voice of Christ, would have his own mic and earphones, and his own screen. When Paul said, "Cue Christ" the switcher flicked on his red cue light.

"Doug, all set?"

Through the glass of the announce booth, Paul saw Doug nod. The switcher closed that mic.

Paul spoke a few last words of encouragement over the loudspeaker.

"Thirty seconds," Eileen declared.

Paul looked up at the slowly revolving second hand, turned to her and grinned. "This is it, I guess."

She paid no attention, focussed on the clock.

"Rudi, Rudi, come and sit." Paul commanded.

"Ach Gott, I have to watch all over again?" But he grinned back at Sydney and Brian, who now seemed rather anxious. How would Paul pull all this chaos together, they clearly wondered.

"Ten seconds," Eileen's voice sounded sharply over the loudspeaker, which was then doused for the show. Grimly she counted out, "Five, four, three..."

"We're on," said the technical producer. On air. Live. Across the nation.

"Fade up!" barked Paul.

Eileen, fast: "Ready two on credits"

Paul, staccato: "Two! Flip the credit. Take one!"

Up came the second credit,

"Fade out credits." Paul flicked his hand at the switcher. "Take the crane! Great! We're rolling!"

And Paul's script for *The Hill*, depicting the ascent up Golgotha and written just in the last weeks, began to roll out live, coast-to-coast, across the Canadian viewer-scape.

CHAPTER NINE
1956

A few days after *The Hill* was telecast, Stephanie sat in the back seat of the Austin beside her little suitcase, unusually quiet. Paul suspected the reason. The Easter holidays were ending. Back to school for her.

"So there weren't a lot of hate letters from the show?" asked Angela.

"No. Sydney was sure afraid. But the reactions so far have been fine, even surprisingly good. Even from clerics."

"And you said you've gotten your next show?"

"A General Motors called *Seat of the Scornful*. Goes out April 17th. But I know he's going to insist on an even worse script, *Tolliver's Travels* for May 29th. But there's a Spanish dancer you could do."

Angela brightened. "Tell me about it."

Paul nodded. "When it's set." He lapsed into silence, Stephanie being his main preoccupation.

Angela turned to look at her daughter and smiled, with no answering look. "You know Stephanie, I'll be home all this term. You'll come home on Saturdays. Every second week, I think."

No reply from Stephanie. Paul knew she didn't like St. Mildred's, the boarding school for young girls run by nuns. When it came time for Steph to enter grade one last September, Angela had enrolled her there before going on tour.

After Christmas, taking Stephanie back to the school had produced quite a scene. Paul prayed it wouldn't be repeated. He had been staying (clandestinely) off and on at Angela's tiny one-room flat on Church Street. But it had felt cramped for both of them, so one day he'd suggested: "I think I'll go up and stay at Harry's for a while."

"What's wrong with my flat? It's close to your office, so convenient for you. That's one of the reasons I took it."

"It's wonderful, Angela, but Harry might build a room in his basement."

"Harry? Is he a carpenter?"

Paul chuckled. "Of course not. But he knows a nice guy in a hardware store who could tell us what to do. We'd both build it."

He remembered the sceptical look, mixed with annoyance, on Angela's face. But build the room they did, spartan of course, adding Stephanie's single bed from the Vaughan Road apartment and a small unpainted desk. All he needed. And now Cay didn't mind as her new lodger was mostly out, save for evenings when, due to his new interest in astronomy, he'd bought a six inch telescope to watch planets, nebulae, and star clusters in the crisp dark air.

They pulled up outside St Mildred's. Little Stephanie carried her suitcase, so Paul offered to take it but she pulled away angrily. They rang the bell, and a sister in a black outfit opened the door and ushered them into the vestibule. "Welcome back, Stephanie, we are delighted to see you again!"

Stephanie didn't reply and another Sister, also dressed in black, took Stephanie by the hand. "We'll go down to the cellar where you can take off your coat and then you'll come up and say good-bye to Mummy and Daddy."

"He's not my daddy," snapped Stephanie and held back. But the nun had a firm grip, and almost dragged her out of the room. Paul grimaced, but then Sister Grace ushered them into a neat but sterile drawing room, where they sat to discuss Stephanie.

The Sister Mary Adela admitted that Stephanie did not seem overly happy, but for the most part was a good little student, and obedient; they discussed what the nuns taught the students at her age. She slept in a room called "the baby dorm" and had made friends with an even younger girl, which made her a little happier. Angela explained again about her tour, that this winter they had danced all over the eastern and southern United States, travelling between cities every day on buses, which, by the way, carried no toilets. But now she was back and would be able to see Stephanie every second weekend, according to rules. The Sister allowed as how this would probably make it easier on the little darling.

Stephanie returned, and Paul found out later that the other nun had stayed below to clean up the vomit, for Steph threw up every time she had to go back.

They went into the vestibule. "Well, goodbye darling." Angela bent to hug her daughter.

"I bet this time, you'll enjoy it," exclaimed Paul! He cheerily gave her a hug, which she resisted. As they turned to go, Steph-anie began to wail and rushed to her mother, clinging tightly to her legs.

Taken aback, Angela gently tried to unwrap her, murmuring, "Don't worry, Stephanie, I'll be right here all spring — we can see you every second weekend, it'll be all right." That only made her wail louder and the high-pitched screams brought another nun. Sister Mary Adela bent and tried to unwrap Stephanie, which meant she only screamed louder and hugged tighter. "Mummy, Mummy, Mummy."

The second nun, obviously more adept at this, with arms and fingers of steel pried Stephanie off her mother and dragged her by the arm through the door, still yelling.

Angela and Paul looked on helplessly. The bewildered Sister escaped inside and hurriedly closed the door.

Paul and Angela walked slowly back to the car.

They drove for a time in silence. But Paul could contain himself no longer. Not only had Stephanie's treatment disturbed him no end, but Angela's clinging ways — so stifling — how many times had she claimed, "You don't love me," when he had done his best to reassure her, over and over. It was all just too much. He didn't know what to do. Having had no experience of what a good relationship should be, no father and mother loving each other, in fact no father at all, how couples behaved, how they related in a happy union — it was all simply beyond him. Was this all there was to life? If he got free, for a time, perhaps... yes, he must get free. Get away now, was his only thought, for good or ill.

He blurted out: "Angela, I've got to get away this summer. I've got to. I'm going back to Oxford to collect some of my things."

Angela, also shaken by the previous scene, did not mince words as she cut him off: "You're not going to leave me!"

"Not leave you, Angela," Paul replied, almost angrily. "I haven't been to Europe for three years. I left a lot of things in Oxford and I have to collect them."

"Just have them sent back! I don't want you to go. You can see what troubles I have. I need you here."

"I have troubles too, Angela. But..." He tried to soften, knowing she was under strain. "I want to travel again. I'm getting the summer off."

"I'll have a fortnight off too, we can be together. We can go to Apple Barrel."

"I've been to Apple Barrel. I want to go back to England. You know I'm getting my M.A. conferred at the Sheldonian Theatre.

"So go over, get your MA, and come right back."

"No, I want to see things. I've never been to Scandinavia. Northern Finland, it's even above Québec province, above the Arctic Circle. Imagine, so close to the North Pole."

"You know I can't come, I have to take class every day. You're just being selfish."

"Selfish? Is that what you call somebody who wants to better himself?"

"You can better yourself here."

And so the arguments would rage on, most evenings when they met for dinner in the tiny apartment. But they would often end in reconciliation, and then lovemaking. They both did really enjoy being together, Paul reflected. But something was still so unsatisfactory. He had to get away and be alone, to think. And to decide on this relationship once and for all.

And what better way than in the birch forests of Lapland?

* * *

As soon as Paul arrived in Helsinki, each day was full: hitchhiking north to Lapland in the back of a truck with a couple of Australian nurses on a load of smoked reindeer meat, which had a roly-poly feel, shifting as the truck bumped along the gravel road, more enticing than any mattress. Later, they all had a real Finnish sauna at the driver's farm. After the welcome heat, birch branches had been fetched and they all slapped themselves, then dashed outside to splash in a barrel of icy water.

Watching the midnight sun at Nordkapp so very far above the

Arctic Circle was the highlight for Paul, then sleeping on a ferry deck on the four-day trip down Norway's coast past indelible
fjords. By the time Paul arrived back in London to stay with Stanley Myers and his new wife, he had forgotten any Angela troubles.

A couple years previously, they had married and now had a little son, Nicholas. Eleanor Fazan, known to everyone as Fiz, had a
lithe dancer's body, athletic rather than voluptuous, large round
eyes in features that spoke of warmth. She told him she'd been
brought up in Kenya.

Paul went over his central problem with Stanley. "You know,
Stanley, I've been with Angela now for some time, but there's so
much... I can't take. I don't know what to do. I think I need to get
free."

"Your letters said she was pretty darned attractive."

"True, but so clingy! She keeps saying: 'You don't love me.' I
do — as much as I can. But when she clings, I kind of draw back."

"So what are you going to do?"

"When I get back? Break it off. I think..."

"You think?" Stanley smirked.

"Well, I'll try, anyway."

But the next three weeks in London took his mind off it. He
saw Christopher Plummer perform, who afterwards asked about
Paul's mother, Rene, with whom he had acted in *Coriolanus* in
Montreal. Peter Dale Scott showed off a stunning new wife, May-
lie Marshall, whom Paul fell for rather heavily, but she was firmly
attached. Ronnie and Rose Marie Duncan came to London and
invited him to dinner. He had drinks with Tony Richardson who
was heading up the new Royal Court Theatre that Ronnie had begun.

Before leaving England, Paul trained north to the Edinburgh
Festival and stayed with Chris Bell and the Oxford Theatre Group
he had helped. He spent a day with pretty red-haired Deirdre

who had travelled with him and the Oxford and Cambridge players all around England. She had married Neil, an Oxford student and electrician on OUDS productions — the son and heir of Lord Rosebery.

But when finally Paul came back to Toronto, Angela happily provided dinners, her lovely body welcomed him under the covers and, for the life of him, he found it impossible to make the break. Routine overtook them both.

Off she went again on tour: eight cities and twenty eight performances in November and December. When she arrived back, they picked Stephanie up from St. Mildred's and went to the Zoo.

A few months ago, Glenn Gould had given Paul's skunk to Riverdale Zoo in the Don Valley. They hadn't expected to see Alice but in one enclosure, a little creature with black-and-white stripes was grubbing for beetles. Most skunks look the same, but when Paul called, the little animal ambled in their direction and finally ended up at the fence. Stephanie had been delighted. "I think Alice remembers us!"

"She sure does," Paul agreed. "She seems happy."

As they left, Paul's thoughts were diverted by Angela bringing up the recent flight of the Sputnik on the fourth of October. That and the foreign minister, Lester Pearson, winning the Nobel Prize for his work on the Suez crisis. But for Paul, this visit was about Stephanie, and he quickly turned his attention to her.

"Now that you're taking ballet, Stephanie, won't it be fun to watch your mother rehearse?" At seven years old, Steph had been taken to her first class in September with the company's ballet mistress, Betty Oliphant, at her studio on Sherbourne. "You know Steph, I like your hair short."

"I hate it!" Stephanie complained. "Matron didn't want to have to do my pigtails, so she just cut them off."

Paul didn't know quite what to say, but Stephanie went on.

"Then Jane," her father's new girlfriend, "took me to Holt Renfrew and they cut even more. I was late getting back to the school, so when Matron found me, she pushed me down stairs, and I tumbled to the bottom." Paul could see her little face go into a grimace, as if to cry.

"But Matron has left this term," Paul quickly reassured her. "If that happens again, you tell Angela or me right away. Other parents must have complained. They don't get away with that stuff forever."

Stephanie allowed that she was happier now.

"And how are you liking Grade 2?"

"All right."

Poor little thing, but what else could Angela do? Since Paul had come back from Europe, his slate had been full. In October, General Motors had moved to Sunday nights, no longer sponsored. Angela had gone on tour and he'd directed four more dramas. So this Saturday, the first time all three would be together, they went out to dinner after the zoo.

To cheer them up, Angela said, "Celia seems excited about the new Canada Council."

"I heard something about that. Wasn't it set in motion this spring? March or something?

"Yes, based in Ottawa. It's already started."

"But why would that excite Celia?"

"She thinks it will give money to artists, and writers, and, well, orchestras and so on..."

"And of course, the ballet company!"

"We hope so. We've all been talking about it. Louis St. Laurent and his Liberals started it, to promote works of art."

"Quite a mouthful!" Paul grinned.

This December 8th 1956 was unseasonably cold. For two days snow had fallen and decorated the lawns and awnings in white.

The company had left the St Lawrence Market, needed as winter accommodation for the homeless, so Paul was driving them to Pape Hall, where they now rehearsed. The double doors were big enough to admit trucks of horse feed stored on the ground floor. They climbed a narrow staircase and along the dusty corridor past the costume department where James Ronaldson, a former dancer, made costumes and gave dancers their fittings. Paul called to say hello to Jimmie, at work up a ladder in his tiny loft.

James called back, "Please keep the door shut, it's freezing."

They went into the dance studio, if it could be called that. One window only four feet wide reached the ceiling and two old iron radiators, three feet off the floor, threw off tepid heat. The ceiling often leaked — when it wasn't snowing. Thankfully in January, when performing at the Royal Alexandra Theatre, they would do class and rehearsals on a warm stage. Here, with nowhere to change into practice tights, the dancers had littered one side of their dance studio with outdoor garments.

While waiting for their *enchaînements*, dancers wore coats and huddled together for warmth. Angela saw her daughter arrive and hurried across to kiss Stephanie, then tore back, threw off her coat, and began rehearsing. Paul and Stephanie found a couple of chairs, and sat to watch. Celia spotted Paul and waved.

Myrna winked at him and Colleen Kenny came tripping over to kiss Paul. They whispered, but stopped when Celia glanced in their direction. Stephanie sat up straight, watching every movement.

* * *

"Sure is cold in there, Angela, don't know how you all do it." Paul drove them home, Stephanie in the back seat.

"That's the way it is, old bean. Now how do you like your new offices on Front Street?"

"Horrible," Paul replied. "More space, but no windows, except at the front where Sydney's office is. Ron Weyman is doing well on the half-hours, Mel Breen has been elevated to director, so he does one occasionally. No one's as busy as me, unfortunately."

Angela turned to her daughter. "How did you like the rehearsal, Stephanie?"

"Okay. Celia does our Chechetti exams. Everyone's afraid of her."

"No Stephanie, we all like her. She has to be like that or she couldn't run the company. She's very nice."

Paul nodded. "On tour, Angela, anyone hear about the November 1st Springhill disaster in Nova Scotia? Forty miners died."

She looked at him, and frowned. "Paul, our alarm clocks wake us up, we roll out of bed, run downstairs, grab breakfast, check out, jump on the bus, none of us ever reads a newspaper. Once on the bus, we fall asleep, but they wake us up for a pee break. When we get to the city, often we don't even check in, we just go straight backstage, put on wet white and makeup, do our hair, and out we go on stage."

"Day after day?"

"Day after day." Angela smiled. "But what else are we going to do? Sit around in unemployment offices wishing we could spend the rest of our lives appearing at the Royal Alexandra Theatre?"

CHAPTER TEN
1957

After Christmas, with Angela off on tour again, Paul turned his attention to directing. He had arranged to meet Rudi Dorn before rehearsals, wondering what he'd make of this Ugo Betti play. At the Newman home recently, Paul had asked what Sydney had up his sleeve for the next show.

"You'll love it," Sydney had said in response. "It's a classic."

"But first," Betty interrupted, "let me tell Paul how we all loved his repeat of *The Return of Don Juan* last night. We didn't catch it the first time. The girls liked it, too." Sydney's wife Betty had a rather sharp face, black hair pulled back in a ponytail, glasses, a bit like a schoolmarm but with a warm personality. She'd been at the National Film Board, but now was a full time mother and apparently the intellectual of the family.

Sydney went on, "It's called *The Sacred Scales.*"

"Scales? What — some Hindu play about a mystical lizard?" Paul grinned.

Sydney looked at him with a gleam in his eye. "The scales are the scales of justice!" He pretended to be contemptuous, clearly delighting in Paul's lack of knowledge.

"Oh God, not a courtroom drama, Sydney!" Paul shot back.

"Not at all. Listen, it's by Ugo Betti." Sydney watched Paul closely, hoping to see a blank look.

Paul shrugged. "I don't think I know his plays."

Sydney, delighted, elaborated: "He's only the most famous living French playwright —"

"Italian," Betty corrected.

"Yes yes, I meant Italian."

Paul frowned. "The most famous living Italian playwright?"

"Well, he's not exactly living," Betty interposed. "He died a couple of years ago."

"Listen," Sydney said, "this is his most famous play. *Corruption in the Courts* — what the hell is the Italian title, Betty?"

"*Corruzione al Palazzo di Giustizia,*" Betty answered.

Paul felt duly chastised. "I thought Pirandello was the most famous Italian playwright."

"Okay, okay, so Ugo Betti is the second most famous playwright, I'll give you that." Sydney was still enjoying putting one over on his arrogant young director.

"Sounds fabulous," Paul said. "But please, get me Rudi Dorn."

And so Paul met with Rudi. "What did you think of the script?"

"What do you expect?" growled Rudi. "I hate all this dialogue." Again he pulled his hand down over his face to contort his features.

"Rudi, look, in this scene here, in the library, we have a guy on the floor, dying. What the hell do we do?" Pedestal cameras at their lowest only went down to three foot six.

Rudi brushed his hand through his short but ample brown hair, and started scribbling on a pad. Paul looked down, trying to decipher the scrawls.

After silence had settled, the suspense began to get to Paul. "So what do you think, Rudi?"

But Paul had to wait for the Oracle to manufacture another miracle.

Rudi pushed away the pad and sunk into his chair with a brooding look.

None the wiser, Paul asked, "So explain it."

"I build set on a ramp. It slopes, look. Four feet at the front for the camera, then down to the floor at the back. Then I distort everything. I distort the perspective. I distort the ceiling. The shelves. Everything. Now you chust shoot, and you got your effect."

"Oh my God," said Paul. "I can't believe this! A set on risers! All distorted! Never seen before. Fantastic!"

And fantastic it proved to be — but not without attendant problems....

On the second day's rehearsal in River Street Studios, with sets taped out on the floor, the double doors opened and in came Peter Garstang, the head of the stage crew, with his assistant Lawrie McVicker. "I was just checking on the design department downstairs, and they're all in an uproar, discussing your show.

"Oh really?"

"Yes, really. Rudi wanted us to bring up these risers so that you could rehearse on them. We never allow risers in the rehearsal rooms. But Rudi insisted. So Lawrie and I figured, what the hell, we'll get some stage crew —"

They were interrupted by Patrick Carney, a sometimes caustic stagehand, struggling with his friend, Dave McFadyen, to carry in the large riser. Paul and his cast stopped rehearsing and watched.

"You'd better not be after blamin' us," said Patrick. "Rudi tells us what the hell he wants, and we build the bloody thing," Irish accent, for sure.

"No matter how crazy," Dave added. "He's the one they're gonna fire, not us, were just doing what we're told."

Paul burst out laughing. "If this show gets on air, none of us will be fired. We'll all get medals."

They shook their heads. No shortage of hubris in this young man, they decided.

These heavy rostra were not just flat but sloped. The actors looked on, aghast.

"You don't expect us to stand on that cockamamie slope and try to act?" grimaced Lloyd Bochner.

Eric Christmas gave out a laugh like a whinny. "I'll have a great death scene on that!"

After they had gone, Paul said, "Let's try that scene right now, while it's fresh."

"I think you'll have to get a new cast, Paul," remarked Lloyd dryly. "How is John Drainie going to prance around on that with his game leg?"

John, rather sensitive about his limp, leapt into the fray. "I'll do that fine! You fellows with two good legs better watch out."

"Come on, fellas," Paul urged, "let's give the scene a try."

Lloyd, always impeccably dressed, immaculately groomed, the quintessential handsome leading man, wore gleaming leather shoes guaranteed to slip off any slope. Charles Jarrott, new to Canada, always in a bright waistcoat, his black hair perfectly groomed, was more malleable. Did he already have plans to become a director himself?

They gave the scene a try, but first Paul urged Lloyd to take off his shoes and try his socks. Teetering precariously on the slanted rostra, the actors proceeded to enact the Ugo Betti scene. And Paul was delighted.

In Studio One, however, on the first day of rehearsal, consternation was palpable. Paul had taken the precaution of warning Cec Johns, the technical producer, of the slightly unusual sets.

"Slightly?" barked Cec as he came into the studio. "These are SLIGHTLY unusual sets?"

"Well, the main thing is, Cec, we're going to have a great show. Isn't that important?"

"All right, if it ever gets on the air!" Cec would never argue about exciting shows with this unpredictable ball of energy. He hurried over to his lighting director, and Paul heaved a sigh of relief.

Later in the dress rehearsal, Paul's excitement in the control booth knew no bounds. "Look at that shot, Rudi!" — as the camera framed what Rudi had expressly designed the set for: Eric in the foreground on the riser, behind him library and actors distorted by the two-inch lens, astonishing. "Rudi, look!"

"Ach Gott, Paul, I watch when you put on camera, I watch again for rough dress, now you want me to watch again? It's too much," Rudi cried loudly. "I can't keep looking at little screens all day. Drives me crazy!"

"Okay okay, Mary Lou, Mary Lou, you look!" Paul was so excited, he had to get some reaction; she was his new African-Canadian script assistant.

"Yes Paul, yes! Ready shot twenty-seven on three." She had to keep her eye on the script or there'd be no show going out live on time.

Paul's excitement even grew when they shot down a special twenty-foot table, which on a wide-angle lens looked a mile long. John Drainie, shrunk by the lens, appeared tiny at the far end and next to him, Paul Endersby sulked appropriately. Smooth Charles Jarrott talked to a bearded Lloyd. Yes, quite a scene.

As they gathered for a party at John Drainie's afterwards, all agreed it had been a bracing experience. And so, it seemed, did the viewers.

* * *

In April, after Paul gave his actors notes in the spaceship set of *Who Destroyed the Earth*, he walked Harry Boyd through the parking lot and down into the basement of the radio building, where they entered the dingy cafeteria, found food, and sat at a small vinyl table.

"Well," Harry commented after Paul had asked him how he liked the run-through, "all those chairs that came up to your shoulders, double-size, what's the idea?"

"Rudi did it to make the actors look half -size. See, they're aliens."

"That's also why they also have white hair?"

"What a kerfuffle! Kate Blake, she has that wild head of lovely red hair? Well, they put so much bleach on it that it started coming out by the handful! Was I upset."

"So was she, I bet."

"They come upon this abandoned planet with no life, and yet evidence of a wonderful civilization, built by great artists and geniuses. Who could have destroyed it? At the end, you find out. But I haven't put the final picture on set yet — I'm saving it. When Powys Thomas pulls the cord and the curtain drops, the actors will see the explanation on air for the first time. Live!"

Harry looked up. "What's the painting?"

"The Crucifixion." Paul sat back, pleased.

Harry smiled. "That's good."

"The last line of the play is: 'They must have done it to themselves!'"

Harry nodded. "My father will enjoy this. And my mother. Tomorrow at nine?"

"Now Harry, about your father..."

Harry interrupted. "Is this one of Brian Freeland's religious programs?"

"Brian commissioned it. He thinks that's the best way to get any message across — through drama." Paul paused. "Now Harry, I have something to ask..."

"Oh, before I forget, Cay cut this out of Liberty Magazine for you. They give annual prizes for excellence in television. Here's a piece on you."

Paul glanced at the first sentence: *Alford is a tall, tense, tweedy Montrealer of 28, blue-eyed, bowtied, with coffee-nerves animation, who snaps his fingers to make his point.* "Oh. Thank Cay, Harry." He put it in his pocket. "Now listen..."

"You're not going to want Dad to take Alice again?"

"I don't have her any more. And he never took Alice."

"Don't you remember when you asked me to look after Alice before you went away that time?"

"Sort of."

"Well, Cay wouldn't let the skunk stay, so I put it in Dad's rectory office. When he came back, he opened his study door and nearly fainted!" They both burst out laughing.

"Oh dear," said Paul. "Because that's why I wanted to talk to you. You see, Harry," Paul had finished his unappetizing meal, "Angela and I have decided to get married."

Harry stopped eating, put down his knife and fork, and stared. Paul grinned. Harry shook his head. "I thought you and Angela were always having trouble."

"We are. But you know, she is kind of highly strung."

"And you're not?"

Paul chuckled. "Well, that's part of the problem, I guess. We both are. Somehow, it's never worked that well. I've gone away, I've tried all sorts of ways to break up, and we're still together. So the only thing we have not tried is marriage. Maybe that will help. So we're trying..."

"Not a really good reason to marry," Harry murmured.

"I guess not. But we seem to have no other alternative. Anyway,"

Paul went on, "could we marry in your United Church? Brian told me that Anglicans are not fond of marrying someone who's been married before."

"You haven't been married before."

"No, but Angela has."

"When would you like to do it?"

"Soon. Maybe June 1st?" Paul leaned closer. "Listen, it'll just be us, Grant Strate is giving Angela away, her parents are in Africa. Lillian Jarvis as Maid of Honour, she's a principal dancer like Angela and even looks a bit like her. Then maybe Sydney and Betty, Rudi and Margaret. I'm trying to get away without my mother and Auntie coming, because they'll bring a pile of friends — but they will anyway. That's all."

"I'll try."

"It's a Saturday. Stephanie can get out of boarding school. Angela's racing like hell to get our new apartment ready, making curtains, even making her own wedding dress. George Crum, you know, the conductor of the Ballet orchestra, he'll play the organ. Nice, but small."

Harry grinned. "Well, if my father gets over the skunk episode, I might get him to do it."

"Harry, Angela will have been on tour all winter, February to June. Guess how many cities?"

"I don't know. About a dozen?"

"Wrong. Seventy cities, Harry. Seventy. All one night stands, travel all day by bus... And that after thirty-two performances in Toronto in January. Can you believe it?"

"She's amazing. You sure you want to marry that whirling dervish?"

"What else can I do?" Paul let the sentence hang.

So on June 1st, 1957, Paul and Angela were married by the Rev. Henry Allen Boyd, and then moved into a new apartment at 29a

Isabella Street. The government also changed, with John Diefen-baker replacing Louis Saint Laurent as Prime Minister. Lots of change, Paul thought. Now to try a new way of life.

CHAPTER ELEVEN
AUTUMN 1957

In September 1957, Paul's new script assistant, Pat Young, popped her head inside Paul's door. "Bernard Slade has just come out of George Salverson's office. Shall I grab him?" Pat was nothing if not efficient. Tall, brown hair and eyes, she was pockmarked from some childhood disease but so charming that everyone liked her. Mary Lou Carter had gone on to another producer.

Paul caught Bernard walking down the long wide office on Front Street. Known for his sense of humour, Bernard was tall, slim, with a prominent nose and sharp brown eyes, and also a reasonable actor. George Salverson, one of the two new script editors, had been trying to get him to write another play. "Bernie, got a second?"

Bernie turned. "What now? You want to ruin another one of my plays?"

Paul grinned. "Bernie, you know that *The Prizewinner* wasn't my fault. Give us a second." They wandered into Paul's office. "I'm doing Arthur Hailey's next play, *Seeds of Power.*"

"I don't want to hear," said Bernard.

"No no, it's important. It's the first television drama about an atomic power station!"

"So what?"

"Look, Art Hailey's important, Bernie. Didn't you know?"

"Of course, everyone knows. So why are you telling me?"

"Because," Paul said with a flourish, "I want to offer you a part!"

"Why? Ah, you want to hire my wife!" Jill Foster was one of Paul's favourite actresses, having played in several of his productions, including *The Hill.* Warm and motherly, she was also good at playing dumb blondes.

Paul wondered how to get out of this one. "As a matter of fact, Bernie, I do want to offer Jill a part."

"So you can offer us a twofer? Two parts for one salary?"

Paul laughed. "The thing is, Bernie, it's pretty exciting. I don't know if you've heard of Chalk River?"

"The new power station? Up near Ottawa. Of course."

"No one has put a nuclear power station in a teleplay before. Art and I thought it up together. Chalk River is leading the world in nuclear power, but we decided to set the plot in India, to avoid controversy. It's about sabotage, and how atomic power might get out of hand."

"And you're going to shoot all this in Studio Four?" Bernard chortled.

"You sound just like Rudi Dorn. In fact, he is doing the sets. But listen, it's the first of a big new series of four plays that the Bank of Canada is sponsoring to sell Canada Savings Bonds. Sydney got me some extra money, and I went to Ottawa and shot inserts at Chalk River!"

Bernie nodded. "Another chance for a fuck-up."

"You're not still thinking about *The Prizewinner*?"

"What else have I got to think about? It was my first play. I wrote it so that I could play the lead."

"I know, Bernie, I know." Paul had taken over the production from Ted Kotcheff, who had come down with a serious flu. When the play went to New York, Bernie's agent, Jay Sanford, sold it like a cracker-jack, though CBC editors only responded after six weeks. But because Sydney had moved fast, he'd slapped it on before the Americans.

"First, I wasn't cast in it, and then, when it went out on air — no sound for half an hour! Jill and I went nuts fiddling with our sets."

"I noticed the technicians coming and going, but never I heard what happened till after the show. We got all the sound in the control room, of course."

"Why the hell didn't they put up a card saying *technical difficulties are temporary?* When I phoned later, they told me they couldn't find the card!" Bernie had to laugh.

"Maybe this role will help; Arthur has quite a reputation after *Flight Into Danger.* I was in Europe when David Greene did it."

"I know, I know, everyone raved. I thought it was pretty good. When both pilots come down with food poisoning, Jimmy Doohan takes over — but he's never piloted a big airplane. Clever. Where is David now, by the way?"

"New York. Doing *Studio Ones.* You don't think they'd give this to me if he were here, do you? Now look, I've got John Drainie in it, and I persuaded Katherine Blake —"

"Didn't she go down there with David?"

"No. Remember Charles Jarrott?" Bernie shook his head. "Well, Charles had come over from England at David Greene's suggestion and stayed with him. Before you knew it, bingo, Kate fell in love with Charles and left David. So now he's fallen for Eileen Jack, who used to be my script assistant. She's gone down to New York instead."

"Ring-around-the-rosy. The Drama Department makes Peyton Place look like kindergarten. So when," Bernie asked, "does this wondrous show of yours go out?"

"October 3rd."

When Bernard left, right away Nathan Cohen stood in the doorway. A scathing theatre critic, he was by no means physically attractive: above heavy jowls, his crinkly thinning grey-black hair was combed straight back. "Paul, this is Arthur Hailey."

In came Art, every inch a gentleman with suit and tie, rather like a car salesman. And in fact, he was still the editor of an automotive magazine. His first play, *Flight into Danger,* had been such a hit here and in America, he was much sought after. A model writer, he sat and pulled out a yellow pad.

Nathan folded his hands across his ample stomach.

What could Paul say? He would have preferred a one-on-one with the author. But he went over a few slight changes and Arthur went off to polish the first television play ever written about an accident in an atomic power station.

* * *

In early November, Sydney and Betty Newman threw Ted Kotcheff a farewell party at their Rosedale home, 3 Nesbitt Drive. Most directors came, a few of the prettier script assistants, and some of the better actors. Ted was a large, imposing Bulgarian given to stating his wishes boldly without regard to crew feelings. But to his cast he was gentle and supportive.

"Hi, Ted," Paul said. "You going nuts again?"

"You mean, leaving for England?"

"Don't you like it here? I mean, look at the freedom we have."

"Yes, but I joined CBC in 1952, stage crew first, then Studio Director, then —"

"— You started directing in about 1955."

"Yep. So now, two years later, time to move on."

Paul shook his head. "What does Sydney think of that?"

"Oh, he's all right with it. He has to be," Ted added with a laugh. "You know, Silvio Narizzano's over there now." Paul had been sad to see him go. "And Hank Kaplan, too."

"I know, they're all going," Paul went on. "I spent three years at Oxford and I stayed on afterwards so I have no hankering to go back."

"My friend Stanley Mann, the writer, is there," Ted added, "and Mordecai Richler. I'm not married, so what the hell, I thought, get moving."

"Angie and I always liked your productions, Ted. We make a special point of watching them."

Ted nodded in appreciation. "What I like here is we all watch each other's shows. You see, a few months ago Silvio recommended me to London's ABC. So I got a contract with Armchair Theatre." Later, Sydney would move to the UK himself to run that series.

"Well, best of luck."

Their hostess, Betty, came over and Paul thanked her for the party. "We'd do anything for Ted." She smiled down at her daughter, Deirdre, coming up with hors d'oeuvres in an incongruous party frock. Paul had only seen her as a tomboy, jeans and ragged shirt, ready to climb the nearest tree. Her pretty sister Jenny, however, suited her frock perfectly.

Paul spotted Sheila Hailey, looking a little lost. "Hi Sheila. What's Arthur up to these days?"

Sheila seemed every inch a Toronto wife: pleasant, cheery, well kept, and full of warmth. "Working on another play about his childhood in England during the war."

"Is he? Hope I get to do it."

"Oh yes, if he gets it on, he'll want you. We loved what you did with *Seeds of Power* about Chalk River."

Paul nodded. "Thanks, Sheila.

Toby Robins came over to give Paul a dazzling smile. His heart looped the loop, and he resolved to find another play for her as quickly as possible. She and her husband, Bill Freedman, had a fine large house in Forest Hill, well beyond Paul's means.

A newcomer to the Drama Department, Gordon Hinch, a former agency producer, was passing out drinks. "Some wine, Paul? Or more gin and tonic?"

"Yes please." Gordon, short, with black hair and glasses, looked like an accountant. "My golly," Paul shook his head, "we keep adding personnel all the time. What do we need a Unit Manager for, anyway?"

"When I find out, I'll let you know." Gordon grinned as they went to find some finger food on a cabinet Betty used for sewing. Sydney had proudly explained he'd made it himself; he loved working with wood.

"Are we going to have you looking over our shoulders?"

"No no, I'm cloistered in an office, checking facts and figures for Sydney, and then reporting to the 'Kremlin'" — where network executives worked. Fergus Mutrie, for example, director of all Toronto television, had just met with Paul and upped his salary, which would place him among the highest paid producers of any department. In three short years, he'd gone from three figures to six, just as Angela had demanded. Fergus added that any time Paul wished, he could take off and do other shows, but he'd always have a place in drama — or on Bob Allen's new *Folio*, a prestige series of operas, ballets and dramas that Paul hungered for.

* * *

In November, 1957, they were rehearsing *Lost in a Crowd* on the fifth floor of the Sumach Street design building, a fairly new — and at last clean — warehouse structure, though its huge round pillars badly interrupted rehearsal space.

"Mind if I say something, Paul?"

"Please do, Vivian."

Paul had seen Vivian Nathan in Sydney Lumet's *Deaf Heart* on *Studio One*, and brought her from New York. She insisted on rehearsing for her role as the Polish mother in costume: mottled blue apron, dowdy dress, and braids wrapped around to frame her face. Since her arrival, Paul had grown to like her enormously. Warm, kindly, and having played on Broadway, she was a consummate actress. Paul had also cast a stunning young Toby Tarnow, a lead on *Howdy Doody* and in the movie *Anne of Green Gables*. She and Jonathan White made an excellent team, Jonathan being blond, Toby with her short, curly brown hair.

"Paul, I love the way you direct us: you leave us free," said Vivian. "But might it help if I talk to Jonathan about his action?"

"You mean, where he's standing?"

"No, his 'action' in the scene." They all listened, full of interest.

"You see, an action, well it's... what you need to ACHIEVE in the scene: your want, your desire, that gives the drive a scene needs."

Jonathan looked perplexed. "So what would my action here be?"

"In this scene, you want her to marry you, don't you?" Jonathan nodded. "And Toby, you don't want to, at least not yet."

Toby nodded. "So I'm trying to find a way to avoid what he's going to ask?"

"Yes. And these needs must be foremost. Jack has written this really cleverly, so it's not obvious, but it's there underneath..." Jack Kuper, the author, had popped up from the graphics Department below, where he worked.

Paul leapt up. "That's terrific, Vivian. So they follow that right to the end?"

"Not really. You see, we can divide the scene into what we call 'beats.'"

"Oh, you mean like the rhythm," Jonathan asked, "like beating a drum?"

"No, we're talking about when one action ends and another begins. In other words, the scene may have one beat, or several. In this beat, before I come in and interrupt, Jonathan, you are trying to get Toby to sit down so you can have a proper talk. But Toby knows that when she sits and lets you hold her hands, you're going to talk seriously about the future."

"I see that," Toby agreed.

"So put another way, Jonathan, your action could be to get her to sit down. And your action, Toby, could be to avoid sitting."

"Terrific!" Paul exclaimed. "Shall we try it again?"

"Another thing..." Vivian went on, "if you don't mind Paul?"

"No, no, keep talking, Vivian. I guess this is the famous Method Acting we've heard about?"

Vivian nodded. "One of the things we often do is improvise. We ad lib, maybe something tangential, but often a key to our emotions. Some actors are better at this than others," and she threw a quick look at Jack, "then we go back to the script, of course. But in this way, we discover new things about our characters and the scene, or our emotional responses. Though sometimes, I admit, on *Studio One*, we've even improvised on air. But it requires a pretty agile director calling the shots."

"I bet it does!" Paul grinned. "I'd be ready for that."

"Let's not rush ahead," Vivian cautioned.

"Okay," Paul broke in, "how about trying this scene with you, Jonathan, saying whatever comes into your head, but trying to get Toby to sit down, and Toby, you using any trick you can, woman's wiles, anything you like, to avoid it. And we'll see what happens."

Toby and Jonathan tried improvising, when Jack leapt up. "This has given me some ideas. I'd like to try altering the scene slightly and bring it in tomorrow. Would that be all right, Paul?"

"Just great — if you wouldn't mind?" He turned to his actors.

They actors seemed delighted at this turn of events.

As the rehearsals progressed, Vivian kept dropping more pearls of wisdom about Method Acting, whose chief exponent, Lee Strasberg, taught at the Actors Studio in New York, where Vivian was a member. Other Method coaches, Stella Adler and a Group Theatre pioneer Sanford Meisner, all used techniques pioneered by the great Constantin Stanislavski at the Moscow Art Theatre, where he had even worked with Anton Chekhov.

It's so great learning new processes, Paul thought. One more technique. He'd see how it worked on live television.

CHAPTER TWELVE
1957-58

Kenya

Full of anticipation, Paul parked along Front Street and hurried to Union Station where the ballet company's bus was due. Through the autumn they had given twenty-eight performances in Hamilton, St. Catherine's, Kitchener, Belleville, Ottawa, Sherbrooke, Québec City, and Montréal. And now, Sunday night, December 1st, Paul had gone to pick up his bride.

When he got there, Dick Butterfield, a handsome blond banker from Bermuda, was waiting for his wife, Lillian Jarvis. They were married in '56, after Lillian did *A Soldier's Tale* in Stratford in '55, with Douglas Rain, and Marcel Marceau in his North American debut and only speaking role. "Lillian called from their lunch stop. The bus driver thought he'd might be fifteen or twenty minutes late," he told Paul. "By the way, that was quite some article on you in the Weekend Globe."

"Yeah, thanks Dick." Paul had brought a copy to show Angela, though he'd only glanced at it. Over the weekend he'd been working hard on a script that Brian Freeland had commissioned him to write on spiritual healing. But now he found the night chilly. "I'll just run into the railway station and wait in the warm."

Once there, he pulled out the article: several pages and lots of photographs.

Paul Alford, this tall, thin, young man with bushy brown hair and a quick and fleeting smile, has great depths of enthusiasm. His lanky figure suggests that he should move like Gary Cooper or Henry Fonda but instead he bounds among his actors like Mickey Rooney.

Oh migosh, is that how the writer saw me? He read on.

His method of handling the play is believed to be more important to establish the feeling of a scene than to adhere slavishly to dialogue as written.

Not exactly. But what the hell.

When working, Alford is a bundle of nervous energy. He finds it hard to stand still and his communications to others are apt to take the form of a series of staccato, unfinished sentences: "I see, that's fine, yes, yes lovely, just lovely. Now let's try..."

Paul grimaced, not sure he liked it. But he couldn't stop reading.

Or, if his ire falls on some object at a difficult time, the utterance may be more pronounced. "This is the most ridiculous table," he said sharply one day. "I'm fed up with it and I want it struck at once!" He finished by thrusting the table off the set himself.

In the studio, he changes shots at key moments by snapping his fingers and saying "take!" or "take it," punctuated by a stream of technical instructions and cues, the latter set up by a script assistant. During the performance, a hundred and thirty shots were taken by the three cameras. All worked by Alford.

He shrugged. Well, I suppose that's interesting how it all works, but how did he get the number of shots? Probably from Pat.

During rehearsals at Sumach, Alford seemed to forget what the performers were saying and began looking for camera shots. He would crouch low and squint between his hands in an attempt to see the scene as the camera would, repeating the process from tabletops and floor, searching for high and low angles as well as lateral positioning. Once the show was in Studio One, Alford worked from the control booth. Under these conditions, technical details flood his time and almost obscure his handling of the artists.

Honks from the bus brought Paul hurrying out to join other friends, lovers, and spouses of the dancers, as the raggle-taggle and worn-out company emerged to collect their bags. Angela was one of the first and Paul wrapped his arms around her heavily clothed body in a big hug. She seemed pleased. "I told Grant and Earl we'd give them a lift, if that's all right?"

"Of course. I'll just go get the car."

They piled in and headed up Jarvis Street towards Grant and Earl's attic apartment in Rosedale. They were all tired, but exhilarated at being back home again. Paul dropped them and Angela said, "See you Tuesday, Grant."

"You've got Monday off?" Paul asked.

"Yes, but Tuesday, class and rehearsals again."

"Oh not Pape Hall! I'd forgotten," Earl said. "Do you think they've cleaned it up?"

Grant chuckled. "They've only just found money to pay us for the December rehearsals — I doubt there's extra for cleaning!"

Back in the car heading over to Isabella Street, Paul gossiped happily about his recent visit to New York. "Wonderful time, Angela: the New York City Ballet, three by Stravinsky and Balanchine. So exciting!"

"Go on."

"Well, I also saw *West Side Story* — "

"Yes, I heard the dancing is wonderful."

"Sure is. Jerome Robbins brought the *Romeo and Juliet* story up to date — all done as a gang war. Best thing down there."

"Lucky you," was all Angela replied.

"I got into a preview of Tyrone Guthrie's *The Necropolis Secret* with Eileen Hurley, and *The Rope Dancers,* an Irish play with Siobhan McKenna — she's terrific. Also, *Compulsion,* which was really first class."

"Did you see David and Eileen?"

"Yes, Thanksgiving dinner with them in their flat in Greenwich Village. He's directing *Twelfth Night* with Maurice Evans on the *Hallmark Hall of Fame,* an hour and a half! I saw bits of rehearsal, which was fun. Oh — and I had lunch with Bill Shatner and Lee J. Cobb. They're both working on *Studio One's No Deadly Medicine.* I saw Lee as Willy Loman in *Death of a Salesman* back in '49. He's an amazing actor."

"You told me in a letter you'd been to the Actor's Studio."

"Yes, Vivian took me. It's pretty small, almost grungy, with raked seats around. I watched a couple of tremendous young actors do a scene, and then Lee spent the rest of the hour talking. I guess they came to hear him, but I wished he'd allowed more couples to do scenes. I picked up a few tips..." When Angela didn't react, he went on, "I've gotten a little something ready. I bet you're tired."

"Thanks, old bean. Yes, I danced Queen of the Wilis Friday night, then Snow Queen in *Nutcracker,* Chiarina in *Carnaval* and Felice in *Winter Night* at yesterday's matinee, and last night, Queen of the Carriage Trade in *Offenbach.* Three performances in two days."

"Oh boy," Paul said, "Right after the snack — into bed." He could hardly wait! A whole month without her.

"I do need sleep rather badly," Angela replied ominously.

139

While Angela unpacked her suitcase, Paul took the grilled cheese sandwiches out of the warming oven, lit candles and put music on the hifi (high fidelity sound). He wanted this to be a romantic evening. But he had his doubts.

At dinner, Angela gave him her news. She had just appeared for a fortnight in Montreal at Her Majesty's Theatre. "Your mother was so nice; she took me out to Apple Barrel on Sunday for a lovely lunch. And I went for a walk on the mountain."

"Oh yes..." Paul wiped his mouth with his napkin. "Remember that night when we took our blankets and lay in the moonlight under the apple trees? The wind came up and blew white apple blossoms all over us. Such a beautiful time..."

Angela lowered her eyes. "That was when we were on holiday. I'm going to be working awfully hard this December." She changed the subject. "Your Aunt Hilda came, too. You know she's directing a play?"

"I heard something about that," Paul said

"It's a huge production. She teaches four days a week in different Catholic schools. She's working hard."

"And Mum is, too." Paul helped himself to another glass of wine.

"Your mother never stops. She's now a District Manager with *Beauty Counsellors*, helping other women learn beauty counselling. She's coming to their head office in Detroit in January, so she'll stay with us on her way."

"I guess she's making more money than she used to."

Angela nodded. "And she seems to enjoy it. She brought several ladies along to see one performance. They were so tickled to come backstage. I introduced them to Lillian, and even to David Adams and Lois Smith. I think your mum liked all that."

"I bet she did." Then Paul brought the subject back... "I looked over the poem I wrote for you that spring on Mont. Saint-Hilaire."

Paul repeated it [see Appendix] while Angela finished her light meal.

"Very nice. I've not seen it since you sent it to me."

"Those were the days, eh Angela?"

"And these are the days now. We're married."

"We sure are. So. Nothing has changed. Has it?"

Angela glanced up quickly and then rose. "I'm off to bed now. I'm absolutely worn out."

Paul's libido had been growing all through dinner. Angela looked beautiful in the candlelight and he desired her as never before. He let her get changed while he cleaned up their simple meal.

As he came in, he saw that Angela had changed into a pink shorty nightie, her flawless legs beneath, and her equally flawless body, a Stradivarius among the dancing instruments of the other girls. Once in his pyjamas, he slid under the covers.

Angela lay as if asleep. He reached over to pull her to him.

"Not tonight, Paul. I'm dead tired."

* * *

In March, the news was full of the Progressive Conservatives massive election victory led by John Diefenbaker. Paul got to direct another play on Robert Allen's prestigious *Folio* and then did a couple more dramas on GM *Presents*, including one by Arthur Hailey, *Epitaph at Little Buffalo*, with splendid Jimmy Doohan.

His main achievement was A *Phoenix too Frequent* by Christopher Fry, whose gifted and sparkling poetic wit had captivated West End audiences. Paul had teamed Donald Harron, a terrific comic actor, with Broadway performer Rosemary Harris, on whom he had developed a huge crush — which went nowhere: she was about to marry the director, Ellis Rabb. Paul had met Mr.

Fry in England and persuaded him to give the rights: so far not one of his plays had been seen on North American television. Another first for Paul.

So this July, 1958, Paul had arranged for the three of them to visit Angela's family in Kenya. Would it help their relationship? He'd give it a shot — and anyway, at worst, he found the idea of an African visit appealing.

"So you're off to see your parents, Angela?" asked Stanley Myer's wife, Fiz, when they'd arrived in London.

"Yes. Celia gave me a whole month's holiday. We're so excited. You know, we danced in sixty-seven cities this winter. Can you believe it?" Angela was helping Fiz prepare dinner in their flat at 100 Eaton Place in London's Belgravia. In a bedroom, Stephanie was looking at a picture book of African animals; Nicholas, now two, was asleep, but would waken boisterously as the evening progressed.

"What are your parents doing in Africa?" asked Fiz.

"I was born in Uganda," Angela explained. "My father was a bank manager in Kampala, Uganda, but during the war, mother and I took home leave and I studied ballet in London."

In the living room out of earshot, Paul quietly discussed his situation with Stanley. "What's the idea of this Africa trip?" Stanley asked. "Last time you were here, you swore that you were going to break up. Now you're married?"

Paul sighed. "I have no idea what will happen. Angie was away all winter, on tour. I couldn't stop myself, I fell for a really pretty script assistant and then, imagine the kerfuffle when I had to tell her that Angela was coming back, and I couldn't really destroy my marriage. So, we're back together again. But you know, Stanley, we have a lot in common. She has a great sense of humour, works like a dog, decorated our apartment beautifully, right near the CBC, she understands me, so in a way, everything works well..."

"Except?"

"Yeah, except in bed. She won't let me touch her. Drives me nuts. We got married, and crash – down came the blinds! I have no idea why. We even tried a therapist. Not much help."

Stanley shook his head. "And you're spending all this money flying her and Stephanie to Africa?"

"I'll try anything to make it work. Before we got married, Stanley, there was no containing her. She was almost sex-crazed, we made love all the time, but once she was married, nothing!"

Stanley grinned. "Sounds like some textbook case for any old psychiatrist."

"You'd think so. But the one we have doesn't know what to do about it."

They eyed each other glumly, and then wandered over to the kitchen. "Maybe dancers are like that," Stanley added. "Though it hasn't affected Fiz. She's directing now, and she's a great chore-ographer."

"You're a director, Fiz?" Paul asked. "You never told me. You're so modest!"

"Paul," Stanley announced firmly, "Fiz just directed the most popular musical in the West End, *Grab me a Gondola*! She also directed *Share my Lettuce*, another hit. She's highly successful, though she'd never tell you herself."

Fiz, not wanting to be the object of attention, turned to Paul. "That Mau Mau uprising is still going on down there. It's a State of Emergency, so I'd be awfully careful."

Angela shuddered. "But aren't there more Africans killed than whites?"

"So it seems."

"Angela's mother," Paul mentioned, "is a matron at a girl's school in Nairobi. That's pretty safe."

Angela nodded. "Betty has to work. My father is retired and lives with another woman at a place called Njoro. We're going to visit them."

"Daddy writes to me," Fiz warned, "that outside the city, things are by no means settled."

"Is your father still in Kenya?" Paul knew Fiz had been born there.

"Yes. But he left my mother, too," Fiz confirmed, "and now he's with a woman called Pat, very nice, it appears. They have a couple of children a bit younger than Stephanie. You must go see them."

"Good," Paul said. "What does he do?"

"He's retired now, but still goes into the Secretariat, that's the Government: Kenya is run by a Legislative Council. In those British Empire days, Daddy , as a senior official, had to set a standard of allegiance to the British Crown. He flew the Union Jack on his car and on the flag post in our garden."

"He's very well-known," Stanley chimed in, "even now."

As they were sitting down to eat, Fiz asked, "When did your parents divorce, Angela?"

"After the war. My mother was a notorious shopper. With my father being a bank manager and away all day, Mother would go shopping and spend money they didn't have on dresses she didn't need. The bank cautioned him and Daddy did try to explain it to her. But mother never really got the picture."

"I'm anxious to meet them," Paul said.

Arriving in Nairobi, they were met by Angela's mother, Betty Firmin, with her African driver. She looked small, almost wizened, but well kept with white hair, a prominent nose and sharp, piercing blue eyes. They drove to the prestigious Norfolk Hotel, *the* place to stay in Nairobi. Built in 1904, its spacious grounds were scattered with round thatched-roof dwellings and protected by a fence.

The next day, they investigated the city. Quite tiny, Paul thought, a hodgepodge of native huts beside modern apartments, a bank or two, and buildings built out over arcades, shading the sidewalks from the sun. Not many whites, mostly natives speaking Swahili (with varying degrees of competence), their many tribal languages making communication difficult. Paul bought a book, *Teach Yourself Swahili*.

After a few days of rest, they set off for Angela's father, Stanley Firmin, and his new wife Dorrie, at Njoro, near Nakuru, some hundred miles away through grassland and scrub, on a plateau over five thousand feet above sea level — not too hot, although just below the equator.

On the way, they made a detour to meet Brig. Sydney Fazan, OBE, CBE, CMG, who had received a letter from his daughter, Fiz, and so invited them to lunch, longer if they could manage it.

When they pulled up, two enormous dogs, baying furiously, bounded up to the car. The Brigadier hurried out, motioning his visitors to stay inside while he talked to the dogs. "Hello hello! Just give Jasper a few minutes to get acquainted and he'll be all right. They are trained to attack, you see. Better than any gun, though I have a few in the house, of course."

The Fazan's were delighted with the news of Eleanor, but they wanted to know more about Stanley, her new husband, so Paul complied copiously. Angela told them of baby Nicholas and the Brigadier drank in every word. "I hope I see Eleanor again one day, but it's doubtful. I do call Kenya home."

Paul could understand them hating to leave this fine house with its eight *shamba* (garden) boys, the usual complement for settlers, and two houseboys, one cook, *mpishi*, with a kitchen *toto* to help, a *dhobi* who did the washing and ironing, and an *ayah* (nanny) who, in Eleanor's time when the parents went out to dinner, would unroll her mat in front of the nursery where the children slept.

Finally, Paul and Angela had to move out into Mau Mau territory.

As they set off for Njoro, Paul prided himself on his bravado, but soon found it disappearing. He began to dwell on the stories heard in the Norfolk Hotel bar: families with children slashed to bits by machetes. Apparently in one case, a houseboy let them into the grounds and Mau Mau slaughtered the parents and two little girls and then looted the house. In another case, the intruders had brutally cut the throats of an elderly settler and his wife in bed. And here he was, "wet behind the ears" taking his stunning and delicious blonde wife and sweet little girl through a kind of No Man's Land into violent danger. He felt his stomach tighten.

"All's well so far, eh Angela?"

"We'll be fine," Angela murmured, with a glance at the back seat. She clearly did not want to alarm little Stephanie.

Nonetheless, his knuckles on the steering wheel whitened as he sent up prayer after prayer for their safety.

But happily, no roving band of guerrillas attacked them. Finally, after what seemed an age, they arrived while it was still light at the Firmin's, enclosed as most homes were by a thick fence of thorn trees and wire.

Angela was overjoyed to see her father, and meet Dorrie. Paul soon took to Stanley: methodical, peaceful, and especially interested in the arts. He even had a Canadian record featuring John Drainie, and knew about Ottawa's Paul Anka, now becoming one of the most popular singers ever. "I just love the arts," Stanley admitted. "Being far away from what you'd call civilization, I surround myself with the odd tidbits."

After a lovely few days, they left. Paul was surprised to see Angela break down in tears. It touched him enormously: she was not given to showing emotion, except, of course, on stage.

At the Nyali Beach Hotel, a splendid Mombasa resort booked by Angela's mother, some sort of dam broke and Angela gave herself to the husband who so longed for her human side to surface again. During the day, they would amble down narrow streets to the old harbour where they'd watch porters in loincloths unload Arab dhows, and spend time lazing on the beach, swimming in the Indian Ocean with natives casting nets just off the beach.

But the delights were not over. On returning to Nairobi, they set off for the obligatory visit to the famous Treetops, where Princess Elizabeth heard she'd one day become Queen. Baboons greeted them and a mother with baby kept opening one of the doors. A toto had to use his slingshot to keep them away. Naturally, the white hunter in charge took a shine to Angela and gave them the special room with three beds, its own WC, and a door onto the veranda where all evening, high in the tree, guests watched bushbuck and waterbuck, a female rogue elephant, and even a mother rhino and her calf come to take the salt lick. All ten visitors, wearing compulsory dark clothing, were enthralled and later sat with the white hunter at a long table — down which a little condiment trolley rolled back and forth on a track in the centre.

But as with all good holidays, it had to end. As they flew back to Toronto to face a heavy schedule, did Paul feel more optimistic about their marriage?

CHAPTER THIRTEEN
1958-59

Hollywood

November. His first day in Hollywood, Paul sat in the old Republic Studios to watch the famed Alfred Hitchcock direct a half-hour in his own series, *Alfred Hitchcock Presents*. The great man looked remarkably like the line drawing that opened each episode. In his director's chair, he gave quiet instructions to individual crew members. The only words Paul heard were: "Action" and "Cut". No running back and forth, as Paul did; so this was the way of film?

Paul's agents, Robin and Hugh French, had gotten him an assignment to direct an episode himself. He found himself warmly greeted by Joan Harrison, slight, with short, swept-back hair in her dark suit. She introduced her associate producer, Norman Lloyd, a former actor. Not tall, with receding sandy hair and glasses, Norman displayed a kindly disposition — which Paul appreciated, feeling rather intimidated at being on the legendary Republic lot.

A production assistant brought in sandwiches and Cokes which Norman took with Paul through to Robert Stevens, lead director on the series, who was next door talking to Margaret Leighton, exuding regal grandeur and refinement. Paul had seen her in Rattigan's *Separate Tables,* a West End triumph, and also on Broadway winning a Tony as Best Actress.

He realized then, here he was, directing an episode on the most prestigious series in Hollywood.

Back in the room, Joan said, "Paul, you'll be happy to hear that we just finalized the deal with Denholm Elliott for your show."

"Wonderful. I last saw him in Fry's *Sleep of Prisoners*. He's a terrific actor."

The next day, Paul began two days of rehearsals, a rarity in series television. After that, on Friday afternoon, Joan and Norman came to watch the simple run through, and seemed pleased. They broke for the weekend — no rehearsing as in Toronto.

Paul was staying with David and Eileen Greene, who had recently moved from New York. They'd both taken up painting, and Eileen ceramics. That evening, Paul saw the results of their efforts and applauded. "It's so good to see you being creative, Eileen. You don't miss working in television?

"I do, actually. But it's awfully nice to do whatever I want."

"How do you like doing Hitchcocks?" David asked.

"I thought I'd be intimidated," Paul said. "But it helps with you guys letting me stay. Exhilarating, I guess."

"No doubt. Now, time for a gin and tonic. After dinner, we'll watch a film of Rattigan's *The Winslow Boy*. Margaret's in it, you know. And I think Denholm Elliott."

On Monday and Tuesday, Paul watched Bob Stevens work, and then started shooting himself. He was taken aback by the speed on set. As soon as the actors repeated their lines, a stage hand marked their feet and the lighting cameraman got the lights focussed while the continuity girl took the actors aside and went over their lines. Once the camera got into position, before Paul knew it, the First AD called for quiet and ran a rehearsal for camera.

All with no input from Paul. But then, this crew had worked together all through the series. But what exactly did the director do?

The First AD (Assistant Director) called, "Quiet on set!"

The noise stopped.

AD: "Turn over sound."

"Speed"

AD: "Roll camera."

"Mark it!"

"Scene twenty-seven; take one."

Pause. The AD looked at Paul.

"Action," Paul said.

The actors went through the short scene, probably forty seconds, and then, the AD looked at Paul again and he realized he should call: "Cut!"

"How was it?" The First AD asked.

"Hair in the gate," the camera operator said.

"We'll go again," said the first AD.

"I'm just as pleased," said Denholm. "I'd like another try."

The rigmarole was repeated.

"Okay for camera? Sound?"

When the affirmatives came, Paul knew enough to say, "Print!"

No sooner were the words out of his mouth, than the First AD ordered, "Next set up! Over the shoulders, Paul?"

Before he could nod, the camera was moving to its new position and adjustments made to the lights, all with such dreadful speed and efficiency.

When Paul didn't know something, he asked, which the crew seemed to appreciate. He had soon realized that, unlike live television, he'd better plan the staging and camera moves ahead of time. Not a method he enjoyed. In fact, he saw that directors had no need of the substantial experience he had — any agent's nephew could do it. And often did!

In the end, Norman told him that he and Joan were both pleased. But Paul couldn't wait to return to his own special way of working on live television.

* * *

In Robert Allen's office, Paul leaned forward earnestly. Earlier, before going to Los Angeles, Paul had directed *Sammy* and *The Dock Brief*, the first plays produced anywhere in North America by John Mortimer, one of London's leading playwrights. "Look Robert, you've really established Folio. It's got an audience. So now, let's do *Under Milk Wood*."

Bob frowned. "That's a verse play for radio."

"I know I know, but I bet we could do it."

Bob shook his head. "Richard Burton is doing it on an American network."

"Yeah, like a film, Bob, with a real village and real houses. Terrible! It's a VERSE play. You have to use your imagination. Let me have a go."

"Think you can get the rights?"

"Bob, I met Dylan one night at the Mandrake Club in London. That's where all the poets drank when the pubs shut at eleven. He was terrific, but full of angst. Drunk when I met him. He died in 1954, poor guy. You know, when I was president of the O.U. Poetry Society, I wanted to get him to come up and talk to us." Bob raised his eyebrows. "Look, I managed to get C. Day Lewis, Stephen

Spender, Louis MacNeice, John Betjeman, I got a ton of famous people. So I sent Peter Dale Scott — he was secretary of the Society — to Laugharne where Dylan lives. But that morning, Dylan had taken the train to London. So he talked to Caitlin, who promised she'd get after him. But nothing happened. Why would he bother coming to talk to a bunch of dumb undergraduates? And anyway, I bet our female members were not attractive enough..."

Bob, amused by Paul's tale, nodded. "All right, see what you can do."

* * *

Brimming with excitement, Paul leapt to open the door to his Isabella Street apartment for Rudi, in his winter coat and fedora. Paul usually went from show to show so quickly, he had no time to catch his breath or otherwise reflect on what he was doing – he just forged ahead, each new occurrence being exciting enough.

"Where is Angela?" Rudi came in and closed the door.

"Off dancing. Nineteen cities in January. But she's home at the Royal Alex for February, when we do this." They went straight into the small room set up as Paul's office. "Rudi, it's going to be such an exciting show — have you read it?"

Rudi pulled a face, as expected. "Paul, what you think? I understand this rubbish?"

"Rudi Rudi, just listen:

"To begin at the beginning:
It is spring, moonless night in the small town, starless
and bible-black, the cobblestreets silent and the hunched,
courters'-and-rabbits' wood limping invisible down to the
sloeblack, slow, black, crowblack, fishingboatbobbing sea.
The houses are blind as moles (though moles see fine to-night
in the snouting, velvet dingles) ..."

Paul had to stop, because Rudi had completely switched off. "Houses blind as moles, Rudi! Moles, they're little blind creatures, so 'they see fine' in pitch darkness! Listen — "in their snouting velvet dingles" — get that, Rudi? Dingles, well, they're little wooded hollows..."

Rudi shook his head. "What, now I design little wooded hollows?" He laughed.

"Okay, okay Rudi, but this, you have to admit this is funny:
MR EDWARDS *Myfanwy Price!*

Paul read with appropriate inflections, but giggling all the while:

*"I am a draper mad with love. I have come to take
you away to my Emporium on the hill...
Throw away your little bedsocks and your Welsh
wool knitted jacket, I will warm the sheets like an electric
toaster, I will lie by your side like the Sunday roast"*

"No? Okay, how about this?" He flipped through pages.

"It is night, neddying among the snuggeries of babies.

"Get that, Rudi? Neddying among the snuggeries..."

Again Rudi shook his head. "Crainford (Head of the Design Department) says you need a village. So I build a Welsh village in studio?" Rudi snorted.

"Rudi, Rudi, those guys have no imagination. Can't they see it's not a play about a village — it's about people. A radio play. Probably the best radio play ever written."

"So give it to those radio guys. What do you expect me to do?"

"You know what I expect us to do — use our imaginations." But then Paul slumped. "But how can we do that if you won't even read it?"

Seeing Paul's switch from ebullience to dejection, Rudi sat up. "Okay, Paul, tell me what you need. Read!" Rudi gestured to the script. "We find elements, okay?"

Paul sighed and nodded. Rudi pulled out his pad and thick pencil, as Paul read:

"Mary Ann Sailors, opening her bedroom window above the
taproom called to the heavens:
"I'm eighty-five years three months and a day!"
Organ Morgan at his bedroom window playing chords on the
sill to the morning fishwife gulls

Rudi: "Two windows."

Paul grinned and went on searching:

"At the sea-end of town, Mr and Mrs Floyd, the cocklers,
are sleeping as quiet as death, side by wrinkled side, toothless,
salt and brown, like two old kippers in a box."

"One bed," Rudi dutifully wrote.

"No no, Rudi, we need two beds. See, right after that comes this bit:

"And high above, in Salt Lake Farm, Mr Utah Watkins counts,
all night, the wife-faced sheep as they leap up the hill
smiling and knitting and bleating just like Mrs Utah Watkins."

"Two beds. And two windows? This is gonna knock their eyes out!"

Paul had to laugh and then, ignoring the sarcasm, went on.

"The Reverend Eli Jenkins, in Bethesda House, gropes out of bed
into his preacher's black, pads barefoot downstairs,
opens the front door..."

"A doorway."

"Yeah, and we just need one; I'll use it for other bits. Oh heavens, here, let me read you this:

"The owls are hunting. Look, over Bethesda gravestones one
hoots and swoops and catches a mouse by Hannah Rees, Be-
loved Wife."

"One cemetery..."

"No no, Rudi, I can play that on the Narrator — oh, I never told you, Douglas Rain is the spitting image of Dylan, if we curl his hair. I met Dylan, you know."

"Big deal — you met the writer. Congratulations!" In spite of himself, Rudi laughed again.

"Rudi, Rudi, it's like you meeting Goethe — "

"If I need to meet him, I put on little wings," Rudi made flapping motions with two hands, "and I fly to heaven."

And so the two of them, laughing, sketching, having fun, went through the whole play figuring out what elements they needed. And then, the chunky Austrian tugged on his hat, dove into his coat, and went out into the frosty Toronto morning, to make what would turn out to be one of the most breathtaking designs ever seen on CBC television.

Paul assembled a splendid cast of Welsh actors, headed by Powys Thomas, Diana Maddox and Sarah Davies, who threaded the play with their delightful lilting accents.

The show got some thirty-five laudatory letters. The distinguished critic Chester Duncan's review said, "It seems to me at this moment that I have never seen a program that excited and satisfied me as much as *Under Milk Wood*." Ron Poulton, in the Toronto Telegram, wrote: "No drama Department of any US network did anything better last season." This was echoed by the well-known TV critic, Dennis Braithwaite, who wrote, "I thought the CBC *Folio* version of *Under Milk Wood* this week was as fine a television production as I have ever seen." The show went on to win the prestigious Ohio State Award that year, which stated: "... exceptional utilization of the TV media. Brilliantly conceived and executed, beautifully staged and performed... A brilliant illustration of CBC creativity, integrity and respect for art."

CHAPTER FOURTEEN
1959

The Hill in England

Seated in the Comet, an all first-class BOAC turbojet flying to London, Paul could hardly believe his luck. He had admired the BBC for years, a Mecca he'd never dreamed of reaching. But he'd received a letter from them inviting him to London to do his own play, *The Hill*, live across the British Isles this Good Friday.

During his splendid dinner with lots of free wine, he kept wondering: what would the cast be like? And an unknown crew? He felt nervous, even though Michael Barry, head of all television drama, had been welcoming. But would Paul feel out of his depth? He'd managed Los Angeles, but now, the renowned BBC?

His old Balliol friend, Tom Espie with his new wife, Ailsa, had invited him to stay until he rented a flat, which he soon found at 25 Cadogan Place near Sloane Square. And of course, dinners with Stanley and Fiz also allayed his apprehension.

Renate Esslin, his script assistant, warned him that the play itself was so different from anything that had gone before, he ought to accept his casting director's suggestion of well-known names, although in Toronto, Paul often preferred new faces. But he would enjoy rehearsing with this experienced cast.

What enlivened his stay was a friendship with a striking and intelligent redhead, Maureen Heneghan, his costume designer. Over candlelit dinners, she filled him in on BBC gossip, and made him feel at home. He found himself inordinately busy, putting this production together so quickly in an unfamiliar environment, and things went smoothly — until he got in the studio.

In the venerable (since 1950) Studio D at Lime Grove in London, the technical producer George Summers announced time for the cameramen to put on earphones and ready their cameras for the first walk-through. The crew had attended a run-through at St. Helen's Church Hall in North Kensington, no rehearsal rooms being available at the Television Centre.

In studio, Rosalie Crutchley as Mary Magdalene, Gwen Ffrancon-Davies as the Virgin, and a number of other stellar British actors, were walking through their well-rehearsed moves on camera for the technical crew. Everything went more or less as planned until Paul told a cameraman, "Go left! Left! Can't you see the shot?"

The voice crackled back: "I'm on my marks."

"Marks? What marks? On the floor? Oh my gawd! Like film?" Paul had noticed some cameramen with chalk in their hands along with their shot lists, but he hadn't paid attention. "Don't tell me you've marked your positions on the floor?"

Another cameramen spoke into his mic. "We always do. That's the way it's done here." Oh yes, a good British understatement: The way it's done here...

"Done! What's this 'done' business?" Paul leapt up, first turning to Renate. "Got a handkerchief? Kleenex? Anything?"

She quickly produced a large white hankie and he grabbed it, tore out of the control booth and onto the studio floor. "Where the hell are those damn marks?" he shouted. Hardly British, of course.

He found some, dropped to his knees and rubbed them out; then went on crawling around, rubbing furiously.

The cameramen stood back, aghast.

He stood. "Look you guys, I told you to take your positions by where the actors are. What the hell is this anyway? We're not a bloody film studio. This is television. Live television. With the most fluid camera mounts known to man. You guys are good, so why not start trusting yourselves, for heaven's sake? Frame your shots by where the actors are, and hey, by how they're feeling — not by stupid marks on a floor like a bunch of automatons."

He didn't wait for the mutiny that he knew was about to take place, but tore back to the booth.

The technical producer told his men on mic, "Don't worry, just keep going, I've rung up."

Soon Michael Barry, head of all drama, came into the control room, an unusual event, apparently. Renate spotted him and nudged Paul.

Paul turned to George. "Give everyone a break, I'll talk to Michael." They went into the corridor, Paul incensed but keeping himself in check. He trusted Michael, an older and kindly supervisor, who had himself selected the play. "Michael," Paul began, "have your guys worked in film? Or were they trained by film technicians?"

Michael nodded. "They come from a long tradition. But what is all this about marks on the floor?"

"Michael, these cameras are the most mobile, flowing, beautiful creatures. Once you lock them down, immobilize them with marks and predetermined heights, you're wasting your most precious resource! I never knew you guys at the BBC were so behind!"

Michael was taken aback. No director had ever spoken this way. "But Paul, you can't break years of tradition."

"Just watch me, Michael, just watch this show when it goes out. It cannot go out with that old-fashioned film technique!" Paul took a breath. "You see those followers of Jesus? They're walking around the studio; they may hit their marks, but you know actors — they move to their own rhythms. The cameramen just have to follow them. Dammit, you've said these are the best crew you have. Well, all they have to do is keep the actors in frame. It's no big problem. I've been on sets in New York, and Hollywood. And listen to the words as the play starts out: "Through their eyes tonight, we shall see His passion.""

Michael was silent. He nodded slightly. "Makes a bit of sense. But do you think they're capable? I mean, some of them have been working this way for years."

"They'll bless me later, Michael, I swear. Look, please, go, have a little chat with them. Blame me. I don't care what you say. Pretend I'm nuts, if you like. Maybe I over-reacted but I can't see them wedged into such darned strait-jackets."

Michael was softening. Paul went on, "The drama department could be facing a disaster. I mean, we have a big crowd of extras, a Chorus in the announce booth, Christ in another, it's a mammoth undertaking. It's costly. We've got to do it my way, or the show won't get on air."

"All right, Paul, let me go down and talk to them."

In the end, this crew and indeed all the BBC did come around, albeit slowly: other drama directors began to adapt to this way of work as it spread through the drama department. But of this Paul was unaware — he was back in Toronto working on his next show. And waiting for Angela, who had been on tour from March to May in thirty-eight cities, with forty-five performances. Would she be "tired" again? How would he deal with that?

* * *

On his new freelance contract, Paul could take the summer off. To get the marriage back on track — mainly those horrible monastic nights — he decided they all should head off across the United States to Los Angeles in his little blue Riley. The beach, the bathing suits, the hot sun, might loosen Angela up and who knows, Hugh French might find work to pay for the summer. Though he secretly hoped not.

Pat Macnee found for them a beachfront flat decorated with tribal statues and huge plants at 19002 Pacific Coast Highway owned by a UCLA professor of anthropology, Councill Taylor. Halfway down the beach steps, Dick Hobson, a writer who had been in therapy for years, stayed in his tiny room under the main floor. During the summer, however, they managed to roust him out for an occasional barbecue.

Paul went for coffee with Pat who lived in one of Topanga's raggle-taggle beach cottages: the ramshackle veranda had been roofed over, and they sat in the shade, gossiping. Pat was never without work, because British actors were in demand and he, like Paul, was represented by Hugh and Robin French — who had invited Patrick and Paul's family for lunch.

After they had run through the Hollywood gossip, Pat asked "In the mood for exercise? We could walk to Hugh's, though it's fairly far. But the tide is low."

Paul agreed and they set off. "Those Hitchcock crews are so darned efficient," Paul began. "If you take the slightest time to rehearse, they get nervous."

"Like you, I much prefer live television," Pat agreed. "But at least Hitch has a different story every week. Most half-hour shows have the same characters all through."

They passed a number of beaches named after the canyons across Pacific Coast Highway: Las Tunas Beach, Big Rock, and Las Flores Beach. After breathing in the Pacific salt air, seeing Western and California gulls wheeling overhead, and beyond the surf a school of sleek dolphins, they reached Malibu Pier. "The Colony's just beyond that," Pat said.

"What Colony?"

"It was first known as the 'movie star colony'. In the 30s, stars used to rent houses here — you couldn't own them — and they'd come with their mistresses for weekends. After a while, they had to put up a gate with security guards to stop onlookers. Hugh has a house right in the middle, number 72. It's a prestige area."

They passed under the pilings of Malibu Pier and past surfers in black wetsuits at Surfrider Beach. A creek running down from the Santa Monica Mountains fed the lagoon behind them. Just beyond, they walked past the row of densely nestled cottages, some broken down as in Topanga, some grandly restored: the famous Malibu Colony. An eight-mile walk.

Hugh French greeted them cheerily. He was nothing if not dapper: a slight grey moustache, short and wavy grey hair, and a distinguished demeanour. No wonder British actors and directors liked having him as their agent. Robin, his twenty-three-year-old son, had recently attended Caltech after leaving Downside, a British boarding school. Despite his fresh youthful face, he had become an effective agent. An unbeatable team, with an office on Brighton Way.

Angela soon turned up in the Riley with Stephanie. Bloody Mary's were the order of the day, with a fine salad lunch in the patio. They gossiped about the Colony neighbours: Rita Hayworth,

Lana Turner, Janet Leigh, all of whom Hugh knew and mingled with. No comparison with Isabella Street in Toronto, Paul thought.

Hugh had also invited the distinguished novelist Nigel Balchin, whose daughter Prudence had been a close friend of Paul's in Oxford. Also Jack Clayton, director of *Room at the Top.* Robin prompted Paul to show his press cuttings from *The Hill,* a horde of reviews, thirty five, in all. "They sure take notice of television drama in England." Paul, embarrassed but pleased, spread them out on the patio table before they ate.

As Hugh leafed through, he said, "Look at these headlines! On the one hand 'Realism is the Death of Art' and then this: 'Passion Story told Most Vividly.'"

Robin added: "Look, '*The Hill* was Just a Horror' from the *South Evening Echo* but then — 'Adversity and a Strong Faith! One of the most moving and touching Passion plays I have ever seen.'"

Hugh held up the Daily Sketch with its big black headline stretched across the page: Agony on TV Jolts Country! "Great notices, Paul. Good for you!"

"Looks as if you caused a stir, Paul," Robin echoed.

Paul grinned. "Just what I hoped for."

"Paul, tell Hugh what you won last year," Robin prompted.

Paul hesitated. "The Liberty Award as Best Drama Producer in Canada."

"Liberty? What's that?"

"A magazine. Every year they choose prizewinners — the only awards we have up there. It just happened to be me this year."

"As it should be, old boy," Hugh said. "I'm delighted."

During a quiet moment after lunch, Hugh told Paul that they would now begin poking about for work for him, but Paul confessed that he felt sufficiently fulfilled in Canada. Budge Crawley had just asked him to direct an episode in the first filmed television series ever done in Canada, simply called RCMP. The great pioneer of Canadian film, Budge had founded Crawley Films in Ottawa and owned a studio in Gatineau. Gilles Pelletier, a French Canadian, played one lead and Don Francks the other. Paul accepted.

With a beautiful beach, rolling surf, hot sun, Angela found a little freedom, so that on the odd, very odd, night she satisfied their mutual desires. Nothing like the sound of waves to foster marital bliss.

* * *

In Ottawa, Paul was taken under the wing of dynamic Peter Carter, a Cockney born within the sound of Bow Bells whose father, a film executive, had gotten Peter at sixteen a job in the industry sweeping floors. Peter had made his way up through the ranks, and was now so experienced that Budge brought him over as the RCMP's First Assistant Director, soon the kingpin of the series.

Peter took to Paul and the two hit it off as never before, including Peter's stunning French Canadian wife, Denise. Peter's initial task as First AD was to bring each show in on time and on budget. Paul was a willing pupil.

First they needed to cast a Native Canadian who, having been mistreated, gave vent to a pent-up rage by smashing his own house (apparently a common occurrence). The climax was a shootout, which Peter and Paul decided to set in an abandoned rock quarry.

But how to find a native capable of carrying an entire show? Well, as usual Peter had the answer: their Lebanese stand-in, Lawrence Zahab, who had never acted. He took this standout part, and Paul cast Denise, another non-actor, as Larry's live-in.

Well, no doubt about it, Larry was up to the task, as was Denise. When it came to the room-smashing scene, the cameraman lit for a general wide shot and then, on "Action", Larry smashed up the place in one tremendous take.

"Let's go again," shouted Paul. Everyone laughed because they knew there'd be no second chance.

Paul found directing this film more enjoyable, as he'd had time to get it right: Budge had budgeted five days shooting per episode. What a difference! In fact, what a pleasure.

* * *

Back in Toronto, Angela continued her nightly rant about Celia Franca, founder of the National Ballet, who was "not giving her enough to do," although in Paul's eyes, his wife was dancing up a storm: lots of juicy acting and dancing roles.

Paul was thinking about the autumn month ahead with Angela away. And after Christmas, her long winter tour. He didn't know what felt worse: lying in bed beside her all night so out of reach, or when she was away, even more distant.

When Paul began rehearsals for a Somerset Maugham play, *Land of Promise*, due out October 4th, a phone call came from Peter Carter. "Paul, we have a great script on the RCMP series. It all takes place in a paper mill."

"Not the Eddie's one in Ottawa? You'll never get permission."

"Budge has it already. But we need to shoot it in five days, and you're the fastest director he's got."

"Yeah, but I'm doing *Land Of Promise* with Robert Goulet."

"Not that singer? He's never acted before."

"No. But he looks like a farmer. Sort of." Paul grinned.

"A handsome one. Who's playing opposite?"

"Bob Allen's letting me bring up Rosemary Harris."

"Again? I bet you're pleased. Maybe after that? I'll tell Budge to wait and slot in a couple of other scripts beforehand."

And so it was arranged.

One evening while preparing the film, Peter took Paul to Gatineau to watch ladies undress at a strippers' bar — none of which interested him. So they discussed casting. "For the girl in the story, Paul, why don't you get some actress you're really keen on? Budge will pay expenses from Toronto. It'll be fun."

Paul thought a bit. "The Gatineau, especially in autumn, is just so romantic: there's a stream outside the hotel where I stay, birds singing in the morning, woods around, tremendous."

"Well..." Peter said, looking at him.

"That Jill Foster, I've always been attracted to her, I don't know why. She's not that pretty, but she's the kind of woman I'd... But she's very attached to Bernie."

"Maybe not if you get her here. I'll get her a room next to yours."

Paul had to digest this: the first time he'd ever done casting with an ulterior motive.

A few days later when Jill turned up, Peter got her booked into the adjacent hotel room.

After the first day's shooting, with their ears deafened by the din of the Eddies plant, Paul provided drinks for his cast and made sure to keep filling Jill's glass. He felt his heart beating: he'd never slept with any cast member. He was both fascinated, and appalled, by the prospect.

After the others went upstairs, Peter coached Paul: "Okay, get changed, and then think up some kind of excuse, like wanting to go over lines, and knock on Jill's door."

Paul, having had enough gins and wine to make him feel confident, went up and changed. Then, pulling on slippers, he opened his door very quietly, tiptoed down the hall, and knocked on Jill's door. Tremendously exciting, though scary.

"Who is it?"

"Me. Your director."

Jill opened the door four inches. She wore a pale blue frilly dressing gown over a filmy nightie. Her big blue eyes stared at him.

"Can I come in for a minute?"

She shook her head.

"Just a second. I need —"

Jill shook her head again. "Paul, I'm a bit tipsy. And I need my sleep. Go back to bed." She closed the door.

Had she guessed what was in his mind? Might it have been in hers, too? Those questions would never be answered. Paul went back to bed, resolving never to let casting revolve around anything but who was the best actress. Although, in this case, Jill was both: very inviting and indeed, the best actress.

Eventually, after horrendous conditions where the noise of the matchstick mill made communicating possible only by hand signals, Budge Crawley deemed the film a success and — as Peter had predicted — Paul had finished it on time. Almost immediately, he was off to Los Angeles to direct another episode in *Alfred Hitchcock Presents, The Icon of Elijah* with the great character actor, Oscar Homolka, in the lead.

CHAPTER FIFTEEN
WINTER 1960

Cancelled Shows

Stephanie had been learning some ballet under Betty Oliphant, and now, as autumn approached, she asked to leave St Mildred's and attend Betty's newly formed National Ballet School. She could live on Isabella Street with Paul, just a few blocks away, while Angela was on tour, adding the title role in *Barbara Allen*, and also dancing in Grant's new ballet.

Stephanie loved the school and, although its youngest student, made friends with Vanessa Harwood, Veronica Tennant, later prima ballerina of the National Ballet, and also Karen Kain, who succeeded Veronica in that position.

Festival (previously *Folio*) was CBC's flagship: a remarkable collection of classical plays, music, ballet, and opera. Franz Kramer, a former student of Alban Berg, was producing music, Norman Campbell directed ballet, Mario Prizak the more esoteric dramas, and Eric Till had just joined. But as a group, not the cohesive ménage of the Drama Department.

For his '61-'62 season, Robert Allen suggested Paul do a Shakespeare play. As the schools were studying *Julius Caesar*, Paul set about creating that for television. The Stratford Festival Theatre having closed for the season, Paul was able to cast some of those regulars, and for the women, Frances Hyland and the glorious Kate Reid. But for Marc Antony, he wanted Bill Shatner.

Next he tackled the settings. Rudi Dorn mournfully wandered into Paul's office. "Ach Gott, Paul, not another show in bed sheets?"

"Rudi, they're togas."

"So... now I build the Colosseum in studio?" he asked. "Big disaster." He chuckled.

Paul repressed a grin.

"All television," Rudi went on, "it's a disaster, why be different?"

"Okay okay, Rudi, so what do we do?"

Rudi shrugged.

"Okay listen, Shakespeare wrote his plays for a bare stage at the Globe Theatre. Props, okay, but no sets."

Rudi looked at him and then, without a word, fled.

What on earth would he do? Paul wondered.

What he did was another remarkable set.

In the foreground, two vast twelve-foot-across Roman columns reached up as though to an almighty height. Against the cyc at the back, Rudi put up four very large Roman columns, also stretching out of sight — the whole giving an impression of great scale in the small studio.

Rome without folderols. The man's a genius, thought Paul, and started rehearsing. And that's when the trouble began.

The Stratford coterie looked down on television, so did not take kindly to an upstart director who'd never done any theatre, or so they thought. Paul didn't bother to correct that. Having spent months together, they had formed liaisons, or rather, cliques. Cutting remarks, muttered and whispered — not always out of earshot — could be heard, many directed at Bill, and even their director.

Bill and Paul, being friends and good at television, tried to ignore all that and get on with the play. But for the first time, Paul did not enjoy his rehearsals. Acknowledged as a master of the medium, he was at least accustomed to respect.

The real clincher came when Mark Antony harangued the Roman crowd. "Friends, Romans, countrymen, lend me your ears." One of the better-known phrases in Shakespeare — usually declaimed from a rostrum in heroic tones with broad gestures. But Bill and Paul decided on a whole other interpretation — the vernacular. Bill would bend over and murmur, "Friends..." speaking directly and quietly as in a small room — where indeed the telecast would be seen. "Romans," he would beckon, "countrymen..." A few of the supposedly huge crowd in the Roman Forum began to pay attention. "Lend me your ears," he pleaded gently.

Some got interested and nudged their companions. Slowly, throughout the famous oration, more and more bystanders became involved. Paul shot them from high on a crane camera, looking down as if from Bill's point of view. He bunched the citizens tight, all excellent actors, handpicked by Paul.

"...He hath brought many captives home to Rome
Whose ransoms did the general coffers fill:
Did this in Caesar seem ambitious?"
On Bill went on...
"My heart is in the coffin there with Caesar,
And I must pause till it come back to me."
He turned, tears in his eyes... The crowd believed him overcome with emotion, but the camera saw his secret hidden delight. Fi-

nally, they erupted in shouts. Marc Antony had won the day.

When the Stratford bunch saw how Bill was playing the famous speech, scorn curled their lips. Conflict for sure. But oddly enough, just what Paul needed: this "us versus them" augmented the antagonistic feelings between Mark Antony and the conspirators who murdered Caesar.

Once they went into studio, however, Rudi's sets appeared stunning. Even the recalcitrant theatre bunch caught their breath. And Bill turned out to be a stunning Mark Antony.

The huge production went on, all two hours, so that by the end, everyone was worn out, most of all Paul.

But he threw his usual cast party back at the flat, where a few selected actors and all three super cameramen, led by Tommy Farquharson, drank and made merry. The phones had indeed rung; audience and newspaper critics deemed it a success.

Nonetheless, Paul was against doing another Shakespeare.

* * *

Before Christmas, Paul was offered an Australian piece, *Shadow of a Pale Horse*, which featured a hanging. It had been bought by the Americans and the BBC, but the CBC put it into production first.

Paul celebrated the holidays with Angela and her gorgeous ballet friends: Myrna Aaron, back in the company after a stint in Italy and Tamburlaine at Stratford, Ontario; Colleen Kenney, now a soloist; and the blonde Jacqueline Ivings, Jocey Tyrell, and Sally Brayley, who would not leave for another year. And their good friends Grant and Earl. But then she was off on another tour: thirty-eight cities till April, after a stay in Toronto in February.

In his January production, Paul cast as the poor fellow to be hanged, Larry Zahab, who after the RCMP had come to Toronto to begin an acting career. In addition, Paul assembled his regular performers: Robert Christie, Hugh Webster, Barney Dylan, Powys Thomas, and so on.

The hanging scene would prove a challenge. Paul wanted it as realistic as possible — Larry would drop on camera, oh yes! And he'd managed permission for a horse and cart in studio — another first.

Larry would stand on the cart, with a noose around his neck. The clergyman, Ivor Barry, would say a few words, then they would whip the horse, the cart would leap forward, and Larry would drop. During rehearsals at Sumach Street, Paul had gotten someone from the Design Department, who happened to be only in training, to come up and rig the harness on Larry.

In the control booth as they started the live show, Paul grinned at Robey Ivy, who had replaced Pat Young. She was older than Paul, a no-nonsense type with red hair piled in a beehive, upright in bearing, which Paul suspected might be due to a corset. The other script assistants were mostly in their innocent and succulent twenties. "Well, let's just trust in God and see how it all goes, eh Robey?" Everyone had their fingers crossed.

"I'll trust more in you than God to pull this off," smiled Robey.

The drama began to unfold, some villagers being for, others against, the hanging. Based on a real incident, there had been a trial of sorts, but hardly a satisfying one.

The horse and cart were brought forward and a loop placed around Larry's neck. Grizzled faces, some praying, some in wide-eyed anticipation, watched. Paul called in the mic to Johnson Ashley, the Studio Director: "Cue the horse."

The actor-driver slapped his reins, the horse bolted, and Larry dropped.

He twisted and thrashed in death throes while a series of quick cuts registered the horror on the faces. But something looked horribly wrong.

"Ready 112 on [camera] one — Paul!" Robey cried out.

"Take one," Paul snapped. "Look, Lynn's crying! Great. Hold the shot."

"Ready 113 on three — Paul! Paul!" Robey cried.

"Dolly in on Lynn. More in! Now take three."

Robey: "Ready 114 on one."

Paul: "Take one. My God, my God, Robey — what acting!"

Robey: "Ready 115 on three. No, he's choking, Paul, he's choking."

Paul: "Take Three. He can't be! He's in a harness."

The commands came out abrupt, staccato, fast.

Robey: "Ready 116 on two. Look, he's twisting. He's trying to... Oh my God."

On screen, Larry was thrashing and struggling.

Paul: "No no, surely he's acting, but —" He could hear the cameramen's gasps in his earphones. "Take two."

Robey: "Ready 117 on three. Do something!"

Paul: "Take three. Just look at that acting! Or is he?"

Robey: "Ready 118 on one. He's not, Paul. He's choking!"

Paul stared. "Take one." The control room began a turmoil.

Robey: "Ready 119 on three. Paul, we'd better stop!"

Paul: "Take three — we can't. We're on air. Don't worry so much, he's acting."

Robey: "Ready 120 on two."

Paul: "Take two. He's slowing down..."

Robey: "Ready 121 on three"

Paul: "Take three. I'm off him — Johnson, get ready to cut him down."

Robey: "Ready 122 on one. Yes yes, cut him down."

Paul: "Take one. We're still off him. But I've gotta go back to him. I've got to. Pray God he's acting."

Robey: "Ready 123 on two. He's not, Paul."

Paul: "Take two. I can't help it. Oh God, Johnson!"

Robey: "Ready 124 on one."

Paul: "Take one. I'm off him. Get in fast, Johnson! Three, flip to a close up."

Robey: "Ready 125 on three. Only two more shots."

Paul: "Wait, Johnnie – only two more. Can you get in safely? Take three."

Robey: "Ready 126 on one. Paul!"

Paul: "Take one."

Robey: "Ready 127 on three. Look, he's not moving!"

Paul: "No, I'm flying. Hold on one. Hold it. Okay, now I'm back on..."

Robey: "...126."

Paul: "Take three. Good! Last shot coming."

Robey: "Ready 127 on one again."

Paul: "Take one. Pull back. More. Johnnie, soon as I fade out, get in there, get in to Larry..."

John Ashley and a stagehand stood ready to run in.

At last, Paul waved his arm widely. "And... fade out."

Larry's form lay on the studio floor, inert.

The booth was now in chaos. "Get a doctor, someone!"

"Done," Cec Johns replied. "I phoned."

Johnson Ashley and others rushed to the inert form.

Suddenly... Larry sat up — a big grin on his face. "Fooled you, eh?"

In the booth, everyone stared, then broke up in relief.

"What a great show!" Trevor Williams, the designer of this show and not at all like Rudi, had watched every shot. "Tremendous, Paul."

So Larry was fine!

But as Paul soon found out, all was not fine...

The CBC had recently set up huge two-inch tape machines that filled all of one room. Shows were now video-taped for later viewing across the nation, so that in the West they could show better quality programs than on kinescopes, as previously. No producer was allowed into the tape room, and no cuts of any kind were permitted, no matter what. So the show was just as "live" as before. But the upshot was that productions could be shown in advance to GM's executives.

The head of sales demanded they take General Motors name off the show. "Too realistic."

No sponsorship?

Well, that provided copy for newspapers all across Canada. But the CBC, undeterred, put out the drama anyway. No agency executives could dictate to a public broadcasting system! Newspaper critics flocked. The consensus ended up that, as usual, the executives had overreacted.

Paul was naturally tickled. But little did he know that his next production would create an even greater furor.

* * *

One memorable play Paul had seen in London was *Point of Departure,* a retelling of the Orpheus legend by his favourite French playwright, Jean Anouilh. So he asked Robert Allen if he could produce it on *Folio*. Robert read it and gave his approval. Orpheus, played by William Shatner, and Eurydice got to know each other in a sordid bedroom in a station boarding house. But the scene itself was inordinately tame, just two lovers on a bed, getting to know each other. No heavy breathing, no locked embraces — the white bed being a sort of island out of time and space. A tender scene, a dramatic scene, in fact, a really splendid scene. All on a bed.

The show went smoothly, and after the last shot, Paul tore off his earphones and ran down to congratulate each cameraman and hug dear Bill.

But this time, even the CBC's own executives proved timid. After some discussions, they cancelled the telecast.

The papers were full of it: the *Toronto Star* headlined: "CBC Cancels Sexy French Play."

The CBC did telecast it a few weeks later, but late in the evening. Paul didn't mind; it just added to the show's acclaim, which was considerable.

In another surprise *The Globe and Mail* elected to publish a photo spread on the Isabella Street apartment that Angela had decorated. As it happened, Bill had come to tea and so was photographed as well. But Paul didn't wait to read the articles spawned by the cancellation. He rushed off to New York for his next production.

Play of the Week's producer, Lewis Freedman, had asked theatre guru Harold Clurman to direct Christopher Fry's translation of Jean Giraudoux's *Tiger at the Gates*. Mr. Clurman, a highly influential theatre critic, had been one of the founders of New York's famous Group Theatre, and had often directed on stage. He was working on his seminal book, *The Fervent Years,* to come out the following year. But he had no idea of cameras, or this new medium. So to work the camera shots, Lewis had decided to bring in an accomplished television director who had also directed classical plays — Paul, who had heard of Clurman and was anxious to meet him.

But what a come-down! On arriving, Paul found that the great man had spent a couple of days in rehearsal just going over lines. Shaped rather like Hitchcock, with a round face and thinning hair, Mr. Clurman in his perennial dark suit was didactic, though articulate as behooved a university professor. But he only worked on the words; he interrupted actors time and time again to give line readings — a complete no-no in Paul's book. Actors should find their own rhythms, with which the cast also agreed.

Harold would sit in his chair, giving line readings, as Paul moved around, framing shots, glancing back at Harold, who would nod. An unnerving experience.

After the show, which had been well received, Paul returned to Toronto with a good-sized cheque and a newly minted reputation. He had seen more Broadway plays, all expenses paid.

* * *

After repeating *The Hill* in Canada, his third run at it, with Kate Reid instead of Kate Blake, who had gone to London, Paul directed *The Beckoning Hill,* by Arthur Murphy, the Halifax surgeon whose previous play, *You'll be Calling Me Michael,* he'd done earlier.

Paul cast Michael Craig, a J. Arthur Rank star, as he now had the stirrings of a desire to make motion pictures. Finally on a freelance contract, he could do as he pleased. So he flew to Halifax and drove with Arthur around Cape Breton Island looking for locations, hoping that with Craig attached, the script might end up as a film in cinemas. The scenic spectacular island stayed with Paul long afterwards. But nothing came the project.

Now, to find an actress with enough star quality to play opposite Michael. After checking around, Paul was finally rewarded by finding a delicious young lady, Martha Buhs. Comely, slim, graceful, she had a lovely voice, great big brown eyes set in stunning features surrounded by brown curls. A new face to boot!

Even as a beginner, on screen she projected such warmth, charisma, and sympathy that she lifted the show, clicked with Michael, and it all went well.

Afterwards, Paul set off with Angela to direct the Giraudoux play again in England for Granada. She had completed her winter tour encompassing thirty-eight cities, plus thirty performances in Toronto in February, and needed a break. Because Betty Firmin, Angela's mother, wanted to retire to England, they helped her find a new apartment in Sidmouth, on Devon's South coast.

As Agamemnon, Paul cast Keith Michell, a movie and television star, and decided on his wife, Jeanette Sterke as Andromache. Jeanette had been rather close to Paul and had travelled with his Oxford and Cambridge Players. Watching her during rehearsals, Paul wondered why he had never asked her to marry him. She was beauty itself, her round face, her kind eyes, such a gentle disposition that would never hurt a fly; she must surely look after her husband with all the innate breeding of her Czech background. Enough reminiscing, thought Paul, just concentrate on directing.

So far as casting went, Paul made his first major mistake — probably his biggest to date. Going out for lunch one day, he'd seen a pretty, slightly pudgy, blonde actress getting off a motorcycle and running in to deposit photos for him to see as Helen. It turned to be Susannah York.

But Paul, the idiot, decided that because Helen of Troy had been the pinup of the day, he wanted the casting director to find him the present-day pinup of British troops. Pictures of Carole Lesley, dressed or undressed, adorned the noticeboards and walls next to the beds of soldiers. She did look pretty, followed directions, and ended up acquitting herself reasonably well. But in the end, a dreadful idea. The critics turned out to be kind on the whole, because the rest of the cast was stellar. And the Irish-Canadian designer Paul had chosen to design his sets, Seamus Flannery, won a splendid long-term contract from Sidney Bernstein.

But Paul went back to Toronto — no long term in England for him.

CHAPTER SIXTEEN
1961-62

After Angela went on tour, Paul directed a teleplay about Louis Braille, *A Touch of Light*. He needed another new face to play the young blind girl. After quite a search, he found a teenager who had studied acting but had never done a TV show. Then, as soon as he saw Roberta Maxwell's extraordinary energy in key scenes, he knew he'd found another star. And in fact, in no time she was doing very well in Stratford and London's West End.

Dylan Thomas's *Return Journey* followed, with Douglas Rain. At the opening of his play, Dylan hurries into a radio studio, and as an homage to Andrew Allan, the great creator of radio's *CBC Stage* series, Paul asked him to play the on-camera director in the booth. Paul went on to direct three more shows, but the highlight of the season for Paul was seeing Ingmar Bergman's two new films: *Wild Strawberries,* and *The Seventh Seal.*

That summer, Granada planned two difficult plays: Harold Pinter's *The Dumb Waiter,* and N.F. Simpson's *A Resounding Tin-*

kle. The latter, incomprehensible but amusing, was part of the new "theatre of the absurd" movement sweeping England. Sidney Bernstein was adventurous, but also cautious, so beckoned a director he hoped would save them: Paul.

Elspeth Cochrane, Paul's British agent, had leased him a flat at one Ilchester Place, owned by the renowned movie actress, Ann Todd. She had played opposite James Mason in the biggest British box-office success of 1945 — *The Seventh Veil*.

Harold Pinter had so far not allowed any of his plays on television. But he had not counted on the persuasive power, and money, of the great Granada mogul. Paul had already seen his *Caretaker* at the Duchess Theatre, where it won the Evening Standard Award for best play of 1960. Michael Codron, Paul's friend from Oxford days, had presented Harold's first major play, *The Birthday Party,* at the Lyric Hammersmith, in 1958. Now Harold's work would be seen by millions across England for the first time. But what an unorthodox choice: this brash young Canadian tackling the idol of British theatre.

Harold came to the first read-through, as always. His plays were punctuated by very specific details: a pause, a long pause, a very long pause, and so on: each length of silence specifically delineated. But Paul was very aware these should not be filled by blank looks while actors counted time: in each pause, the characters must search for a response, be it panic, subterfuge, retaliation, or making a decision.

After the read-through, Paul took his author aside. "Harold, I think it might be better if you don't come to rehearsals for a while."

Harold looked at him in alarm. "Why not? I always come. I'm the author."

"I know, Harold, and believe me, I'm in awe of your abilities."

"So what's the problem, old boy?" growled Harold.

Paul was not deterred. "To get the pauses right, Harold, I may...

well, have to do some improvisations. You know, try scenes in different ways."

"You want to experiment?" Alarm filled Harold's face.

"Believe me, Harold, in a week or so, when you come back, the lads will be word perfect — and pause perfect. I promise."

Harold looked at him askance. And then, after "a very long pause", replied, "They told me about your reputation. You're supposed to be the hot new TV director. They showed me *The Hill* so I approved you. I was an actor myself, you know. If that's the way you want it, I'll oblige."

Better move fast before he changes his mind, thought Paul. "Thanks a lot, Harold, you won't regret it." And out they went, Paul rejoicing, Harold less so.

Paul hoped he had not bitten off more than, as the saying goes, he could chew.

Later, when Harold returned to watch a run-through, he said, "I don't know how you did it in a week, Paul. With a bit more rehearsing, it might just be all right."

And all right it was. Many TV critics, as was expected, couldn't make head nor tail of it. But those in the know thought it splendid. Harold Pinter was a stunning and original playwright. Paul resolved to get one of his plays on Canadian television.

Next, Paul directed *A Resounding Tinkle*. Its author, N.F. (Wally) Simpson, a sprightly, thin-faced Britisher, had a lively sense of humour. More important for Paul, this "absurd" play gave him a chance, after begging for live music, to hire as composer his longtime friend, Stanley Myers, quirky but brilliant, who had never done any television. Another risk.

But it did set Stanley off on a great new career.

One of the headlines in the many papers tickled Paul and Wally — "A Resounding Tinkle — a Resounding Clanger!" Like this critic, most could not make head nor tail of it.

After that, Paul took a shot at his first B-movie called *Backfire*, a five day shoot that gave Paul a rather unpleasant taste of the old days of British film making.

* * *

Back in Toronto at the start of the '61-'62 season, Paul and Angela were invited to dinner by Robert's wife, Rita Greer Allen, herself a broadcaster and writer. She was a very smart lady with attractive features and the most irresistible lips — resisted by Paul, though, because she was the boss's wife. But Rita was no cook. At every dinner she served roast chicken with roast potatoes and one soggy vegetable, never properly cooked. Nonetheless, the wine flowed and Robert, who believed in "early to bed and early to rise", usually went off to sleep around 8.30. He was known to call actors at dawn to negotiate their fees while they were half-asleep.

The Allens talked of their admiration for Angela on stage, and then turned to the recent name change of the Canadian left-wing party, the CCF (founded by Peter Scott's father, Frank) to the New Democratic Party. Then, Robert broached the subject of another Shakespeare.

"That lets me out," said Paul stoutly. Angela looked across the table at him in alarm.

"The schools are doing *Macbeth*, this year, Paul. We thought to do a five-part school series, then knit it together for *Folio*."

"Why not get Eric Till or Mario Prizak or someone? I've had enough of those Stratford actors."

Angela looked up. "Paul, you did so well with *Julius Caesar!*" Paul had gone freelance, so every show meant income.

"Paul, your production was excellent," maintained Bob.

"Yes, and we thought I should introduce each episode of *Macbeth* on camera," Rita told him. Paul knew Rita's engaging and warm personality would enchant the students. "I'll want you to come on camera, too, and describe how you saw the play."

That did sound interesting. "Rita," he answered impulsively, if you're doing that, I'll direct." ·

And so the matter was settled.

This play presented Paul with an even greater challenge, centring as it did on one Scottish thane and his Lady wife. Eva Langbord felt that in Toronto, no perfect choice came to mind. So, prompted by his new Script Assistant, Dorothy Gardner, Paul rang his English agent.

"Elspeth, I'm going to do Macbeth."

Elspeth Cochrane sounded delighted.

"But I really want some Scottish guy for the lead. None of your tired old British actors. It's for schools and then CBC Festival. I want plenty of action, so I need a vigorous and exciting Macbeth."

Elspeth promised to ring back.

"The best I can come up with," she later announced, "is a young Scottish actor who just did his first lead as *Alexander the Great* on BBC, Sean Connery. Not a lot of experience, I'm afraid, but I thought he did rather well. He's played football, so he might be what you want. But of course, you'd be taking a risk."

Paul sounded delighted. "I love risks! He sounds perfect, Elspeth. I'll put Bob in touch with his agent..."

The next problem was Lady Macbeth. Frances Hyland was too slight and elfin, and Martha Buhs too young... But an actress had just arrived from Australia, Zoe (rhymes with Joe) Caldwell, not tall, but with lots of authority although only in her twenties, just two years younger than Paul. So he cast her.

For the Lady Macduff murder scene, Paul had decided to add a vicious chase, and even a rape. So he chose the attractive, long-haired Sharon Acker, whose succulent body every drama director, including Paul, hungered after.

Bob freed up the great Austrian designer, and when they met in Paul's apartment, Rudi's first words were, "Ach Gott, Paul, not more talk. These old words! Sets switching off all over Canada!"

"Rudi Rudi, it's going to be exciting. I found a Scots actor in London."

"Scotch with Shakespeare? Sure. Then no one understands."

Paul ignored that. "And I found a new actress, too: Zoe Caldwell. She's Australian."

Rudi mumbled disconsolately, "Another accent..."

"So listen, Rudi, two new faces for our leads. Exciting, no?"

"All talk? Drives me nuts. So what now — you want a Scottish castle? You know what studio we got?"

"Four?"

"No," spat Rudi, "they give us that Variety place up Yonge."

"Oh my God, Rudi, not that long, narrow studio? It looks like a corridor. We can't do it there."

Rudi nodded unhappily

"What the hell do we do?" Finally, Paul had met his come-uppance — no decent show...

Rudi brightened. "Tell me what you need."

"How do you mean?"

"You think I read all those old words? Tell me elements." Out came the design pad and thick stubby pencil.

"Elements?" Paul began to think. "Yes yes, elements."

Rudi grinned. He liked pushing his friend.

"Hmm. Okay, the play is about the throne of Scotland. Banquo is king. Macbeth murders Banquo to become king himself."

Rudi wrote on his pad. "Throne. I give you throne."

"He's pushed into it by his wife. Big famous scene when Lady Macbeth comes down stairs, sleepwalking, wiping blood off her hands. Same stairs Macbeth walks down after killing Banquo."

Rudi scribbled. "Stairs. We got height there. I give you big big flight of stairs."

"Okay, Rudi, a throne, a flight of stairs — oh — a funny scene when they keep knocking on Macbeth's gates, but the gatekeeper's too drunk to open them. Eric Christmas — he's such a good comic."

"I build you huge gate," Rudi said.

"But what the hell do we do about the 'blasted heath'?"

"The what?" asked Rudi.

"Sort of a barren moor. Three witches dance around a cauldron."

"What's a cauldron? — Okay, okay, we do it against cyc."

"Yeah yeah, I like the idea of the play being out of time. No fussy folderols like on US television. Same with costumes. Can we get Horst Dantz?"

Rudi shook his head. "I design for you. I give to Horst. He likes that for sure. No work."

But much more work for the makers of the costumes — Rudi designed thick slabs of felt built out beyond the shoulders and draped in clean lines over the bodies, giving everyone, including Macbeth, a massive look in keeping with his sets.

"Okay? I go now, yes?"

"Yes." And with that, the great genius departed. Paul sank back; thank heaven for someone like Rudi.

When Rudi came back with sketches, Paul had never seen anything like it: an enormous built-up throne with massive square arms, and a long flight of stairs going up one side of the studio into the darkness. Gigantic thundering beams criss-crossed the whole studio, giving a brooding oppressive weight — one could almost bite into the darkened murderous atmosphere and smell the heavy clouds, the louring mists of northern Scotland. At the opposite end, vast timbered gates barred shut by a great plank in iron brackets.

Then Paul got an idea. For the witches to be shot in silhouette, why not three lithe dancers from the National Ballet? He'd always found Jacqueline Ivings so attractive, luscious, long- limbed, blonde, and he cast two others from the corps de ballet. Grant Strate would choreograph the witches' ring-around-the-rosy that opened the play.

One night Paul got a call from the Toronto Constabulary. The police had apprehended a scruffy, bearded, foreigner walking along, proclaiming nonsense aloud. "Is this Mr. Alford? We have someone here who claims to know you. We suspect he is here illegally, and perhaps should be committed — name of Sean Connery."

"Oh Lord!" exclaimed Paul, "put him on the line"

Paul was full of the most abject apologies. "Please, please forgive these darn Toronto police. Let me talk to them."

Paul confirmed in no uncertain terms that Sean Connery was indeed a distinguished actor, flown in specially to play *Macbeth*. Would they please bring him to Paul's apartment right away, so he could offer him a large dram o' Scotch in compensation.

Sean posed his own challenge. Having been brought up poor, delivering milk in a horse-drawn wagon to make a living, he had never read or studied *Macbeth*. Impossible to learn that part in ten days! But Zoe Caldwell, a classical actress, had made short work of her lines, so most evenings she helped Sean.

These rehearsals were strides ahead of *Julius Caesar*. Paul even began to think he might have a good show.

And wonderful it was. Never mind that on air, some of Shakespeare's better known lines were often improved upon by Sean. Did it shock Shakespeare scholars? Perhaps, but the schools were entirely satisfied. Especially with the rape and murder of beautiful Sharon and a splendid fight scene at the end. A vigorous and entertaining Macbeth, in which Zoe and Sean were just magnitficent.

* * *

Right after Macbeth in the autumn of '61, during Paul's production of Christopher Fry's *Sleep of Prisoners,* Angela prodded him to buy a house. On October 31 they took over 212 Briar Hill Avenue, half way between Avenue Road and Yonge Street, just north of Eglinton.

While Angela had been away, Steph and he had come to understand each other and grow closer. Paul even came to regret the way she had been relegated to a sunroom on Isabella Street — so found himself thrown into this rash, wild enterprise of actually tying himself down with a seemingly large house. Angela loved it and spent what little spare time she had making curtains and buying furniture in stores like the Salvation Army. Now Stephanie had her own decent room, and in the end Paul wondered why buying a house had taken him so long.

In January Angela went off with the company and danced in twenty-nine cities in the southern US in January and February, and then after a month in Toronto, another seven cities in Eastern Canada, twenty-four performances in all. Quite a tour!

In January of 1962, Paul chose another Christopher Fry, *The Lady's not for Burning,* led by his discovery, Zoe Caldwell, opposite Donald Harron. More lovely verse.

During that winter, Harold Pinter, trusting Paul now, gave him the rights to two short plays, *The Collection*, and *A Slight Ache*, starring William Hutt and Neil McCallum. This caused a slew of hate letters from the Middle West, but Harold, on seeing a kine, seemed pleased, especially as he'd never before allowed a play on North American television. Another first for the director.

One day the next summer, Rudi spoke about an incident he'd experienced as a foot soldier in the Austrian army. How odd, Paul thought, I might actually have been fighting against him. They decided to write a play about it.

At eighteen, little tubby Rudi, having studied architecture, was conscripted into the Engineering Corps. When the German army was in full retreat, an officer ordered him and another soldier to blow up a bridge to stop the British advance. But this bridge separated the villagers from their fields. The mayor begged them to leave their bridge intact. Conflict!

That night, Rudi's character meets a scrawny urchin girl hiding in the basement, and falls in love.

The next day, hoisting a flag, the villagers surge across the bridge with a cheering welcome for the victorious British. But Rudi has already mined the bridge and tries to stop them crossing. Caught in the crowd, he calls again and again to his urchin love: "Don't cross!"

Too late, the bridge blows up.

Paul's friend Powys Thomas had been a founder of Canada's nascent National Theatre School, and gave Paul his three best students: Donnelly Rhodes, Heath Lamberts as the young Rudi, and Diane Leblanc, all new faces. Rudi called it *The Broken Sky* (*Der zerbrochene Himmel*), their first collaboration as authors.

Later that autumn Paul did Fry's *Venus Observed,* and cast his discovery Martha Buhs, who had changed her name to Henry after she married Donnelly Rhodes, the son of a distinguished Winnipeg critic, Ann Henry.

And then in the winter after more shows, he undertook his greatest challenge: a documentary. Paul had never made one, nor had the faintest idea how to proceed.

CHAPTER SEVENTEEN
1963

The Holy Land

In February, Paul was handed a real treat by Brian Freeland: the Holy Land. The idea was to capture on film images that Our Lord might have seen two thousand years ago as He walked His land, preaching and healing.

Paul, Brian, cameraman Norman Allin and his assistant Matt Tundo, and a quite pregnant continuity girl Helen, arrived at Lod airport in February, got into a prearranged van and drove the forty miles to Jerusalem's New City, where they checked into the King David Hotel. Reconnoitring the next day, Paul felt his heart sink — Israel looked just as modern as North America. And to boot, native-born Israelis had a nickname: Sabra, a prickly cactus fruit. They resembled the fruit rather too closely. What kind of a film would this be?

Leaving Israel, they crossed through the concrete and barbed wire barrier of the Mandelbaum Gate on the Green Line at the western edge of the Old City. The contrast at the renowned American Colony Hotel in the Hashemite Kingdom of Jordan was enormous: old beige stone walls, pleasant staff, spartan but comfortable rooms, and a lounge fire, so welcoming this chilly midwinter. For their guide (and bodyguard) the Jordanian Tourist Police assigned Moussa Taha, a warm and pudgy companion.

The Old City in East Jerusalem — what a revelation!

Golden stone, hidden markets, calls to prayer, bells at night, hurried meals, calls from the minarets: "Allahu-akbar", kids racing past, people tugging, "buy, yes, buy!" fly-covered sweets, strong coffee, roofs over markets, so much to be explored, torn tapestries, hidden doorways, rats, hawkers, beggars, blind men, vistas, monasteries, tradition...

Here at last, Paul could walk the land where God had been made flesh. Now, he could know Jesus better by feeling how hot or cold He'd been, where He walked each day, what clouds He'd seen, what rain cooled Him, what clothes He'd worn. Imagine! Paul now listened with his own ears to the same murmurs in alleyways, the brays of ambling donkeys, the dawn calls of roosters. Whatever they could find and film from that era — a lot, even now — would illustrate for viewers the key Christian rituals: the water of baptism, round flat bread broken among friends, the amphoras of wine.

But first, St Peter's Gallicantu (Latin for cock crow) in whose cellars they filmed a dungeon resembling the one in which Jesus had been held — accessible only through a hole in the floor where captives, and later their food, were lowered. Horrible.

But then, another revelation — the Kidron Steps. Paul asked Norman to hand-hold the little Arriflex and stride slowly down these huge old flagstones on which the very feet of Jesus had trodden into the Kidron Valley and on over to the

Garden of Gethsemane.

Later, when they went to film in the Garden, the weather gave itself to rain, so they went into the Pater Noster Church with the Lord's Prayer written on the walls in hundreds of languages. They sat, wrapped in thoughts, while Brian told them to imagine the simple disciples listening to their great Rabbi, twelve guys hidden away — such a far cry from Westminster Abbey.

When the weather turned sunny they drove to Bethany, a clump of mud houses whose villagers lived much as in the old days. But how to film Mary and Martha? They found a guard and got into the supposed tomb of Lazarus. Paul recalled pictures he'd seen at Ronald Duncan's of the sculpture of Lazarus done by the great Jacob Epstein, who had also done a bust of his good friend Ronnie.

The others drove back to Jerusalem, but Paul walked in order to feel as Jesus must have felt, travelling to visit chums in Bethany.

Next, down into the Jordan Valley by the Old Roman Road. They pulled up near the ancient Greek Monastery of the Temptation, hewn out of rock in the sheer cliffs. They carried equipment up the long, tortuous stairs where, from a balcony, Paul and Brian hung onto Norman's legs as he leaned far out and shot, twisting and turning, into the depths below, for the sequence when Satan offered Jesus dominion over all the world.

On to the Dead Sea, and up the valley to find the famous Jordan river. Pushing through tall reeds, the little crew got a shock at the muddy, polluted creek, the mighty Jordan of the Bible. As Norman filmed, Paul sat and imagined the crowds gathering around John, a latter-day hippie in a camelhair cloak (how scratchy!) while a scrubby, bearded young man (dressed like anyone else) submerged and re-emerged with an explosion from God filling his mind — He knew, yes, how He knew...

Crossing the desert again and filming in the extreme heat, they looked up at distant, huge, long escarpments westward toward

Jerusalem. Brian told them how, after baptism in the muddy waters, Jesus came here to be alone, sleeping under the stars, knowing where it would all end if He followed his destiny. Then among fly-ridden dogs and cats in the cool of a vine-hung garden of a simple Jericho restaurant, they ate a tagine (stew) with a dessert of sweet oranges, as in His day.

Later they visited the distant Jerash and ten towns of the Decapolis, centres of Greek and Roman culture, where Jesus also preached. They filmed a donkey yoked with an ox tugging a handmade wooden plough, the simple farmer plodding behind, and later, a woman carrying sticks on her head.

Back in Jerusalem, they shot in the grounds of the Church of St Anne: the finest Crusader architecture in the Eastern Mediterranean, where they paused to hear boy choristers singing a mass and to reflect on Jesus healing the blind man beside the now garbage-filled Pool of Bethesda. What kind of dirty, grimy, unhealthy places were these seats of profound holiness where often all day, Jesus would squat in the dirt, telling parables of the Kingdom of Heaven.

To capture the feeling of a market as it existed two thousand years ago, Moussa found them a shop where they hid the camera behind hanging jellabas and shawls. Keeping well out of sight, Norman banged away on a long lens at beggars and woman sellers who had walked in from the countryside, often miles, with their babies, "the maimed, the halt and the blind."

After they had sent back their first rushes, Paul and Brian arranged a time by telex to speak to their editor, Noel Dodds, assigned by CBC's film department. Full of excitement, they phoned, in spite of the cost. But he and his supervisor were less than encouraging. Flabbergasted, obviously at sea, they offered constructive comments, none any use. The crew never suspected that Noel was actually the finest editor in the film department.

That night as Paul, depressed, lay in his bath to wash off the day's dust, he heard a knock. "Come in?"

Brian came to sit.

"I'm awfully sorry, Brian. I thought we were doing so well."

"Don't worry, I have every confidence that we're getting great stuff," he said warmly. "When we get back, you'll put it all together brilliantly."

Well! His producer must have felt the strain and still he sounded confident — a true leader. Paul dressed and went down to join the crew, imbibing a little more arak than he should. Midway through their shooting, the little group felt abandoned.

Eventually, they had to fly to Cyprus, change to a second passport (because the first carried a Jordanian stamp – no double entry) and then fly back to Israel to shoot by the Sea of Galilee, Capernaum, and the Mount of the Transfiguration. They set out north along the coast and then turned inland for Bellevoir, an extraordinary tenth century Crusader castle overlooking the valley of the Sea of Galilee.

Sea? It looked like a small lake!

Down they went to stay at the elegant Galei Kinnaret Hotel on the shore.

The next day at the Church of the Multiplication, commemorating the miracle of the loaves and fishes, they were asked to sign a visitors' book by an aged Franciscan friar.

On inspiration, Paul asked, "Have you been doing this a long time?"

"A very long time," came the answer. Would his crew mind waiting while the aged monk went into the basement and retrieved books from 1929 or 1930?

Paul's clergyman father, before being committed to Ste. Anne de Bellevue Military Hospital from shell shock, had visited the Holy Land with Paul's mother on their honeymoon. Rene's wealthy mater (Paul's grandmother) had given the couple a round-the-world trip. (Later in her will, she left everything to Paul's Aunt Leo, forgetting entirely Rene and Hilda, and thus of course her grandson.)

They searched and found on the page the very signatures and dates of his mother and long dead father. Such an exciting moment. Confirmation of a trip he had only vaguely learned about. He felt as if they were with him now.

Driving by the Galilee toward Capernaum, Brian asked them to stop as they passed sloping meadows with asphodel in bloom, the site of the Sermon on the Mount. As Norman shot, Paul imagined the hundreds sitting around as in a music concert, kids running and playing, babies nursing, old and young men and families — after all, with no TV and nothing much going on, a real Happening among happenings. The wretchedly poor, and the sick, forgetting their ill fortune with the murmur going round, "He's coming soon!"

At Capernaum, though scattered with tourists, Paul managed to shoot among the ruined Roman pillars. The next day, not bothering to stop at Nazareth, the "city on a hill" — now full of open garages and garbage, they climbed the twisting road up Mount Hermon. Luckily, low heavy clouds gave Norman the opportunity of shooting the Transfiguration and the Ascension.

* * *

Paul had never made a documentary. So he relied on Noel. In the tiny editing room, he watched as Noel cut the 16mm film. Using a hot splicer between film reels on each side, Noel would pull the film through his viewer, stopping when he reached a possible cutting point. He'd pull it back and forth until they agreed on which frame to cut, losing it in the process. From his 'trim bin'

Noel would select another strip of film, then scrape each end with a razor blade to get rid the emulsion, paint glue on with a tiny brush and, in the hot-splicer, clamp the two ends together and wait, perhaps a few seconds. Each time a cut was changed, a black frame was inserted to replace the lost one, so that screenings were peppered with black flashes.

Noel was not used to having a director sit next to him — especially one as ebullient and excited as Paul. So at lunch hour, Noel would lie flat on the floor, trying to shut out the explosive morning. A South African, with a round face, a quick wit, and an innate brilliance, Noel exhibited a talent equal to that of Paul's other soul mate, Rudi Dorn. The film department hadn't realized what a genius they had in their midst until they saw the superbly edited film, with stunning black and white photography by Norman Allin.

Brian oversaw *The Dark Did Not Conquer,* a total collaborator, especially with the script that Paul wrote, laying voices of his actors on the sound-track to illuminate scenes: Douglas Rain as Christ, for example, or the blind man rushing off crying at the top of his voice, "I've been healed, I've been healed!"

Of all the films made that year, Paul's first documentary was the one submitted by the CBC for the Wilderness Award.

CHAPTER EIGHTEEN
1962–63

Breakup

June 1st, 1962. "Can you believe it? This is our sixth wedding anniversary, Angela!" Paul picked up the menu.

Angela, dolled up for the special occasion, nodded as she studied the menu. "Amazing how time flies."

After her winter tour, thirty-five cities with countless performances, Angela had gotten home in May. And tonight, Paul was taking off from his hectic schedule to celebrate. He had something on his mind. When he ordered champagne, Angela looked up: "We are putting on the dog tonight!"

They chatted about the new guild for directors being created. "They want to establish a schedule of rates of pay and working conditions to form a basis for an agreement with independent producers."

"What a good idea."

"Yeah, but it won't apply to us at CBC unfortunately. We're on staff. It would have if the RCMP series ever continued." They went on to talk about inconsequential things, Angela knowing full well Paul was avoiding something. They talked about how well Stephanie was doing at the National Ballet School. She would soon be completing ninth grade and at fourteen seemed to be flourishing. Finally, as they sipped their drinks, Paul looked at Angela. "It's been quite a six years..."

"Longer."

"Seven? Eight?"

"Nine and a half."

"I guess it hasn't been all that smooth, has it?"

Angela shook her head. "We both tried!"

"Yes. So hard to for a marriage to succeed when one is often away and otherwise we work all the time."

"I'm only too aware of that." Angela dropped her eyes, as the waiter took their orders.

At last he said, "Angela..."

She kept looking down at her plate. "Yes?"

"I've been offered a job." Angela looked up. "A good one. In England. Granada. A year's contract." Angela stared, absorbing... "Elspeth settled it. October 1st. Apparently, they've offered me more money than they're paying anyone else. Supervising producer. Running things. So I was wondering..."

Almost without thinking, Angela blurted out, "You must take it, Paul. It's a step forward. Don't let anything hold you back."

"I thought you might say that." He smiled. "But... the thing is, could our relationship stand a year's separation?" He paused. "So I'm wondering... Would you come, too?"

"You mean leave the National Ballet for the 63-64 season?"

"Only for one year."

"A year? What happens if you do well? It could go on..."

"Yes, but," Paul went on, a bit desperately, "there are lots of ballet companies over there."

"I know, darling, but it is a bit of a shock. Will you let me think about it?"

"Of course, of course. I won't sign anything until you say."

"No, go ahead, sign. You must sign. It's just..." Angela paused again for a while. "It means holding onto my marriage, or holding onto my ballet."

"Don't think about it that way."

"I must. If we want to make the marriage work, I'd have to come."

"Well... It might be a way to renew our relationship. I mean, a new environment, exciting ballet companies all around, me with a big new job, we can give our relationship one last try."

"It might work," she replied. "One last try...."

Shortly afterwards, the Royal Ballet, led by Margot Fonteyn and Rudolf Nureyev, came to town. What excitement! Angela and Paul, and indeed most of the National Ballet company, went to several performances. Nureyev's agility, elevations, and technical ease nabbed everyone's heart, and Margot was grace personified. One evening, Paul thought a young Canadian dancer, Lynn Seymour, almost stole the show.

At the closing night's glittering reception, they met Sir Frederick Ashton, the renowned British choreographer who was due to take over the Royal Ballet the following year. He liked Angela at once and insisted that they call him Sir Freddie. Angela also chatted with Margot and made other valuable contacts in case she went to London.

But resuming classes, she kept her thoughts to herself. Then one evening at dinner, she announced, "All right, Paul, I'll go with you."

Stephanie had auditioned for the Royal Ballet School and got in, a real "feather in her cap". But all three agreed it would be better for her to stay in Toronto at the National Ballet School. A lovely couple, Jane Smith and her husband, agreed to have Stephanie board with them while her parents left for the season.

The rest of the summer, Paul worked on *The Forest Rangers*, with Gordon Pinsent and Graden Gould, a series Maxine Samuels had put together. Known by some as the Dragon Lady, she had sold it to the CBC. A fine group of children, Ralph Endersby, Peter Tully, Susan Conway, Syme Jago and others, filmed out at Kleinberg in a recently built studio.

While working on *Forest Rangers,* Paul put together with Noel Dodds another documentary, *Journey to the Centre,* from unused shots from the Holy Land. A meditational film, it used out-takes of churches and monasteries that marked key moments in the ministry of Jesus. The narration, read so well by Budd Knapp, provided just the right reflective touch.

And another delight was the film *Mother and Daughter* Paul made to showcase his wife and stepdaughter. He had approached Ross Maclean, acknowledged genius producer of a short-lived miscellany called *Telescope.* In a bare studio with a cyclorama, Norman Allin shot Angela and Stephanie in practice tights and leotards. The brilliant young Canadian Harry Somers composed the score. In his editing room, Noel Dodds put a magic touch on the proceedings, running certain sequences backwards and then forwards, superimposing shot upon shot as though the alter egos were dancing. The NFB's Norman McLaren later borrowed this same technique for his famous *Pas de Deux.*

* * *

In London, the couple rented a tiny flat in a sprawling complex known as Dolphin Square. But after their ample Briar Hill home and garden, they found the one bedroom apartment rather depressing.

Sidney Bernstein, the owner of Granada Television, had persuaded Tennessee Williams to allow his plays for the first time on television anywhere. Paul chose *The Rose Tattoo* and his friends, Hank Kaplan and Silvio Narizzano, selected two others. For the Italian mother, Paul cast Katherine Blake, now in London, and for her daughter, Lelia Goldoni, whom he had seen in John Cassavetes' *Shadows*. The tiny role of Salesman he gave to a young actor from Nova Scotia, Donald Sutherland.

"So how are rehearsals?" Angela asked one day as she cooked dinner.

"Fine, fine." Paul poured them both a gin and tonic. "Thanks for cooking again, Angela."

"That's all I seem to be doing here. Restaurants are so expensive."

Paul agreed. "I thought, having this supposedly super salary, that we'd be out every couple of nights, but it's not even once a week. Lucky Pat Macnee invited us. His new series *The Avengers*, with that sexy Honor Blackman, is a big success. My old boss Sydney Newman thought that up, you know."

"And David and Eileen Green phoned us for dinner next week."

Paul sipped his drink. "Anyway, to be perfectly frank, I'm not really enjoying England. I thought I would love it. My memories of it all were so good.

"And so were mine, old bean," Angela agreed. "But I have to admit..."

"Go on, finish the sentence."

"I'm a bit depressed, too. I like taking class, I like seeing ballets with our friends Pat and Clive Barnes, the ballet critic, but... shall we get away down to Sidmouth for Christmas? Mother's lonely."

So Christmas they celebrated with Betty and came back to London, somewhat cheered.

* * *

At Granada's Golden Square office, Paul often went for a drink in the pub opposite with Australian Tim Hewitt, Head of *World in Action,* Britain's top public affairs show. One evening over a pint of bitter, Tim asked, "Ever done a documentary, mate?"

"Two or three. I mainly do dramas. Did you see my *Rose Tattoo*?"

"No, but I heard it was the best of the lot."

"Oh? Thanks!"

"I've been wondering, why don't we do a show together?"

Paul grinned. "I'd sure be up for that. I don't even have a play now."

"I've been wondering. Ever think about England's class system?"

Paul nodded. "I'd have lots to say about that..." Paul from Canada and Tim from Australia had both been surprised by how entrenched it was.

Tim ordered another half for them both. "You know that old Jesuit saying, give me a child until he is seven, and I will give you the man?"

Paul perked up. "Yes yes! So let's look at seven-year-olds."

Tim thought a bit longer. "We'll go see Sidney." Simple as that.

In 1954, Sidney Bernstein had founded Granada television as one of the original four ITA franchises when commercial channels were first permitted. Sidney, a lifelong Socialist, had inherited some money and increased it by owning cafeterias on throughways. He ran the company like an old-time mogul, but always accessible. So they met Sidney in the boardroom.

Sidney liked the idea. But after a moment, asked, "Why not call it *7Up*?"

Being the name of a soft drink, this title they both thought terrible. But any suggestion from Sidney was law. He gave them *carte blanche,* and told them to start right away.

Paul got two young researchers, Michael Apted and Gordon McDougall, Cambridge graduates and brand new to television. He described the project and sent them off to find photogenic children. Remembering his hikes over the Yorkshire Dales, he asked Gordon to go to Yorkshire and also to Liverpool, because of its colourful accents. They chose two bright lads from there, and Nicholas from a remote Yorkshire dale; little Paul, from an orphanage outside London came a bit later.

Michael Apted poked about the London boroughs. In the East End he found three girls and three boys, among whom was Tony Walker, a would-be jockey. To match these, Michael also turned up an upper-class trio.

Next Paul got an experienced cameraman, David Samuelson, and off they went to Lancashire, to start shooting — always using a tripod. Finally, on a bumpy country lane in Yorkshire, Paul got David to film off the back of their station wagon. David did grumble, but confessed he loved holding the camera in his powerful hands, protesting all the while that the labs would reject his footage when they saw his rushes.

Paul was not a little appalled to discover that how the Brits were still using techniques he deemed impossibly old-fashioned. Oh dear, he asked himself, am I going to cause as much trouble as I did with *The Hill*? It came to a head the day they shot Tony going into school. Paul wanted David to run with Tony at the height of a seven-year-old. "I'm sorry Paul, I can't send that to the lab. I'll be fired. It's too shaky."

"David, don't worry, it's got to be shaky, it's a child, running."

"It's all very well for you , you'll be back in Canada; but I'm stuck here. I'll be out of a job."

"David, Sidney Bernstein is fully behind all this. He'll defend you, I promise. Can you imagine anyone tougher?"

David looked at him, then nodded. "All right, I'm not saying I don't enjoy it. In fact, I love it. I was just afraid what they'd say. But if Sidney's behind us..."

And so the matter was settled. Later hand-held cameras became the norm in British documentaries.

But shooting had its surprises. Paul brought all the children together in London: posh kids and orphans, farmers' sons and East End girls, Lancashire and Kensington, the whole lot. First they went to a zoo where David shot their reactions, especially to a huge polar bear.

The climax of the outing was to be a party. Two extra cameras were ordered, and a table in the centre laid with all sorts of goodies.

The cameras were readied, as was sound.

Paul said, "Roll cameras."

"Camera one, speed!" David said.

"Camera two, speed!"

"Camera three, speed!"

"Open the door."

In came the children.

Paul watched.

Nothing!

The youngsters saw food — cookies, candies, soft drinks, milk — and rushed to the table without a word, never even looking at their neighbour; they all just tucked in silently like little angels. So much for that climax.

In British documentaries, the director always submitted a script before getting a go-ahead. But Paul had no script. As usual, he had intended to let the material speak for itself. So when Lewis Linzee, the editor, saw the rushes he growled, "What do you expect me to do with all this rubbish? They never sent me a script! How will I know what to do?"

"No script, Lewis. We'll edit the film together. Then I'll write the commentary."

Lewis looked at Paul as if he'd gone mad — some stupid Colonial — and almost said, "I quit." But he was a salaried employee...

So Paul sat patiently with his editor, assembling a rough cut. Once Lewis felt comfortable, he turned out some excellent editing.

They had chosen more children than needed, so they decided to concentrate on certain ones that Paul selected. The trainees he brought to the mixing studio to keep on learning. Indeed later, he asked Tim to add to his own end credit the names of Michael Apted and Gordon McDougall. After Apted took over the series, on *14Up*, he single-handedly took Gordon's credit off.

Once the film was pretty well put together, though not polished, Paul and Tim showed it to Sidney. But now it ran forty-five minutes.

World in Action ran only twenty-five. Good old Sidney Bernstein loved *7Up* at the longer length. He persuaded the network to add fifteen minutes and run it exactly as Paul had made it. Now that, thought Paul, is how all television should work. But would North America ever change?

The film aired in May, but Paul had left England. It proved a major success, causing Granada to repeat it on New Year's Day, and enter it at the Prague Festival where it won a Special Diploma.

* * *

One day, while Paul was planning *7Up*, Angela proposed a rather novel idea: "Paul, let's buy a house."

"What?"

"Well, it might cheer us up. I'd love to decorate one."

For the next month they searched, and finally found in Pimlico a derelict townhouse at 42 Cambridge Street, five minutes' walk from Victoria Air Terminal. All sorts of complicated and prolonged negotiations followed with building societies and Canadian banks but in the end, Paul bought the house. His two youthful architects proved suitably adventurous, opening up two floors, putting in a balcony dining room and adding a two-storey window — although it looked out only onto a tiny back yard. Angela, while taking classes with different companies, began choosing colour schemes and buying furniture in cheap, hidden-away antique stores.

After the editing and mix was over, Paul sat with Angela at dinner, and announced, "Sidney Newman wants me to join BBC."

Angela stopped eating and looked at him.

"Yeah. Become supervising producer of a new series he's doing of ninety minute shows. Less salary than at Granada, but lots of prestige, he said."

"Oh?" Angela appeared less than enthusiastic.

"And Philip Mackie at Granada, he wants me to do a new series made up of three half-hour plays on the same theme in each ninety-minute episode."

"Lucky we're getting this house," Angela said. Not a lot of joy in her tone.

"I only told you to cheer you up. Frankly, I'm not keen on any of it. Philip's plan would mean us living in Manchester for months..." He paused. "Did you hear that Lester B. Pearson got a minority government in Ottawa? Yes, on April 8th. He's our new Prime Minster..." He trailed off.

Angela nodded. "It seems so far off."

"Too far!"

Angela looked up. "So?" She paused. "You might think of going back?"

"Well... I keep seeing our little house on Briar Hill Avenue, our garden, and our life there. *Forest Rangers* is rolling all summer again, more film experience for me. I could write Bob and find out what's up."

The thought of going back to Canada gave them both a lift. And then, wouldn't you know, Angela got offered a six-week contract with Britain's Western Ballet Company.

"I'll manage fine, Angela, don't worry. Take the contract while it's offered. I'll go back, get the house ready, and find someone to help me with Stephanie."

Angela looked at him with some tenderness. "Thanks, old bean. I might just do that."

And so, with the Pimlico house almost finished, they both decided on Toronto, dreading what they knew was likely to happen.

* * *

The fateful day arrived when Paul, full of apprehension, drove out to the airport to meet Angela on her BOAC flight from London. Once out of the bustle of the airport and on the throughway, Paul told her about his rehearsals in Sumach Street on Harold Pinter's first and most formidable play, *The Birthday Party*. Finally, he asked, "Glad to be home?" He kept his eyes on the road. They had done their best, were such good friends, but both knew the marriage could not survive.

After a pause, Angela said, "Is it still?

"What?"

"Home?"

"Of course, of course."

"But I thought, we discussed..."

"Yes, yes. I know. But..."

Neither of them said anything.

"You know," he said, "when the awful moment actually comes, I don't know if I'm really up to it."

"Neither am I, right now."

Another silence followed.

"Shall we just tough it out for a bit longer?" Paul murmured.

"Good idea." Angela leaned over, put her small hand on his on the steering wheel, and gave him a kiss. "Stephanie will be pleased."

And that, for the moment, was that.

But the nights were still driving Paul to distraction. He decided that perhaps he should get away again, and so went to see Ross Maclean about doing another *Telescope*.

"Ross, how about a film this autumn on the Gaspe Coast? It's never been covered by an English filmmaker. At least, I don't know of any."

Ross agreed. Paul went with a cameraman, Mogens Gander, to Shigawake to recreate film scenes from his boyhood — *October Beach,* a forerunner of what was to become *Isabel.*

How Paul had loved walking below the great red cliffs, or feeding the pigs back the Hollow, or lying on a load of hay behind a team of horses trotting along the brow above Uncle Joe's abandoned sawmill and their pig pasture — all slowly returning to the dense woods of yesteryear.

Noel Dodds put together a terrific rough cut. But Ross and CBC brass were not enthralled. Undeterred, Paul finished the film and wrote the narration, and out it went, to excellent notices. Fletcher Markle, once lionized on American networks, had returned to introduce Telescope, and so opened the film.

Another step on Paul's path to becoming a filmmaker.

* * *

With Charles Israel, they devised a *Festival, Let Me Count the Ways*, that would require a lot of film inserts. To play the wife of the troubled husband haunted by her death, Paul got Bob Allen to bring in Teresa Wright, an Oscar-winner for best supporting actress. He flew to New York and convinced the superb actor, James Daley, to come to Toronto. A kindly father with four children, he introduced Paul to a graceful teenager named Tyne, who kept offering them cups of tea.

That production became Canada's entry for the Prix Italia.

After his next, *Spring Song*, with again the lovely Martha Henry, Paul flew down to direct one of Bill Shatner's *For The People*, all shot on the streets of New York.

Arriving back at Toronto airport, he was met by a familiar figure, smartly dressed, trim, elegant, blonde hair gleaming under the lights. She had finished her National Ballet tour in April, forty-four cities. They embraced, threw the luggage in the trunk, and drove off.

"How was the show?" she asked her husband.

"Pretty darn hard, actually. Up at five, shooting all day on those crowded streets — first time a series has ever been shot outdoors on New York streets. I usually had dinner with Bill — always a new young lady with him — and then into bed. I'm still worn out."

"So... not a good time to discuss..."

Paul sighed. "Shades of the last time we drove home from the Toronto airport?"

Angela nodded.

"No. It's okay. Go ahead.

"Well, I've been looking for a house to buy..."

"Oh yes?"

"And I think I've found it."

"Where?"

"Near Bathurst Street, below Bloor."

"I see." So, it was finally happening. His stomach churned.

"Not expensive. I'll have to fix it up, of course."

"But you'll love that." Amazing, this break up: something they'd both been facing and dreading for months, probably even years. Now so mundane.

"I've told Stephanie."

"Hasn't she been... rather expecting it, poor darling?"

Angela nodded. "I think so. An elderly couple owns the townhouse. They've seen me dance, so they're giving me the mortgage themselves." She smiled. "They love ballet and know that I've been with the company a dozen years."

"Very nice of them, all the same."

"Yes, it is," Angela went on. "It's a converted duplex on Brunswick, quite central. I'll decorate the one-bedroom apartment downstairs and rent it out, to help with the mortgage. Upstairs there are two bedrooms on two floors, just right for myself and Stephanie."

And so it came about, with little emotion, no screaming, no frantic arguments, in fact just two friends discussing the most important moment of their lives. As if they were choosing a restaurant for dinner.

Luckily, Paul got an offer from Granada to direct an Albee play in ten days; he wouldn't have to moon around an empty house. And then he'd hurry back, because Bob wanted him to do another Festival in June.

Now, tell his mother and aunt and then, sadly, go his separate way.

* * *

Once again in London, Paul directed T*he American Dream,* and *Sandbox,* the first Edward Albee plays ever allowed on television, telecast May 25th. This gave Paul a chance to cast Cathleen Nesbitt, nearly 80. While starring in the West End during WWI, she had been engaged to the poet, Rupert Brooke. [for his poem, *The Soldier,* see Appendix] Imagine directing an actress who had been loved by one of his favourite poets! He also enjoyed staying in his very own house in Pimlico — comfortable, though not fully furnished. He decided to ask, and pay, Angela to come over and finish it properly.

What made the whole experience more palatable was meeting, at a party at Canada House, a tall, slim, striking RADA student, Susan Clark. One look into her clear green almond-shaped eyes and Paul was smitten. She accepted his invitation to dinner, repeated several times. And as soon as they got back to Toronto, he cast her in his next Festival, *Horror of Darkness* with Neil McCallum. Soon, she too was off to Hollywood, another TV star.

But first, he and Robert Allen picked up a rented van, drove to Briar Hill, and took the day to load Angela's furniture and bring it to her new home. As they drove down to Angela's, it struck Paul forcefully: they had well and truly separated. His marriage was over. He would never again be coming home to share Angela's dinners. Never again discuss her problems, or his own. They had so amicably agreed on a proper settlement, with money to help her and a down payment on her house. But still, the pain began to bite deeply. It infused his whole being. Everything ached. His heart plummeted. Gloom descended. Next to him, Bob sensed his agony.

That drive in the furniture van Paul was to remember the rest of his life.

PART TWO: GENEVIEVE

CHAPTER NINETEEN
1965

Early in July, a young actress Paul had flown to Montreal to meet came down the path to Desjardins, a restaurant on Guy Street considered to have great seafood in a city of fine dining. Emma Hodgson, Radio Canada's casting director, had warned Paul (through Eva Langbord) to meet Geneviève Bujold in a proper environment; she was used to the royal treatment.

Anouilh had updated *Romeo et Jeanette* to contemporary France: the Montagues come from an upscale bourgeois family, and the Capulets somewhat lower class. Paul had explained all this to his supervising producer. "It's a terrific play, Bob. Passion! Torment! Free-will, idealism, all that stuff." He'd waited till they'd had their obligatory chat about current events, including the Canada Pension Plan passed earlier. Now everyone in Canada, not just the high earners, would have an income after they retired. And of course, they talked about the much debated new flag, a red maple leaf on white with red side bars.

Bob said nothing, brown eyes just watching, fingers tapping the desk.

"So let's update it to Canada now: make the Montagues English, from boring old Toronto and the Capulets, French from Quebec. What do you think?" Bob's cherubic features hardly changed, and then, as was his habit, he puffed and leaned forward. "You think you can find a Jeannette?"

"Montreal's crawling with beautiful young actresses. Won't it be great to have a fresh face? I'll check with Eva Langbord."

"Montreal! You mean, pay board and lodging?"

"Oh Bob, come on! Yes, only for Jeannette and her family. Let's break out, let's get something going here..."

Bob had finally agreed, so now, Paul was sitting by a Desjardins window, awaiting Emma's find: "She's tops, Paul, the best theatre actress for her age. She made a wonderful film with Michel Brault: *Entre la mer et l'eau douce* with Louise Marleau, who's busy right now. She's just back from a hard tour all over Europe and Russia with the *Théâtre du Rideau Vert.* Before that, she never stopped: theatre at night, acting on radio by day, rehearsing television — she's worn out. She's taking the whole summer off. She told me, 'Don't offer me anything, Emma! And not even this autumn.' She does need a rest, Paul. So... well... good luck!" That challenge had only quickened Paul's interest and determination.

He saw through the window a slight but clearly determined young woman stride up the path, swinging her purse as if nothing in the world could stop her. In she came and scanned the room. A deferential waiter directed her to Paul's table. She came forward and they shook hands firmly. His preeminent position in English television needed little introduction. But could Geneviève speak English?

Paul soon found she did, albeit poorly, but enough for conversing. She quickly corrected Paul's pronunciation of her name –

Junn-veeyev. Her pixie face, frank brown eyes and slightly tousled hair, and especially her confidence, all impressed him. Before they had even ordered, he knew he had his Jeannette.

Now, convince her to come to Toronto. They began the main course, Paul having chosen a light pasta, Geneviève a salad. Paul told her about the play and something of his other Anouilh productions: *Eurydice* (*Point of Departure* in London) and *Antigone*. He was a fan of the great French playwright.

Nothing was decided at lunch, as she'd think it over. Paul flew back to Toronto, worried. All through lunch, an unstoppable desire had grown — he wanted so much to direct this dynamic and fiery actress. But would she get back to work this soon? And come to Toronto? No clear sailing ahead. And while they waited, Bob could not announce the play.

Finally Emma let Paul know that she had agreed. He bounded into Robert Allen's office full of cheer, but Bob stopped him by saying they'd have to audition her.

"Bob! She's known all over Quebec. Even in Europe."

"But not in Toronto. She'll have to fly in."

Paul felt crestfallen.

"You see, if she's any good, then we'll have to pay accommodation for all the French Canadians."

"Only Jeannette's sister, brother, and father. Three. Come on Bob, let's do another first for the old Corp. Time we got our two solitudes together, eh?"

The morning she flew in, Paul met her and brought her straight to the *Festival* offices. While driving, he told her which scenes he'd like her to read. But she seemed oddly nervous. "I've never been to Toronto. I hate coming. And I've never had to audition."

"Yeah. Usually, nobody asks me to audition actors, either. But it is kind of special — we've never imported a whole French cast. Damn well time, of course, but still... Let's just go along with it. Afterwards, I'll take you to a nice lunch and you can fly right back."

Geneviève shrugged.

"Then maybe next week, I'll come to Montreal, stay out in Mount Saint-Hilaire, and together we'll find the rest of Jeannette's family."

That seemed to reassure her. But when they entered Bob's office and saw Eva, Geneviève quailed. He even got nervous himself, which didn't help.

She started to read nervously, with Paul feeding her Romeo's lines (not very well). She began to lose what little English pronunciation she had, and even forgot what was going on in the scene. In spite of himself, Paul was surprised: was this Montreal's greatest actress? He even noticed Bob and Eva exchange glances.

Oh Lord! All over but the shouting? What would he do now?

He was still convinced she'd be terrific, once she got into the role. But how to get that far?

The next few days, Paul made his case to Eva and eventually got her on board. Then they both worked on Bob. Finally, thanks mainly to Paul's decade of directing successful dramas, he prevailed. But would it be worth it? How many risks could he take and still come out on top?

Paul flew to Montreal and stayed at Apple Barrel. He and his new actress struck up quite a partnership. With Emma, they met other French performers. Paul was amazed at the yeast bubbling up in Quebec culture, in theatre, film and dance. Geneviève's young but distinguished director Michel Brault and his wife Marie-Marthe invited them to dinner. Michel with Pierre Perrault had won Best Film at the Canadian Film Awards of 1964 for *Pour la suite du monde*. They spent time with Claude Jutra, also a winner for his *À tout prendre*.

Paul was only too aware that he himself had never made a motion picture. He certainly had been trying. "So try harder," Geneviève told him. "The result counts!" — as she would often repeat.

They selected a pretty blonde actress, Nathalie Naubert as the sister, Julia, Jean Doyon as the brother, Lucien, and finally as the father, Georges Groulx, one of the great comedians of Quebec theatre.

Paul found another newcomer in Montreal, Michael Sarrazin for Romeo. Tall, skinny, with a wistful countenance and soft brown eyes, he would make a complete contrast to the fiery Geneviève. An ideal cast.

* * *

"Quite a challenge you set yourself!" Leo Orenstein, remarked as he passed Paul in the corridor.

"Really? How so?" Paul fell into step with his director friend.

"Bringing in all those French Canadians. I've heard they're all great theatre actors. But have any been on television?"

"Oh sure, on Radio Canada, I think. But I guess you're right," Paul replied. "They've never done English television."

"Ever since I did Marcel Dubé's *Zone*, I wanted to bring in more of them."

"*Zone*, with Gloria Rand? She was terrific, Leo, so beautiful! Yeah, I loved that show. Now she's married to Bill Shatner, did you know?" Leo nodded, and they went into his office and sat down. "I have my first read-through at Sumach Street at two today." Paul shook his head as Leo offered a cigarette. "There's such a wonderful energy in Montreal right now. Geneviève introduced me around. Marvellous actors, lots of theatre, they're even making films — how come we aren't doing that? They're bursting with energy."

"Well, I still think you're a bit of a pioneer."

The word "pioneer" rang in Paul's ear for some reason. "It's hardly a risk, these actors. I think Geneviève is doing us a favour."

"Bob Allan doesn't think so."

Paul raised his eyebrows. "Oh, what have you heard?"

"The word is she reads so badly, he is worried. So is Eva. Doesn't that make you nervous?"

"Not really." Had he ever been nervous before rehearsals? Certainly not. Too much self-confidence? Who knows? He loved all the excitement, the live shows, why be nervous? "Well, we'll all know in ten days. You going to watch?" Paul got to his feet.

"Oh yes, I'll be watching!" Leo smiled. "I'd really like to use French performers myself. We all would."

"Well," said Paul, as he left, "it could be a beginning..."

* * *

During rehearsals Paul kept working on a shooting script. He would scrawl thick pencil lines across the page of dialogue to mark the cuts from one shot to another. As actors grew into their roles and adjusted their movements, cutting points changed. The movement, as organically dictated by the play's emotions, had to rule — let it all flow was Paul's viewpoint: camera work must grow organically from the emotional sweep of the performers and script.

In the evenings, he would transcribe his rough line-scribbled script into a second with neater ruled lines, and often go to a third. Dramas usually had three cameras, sometimes four: at the end of each line, the camera number was written. Below the line in the margin, the shot was described: cu Geneviève; w2s (wide two-shot) Georges and Nathalie. He wrote notes in the margins for special lighting, or sound effects that Bill McClelland would provide. Also cues for Johnson Ashley, his favourite studio director.

Later, the script assistant numbered these shots and after the last run-through sat up well after midnight typing separate "shot lists" which each cameraman attached to his mount.

Too busy to socialize with her new director, Geneviève spent evenings coaching George Groulx with his lines: he couldn't speak a word of English, The Quebec cast ate together, talking, laughing, having fun.

Finally, ten days of rehearsals, standard for a ninety-minute show, ended with a run-through in Sumach rehearsal rooms. Bob Allen came, with Rudi Dorn and other art department members. Bob, an observant and perceptive executive producer, gave Paul notes privately while the actors took a break. Most of his suggestions were helpful, though by no means orders, as in American television.

Shooting in Studio Four went well: Geneviève turned out to be terrific and the rest of the cast matched her. *Romeo and Jeannette* had introduced Geneviève Bujold and Michael Sarrazin to English Canada. Afterwards, English and French mingled at Briar Hill Avenue for a bang-up party.

The next morning, Paul drove his lead to the airport, both of them weary but happy. Being so involved in the play, they'd had no time to look ahead. But underneath it all, Paul felt that they had reached beyond the simple relationship of director-actress.

But now she was off to Montreal.

CHAPTER TWENTY
1965

Now what? Paul wondered, as he rattled around the empty Briar Hill house. He began working on *Indian Summer*, a script he hoped to film, but his thoughts returned again and again to the little gamine who had made such an impression. Finally, he decided to drive to Apple Barrel, and see Geneviève.

His mother and Aunt Hilda had a small apartment on Chomedey Avenue close to the Montreal Forum. While Aunt Hilda was still teaching at convent schools, his mother was busy with Beauty Counsellors. But she was happy to come out to Apple Barrel on the weekend with Hilda and cook roast beef and Yorkshire pudding for Geneviève.

The actress duly arrived and pronounced that she loved the cottage: the yellow walls, the stone fireplace, the simple plank table John Molson had given Paul's mother, as well as the metal sign "Apple Barrel" he'd also had made in the shape of a barrel.

"Nothing like roast beef of old England, eh Geneviève?" Paul said as she tucked into her laden plate. She complimented Rene, not only on her cooking, but also on her son's directing: "He's the best TV director I've worked with."

"Thank you, Geneviève," Paul said. "But the next step for me had better be a motion picture."

"I certainly hope so, Paul." Her brown eyes looked steadily across the table.

* * *

Paul invited Geneviève out again a couple of days later, and they walked up through the apple orchard onto the mountain road leading to the cratered lake — the same trail he had enjoyed many times after coming back from Oxford.

How the last fifteen years had changed him! Confident, rested, happy to be with this new lady, he felt buoyant. Geneviève was also in good form, revelling in the woods, the lake, and then the trail taking them to the highest point of Mont Saint-Hilaire. Paul talked about his time at Oxford and about Angela, which marriage had ended the previous year. Geneviève, too, had been married, but only briefly, so both were free.

Reaching the peak, they faced the distant Montreal mountain and its huge Oratoire Saint- Joseph. The wind tugged at them and clouds reared up in billowing patterns. In the high chill air, his arms went around Geneviève and she turned and clung to him. Their lips met, a kiss long enough to consume his heart. This girl he had grown to love — could she be loving him back?

They broke apart. "We'd better get going. Looks like rain."

Sharing no more words, they hurried back down in single file. After rounding the lake, the promised rain arrived. "Damn, we should've brought coats."

"Why?" gasped a drenched Geneviève. "It's only water, I love it!"

As the rain increased, they hurried down the mountain road, leapt the tussocks under the apple trees and plunged into Apple Barrel.

"Into the shower," Paul ordered and Geneviève complied. When she came out wrapped in Rene's old dressing gown, Paul suggested she get warm in the bedroom upstairs. "I'm going to shower myself."

While he was washing, he pondered, should he go and dive under the covers, too? But no such decision was needed. His body, with a mind of its own, carried him swiftly up the stairs. And into bed he dove..

* * *

One evening before going off to see a play in French, they met at Desjardins again for an early supper. Paul noticed Geneviève seemed unusually anxious. He said nothing, but after they had ordered, she leaned forward. "I have to go to Paris next week." She looked at him.

He looked back. "Why?"

"Well... I have to do the preparations for a film."

Paul's first reaction was to beam. "How exciting? What film is it?"

"It's called *La guerre est fini*. Directed by Alain Resnais."

"Alain Resnais? The top filmmaker in Europe?" Paul was astounded. "Will you ever forget *Last Year at Marienbad?* Breathtaking — I even invested some money in its distribution in Toronto, which of course I lost. Do you have a nice little part?"

"I think so," Geneviève dropped her eyes. "It's the lead. Opposite Yves Montand."

"The lead?" Paul stared. "Opposite Yves Montand? He's the biggest star in Europe today."

Geneviève nodded. "It's going to be fun."

"Oh boy, is it ever!"

But then, as the dinner progressed, Paul could see all hope for them withering. A big star in Europe? She'd never come back. The end.

* * *

After Paris, Geneviève returned to her home in Montreal, while Paul in Toronto headed into a heavy season of work. Geneviève did more plays on Radio Canada before returning to Paris, but her phone calls grew frequent. She had been photographed for the cover of *Elle* magazine; in fact, lots of French papers were after her — which Paul understood only too well. Who'd ever withstand that lure of fame in Europe's finest capital city? She was lost forever.

Geneviève flew back to Paris for the shooting, but a small ray of light broke like an Eastern sunrise: Leonard White, head of drama at ABC London, suggested Paul repeat his successful production of *Neighbours* Leonard had seen in Canada.

London! A good deal closer to Paris. Paul accepted at once, and phoned Geneviève. What would she say?

She was thrilled. So at the beginning of November, Paul flew to London. Ossie Davis was busy, so Paul cast the comedian Dick Gregory who had never acted, but had some star power. Ruby Dee agreed to repeat her role, and his old flame Toby Robins, now in London, played the wife.

As soon as he could, Paul crossed over to Paris. He had only been once before, acting in Tony Richardson's *Duchess of Malfi*, when he had stayed in a humble student dorm on the Left Bank. This time he gave the taxi the address, Hôtel du Quai Voltaire, on the banks of the Seine. When he arrived, Geneviève leapt up from the little salon and they embraced as never before.

The lift took them to their small bedroom on the fifth floor, where she had ordered champagne so they could toast the adventure. Out the window, lights were winking on across the Seine. Paul stared out at the Louvre and on the right, the Pont Neuf. Geneviève seemed as excited as he was. After his second glass of champagne, he blurted out, "Geneviève, I thought I'd never see you again."

"You silly man. You know I will never leave you!"

* * *

When she was free, they strolled across the Seine into the Tuileries gardens, then up the Champs Elysées and around the Arc de Triomphe. Passing a newsstand, Paul got a twinge as he saw Geneviève on several covers. Oh yes, she was on her way. And him only capable of directing television dramas. More than ever, he longed for a real motion picture.

Alain Resnais invited him to watch a scene between Geneviève and Yves Montand in a metro station. What impressed Paul was, during the takes, the crew all crouched down behind the camera so no getting into actors' eye-lines: the performers had the world to themselves. Technicians, as they crouched, faced the ground — as if kneeling in the cathedral of their art.

After the shooting, Geneviève brought Paul to lunch with her co-star and with her powerful agent Lebovici, who handled just about every major singer and star in France. Had he taken a great shine to Geneviève? Another worry?

They went to hear the Montreal singer, Monique Leyraq, introduced on stage by the great French actress, Madeleine Reynaud, who knew of Geneviève and embraced her when they went backstage to see Monique. Were Canadians taking this capital by storm?

In November, Paul brought Geneviève over to London for her first view of the Pimlico house. She loved it, and couldn't wait to come and start cooking there herself. The romantic interlude was continuing.

Michael Langham, artistic director of Stratford, Ontario, came for drinks and asked Geneviève to play three leads the following summer. She turned him down. The stunning Honor Blackman, Pat Macnee's leading lady in *The Avengers*, came to dinner with her husband; Paul had seen her house, designed by his two same architects. On Saturday at the last great flea market on Portobello Road, Paul managed to dodge Geneviève long enough to buy, in a small but elegant jewellery shop, an engagement ring, an emerald surrounded by tiny diamonds.

On Sunday November 11th, Westminster Abbey being only a short walk away, they stood in sorrow at small crosses lining the walks for the thousands killed in both wars. That evening, on the top of the bus heading to Notting Hill Gate for dinner with Ted Kotcheff, Paul offered Geneviève the engagement ring — albeit with baited breath.

Bless his soul, didn't she accept?

Now, an engaged couple, Geneviève left to finish her film in Paris and Paul went on to direct the British version of *Neighbours*.

* * *

"Never", as in "I'll never leave you," is a very big word. Paul wondered, did it mean: Well, at least not for the next two weeks? Or even two years? There he was, back in Toronto, with Geneviève shooting in Paris, and talk of the future being avoided — what would come next? Would she fly back to Montreal? Or to Toronto? Would in fact *amor vincit omnia*?

With great trepidation, he made the fatal phone call.

With alacrity, Geneviève replied, "Of course I'm coming back to you, silly man. Did you think I wouldn't?"

Geneviève took to her new house on Briar Hill Avenue with ease. Almost fiercely, she set about cooking, housekeeping, adding furniture, rearranging, and making Briar Hill comfortable for them both.

Paul plunged into an adaptation of *Crime and Punishment*, entitled *The Murderer*. Geneviève agreed to play little Sonya. The story being Russian, Paul chose as designer the great Nikolai Soloviov, who by now had beaten throat cancer but, with voice box removed, he had to speak through a hole in his throat, covered by a graceful cravat.

"Paul," he gulped as they met in his small third floor office, "part of story is big square."

"Yeah. I've been thinking about that. It's so essential. But maybe we should ask George Salverson, our story editor, to rewrite? I mean, how on earth can we do Saint Petersburg in that tiny studio?"

"Look, Paul!" Nikolai croaked, as he rose excitedly. "We build set in parking lot at Sumach."

Paul was shocked. "Great idea, Nikolai, but what about the guys in props, the painters, the draughtsmen, the carpenters..."

Nikolai slammed his fist on the table. "No problem! Problem is for best show! I will put sets for one week only. We go see Leonard Crainford," head of the design department.

With Nikolai's reputation, and probably Paul's — much to the annoyance of everyone else, they managed the impossible. A first, and probably a last!

Half way through rehearsals, Nik took Paul out into the parking lot to see his half- finished set on a mass of uneven gravel. It really looked forlorn. Awful, Paul thought. He turned to Nik, who shrugged. "We shoot at night."

"Yes, of course. At night."

"'At's it!"

"But we planned on snow. It's mid-December! Where the hell is it?"

"Saint Petersburg." Nik shook his head disconsolately.

"Three days from shooting... What's the forecast?"

Nik sighed. "I not listen to news." He shrugged, and looked rather cowed, unusual for him.

"Can we truck in snow?" As it turned out, that was well beyond any *Festival* budget.

"Are you worried?" asked Eric Till, the handsome new British director. Word had gotten out about Paul's folly.

"Not in the slightest," Paul said with bravado. And in fact, for some reason, he was not. He just prayed hard, and counted on the Lord to do His job. Who else could control the weather?

But the next day, and the next, no snow.

Bob Allen, a wise supervising producer, had likely made contingency plans, but Paul had not. Lots of gossip in the Drama Department, his script assistant reported. Paul Alford was headed for his first big disaster.

But on the morning of the shooting, Paul awoke to see, out the window, heavy snow falling. "Praise be," he shouted, waking Geneviève. "The Lord has spoken! Jeepers, I've got to get to the parking lot fast, and put up ribbons and signs — no walking on the virgin snow!"

But these outdoor sets were not the only "first" the show became known for. *The Murderer,* played by Paul Kozlik, had to walk up stairs and along a corridor to commit his murder, a crucial element in the story, or so both Paul and Nik felt. Before rehearsals, Paul had rung Vic Ferry, the technical producer of *Festival.*

"Vic, I've heard they are developing a camera for television that is hand-held."

Paul could imagine him grimacing at the other end of the line. "Not possible."

"Vic, please. Ring someone in New York. See if they have one. I don't care if it's been tested. Get it up here for the show. We need it."

What Vic actually replied bore little relationship to what he was thinking.

At the end of rehearsals, Paul held the usual run-through in the barren Sumach room. When Vic Ferry came in, he announced that the experimental camera had indeed arrived.

During the shooting of The Murderer, the CBC — and cameraman Tom Farquharson in particular— made television history by using the first hand-held camera on live North American television.

* * *

After the show, which Bob Allen deemed a resounding success, he called Paul in. "You think Geneviève would do another show for us?"

"Of course, Bob. What did you have in mind?"

"Ibsen. *A Doll's House*?"

Paul had only done one Ibsen with Esse W. Ljungh. "I'll ask her, I'm sure she'd love to play Nora. Do you have a date?

"You start Feb. 20."

Geneviève got the script from Paul. After making sure her contract was signed, she spent all the next day in bed, reading. From then on, she never looked at the script again. Word perfect in rehearsals, she grew into the part as though born to it. Paul had found himself quite an actress.

Paul decided the show needed film inserts, so he brought Tommy Farquharson to a home in North Toronto that did look like a perfect little doll's house. Completing the cast was Michael Learned and her husband Peter Donat, with Paul's old stand-by, Toronto's top actor, Douglas Rain. Another trophy show for the engaged couple.

* * *

Still hoping to make a motion picture, Paul tried setting up Charles Israel's teleplay *Let Me Count the Ways* as a film, starring James Daly and Teresa Wright. But even with that stellar cast, he couldn't get financing.

Paul then wrote a winter hockey story set on an outdoor rink, *The Simpleton,* for Budge Crawley's Gatineau Studios. In the end Budge wouldn't commit to the finance, so that didn't get off the ground either.

But Budge wanted Paul to direct his own pet script, *The Strange One*, the story of a Canada Goose from Scotland blown off course to Ontario. He had even built a wind tunnel for shooting geese flying. But that film, too, went nowhere.

Finally, Paul thought up *Indian Summer,* a last love affair between a man in the autumn of his years and a lovely European — which fitted James Mason and Monica Vitti perfectly. She had burst on the North American scene in Antonioni's films and had even appeared on an Italian postage stamp. Paul wanted to shoot it in the Gatineau, with leaves turning from green to brilliant orange and red and then slowly dying, matching the love affair. He knew it could be shot cheaply and got Lindsay Galloway, the *Forest Rangers* screenwriter, to write a first draft. Elspeth Cochrane, his London agent, also represented James Mason, so Paul flew to meet James in Geneva. But the script was deemed not ready, and like his other film projects, it also went nowhere.

So Geneviève and Paul decided to take their minds off work and go to Bonaire, in the Netherland Antilles — the first real holiday Paul had ever taken. Glorious! Just the two of them in a little shack, warm sand, snorkelling every day.

When they came back, Paul arranged another Dylan Thomas script to direct and Geneviève flew to Paris for her second French film, *King of Hearts,* starring Alan Bates, and a stellar French contingent. The director, Philippe de Broca, had made, among other hits, *The Perils of a Chinese in China*, with Ursula Andress.

Then Paul directed two episodes of *Wojeck*, Ron Weyman's new television series about a city coroner. He enjoyed working with Ron, Rita Allen's brother and a former officer in the Royal Canadian Navy. This series was a first for the CBC, shooting on the streets of Toronto and in Ronnie's actual house. The crew was full of the talk of the new Medical Care Act, to pass July 12th, headline news. It meant everyone in Canada would get free doctors and hospitals.

As soon as he could, Paul flew over to be with Geneviève; they stayed at a charming little hotel in Ermenonville, near the location. Philippe de Broca, a short, gnome-like and energetic director with a long nose and sparkling eyes, was shooting in near-by Senlis and in an abandoned castle. His wife, Michelle, a forceful producer, had taken a shine to Geneviève, so they got on wonderfully. Evenings at their hotel, Philippe hosted splendid fun-filled dinners. He was actually two years younger than Paul but already had an impressive career. Whenever would Paul get a film of his own?

On the occasional weekend, Michelle invited them to the de Broca home at Carièrres-sur-Seine outside Paris. The ménage at 29 rue Victor Hugo was unlike any other, what with young Jaya and their live ocelot Charlie.

"Oh Michelle," Paul asked, "you and Philippe have a son?"

"Not at all," Michelle snapped, fiercely. "You see, when we were shooting in Nepal —"

"The film with Ursula Andress?"

"Yes, a little orphan Nepalese child kept coming to the set, deaf and dumb obviously... About five years old, I would say. We couldn't get rid of him. He was very nice, I must admit, but finally," she spoke brusquely, "we moved several hundred miles south. And I was astonished, *oui,* that same little boy, Jaya, he found us! No one knew how he made the trip. He had no money, no food, no way of coming, but there he was."

"Amazing!"

"Absolutely. So Philippe adopted him. He never thinks ahead, you know. So we brought him back to Paris. But who do you think looks after him?"

Paul knew, of course. Poor Michelle. And Charlie the ocelot? He and Geneviève had been disconcerted on entering to see this fierce animal with its yellow eyes and huge paws staring down at them from the stairway curving above the small vestibule. Even worse they had the muscular body rub against their legs under the table. As big as a medium-sized dog, he would lie in wait for guests when they came out to go to the bathroom, so Geneviève insisted on being accompanied.

CHAPTER TWENTY-ONE
1967–68

Isabel

Back in Toronto, Geneviève got another call from Paris. Would she appear opposite Jean-Paul Belmondo in Louis Malle's *Le Voleur*?

"You must go, Geneviève. You will have worked with the top three directors in Europe, Alain Resnais, Philippe de Broca, and Louis Malle — I'll never forget his film *The Lover,* with Jeanne Moreau. Go. I've got a break; I'll come for a while."

So when Geneviève left, Paul served on the jury of the Montreal Film Festival, making friends with another juryman, Milos Forman, the young Czech director whose *Loves of a Blonde* had caused a stir in North America.

In Paris, Geneviève rented an apartment on the Left Bank from an Italian photographer, Murella Ricardi, at 2bis rue de Verneuil. Paul arrived to find himself in a large room with big bookcases and huge windows, and a long comfortable sofa down one wall. Above, a mezzanine bedroom looked down, behind which Paul found a sunny boudoir where he could work on his new inspiration for a film.

While Geneviève was shooting, Paul wandered in the Tuileries and Champs Elysées, letting his film idea blossom. Geneviève's parents had been born in St. Simeon de Bonaventure, about thirty miles from Shigawake. So what about a motion picture in which Geneviève would be stuck on a Gaspe farm? As the film progressed, every door of escape would slam shut.

Nights were filled with happy dinners, sometimes with Louis and his extraordinarily beautiful wife, Anne-Marie, and days were filled with writing his new film.

Back in Toronto, Bob Allen told him that the CBC was moving to colour. Would Paul please direct the first play on this new network?

Why not a play performed in both English and French? So he chose Marie-Claire Blais' delightful *La roulotte aux pupées,* or *Puppet Caravan.* Geneviève would play the puppet, and the bilingual cast would include Jean Doyon (from the Anouilh play) and François Tassé. Paul taped the English version in Toronto on December 8th and the French with the same cast in Montreal on March 12th.

Before these tapings, Paul asked Budge if he might borrow an empty cottage to work on his screenplay. Budge did own a shack in the Gatineau and in October Paul went there to finish *Isabel.* He came back full of excitement, only to be met with real resistance.

"If you want to shoot this as a feature film," Bob Allen said, "why not go to London? Or New York?"

"When I was in London, Kotcheff said the same thing and so did Narizzano: stop thinking about Canada. Ted has already made films over there, and Silvio, too. But Bob, this is my country. I intend to stick it out through thick and thin."

"Paul, no one has made a truly Canadian film. Harry Horner tried for years, he's a reasonably well-known production designer in the US; but he failed."

"He's not a director."

"What about *The Luck of Ginger Coffey*?"

"Okay, so Crawley Films made it in Canada, but it was directed by an American, starring British actors Robert Shaw and Mary Ure. It originated out of Hollywood, too."

"No one knows Geneviève in the United States," Bob went on. "Producers in France have tried to get their films distributed in America. They always fail."

"Look at our television industry, we do marvellous shows —"

"But David Green, Arthur Hiller, Hank Kaplan, they all went south."

"And I stayed, Bob. I don't care, I'm going to make *Isabel* here in Canada."

Still seething, he reported the conversation to Geneviève.

"Remember that agent Stevie Phillips?" Geneviève said. "You met her in New York. She's building quite a reputation with young stars."

"Yeah," Paul said, "with Judy Garland's daughter, too, I think?"

"Yes, Liza Minnelli. And that new young actor, Robert Redford, she's handling him."

"But where does that get us, Geneviève? She doesn't handle me. No directors."

"Meet her anyway."

Down they both went. Stevie announced she'd gotten him an interview at Colombia Pictures, and after it, he reported, "Geneviève, you should see their headquarters! Big stuff. I finally got through enough doors to Mr. Big himself. He sat in a huge office.

He was certainly gracious."

"How wonderful!"

"Sort of... Listen: once I'd introduced myself, he said he had thought I was somebody else! So he thanked me courteously and showed me the door." He grinned.

Geneviève shook her head.

"At Paramount, some guy did say he'd bring it to the attention of Mr. Bluhdorn."

"I've heard of him," Geneviève said. "He ran a nuts and bolts company, and just bought the whole studio! Paramount is in an uproar. It's never happened before."

"Well, maybe I can meet him."

Stevie had insisted they stay at the prestige Hotel Pierre and one day their phone rang. Paul listened, then put his hand over the mouthpiece. "Geneviève, it's Paramount. Bluhdorn's secretary! He'll meet us! Three this afternoon in his office."

Geneviève paused, then shook her head. "We're not going."

"What?"

"If he wants to see us, he'll have to come here."

Paul could scarcely believe his ears. But Geneviève was adamant.

Paul shook his head and then spoke the fatal words. "We'd love to see Mr. Bluhdorn. But he'll have to come here."

No one was more surprised than Paul, perhaps Geneviève, too, when the secretary rang back to say Charlie would be right over.

The new owner of Paramount had an owlish face and large black glasses. Already balding, though probably in his 40s, he seemed the epitome of a dynamic, energetic owner of a large conglomerate.

Charlie, as Paul began to call him, confessed that his wife was French and knew all about Geneviève. So yes, Paramount would finance *Isabel* — the tiny Canadian film to be shot on the Gaspe Coast wilderness.

* * *

Had Paul taken on too much again? No film crews in Canada, no film series shooting, and now they were headed into a remote area with no caterers, no facilities, and he was supposed to deliver a motion picture to a world-wide distributor.

The first thing he did was call Peter Carter, his chum from the RCMP series. "Peter! The film's on! We've got to find a crew, we've got to... well, do everything, I guess."

They raided the National Film Board. Cinematographer Georges Dufaux had shot lots of documentaries, and his kid brother Guy wanted to start so they joined in. Georges recommended an NFB gaffer who knew something, though not a lot, about lighting.

Peter became Production Manager as well as First Assistant Director, and Peter wanted Joyce Kozy as continuity girl, so she also became Production Secretary, Unit Manager, and organized everything — all for $1.70 an hour. Geneviève wore Joyce's cheap green turtleneck sweater in many scenes.

Casting was easy. Paul had often worked with Gerard Parkes, an Irish actor who took risks and would make a perfect Uncle Matthew. Going further afield, he found Marc Strange, slightly overweight, to play the mysterious stranger. Al Waxman, just back from a British movie, trooped down to the Gaspe to play a van driver. The others Paul would later cast among the denizens of Shigawake, including cousin Elton.

The next hurdle — permission to shoot in the Old Homestead, which had been built by his great grandfather. Auntie Lil had left it to her son, Paul's cousin Henry. But previously Paul had written a poetic short story, *A Sheaf of Wheat,* lovingly describing his

Aunts and Uncle and the hired hand, Tim Smith. Out of ten years of fiction carried weekly in the *Family Herald*, it had been selected for a hard cover book. But cousin Henry took exception to his family being portrayed in a newspaper, and warned Paul never to set foot in Shigawake again. No one else had found the story the least bit derogatory. Now, Paul had to get Henry to let them film in the Old Homestead.

This Principal of Montreal High, the biggest English high school in Quebec, would be a hard nut to crack. But Paul's mother, Rene, with the help of Henry's son, Ted, worked on him until he agreed. At last the location was set.

What about that emerald engagement ring? Both had been married before. But Rev. Brian Freeland managed to get permission from the diocese, and on March 18 in a small ceremony at Hart House Chapel at the University of Toronto, Rev. Brian married Paul and Geneviève in the presence of two witnesses, Robert and Rita Allen. Geneviève wore a short burnt-orange dress under a stunning fluffy white coat and carried a little white bouquet.

After the simple ceremony, they all went to lunch at the Royal York Hotel. But that afternoon, Paul still went to a meeting with Peter Carter about *Isabel*.

Joyce booked sleepers to St. Godfrey and, with a strong March blizzard blowing, they boarded the train. The next morning they awoke to find themselves stuck in snowdrifts. Stranded for hours in the middle of nowhere, Paul wondered what on earth he had done. Was it all a dream – or a nightmare? To relieve his mind, he worked out with Georges how to shoot the opening scene of *Isabel*, taking place on this train. The crew members were all excited by their new adventure — save for Michel Desruelles, the Parisian make-up man Geneviève had insisted on bringing. He was frankly terrified. Never had he been in such a wild, remote and obviously dangerous place as the Gaspe coast!

But Paul could not escape the nightmare nagging him. Here he was, stranded in snow with an untried crew, a cast from Shiga-wake who had never acted, with his own novice script — all sitting squarely on the shoulders of a Producer-Director who had never before made a motion picture.

What would that future bring?

* * *

As it turned out, after the first week or so, the crew melded into a smoothly working unit. The rushes were sent by bus to Montreal, where Peter had twisted Harold Greenberg's arm to get him to open the first 35mm processing lab in Canada, and then to give them, as its first film, a huge discount. The rushes came back by bus every week, and then the crew would troop to the broken-down cinema in New Carlisle to watch them silent on its old projector. Peter saw to it that the "Props" person was a local, Arnold Mackenzie. He'd pop down to the wharf every morning, bring back a mess of lobsters on which everyone feasted, adding delicacies such as cod tongues and fiddleheads.

During shooting, major studios always sent an important executive to see how things were progressing. Paul and Peter hatched a plot: Joyce Kozy would arrange the executive's flight to Montreal so as to miss the Gaspe train and spend a day in Montreal doing nothing. Then spend another night on the Ocean Limited train. The next morning, in his shiny shoes and spiffy black suit, Norman, the executive, arrived at the little St. Godfrey station. Elton met him in his messy farm truck smelling of manure, and drove him to "the set" by back roads through fearsome untamed woods. Certainly not normal for big execs!

"What's that rifle doing, Elton?" Norman asked.

"Well, I'll tell ya, me son, it's the spring of the year, and them bears gets terble wicked... Ya never know. Best be safe, eh?"

Norman shifted uneasily and gripped the floppy door handle.

Now this film dealt with the supernatural, so the crew had become afraid of entering the house at night. Rumours of ghosts abounded. And well they might, because several generations had been born and died in the upstairs rooms.

When Elton arrived with Norman, the crew was primed to rejoice. Usually, when a "suit" turns up, directors and crews resent the interference. But this crew fêted him — they had nothing to hide. They fed him lobsters, then showed him a small bedroom in the ghost-ridden house. At lunch crew members had made sure to drop several stories of fearsome apparitions seen in the night.

Later, when Norman asked about accommodation elsewhere, Joyce explained, "No hotels open in winter, Norman. Just ours which of course is fully booked. But you'll be quite comfortable in the old house here."

Paul added, "And every three days there is a train..."

"Three days?" Norman turned white.

"Yeah. Oh! There's one leaving in an hour — we could get you on that, if you're quick."

Well, Norman was quick. And that was how a Paramount executive came for two hours to supervise *Isabel*.

* * *

Back in Toronto, editing with George Appleby, another superb craftsman, Paul heard that the government had announced ten million dollars to assist filmmaking in Canada. His friend, Michael Spencer, a pukka British ex-Army officer and former filmmaker, had been doing his best to convince the Canadian government to set up a body to do just that. He later confessed that *Isabel* and Paramount had been the lever he'd needed. The next year, the

Canadian Film Development Corporation was announced with Michael as Executive Director.

While all this was going on, the country was filled with "Trudeaumania" electing Pierre Elliott Trudeau as prime minister on April 20, 1968, which was to continue till June 4, 1979. He became a friend of the couple, often invited to their films.

During the summer, Geneviève was asked to play *St. Joan* (which would win her an Emmy nomination) in the Shaw play that George Schaefer was directing for NBC's *Hallmark Hall of Fame*. Stevie Phillips had arranged to rent Candice Bergen's lovely but tiny apartment overlooking Central Park. Paul flew down, but realized that when she was working on a difficult part, the last thing needed was a husband. So back he went to his editing room.

Full of confidence, and not knowing anything about how a big (or in fact any) distributor worked, Paul brought his heavy rough cut — quite rough — down to New York to show Stevie and Charlie Bluhdorn: the 35mm print took ten reels and another ten of magnetic dialogue tracks, but with no sound effects or music. He supposed, erroneously, that agents and studio executives knew what rough cuts were. They did not.

Stevie had invited Robert Redford, Liza Minnelli and several others to the screening, and the excitement was palpable. Paul squeezed Geneviève's hand in anticipation. But halfway through, the screen went white and flashed with flames.

When projectionists got too old to handle the normal cinema chores, their union assigned them to comfortable head-office screening rooms to give the old fellows a sinecure before retiring. These two aged projectionists dithered about, so Paul had to rush back into the projection booth. 35mm frames were now joined by Scotch Tape. One taped splice had jammed in the gate, stopped the film, and the hot projection beam had set it on fire.

Now what?

Fortunately, the booth came with an Italian splicer, an advance on the old hot splicer used by Noel Dodds. Paul quickly had the old technicians unthread the film. He counted the burned frames, cut them out, cut the same amount out of the magnetic track, spliced them back together, and had it thread up again.

He went back to the screening room, and the film proceeded.

Thankfully, Charlie had not yet learned the way big moguls behaved, so he accepted this mishap (with which they all sympathized). Paul and Geneviève jollied everyone up so that in the end, the screening passed muster.

Later, while working with two sound editors, Paul got a phone call from Paramount's chairman asking him to fly down to direct Robert Redford's skiing film, *Downhill Racer*. After all, didn't Paul come from Canada where they had snow?

But Paul, lacking "an eye for the main chance", turned him down: editing *Isabel* came first.

The National Film Board in Montreal had the only mixing facility in Canada. Paul convinced them to let him use it for *Isabel,* with its top mixer Joe Grimaldi. And thus got the film finished.

Next came distribution. Genial Charles Boasberg, head of Sales, suggested Toronto for the opening. Paul, knowing (correctly in fact) the ways of Toronto critics, insisted *Isabel* open first in New York City. Already at one private screening, a Toronto critic had, against all protocol, lambasted the film. So they decided to open in July at the 72nd Street Playhouse. The critics were uniformly delighted.

That autumn, Toronto was another matter. As Paul predicted, the Toronto Star tore their film to pieces, albeit a difficult task in the face of so many good u.s. reviews. Nonetheless, Paul was surprised when he went down to Nat Cohen's prestigious Towne

Cinema on Bloor and saw ticket buyers lined up two and three deep around the block.

The good old *Montreal Star*, September 20, headlined its review: Unforgettable *Isabel*, a brilliant Canadian film. The film led the box office for all films that month in Canada.

CHAPTER TWENTY-TWO
1967-68

One night, when Paul came home to Briar Hill for dinner, he noticed that Geneviève seemed excited. "How did it go today? You were seeing a doctor, weren't you?"

"A gynaecologist, as a matter of fact."

"What? You're not pregnant?" Paul could hardly absorb the enormity.

"Well," Geneviève announced, "I am."

Paul let out a whoop of joy. "But" she went on, "I asked him about having the baby here in Toronto. You want to be present when our baby is born?"

"I sure do."

"Well, the doctor gave me one of those condescending smiles, and said, 'Don't worry, my dear, you and I are quite capable. Just let your husband go have a nice dinner, and when he comes back, we'll present the baby to him.'"

"The creep!"

"Exactly what I thought."

"So what about another doctor?"

"That's the way they all work in Toronto hospitals. No fathers allowed."

Paul's eyes blazed. "Well damn it all! Let's move!"

Geneviève looked at him, brown eyes softening. "Just what I hoped you'd say..."

"Now that we're both working in motion pictures — why the hell stay? I mean, we can live anywhere."

"With good doctors?"

"Yes sir!"

First they went to Paris, thinking they might move there.

Doctors were practising a new system called *l'accouchement sans douleur*, also known as the Lamaze method, developed in Russia. But though she learned something about "birthing without pain," Geneviève did not take to the supposedly famous doctor nor his assistant.

On their way home, they stopped in Montreal to check out Hôpital Sainte Justine. There, she met a Dr. Noel, whom she did like. So they decided to buy a house in Montreal.

Before long they found an old castle-like hulk on Redpath Crescent, an exclusive street that curved up into the mountain park. The five floors needed a good deal of renovation, and had been sitting on the market for a couple of years. Having sold the Briar Hill house, Paul was able to fund the down payment.

The house had a storied past. Built in 1922 by the Smith family, it often hosted dinners with evenings of port and cigars. Mr. Smith had died, and Mrs. Smith had become friendly with Stephen Leacock, the great Canadian humorist lecturing just down the block at McGill. She even ended up buying a small house in Orillia, Prof. Leacock's main base. One might speculate on their relationship, but to outward appearances they were just friends. Paul found a Leacock pamphlet: *Christmas*

Convivial and Pleasant at Number Nineteen (as 1272 was then known) *Redpath Crescent.* He framed it and hung it in the powder room.

RENE

I think it has to be confessed
Our René is a perfect Guest.
At every Dinner, every Dance,
He shows the Grace of cultured France.
The Flood of Life he loves to swim in
With old, old Wine and young, young Women.
To Whiskey, Cigarette, Cigar
He says "Je ne refuse pas."
Oh, noble France, if you have any
More wandering Sons as nice as René,
I pray you send them, one and all,
To Redpath Crescent, Montreal.

Although the whole house needed work, Geneviève decided first to prepare the second floor master bedroom for her baby. Between the baby's room and smaller front bedroom sat a bathroom with the original plumbing from 1922, an antique marvel with a walk-in shower and the original white enamel taps.

Paul had long been friends with the great architect Moshe Safdie, designer of Habitat 67. Out of friendship, he redesigned the top floor and kitchen, losing money in the process. But the result was a lovely large master bedroom for the loving couple, with a picture window looking out towards the St. Lawrence and its two big bridges. The casement windows they kept.

Now the next question: Who would look after the baby while they worked?

Housekeepers in Montreal were expensive so Paul suggested they try Paris. "I bet we could find someone nice and motherly who would love a chance to emigrate."

Geneviève agreed. So off the two flew to their favourite Hôtel du Quai Voltaire. Mme Muller, the owner, had taken rather a shine to the petite actress and was delighted to find Geneviève pregnant.

An advertisement in *Le Monde* brought some two dozen women, among whom they agreed on Madame Pecetto, large, heavyset, with reddish hair, motherly, who had once owned a restaurant on Montmartre. It had been so successful that she had shut it down to enlarge it— but when it reopened, having lost its atmosphere, it also lost its clientele. So Madame Pecetto went broke, and followed them back to Montreal.

In the early morning of July 10th, 1968, Geneviève woke Paul with the news that the baby was on its way. Paul drove her in the little green MG to Hôpital Sainte-Justine, and stayed at her side as she did the required breathing. Dr. Noel turned up, and the birth began.

Two little legs appeared first. Geneviève panicked. "It's dead!"

Dr. Noel, cigarette in his mouth, smoke partially closing his eyes as it drifted upwards, tickled the tiny foot. It kicked.

He grinned. Geneviève relaxed.

Right after Matthew James was born, Dr. Noel gave him to Geneviève and Matthew lay on his mother's breast, looking around. In his next film, Paul put these words in the mouth of his actress:

"Well, it was so good to start pushing at last, and you're so busy, with natural childbirth, you — well it was all of a sudden really, the head came out, and then, almost in one push the body — un garçon, the Dr said and lay him on my breast. He lay looking around with big eyes, not seeing, I know, but with such strange... Wisdom. David was crying of course, and I could hardly see..."

1967 had been a banner year for Canada, its Centennial, with

Expo 67 over on St. Helen's Island in the St. Lawrence. Excitement thrived, especially in the arts. The Canadian air force, army and navy had been unified as the Canadian Armed Forces on April 25. Previously, as Minister of Justice, Pierre Elliott Trudeau, had liberalized the laws concerning abortion and homosexuality, when spoke the iconic phrase: *The government has no business in the bedrooms of the nation.*

After screenings of *Isabel* for friends (including the Trudeaus), they would invite the audience back for parties where the team would glean criticism and thus adjust the film. Madame Pecetto proved not only a fine housekeeper and nurse, she also cooked good dinners. Then the couple had to fly to New York for *Isabel's* opening at the 72nd Street Playhouse.

Their press agent, Lois Smith, often held screenings for opinion makers. Late one evening, Paul decided to go to the one for Broadway performers, believing serious actresses would attend. But within fifteen minutes, the hyped-up singers and dancers from musicals decided they'd had quite enough of this bleak, icy, Gaspesian landscape and its repressed actress. They leapt up into the aisles, dancing and yelling: "Man, Isabel, you got a problem!"

On his way home he wondered how to break the news that their creation was such a flop.

Amazingly, Geneviève pooh-poohed his reaction, calmed him down, and said she was sure the critics would like it.

And so they did. Lois had arranged for lunches with many of them, the venerable Archer Winston, a dean of film criticism, and Judith Crist, also widely read. New York critics took film as a serious art, assiduously researching each film's background and intention, seeking to judge it properly and thoughtfully — a practice unknown in Toronto.

The next few days in their hotel room, the couple devoured

their glowing list of press cuttings. But was this luck just too good to last?

* * *

Geneviève made sure they mingled with the French community in Montreal. Cultural activities were blooming. A couple of years before, the NFB director Don Owen had gone to shoot a half hour documentary called *Nobody Waved Goodbye*. After a time, the Board sent him telegrams: come home, no more money, stop shooting and return at once! But Don ignored them and kept right on sending back rushes. He made sure not to return until he had a whole feature film. What could the Board do but let him edit it? It won awards and was considered one of the best films of that year.

The French Canadian filmmakers on the other hand, with no access to money from English distributors, made doubly sure to give their audience what it wanted. Denis Héroux led the charge with a film called *Valérie* (1968) followed by *L'Initiation* in 1970 — both of which "undressed *la petite Québécoise*". Actresses well known in theatre and television dutifully disrobed for the movies. The public were delighted and flocked to the cinemas. Claude Fournier quickly followed with a film entitled *Deux femmes en or* (1970), lightly translated as *Two Brazen Women*. A third, more serious filmmaker, Gilles Carles, made *La vraie nature de Bernadette*. The Canadian Film Awards, struggling since 1949, now found itself with several interesting films to judge.

On October 4, Paul and Geneviève flew to Toronto's Royal York Hotel for the ceremony. Introduced by Fred Davis, the craft and acting awards went to *Isabel*: Georges Dufaux "Best Cinematography", George Appleby "Best Editing", Gerard Parkes "Best Actor", and Geneviève Bujold "Best Actress". Paul waited confidently for the announcement of Best Director. Lo! it went to Don Owen for *The Ernie Game,* which then went on to win Best Film.

Paul had seen so many rejections over the years, it hardly bothered him, and joined in celebrating for his pal Don. But the time had come to think up his next project. What on earth would it to be?

CHAPTER TWENTY-THREE
1970

Act of the Heart

Earth, air, fire, and water, the four elements. *Isabel,* Paul considered his "earth film". This time he pondered the question of fire and, once he was ready to do some writing, he told Geneviève he'd have to go away, as when he wrote *Isabel.* A friend offered a cottage in the Laurentians and he went north to write the script that eventually became *Act of the Heart.*

Geneviève was again central to this story, but this time, he brought her as an innocent *Gaspésienne* to Montreal to teach French to the son of a wealthy widow. He wrote scenes for their Redpath Crescent house, just as he had shot *Isabel* in the Old Homestead. The Gaspe girl was religious and thought of herself as "special", but then fell in love.

They had occasionally met Robert Redford so Paul created for him a musical Augustinian monk arranging a concert. For the widow, because they knew her from Paris, he wanted Jeanne Moreau.

Half way through the writing, Geneviève rang. She didn't like being alone with Matthew and Mme Pecetto in the big old house. "I won't bother you, I'll make meals, and you can write all you want." So up she came into the Laurentians; Paul continued writing and in two or three weeks had a finished script.

Now for the first hurdle. Geneviève had not seen it. Would she accept the role of his lead character, Martha? They'd always agreed that she would only play in a film if she liked it. So with some trepidation, he handed her the script.

The next day, as was her wont, she stayed in bed reading it. Paul diverted himself with needless odds and ends, wondering if he had a star or not. That night at dinner (prepared by Mme Pecetto) she announced she loved it.

Right-oh! Now for the rest of the cast. In Paris, he got the script with Louis Malle's help to Jeanne Moreau. She turned it down. Being madly in love (again), she didn't want to leave Paris. So Paul cast Monique Leyrac, the singer who had never acted. As for Robert Redford, Stevie told them he admitted liking the script but had other films on his mind. Then Paul remembered a young Canadian from *The Rose Tattoo:* Donald Sutherland, tall, blonde, now making Bob Altman's *M*A*S*H* with Elliott Gould. Donald accepted. Later during filming he told Paul that he was pleased to work on a film of this kind after doing what he then described as a piece of rubbish. That "rubbish" turned out to be a huge hit.

The film was to be built around a cantata that the monk would conduct in the Oratoire Saint-Joseph. Paul wanted it written before shooting. His friend, Harry Freedman, who had often composed for Paul's shows, agreed and began writing long before they had the money. Paul arranged the words for The Flame Within from the Bible; it would be the only music in the film — the first (and perhaps only) time that music had been written for a motion picture before the script. Later, Elmer Iseler, director of the Festival Singers, recorded it on a vinyl LP with Universal Records.

Stevie started setting up the film. Not for a second did Paul doubt, even with his lesser cast, that Stevie would fail. After all, didn't it concern matters of the spirit? As always, Paul kept his feet – as Mel Breen once said — firmly planted in mid-air.

He went about picking his crew. Peter Carter came to run everything; they were such great collaborators. No production designers with motion picture experience existed, but one evening Claude Fournier invited them to a party. Paul met his pretty partner, Anne Pritchard, a blonde interior designer with devilishly bewitching pale blue eyes. He hired her at once, and she ended up doing the costumes, too. They tried to get Georges Dufaux but he was shooting a documentary. So Geneviève rang Alain Resnais, who recommended Jean Boffety, cameraman on his last film, *Je t'aime, je t'aime*. Dave Howells, a senior sound technician, got released from the NFB. Paul now had his crew and his cast. All he needed was financing.

"How are we coming, Stevie?" Paul asked on the phone.

"Paul, we just got the script a month ago. You only gave us your new cast last week. I'm not a magician."

"Yes you are, Stevie. I'm counting on you."

Isabel had come to the attention of the great Hal Wallis, an old-time Hollywood producer (*Casablanca*) who was looking for his Anne Boleyn in *Anne of a Thousand Days*. Look no further, Stevie had said, but Universal has to fund Paul's film first. After all, Charles Champlin of the Los Angeles Times had given *Isabel* a great review.

In the end, Universal agreed to fund both.

Looking ahead, Stevie had warned that Universal was a bureaucratic morass and took business seriously. Paul would need a lawyer, so he rang Timmie Porteous, a sweet little red-haired fellow from Bishops College School Paul had known, now a big executive assistant to Trudeau. Tim suggested Donald Johnston, who had just formed the law firm of Mccarthy, Monet and Johnston. Donald had directed a McGill Red-and-White Review and played the piano rather well, so Paul threw him into negotiations with Universal. Being married to Heather McLaren, the prettiest small-boned blonde from Nova Scotia, was no detriment. They had two baby daughters with a third on the way.

Before Christmas, Joel Katz, a former producer whose religion excluded Christmas, flew to Montreal and Donald had to spend his entire holiday negotiating. Heather was not pleased.

Michael Spencer, his new Canadian Film Development Corporation under way, badly needed a film to start the process. With his British background, he didn't want to take a risk, preferring to work with someone "tried-and-true". So he rang Paul. "I hear you're making another film."

"I am, Michael."

"I've talked to my Board, and we've decided to invest."

"Sorry, Michael. You can't. Universal is doing it."

Silence at the other end of the line.

Then Michael went on, pleading. "Now Paul, you have to let us in. For the good of Canada. We expect to invest in several films, if this goes well. We should partner with a big American distribution company. It would be good for Canada. You've got to be patriotic."

Paul had to think that over. Michael Spencer had certainly touched a nerve. "Okay, Michael, I'll let you guys put in half."

Accordingly, Act of the Heart was the first (and only!) film the CFDC had to beg to finance.

Paul was adamant about getting the final cut, although that privilege was rare for a director. He had gotten it on *Isabel* and insisted on doing so again. Nothing for it, but Joel Katz had to give in, reassuring Geneviève and others that what was in the script would end up in the final film.

Right after New Year's Day, Paul began shooting. But clear sailing?

Not exactly.

The first scene was a hockey game between teams of twelve-year-old boys on Westmount's Murray Park. Later, in editing, two McGill students who ran commentary on McGill games and knew the lingo, hilariously parodied the great Foster Hewitt. But that day, the claws of the American eagle tried to reach across the border. Johnny Douet had adamantly refused to join the American technicians union, IATSE. He had been a wonderful grip on *Isabel*, and Paul was determined to include him. The union's head office in New York rang technicians to say they must strike the set — or they'd never work again. So far in Canada, no one had dared go up against IATSE. But Paul, with an NFB director friend, invoked the Taft Hartley Act and rejected any interference in Canada's internal affairs by a foreign country. He threatened to take the matter to Ottawa.

He sent a simple message to the crew: "Boffety, Douet, Peter and myself will be at the rink. If you want to join us, come and work on the film right to the end."

That night his sleep was restless: would they come? Or would the union win?

The next day at the rink, lo! The entire crew turned up. The union had been beaten.

Johnny Douet proved his mettle in a skating scene on Beaver Lake. Everyone knew how to skate — but what about a dolly shot on slithery ice? The Elemac would never work. So Johnny rigged up a platform with skates underneath, and he and his skating grips pushed the camera wherever the actors led.

The monk and his soloist, Geneviève, were to give a concert in the vast Oratoire Saint-Joseph. So Paul would need not one, but three, choirs. He added *Les petit chanteurs de Montréal*, and a United Church women's choir. The Oratory had been erected in 1912 to commemorate Brother André, a humble priest (later sanctified) who'd lived in a shack. The roof of this towering landmark was two hundred feet high with a dome eighty-five feet in diameter, and the largest organ in all North America. Paul was not one to think small.

With no money to pay extras, Paul advertised that Geneviève, already a star in Quebec, would be singing and Donald Sutherland conducting, and anyone could come for free to watch—if they stayed for four hours. Against all predictions, three hundred people turned up. Harry Freedman donned a wig to resemble Donald Sutherland (not a real conductor!), the great crescendo of the organ boomed out, and Geneviève sang her solo. All with no budget for extras.

After the monk succumbed to love for his chorister, Geneviève earned money by singing in a *boîte à chanson*. Gilles Vigneault, Quebec's premier chansonnier, had written *Mon pays,* the Battle Hymn of the new Quebec, and his happy birthday was sung all over the province. Paul asked him to compose Martha's songs, and even to act in the film, playing the old rink tender (shades of his former script, *The Simpleton).* Jean Duceppe, leading light of Montreal theatre, agreed to improvise a memorable scene telling off Gilles for working too much overtime cleaning the rink.

Charles Bonniwell, in a black suit, sparkling shoes, and flowered shirt, flew up from Los Angeles to watch over the production. Much to his discomfort, Paul put him to work doing accounts, as he had done with the Paramount rep, Bob Crawford, on *Isabel.* Charles kept asking, Where is *"Gillus Vigg-nolt"*? Which tickled the crew and became a catchphrase for big studio interference.

Concerned with melding the "two solitudes", Paul devised a prophetic scene in the sunroom of Redpath Crescent with Claude Jutra, François Tassé, Jean Dalmain (Monique Leyrac's husband) and others who improvised on the theme of Quebec's separation from the rest of Canada.

All that was left now was the editing. And to find out what reception would be given this unashamedly Christian film dealing with sacred and profane love.

* * *

Anne of A Thousand Days starring Richard Burton and Geneviève was scheduled to shoot all summer in London. Thus Universal brought over Geneviève's family, and indeed Paul's editing crew, James Mitchell and his assistant Donna Nichol, to cut *Act* on Wardour Street. Jim was somewhat thrown by his director sitting next to him, deciding every cut. In the American system, the director only turned up near the end, made a suggestion or two, and left.

With little Matthew and Mme Pecetto, they set up house on Cambridge Street. Their stay was enlivened by dinners with Elizabeth Taylor and Richard Burton who, in the great Welsh tradition of storytellers, could hold forth for hours with his enviable store of theatrical tales.

One day Paul went to Hampton Court Palace to watch Geneviève shoot: a hundred crew members lay around in the sun while only director Charles Jarrott, producer Hal Wallis and the cameramen worked, setting up shots. Charles, whom Paul had trained while at the CBC but who had never directed a motion picture, had been chosen by Hal, who wanted an amenable young director.

At the beginning of September, they returned to the editing

rooms in the basement of Redpath Crescent. Madame Pecetto provided her usual splendid dinners, and Paul and Geneviève often entertained, especially during the Montreal Film Festival each September when visiting foreign filmmakers and stars, Russian, Indian, many nationalities, would enjoy dining in a private home away from their stark hotel rooms.

One evening, Paul found himself helping clear up with Madame Pecetto who was finishing another glass of wine. He asked the question he had often wondered about: how had she come to own a restaurant on the renowned Montmartre?

Well, she told him, she had run an establishment in Algeria. She had found a goodly number of pretty young Algerian girls to service the officers of the French Foreign Legion — and even, she divulged proudly, cabinet ministers when visiting. When the French withdrew from Algeria, she got compensation from the very ministers who had been her clients. The reparation? This restaurant on Montmartre.

When Paul got to bed, he passed it on to Geneviève. "Imagine, Matthew brought up by a notorious Algerian madame!"

"I've suspected it all along, darling," Geneviève said. "Who cares? She looks after Matthew well, she's a good cook, what more do we want?"

And so the matter was closed.

In early October, Universal's executive in charge of the film, Jennings Lang and his wife Monica flew up for a fine cut screening of *Act of the Heart* at the National Film Board. Paul had invited others, too; after screenings, he usually held a party with lots of drink. As guests loosened up, they would talk to him or his editors and their criticisms helped.

Paul and Jennings arrived back at the house before the others; Monica had stayed in the den to read. Paul was putting on a record when out of the corner of his eye, he saw Monica gesture to her husband questioningly.

Jennings mouthed a word Paul had no trouble understanding: "Disastah!"

What did that presage?

Paul had the right of final cut. And he thought the audience had loved the show. But still... what would happen when he brought it to Los Angeles in the middle of December?

Into Universal's screening room trooped Lew Wasserman, Universal's chief, and his associates, "the suits", as they were called.

As the film progressed, with its great cantata, Paul saw from the back Geneviève overcome with emotion. Happily, this had its desired effect. The men from the famous black tower at Universal City were properly impressed, even moved, so now were behind the film. Of course, Jennings had to exhibit the usual about-face of so many film executives.

The Wassermans invited them to their home, with its Henry Moore sculpture prominent in the driveway and famous paintings on the walls. Lew, tall, angular, a courtly gentleman, was most polite, not at all the image of an agent, which he had once been. Paul was surprised to learn that not only Jennings's salary, but also his house and car, were dependent upon the whims of Universal executives. If fired, he would lose everything. No wonder executives lived in fear of their lives. Stay well away from such a system, Paul told himself.

Next stop, a Royal Command Performance in London for *Anne*, arranged by Hal Wallis. Geneviève gracefully met the Queen and Prince Philip while Paul flew to France to arrange French subtitles for his film and talk to Henri Michaud, head of world distribution for Universal Pictures.

Next event: the Academy Awards at the Dorothy Chandler Pavilion on April 7. *Anne of a Thousand Days* had the most nominations, including Geneviève as Best Actress, with their main competitor, *Butch Cassidy and the Sundance Kid.* Geneviève wore a dress designed by Anne Pritchard. They sat with Richard, Elizabeth, Hal, Lew, and other executives. But Richard and Geneviève were both passed over, as was their film. Best Picture was won by *Midnight Cowboy,* the first X-rated picture ever to win.

Paul felt sorry for Geneviève but they had both expected that. Afterwards at the awards dinner, they mingled with celebrities on the dance floor. Paul was especially impressed by dancing beside Raquel Welch, whose poster from *One Million Years BC* was unforgettable.

The matter of the Cannes Film Festival was broached. Paul had heard that Favre le Bret, the founder and long time director, had talked and laughed all through *Isabel,* so Paul was not keen to repeat that.

American films were dubbed after, and not before, their North American opening, and arrived in Quebec months after the English version. Paul wanted to change all that and open his film in both languages on the same day. Breaking such an entrenched routine took some doing, but in the end he won. Other studios followed, and from then on, Quebec audiences no longer suffered as second class, and watched their own versions as soon as English ones opened.

When the film premiered in Montreal, Mayor Drapeau, a fan of Geneviève, arranged his motorcycle escort, trained during Expo67 to whisk presidents, prime ministers and their delegations across the city. The English version opened at seven o'clock at the Place du Canada. Afterwards, the couple got into a limousine with the mayor and watched as their motorcycle escort raced ahead, stopped traffic at each intersection to allow the motorcade to sail through, then the rear motorcycles raced past to do the same again at the next intersection, until they reached the Rialto Cinema on Park Avenue, where Paul and Geneviève presented the premiere in French.

The couple received extraordinary reactions: the covers of *Macleans,* and of *Weekend Magazine* with a title that read: "Paul & Geneviève — our Dick and Liz?" Inside *Macleans,* John Hofsess wrote a glowing review: "Alford's *Act of the Heart* — a Canadian film that ranks with the work of Bergman and Fellini."

In New York, the couple was fêted once again and the film made several "ten best" lists of US critics.

Paul decided to show a pile of reviews to Geneviève.

"Paul, you know I don't read reviews, I hate them."

"We got forty-five from all across America, almost all good."

Geneviève nodded. "But what did Toronto say?"

Paul chuckled. "They killed us, of course. What did you expect?" Geneviève giggled, along with him.

Next came the Canadian Film Awards, October 3rd at Toronto's Imperial Theatre. Although Geneviève won Best Actress, Don Shebib's actors, Paul Bradley and Doug McGrath, won Best Actors. Paul was expecting to be passed over once again, but this time he did win Best Director. Would the film go on to win Best Film? No, sir. Don Shebib's *Goin' Down the Road,* took that.

CHAPTER TWENTY-FOUR
OCT 5TH TO DEC, 1970

Paul and Geneviève were having breakfast when the doorbell rang. They looked at each other — a bit early for anyone to come calling. Donat Lalonde, the cheery gardener who looked after all the residents of Redpath Crescent, stood leaning on his rake. Heavy set, dressed in his loose working clothes, he was a familiar sight; Paul and Geneviève often awakened to the sound of his hand-driven lawn mower outside their window.

Donat could be counted on for all the latest gossip. He would often come to the side door for a chat with Madame Pecetto, who spoke French, too. Housekeepers on the Crescent would get their up-to-date doings of employers through Donat, so Paul never minded Madame Pecetto catching whatever scoop she could: she would pass it on later in the day.

"What's up, Donat?"

Donat jerked his head across the street. Paul followed his look: two police cars were drawn up outside the house of the British Trade Consul, James Cross.

To Paul's right stood the home of the US Consul General, and to his left the large home of the Chancellor of McGill University. Directly across the street lived Kit Lang, daughter of the Montreal Star magnate, and next, the Trade Commissioner in question. "What are they doing, Donat?"

"Well, M'sieur Paul," Donat scratched his chin, "I seen two fellas go in, dressed in raincoats. Dey come out with Mr. Cross, get in a car and drive away."

Paul frowned. "Why the police cars?"

Donat shrugged. "Mrs. Cross, she's still in dere, maybe she phoned." He shrugged again.

"Thanks, Donat," Paul said, "keep me posted, eh?" He went back into the kitchen to tell Geneviève. They switched on the radio in their breakfast nook and soon heard that the FLQ (Front de libération du Québec) had kidnapped James Cross. They had been putting bombs in letterboxes to encourage the separation of Quebec from the rest of Canada. To cap all that, five days after kidnapping Cross, they took the Minister of Labour, Pierre Laporte, and left his body, strangled, in the trunk of a car to be found on the 17th, the day after the War Measures Act passed by Prime Minister Trudeau, calling out the Army at the request of Bourassa, Premier of Quebec, and the Mayor of Montreal.

A few days later Geneviève heard that some of her friends were arrested and put in prison. "They've even arrested, Pauline Julien!" Geneviève exclaimed. "She'd never plant a bomb. What are they doing? The guy she lives with, Gerald Godin, he's a poet."

Paul knew Pierre Elliott Trudeau to be a statesmanlike prime minister — Paul and Geneviève both liked him. So what were they to make of all this? Paul at this stage was not politically engaged; his quest had been for matters of the spirit. And now, he was thinking about his next film.

* * *

Paul always enjoyed tracking down a new film. His idea for *Isabel* had been finished and distributed within two years. That pattern had been repeated with *Act of the Heart*. So why not this time?

The image haunting him was of a pioneer woman in a long brown skirt on the brow of a cleared field. He wanted the story to be allegorical, representing the great women pioneers who had built Canada. Now to find out about allegory. McGill pointed him to Paul Piehler who had recently arrived from UC Berkeley in San Francisco. The professor had recently seen *Isabel* and been taken by her encounter with the darker aspects of her ancestral Gaspe homeland. He had also been at Magdalen College in Paul's day, and had as his tutor the great CS Lewis. While teaching in Finland, he had married a stunning Swedish sprite, Maj-Britt. For a busy academic, he was unusually amenable to meeting and the two really hit it off. The film-maker felt he was now on the way.

His first two films had been written for specific locations, so for this third one, where? What about a wilderness, untamed, and why not beside a river? Rivers had been important transportation highways, in Paul's mind, and were also of tremendous symbolic significance — rivers of time, deep, dark, mysterious. His former English teacher, Lewis Evans with Betty his wife, had a family home in Tadoussac. Lewis was a consummate sailor and owned a small sailboat in which Paul had often sailed the forbidding and uninhabited Saguenay, one of the deepest rivers in the world flowing down from a northern wilderness between ominous black cliffs. A perfect setting.

What next? He needed an art director versed in early North American construction, so rang John Bland, head of McGill's School of Architecture. Professor Bland pointed him to a bright third-year student.

Paul dialled. "Hello. Is that Glenn Bydwell?"

"Yes."

"Paul Alford here. Wanna come and talk about the sets of my next film?"

There was a silence at the other end of the line.

"Have you not heard of me?"

"I think so," Glenn mumbled.

"Well then, can we meet?" Paul asked.

"I live out on the West Island. I might come in next week."

"Next week? No! Right now. I'll expect you here within the hour."

Glenn did turn up. Paul, who loved bright people, hired him on the spot.

Next step? Advance financing. On Sept 10th, Paul wrote to Michael Spencer, now Head of the Canadian Film Development Corporation:

... even after my ideas are in final screenplay form, it may be difficult to sum them up concisely. Let me at this point describe the direction my film will take.

I have been preoccupied, recently, about the problem of man's environment. Both Isabel *and* Act of the Heart *are concerned with the forces working on, and the development of, the Inner Man. And it is the exterior landscape that provides the symbol through which human consciousness, i.e. the Inner Man, grows. From the early civilizations, which began incidentally along rivers, Man has searched through his Hero figures (Gilgamesh, Odysseus, Christ, etc) for the Earthly Paradise, and these epic explorations have been the means whereby human consciousness has progressed. As civilization developed, the images and symbols have lost their force and now need redefinition. Our exterior world has disintegrated, our man-made landscape is a wasteland. In my next film, therefore, I have chosen to go back to a time when our explorer forefathers came to the New World and founded their settlements along river banks. Their search was, like Aeneas, for a kind of Holy City. Just as the hippie commune is a significant symptom of today, so my film will merge Hippie and Pioneer. For my Pioneer Commune, I have found a glorious location on the banks of the Saguenay River, one of the last rivers that afford great untouched vistas of raw wilderness, and in which, allegorically, present and past can fuse.*

The place I have chosen is completely closed by snow from mid-December to March. Therefore work on the location must begin this autumn, before the shooting, even before the screenplay is finished. For the sets to look authentic, they must have weathered at least one winter...

In the end, Paul got an advance of twenty thousand dollars.

Paul and Glenn took off in his tiny MG for the summer village of Tadoussac, in autumn largely abandoned. At the mouth of the Saguenay, it sprawled across cliffs and a granite promontory that reached out into the Gulf of St. Lawrence. One of the tributaries, the Ste Marguerite, like most good salmon rivers was privately owned, this one by Alcan. Happily, its chairman lived on Redpath Crescent. So Paul had visited the nearby grey stone mansion and "R.E.P" Powell agreed to the filming.

From Tadoussac they set off north towards Chicoutimi. They pulled up at an uneven path and trekked in to the confluence of the Saguenay and Ste. Marguerite. There they found a perfect grassy knoll. Glenn, having brought his clipboard and a thick lead pencil, sketched out a possible design — a large, squared-timber building flanked by two wings on each side: archetypal, symmetrical and pure. Back they trudged to the main dirt road.

"Now, let's try to see that highest point, Cape Trinity."

Glenn objected. "It's getting late..."

But off they went again and down another rough trail, over roots and through tangled brush to where a great set of pylons held huge electric power cables over the river.

Because of the War Measures Act, the military guarded every important infrastructure. On seeing these unexpected visitors, they levelled their machine guns.

Paul leapt out of the MG and started towards them.

Their fingers tightened on the triggers. "Stop!" They called again.

Paul didn't stop, he just kept going. "If you kill me, you can be damn sure there'll be hell to pay! We're unarmed, we're filmmakers, we just want to look over the river." He kept on going.

The soldiers relaxed and showed Paul and Glenn a track to the actual brow. But as dusk was descending, Paul complained, "Too dark! We can't really see."

The head soldier by now was friendly. "Wait here."

Before long, Glenn and Paul were surprised to see a huge star shell bursting over the river, illuminating the whole bank. And then another. Paul got the view he wanted. They turned back and heartily thanked the military for breaking all the rules.

* * *

Towards the end of October, after Geneviève had appeared on the cover of Time magazine, as they were having breakfast, she suggested. "Why not go over to England? You've been having trouble getting your new script written."

"Whatever for?"

"On other screenplays you went away. The English house is empty. Why not fly there? It might help to be alone."

Paul frowned slightly. "I'm not ready to write yet."

"Paul, once you get away from babies and Mme Pecettos and me, ideas will come. All you have to do is jump on a plane! Over there, you'll be free as a bird." She went on spooning out her grapefruit.

Paul absorbed this. "Well, maybe I'll give it a try. Will you be all right here without me?"

"Oh yes. I have Mme Pecetto and Matthew and lots to do, I'll be fine." So ironic, in fact.

So Paul found himself in London, alone in his Pimlico house, with his trusty Smith Corona portable (typewriter). Now, just bang out the next script...

But what should the story be? He had no idea.

He had enjoyed having his own way far too long. A difficult and thorny path to enlightenment lay ahead. He knew it not, of course. Only that, as the days progressed, he got more and more miserable.

That conversation in the kitchen with Geneviève... Did it really sound like her? Could she have wanted him out of the way, for some reason? The script, the story, why on earth would it not come? Because no state of grace had descended? What did that mean? Were dark forces grappling with his soul? As a symptom of his spiritual unease, his physical body began to break down. He felt lost in tangled nightmares, thrashed about in an underbrush of thoughts, and few the flashes of understanding would come to illuminate his darkness.

Days passed with nothing written. Oh yes, he was about to enter his "dark night of the soul".

Finally in December and the approach of Christmas, he wrote to Geneviève:

What a dark night, what a week, I hardly know if I'm emerging. I've started to write now and I have no idea where I'm going or what I'm doing; it's been awful, this certain knowledge that the film is no good and won't work at all. I mapped it out more or less by Tuesday, but realized how awful it all was. It's like living with a corpse, although I'm not sure if it's dead or just lying in wait...

* * *

Two days before Christmas, Paul arrived home, and Geneviève greeted him. He went upstairs to unpack, shower, and take Geneviève out to a welcome dinner at the Café de Paris, their favoured haunt.

After they had begun their first course, Geneviève asked, "So, how did the screenplay go?"

Paul shook his head. "It's terrible, Geneviève. I'm desperate. It was just awful being alone. But now that I'm back with you, everything will be all right, and the script I'm writing for you will flow." He looked up and smiled.

Geneviève said nothing and changed the subject. She talked about Prime Minister Trudeau, who had announced that all troops stationed in Quebec would be withdrawn by January 5th, and about Matthew's doings and what Madame Pecetto had been up to. When the main course came, Geneviève put down her knife and fork.

"Paul, I'm leaving you in the morning with Matthew and Madame Pecetto."

Paul looked up, scarcely believing his ears. "You're what?"

"I'm taking the baby, and we're going to Don and Heather's while I sort myself out. I'm sorry. But that's the way it is. It's been arranged." She put her hand on his arm. "You'll be all right, won't you?"

All right? Paul had been hit by a truck. He couldn't absorb what she was saying. She and the baby were going to leave him and stay with his own lawyer? In their den, the Christmas tree had been decorated and presents gathered. And here he was, about to celebrate Christmas with no housekeeper, no wife, no little son.

And no leading actress.

CHAPTER TWENTY-FIVE
1970 – 1971

How Paul longed for a Virgil as he began his descent! But there he was, without a guide.

He got in touch with his best friends, Moshe and Nina Safdie, only to find that their house had burned down while he'd been in England. Apparently, Oren, their six-year-old son, had woken in the middle of the night to a house filled with smoke. He'd leapt up, rushed to his parents' room and banged on the door until they got up. When they came down the outside stairs in pyjamas into an icy December night, Oren wanted to run back to save his turtles, but right then all of a sudden the house blew up. So the Safdies had rented an apartment down at Sherbrooke and Peel, where Paul now often ate dinners, trying to absorb what had happened to him. In a daze, in denial, he prayed that these doldrums might end and regeneration begin.

His mother and aunt had gone off to their sister Leo in Tangier. His large empty house offered no consolation. But Glenn called to show his designs and photos of the buildings he had constructed on site during the autumn. Paul had an inspiration: "Let's go to the Saguenay! Tomorrow." Anything to get away from the overarching gloom and blackness enwrapping his soul.

Off they went in the little green MG with the help of money saved from the previous film. They arrived at dusk by the brooding river, shrouded in mist, banks covered in snow, a foghorn sounding its mournful knell as they waited for the ferry to take them across (the Styx?) to Tadoussac. A dinner with perhaps too much wine almost kept Paul's rapidly developing panic at bay.

During the autumn while building his beautiful structures of squared timbers, Glenn had become friendly with and enlisted the local craftsmen. They did their celebrating on New Year's Day, because absolute tradition required attendance at the mass on New Year's Eve. Now the two of them had to visit Hector Gauthier, the village chieftain without whose assistance Glenn would have gotten nowhere. His party was *de rigeur.*

They square-danced and drank homemade hooch, and then went on to Emile Savard's, the extraordinary craftsman who had built the sets. Glenn had appointed him their winter guardian. An accomplished salmon-smoker and fine fiddler, with two foot beaters for rhythm, he kept his guests dancing hard. All this helped allay, albeit briefly, the encroaching terrors.

Deep snow lay everywhere and they emerged to find the little MG stuck in a drift. So Paul got out and they both pushed. Once up to the road and in gear, it took off down the hill with the two of them, drunk, chasing after it, and wedged itself in another snow bank.

Glenn had searched the Saguenay region for two working oxen required by the film. No luck. But Elton Hayes had found a farmer willing to train a team in Shigawake. So off they went to see him. So long as he was on the move, Paul felt better.

The ferry across the wide St. Lawrence was making its final trip, wisely as it turned out. And it did get stuck in the ice. For seven hours, Paul tried to read while Glenn did more sketches for some furniture he was going to build. Finally they docked at Rivière du Loup and drove off. With minor mishaps, like running out of gas, they made it to Elton's farm. More celebrating and some decent planning followed.

* * *

Back in Montreal for the rest of the winter of 1971, Paul started on the script again and got a completed screenplay for *Journey*, still far from what he wanted, for he was still not in any state to write creatively.

Geneviève had to move out of Donald Johnston's. So in a fit of complete idiocy, hoping his wife might come back, Paul suggested that she and Matthew move into his home at 1272. She had been saying she only needed time. Were she in her comfortable home again, Paul reasoned, sanity might return. So he rented a small apartment in an ugly high-rise across MacGregor that blocked the view from his Redpath Crescent home. In another fit of foolishness, he still used his basement office, though not allowed in the house. How to twist the angst-filled knife...

Glenn's parents had not been pleased with him dropping out of university, so he moved in to the apartment and worked at designing every hand prop and every stick of wooden furniture to be carved by Tadoussac craftsmen. Paul began casting the twelve followers of the leader, confident the film would shoot as planned. Had it not always happened?

First, the female lead. Paul flew to Los Angeles to see Jane Fonda, another perfect vision of his pioneer woman. He sat cross-legged on a steamer trunk in her Venice home as her little daughter, Vanessa, the same age as Matthew, played on the floor. He outlined the film and talked all about Yin and Yang. For Yang, he needed a "rock" to play Boulder Allen and Jane suggested Oliver Reed, a British actor. Jane would be the river, the Yin. The meeting went well, but a week later, her agent said she was not available.

Struggling with his continuing depression and turmoil, Paul flew to Copenhagen where Oliver was shooting a film with Diane Cilento, the gorgeous British actress. Paul had seen her on stage as Helen of Troy and fallen for her. She did try to cheer Paul up, but his main target, Oliver Reed, seemed either stoned or drunk most of the time. However, if the film started in May, he agreed to star in it.

Financing! The CFDC never invested more than a portion of the budget, so Paul had to find private financing, and a distribution contract. With a script incomprehensible to most people, let alone financiers, Paul got nowhere. But he kept on assembling a cast, hoping somehow the leading lady would drop in his lap. He even called Joni Mitchell, a "name" who told him she would love to be in the film. But in the end, Paul was not sure he should hang a whole film on a singer who had never acted.

For the essential folk singer, Paul rang his old friend Leonard Cohen, but Leonard was busy. Glenn found a young bearded Tennessee draft dodger, Jesse Winchester, who proved amenable.

Every weekend, Paul would walk up Redpath Crescent, knock on the door, and Madame Pecetto would present his son, wrapped in winter clothes. They'd go for a toboggan or walk on the mountain: his only, and painful, contact. Afterwards, the stout oak front door that he had refinished himself would shut as his little son toddled off inside and he would curl up on the icy steps and let the tears come.

One day when he went to get Matthew, Geneviève answered. Paul saw the shock in her eyes. He'd sprouted a scraggly beard, he looked haunted, distraught; later she said she hardly recognized him. She asked how things were going, and he confessed that Jane Fonda had turned down the film and he feared it might never get made.

She thought for a moment and then, to his astonishment, told him that she would do it for him.

What would that mean? Would they get back together? Hope fluttered in his battered heart. Now, he had his lead. With Geneviève and Oliver Reid the film would go ahead.

* * *

He had run out of grant money by now, so paid for everything on credit cards. Glenn was loyally working without pay, so long as they ate properly. Paul moved into high gear to find financing.

But even with Geneviève, still no luck. His script was simply not commercial.

Time passed. May went by, so Oliver Reed dropped out. Unable to meet his rent any longer, he and Glenn were about to become homeless. Donald Johnston offered his mother's apartment on Ridgewood Avenue: she had passed away two weeks earlier. So Paul and Glenn moved into the deceased lady's gloomy flat, her old worn furniture and cupboards of clothes still untouched.

On *Wojeck*, Paul had worked with John Vernon, hardly a "name", but Paul got him to accept the role, and again he had his two leads. But Glenn met Jesse Winchester one afternoon to find he had shaved his beard and cut his hair in military fashion. No film for him! Now the crucial part of Jude, the folk singer who must write eight songs, had to be re-cast. Calamity followed calamity.

Glenn finally found a bearded young singer, Luke Gibson, living on his own commune, and he signed on. Optimistically, Paul kept assembling a crew: Peter Carter flew in from Toronto to help him prepare a budget, and from Paris, Jean Boffety agreed to return as cameraman.

They now waited for the Canadian Film Development's meeting in July. Surely Michael Spencer would come to their rescue. Elton Hayes arrived from Shigawake in a bushy beard grown for the part. Peter Carter, drinking his half bottle of Scotch every night, spent each morning in a haze. He was on tenterhooks, too, hoping that his first film as director, Gordon Pinsent's *The Rowdyman* with Larry Dane (Zahab) as producer, would get funding.

The fateful day came. The meeting ended. But no word. Michael Spencer, after meeting all day and unaware of the angst felt by many waiting cineastes, did not bother to phone.

But Peter and Paul had spies out in Toronto. One got hold of a board member and passed on the news. Peter's *The Rowdyman* was accepted. *Journey* was not.

Glenn had taken a leave of absence from University and lost his year. Elton had left his farm and grown a beard; others had given up good paying jobs. Paul, at the end of his card limits and credit at the bank, had finally hit rock bottom.

But some deep survival instinct welled up, and he tore off to see Donald Johnston. Heather gave them dinner, and the two fiddled the budget down to half its size. Donald phoned Mel Hoppenheim, provider of equipment, and got him to invest one-half his equipment rental fee. Harold Greenberg agreed to invest half Astral's lab fees. An old friend of Paul's from Bishops College School kicked in a good amount. Donald, the lawyer for Astral Films, pressed them to accept *Journey* for distribution. Hey Presto!

Paul and Donald then managed to corral Michael in his own home the next evening. Donald twisted his arm and Michael agreed to approach his Board by telephone.

The Board agreed. Journey got its full financing. The film was on.

CHAPTER TWENTY-SIX
1971

The *Journey* Experience:

PAUL ALFORD'S UNDERSKY by Rick Kline, The Official Scribe

"This film will be a product of our collective minds and bodies." Paul Alford was talking to his cast and crew on the first day of production of his new film, *Journey*. Everyone listened and smiled politely and went right on not believing him. They'd been on too many productions where directors started out talking like synergistic Buckminster Fullers and ended up swaggering around like miniature Hitlers. But as he spoke, thin beams of light broke through the clouds and fell like descending grace on the little group — a kind of cosmic "right on!" and a promise of things to come. But no one noticed and the meeting broke up, leaving the people free to wander around the community that Bydwell had built for the movie.

This was Undersky, a combination of all the country roads James Taylor had ever travelled, complete with a square timbered house, hand-made pegged furniture, and an enormous thatched roof barn, all of it surrounded by mountains and bordered by the Saguenay and Marguerite rivers. The community members, who in more normal times were merely actors, included Geneviève Bujold, John Vernon, Luke Gibson, (Kensington Market Rock Group,) Gale Garnett (an AM radio folk-singer, of "We'll sing in the Sunshine" fame) Gary McKeehan (Perth County Conspiracy, a combination commune-theatre-rock group) — all there to make a film. No one would have guessed at the outset, except possibly Alford, that the same people would in large part become a real community, but they did.

Removed from family and friends and their familiar urban environments, they'd been exiled by the powers that be (Alford) to an imaginary village called Undersky, located near an only slightly less imaginary village called Tadoussac, in northern Quebec. Having abandoned their normal lives, there was little left to order their present existence except the film — and the very film, with its emphasis on dream and the way dreams became realities, didn't make things any easier.

Journey's script began to unravel from its seams: the actors were forced into a kind of existential confrontation between themselves and their characters. And since there was very little left of the actors' old selves, the actors more often than not lost the battle, succumbed completely, and became their characters. Half way through the film, Luke Gibson confessed; "I haven't been me since three days before I came here."

The crisis reached its peak by the fourth week as actor after actor tried to come to grips with the various realities by which the film was affecting their lives. At a week-end party, Alford's ex-wife and current leading lady Geneviève Bujold, slipped him a small note on official Peanuts stationery. Right next to Linus and the bubble reading "the greatest potential is the biggest burden," she had written: "I have faith." Mere techniques and reason had by this time been exhausted. Faith was the only thing left.

This was revolution from the top: Alford himself had caused most of this confusion by launching a cultural war on his own script. After twelve rewrites and innumerable script conferences, many of which he spent padding around the room muttering: "Not enough truth, not enough truth," like some blind prophet, he remained totally dissatisfied. The dissatisfaction crystallized into distrust and he began systematically to explode his script at every turn with suggestions from actors and production people, rewriting whole scenes, or creating new ones out of improvisation. The effect of all this on the actors was decisive.

Alford again: "All movies have a life of their own; it's only a question of how far the people involved are willing to surrender themselves to it." In *Journey*, by choice and through circumstance, the surrender was nearly complete. The resulting movie, though not radically different from the original script, was totally transformed by three dozen cast and crew having lived it completely for two months. By the end, nothing was being done the way movies normally did things.

In the beginning, Alford tried setting up a shooting schedule so that everyone would know at any moment what was being shot and what their part was in it. This procedure proved to be totally out of the question. Weather rolled down the river like a bowling ball down an alley — you could see it coming for miles, but its actual effect was always unpredictable. Changes would come in five minute shifts: first sunlight, then clouds, then rain, then sunlight again, and fog and rain, all in varying patterns, wreaking havoc on the film's continuity. Behind all this demonology was the river, this Saguenay — at 900 feet, the deepest river in the world, carrying beneath its surface icy arctic currents which profoundly disturbed local atmospheric conditions — and the minds of the local weatherman assigned to chart these conditions. Given this problem, the weathermen had long since weirded out. Call them from the set in the pouring rain, drenched to the bone, and ask them for the forecast? They'd cheerfully tell you it would be sunny all day. They'd know it was a lie, of course, but they'd learned after all these years that cheerful lies go down a whole lot better.

Bogged down by this combination of bad weather and prevaricating weathermen, Alford's precisely detailed attack on the film soon faltered, then retreated, and finally turned into a rout as the local weather deities displayed the full range of their power and perversity. Shortly afterwards, Alford surrendered, leaving the whole company truly "Under Sky," dependent for its shooting schedule, its locations, the whole pattern of the film's day-to-day life, on the motions of the clouds. It became common to see gofers, gaffers, actors, and assorted production people all walking around looking up at the sky in some vain attempt to determine what they should be doing.

This continuing disorientation is part of Alford's basic philosophy. "When things are really upset," he says, "a little confusion clears the air!" — confusion elevated to the status of a technique. Alford creates the outlines of a world, places his company inside it, and films the result. It is a technique that works perfectly with *Journey's* script, for the movie is very much concerned with "how things you create have a way of taking over." It is a dream-vision, structured internally by a series of dreams-within-the-dream, which incarnate into increasingly tangible forms of reality as the movie moves on, appearing at first as fleeting thought, then as recollected dream, then as a hallucinated obsession, and finally as nightmarish reality, confronted and disarmed.

Side by side with this dream world is the real story of the community, of the heroine's impact on their lives, of the whole feeling of life as it is lived out in the country, including its less idyllic sides: pigs are slaughtered, bulls mount cows, people take shits and calves are born: realities she must learn to accept. The girl lives in a dream; she must learn to live in the world, and she can do that only by living out the dream in order to be released, to find her authentic self. It is the old Cocteau theme set to music: "I must live out my dream, and thus become real."

A couple of unplanned dramatic incidents: (told by the Company Scribe)

Night flight

Today Geneviève, Paul, Elton, Boffety, John Vernon, Patrick Spence-Thomas (sound) and Tim Hurson (1st AD) flew to Quebec City to see an assembly of the film in a Quebec laboratory and have a press conference — a simple trip: up by six and back by five this afternoon.

They got more than they bargained for.

The assembly went fine, and the press conference was its usual success. Only on the flight back did things begin to get, well, funny. Geneviève noticed that the plane was making strange noises as it circled La Malbaie airport. Then the pilot turned to announce that he was having trouble landing; the indicator light showed that the landing gear had not locked. He had no way of knowing whether the indicator had failed, or whether the wheels really weren't down. They circled around for a while longer; his passengers were alarmed to see him take out his instrument manual and begin reading studiously.

John Vernon's face froze into a Zen-like smile; Geneviève Bujold settled back with a slightly bored attitude ("Such an undramatic way to die"). Jean Boffety tried to be comforting with his wine-red face completely white. Elton, usually the heartiest of the Undersky inhabitants, turned ashen grey beneath his beard. While people sat around waiting for their lives to end, Paul huddled with Tim Hurson, deciding his schedule for the coming week, visibly annoyed at this unscheduled delay. Tim, meanwhile, trying hard to emulate the master, cast significant looks at everyone. Meanwhile, the pilot headed back for Quebec City, where the airport facilities could deal with crash landings. They were further disconcerted by the ambulances and fire trucks lining the runway.

The pilot tried touching down to see if the gear would in fact buckle. It did not and they landed successfully, not without a few bitten lips and white knuckles.

Straight away everyone headed for a bar. Two hours later, well soused, they took off in three separate small planes right back to La Malbaie and safety, drunk — with success?

THE PIG KILLING

Death. Cut with equal parts of wind and rain, it swept through Undersky all day today. Everyone felt it. Never had it rained this hard before, heavy, metaphysical, falling everywhere. Outside and in the barn, three pigs were being slaughtered one after another to cover the various angles and the close-ups.

The actors taking refuge in the main house sat quietly, woodenly, with ashen faces, singing old rock-and-roll songs, afraid to stop because the silence might bring to their ears the squeals of pigs as knives sliced into them. Outside, other animals were going berserk from the smell of blood and scalded flesh. Saul, the bull, pulled back to the end of his tether; geese and ducks agitated loudly and the one frantic calf raced away. From inside, the actors heard Alford's voice: "Fantastic, fantastic! Patrick, did you get the sound of the thunk as the hammer hit the pig's head?" The crew wrestled with their consciences.

In fact, they did rebel and tried to start an actors' strike, but Alford set Elton upon them, and he, as a farmer himself, finally put that to rest.

Norman Mailer once said that no-one should eat meat until they've visited the Chicago slaughterhouses. Up to this day, most of the actors thought meat came from little plastic trays in Steinberg's meat department. What a rude awakening. Inside, Luke Gibson, a confirmed vegetarian, nodded as he played his guitar: "I think it's a good thing. Those middle Americans are really going to have their minds "blown.""

FAMOUS LAST WORDS FROM JOURNEY

Anonymous gofer: Will you please tell me what it is I'm looking for?

Geneviève: Paul, talk to us. Paul: I'm listening.

Paul: Shall we go as we go?

(About the film) It would really be good if it were good.

(Looking at a bunch of actors basking in the sun) If everyone were starving and hungry and miserable, it could really be much worse.

Tim: After watching the pigs being carried into the barn by their ears) Elton, why are their ears so red?

Elton: Ah gee, Tim, I don't know. Maybe they got too much sun.

Tim again: (At an interior) All right, clear the room — of everybody but non-essential people.

Paul: (With the actors, auctioning off lines he's just made up for a scene he's just invented) Out of what? Who wants to say "Out of what?" That's a brilliant line. Now who wants to say "Out of what?"

Ratch: I'm interested in human values and all that shit.

John Vernon: (On the film) This could be a fantastic commentary on ... on ... on something.

JOURNEY AS VISIONARY EXPERIENCE
by Prof Paul T. Piehler

Throughout most of history there have been two radically different types of experience open to mankind: the prosaic or everyday experience, and the more important visionary experience.

The peoples of western Asia and of the Mediterranean basin from whom we draw our fundamental cultural identity carried on most of their important business of life through the medium of visionary experience. A nation in a state of crisis would call upon its soothsayers and dreamers to sleep in the temples of the gods until the right dream or vision was vouchsafed, showing the correct course to take. In fact, the Egyptian Pharaoh or the Babylonian Priest-King was in reality just the best dreamer, the principal visionary of his people. The greatest of these visionaries expressed their experience through poetry, myth, sacred book and epic, and in the Middle Ages, allegory. Up to the period of the Renaissance, all serious art was visionary in nature, and the greatest poets, Virgil, Dante, Chaucer, Spenser, were its foremost practitioners.

The visionary experience is essentially unifying — it implies a harmony of the intuitive and rational faculties — abandoned in that Faustian compact that gave man control over the material world, on condition it seems, that he cease to associate it with the spiritual world. Since that time, man's spiritual and technological faculties have gone their separate ways, with the result that the man of vision, the artist, has become increasingly alienated and embittered — as prophesied in Eliot's "The Waste Land" (1922). We see grim and negative evidence that a failure to grasp the spiritual dimension of the physical world will lead to the extinction of life on earth — life, in its true form as meeting place of matter and spirit.

The way forward is the way back, to a reintegration of physical and spiritual, and the artist must lead the way. The first duty therefore is the recovery of Visionary Allegory, the greatest of the artistic achievements of western man, in the expression of a unified comprehension of the world around us.

It is thus an enormous pleasure to welcome the creation, in Canada, of Paul Alford's film *Journey*, one of the first works of this decade to express this unified vision for which we are searching. It faithfully follows a form hardly seen in English since the Renaissance — a form at once archaic and yet now ultra-modern which may well leave audiences somewhat baffled and yet strangely moved. Its setting is both a perfectly visitable locale of almost unearthly beauty on an inlet of the Saguenay River in northeastern Quebec, and at the same time, a place outside normal time and space, the place of vision. The medieval allegorist would have no difficulty in recognising it, knowing that an ordinary landscape can at times glow with the lineaments of the pastoral vision, or the Earthly Paradise. The mediaevals lacked our sharp distinctions between place and state of mind, and were the better for it.

Rivers, sources of both fish and transport, were at once Rivers of Time; High Places might be climbed to look for a lost sheep or, indeed, for a vision of Truth. Their waterfalls flowed with real water but could also loosen a girl's dammed-up passion. Thus it is in *Journey*. There is nothing of romantic vagueness here.

What makes *Journey* a visionary allegory in the ancient and most modern sense, is the journey itself. Visionary experience was never lightly conferred; Dante himself did not achieve it until angst and terror had brought him almost to the point of death. So too the heroine of *Journey* is plucked from the river where suicidal frenzy had driven her.

And so she finds herself rescued into the visionary otherworld, which is perhaps no more than an eccentric upcountry commune, where the slow uncertain process of soul healing takes place; for *Journey*, like all serious visionary allegory, is therapeutic and reintegrative. And again, in accordance with the ancient tradition, the healing takes place in a kind of pastoral paradise which reconciles the polar opposites of city and wilderness, reason and intuition, the two mighty opposites whose antagonism is pulling man apart in our modern world.

In one highly significant respect, Alford breaks with the tradition of earlier allegorists. Soul-healing in past allegory often involved a mysterious feminine figure with deep powers of understanding and consolation. In Alford's allegory there is no such a figure. Thus, in her search for herself, Saguenay has no one other than the equally tormented figure of Boulder, leader of his pastoral community, to lend help and strength. Thus, the process of soul healing that Saguenay undergoes is considerably less complete than one would expect to find in a medieval vision. By the end of the film, Saguenay has passed through a critical stage of psychic reintegration but has not yet achieved any deep enlightenment.

This circumstance is, I believe, indicative of the insight and essential honesty of Alford's vision. Today we are far from recovering, even on a visionary level, the kind of spiritual authority which medieval visionaries had no difficulty in achieving. It is as if these mysterious soul powers that once guided our psychic destinies have decided that this time, we must learn to do the job ourselves, no matter what extra sweat and anguish is caused. Nonetheless, what remains most striking in Alford's vision in *Journey* is that after decades of artistic disintegration and decadence, we have in this film a searching and honest attempt to recover the ancient neglected mainstream of western artistic achievement, a vision of soul-healing and reintegration.

CHAPTER TWENTY-SEVEN
1971 - 72

The shooting was over. As he drove back to Montreal alone in the cab of the large equipment truck, Paul finally pondered: would he now for the first time sit down and properly discuss the future with Geneviève? He longed for, and at the same time dreaded, that meeting.

During the shoot, they had lived in separate houses and had fallen into the relationship established over many shows: director and actress. No question that Geneviève still admired him as a director, as did Paul her. But not a mention of their future crossed their lips. That now lay ahead.

When shooting ended, the cast and crew voiced their good-byes, some tearful, most happy to get back to their families, but still sad that the overwhelming experience was over. Gail Garnett, who played Morgan (after *Morgan le Fay)* the repository of dreams and seer of the community, told Paul later: "You know, when we left, we cried. We had not only lived our roles but a whole new life style. *Journey* was an experience that none of us will ever have again."

Shooting had run somewhat over budget due to an inexperienced production manager because reduced financing hadn't allowed for a proper executive, so no cleanup crew remained. The producer-director, the production designer, and young Bert Tougas, a great favourite of the crew who called him Bertie-Bert, had to go round themselves with bags and rakes, cleaning debris, checking bushes for burned-out bulbs, empty containers tossed aside, all the detritus of a film crew. It absorbed Paul's last ounce of energy. Finally, Glenn drove back to Montreal in the dysfunctional MG, and Paul was left to return the equipment. Late that day, worn out, he got into the truck and set off overnight at no great speed, due to the fragile equipment in the back, to meet the deadline at the rental house.

Paul wondered over and over, what should he say? Did the fact his former wife played in the film show she still had an undercurrent of feelings for him? Would they come back together as man and wife? Now that actual shooting was not taking up his every pore, every moment of waking consciousness, he focussed on this one meeting. What would his future life be — more films with a beautiful young star? More children with a mother to look after them? Or an arid home on Redpath Crescent, empty of life, striding room to room, restless as always, seeking, questing after some kind of healing enlightenment?

Being in charge of the shoot had developed in him a new courage. He now had the sense to recognize that his own house should properly belong to him. He would move back. Geneviève, who had walked out with his child and his housekeeper, would now, if she did decide to separate, have to find her own accommodation.

Having dropped the van at the equipment house by its deadline of eight am, Paul got his suitcase, grabbed a taxi, and went straight to 1272 Redpath Crescent, where Geneviève, Matthew, and Madame Pecetto were ensconced. Not having a key, he rang the doorbell. Madame Pecetto answered it, inscrutable as always, and ushered him into the kitchen where Geneviève was having breakfast.

A few pleasantries followed about the film cleanup, the farewells of the crew, and how Matthew was doing. Then, with his back to the unlit fireplace, Paul asked, "Well, Geneviève, what's the decision. Are we getting back together?"

The fateful question had been asked. It reached into the very depths of his being. His whole future hung on her response.

Geneviève looked down at her breakfast plate for what seemed a very long time. Then she looked up. "Paul, my darling, I'm afraid it's over. Nothing to do with you. It is just... I cannot come back."

Paul stared.

"The last few days, I've gone back and forth. I knew you would ask me that." She sighed. "I've finally resolved it in my own mind, and in my heart."

Paul did not move.

"I'm sorry. There is no going back. What has been, has been. And what is, is. I still love you. I probably always will. But no, I cannot be your wife. I shall move out with our son, and Madame Pecetto. She has been saying recently she'd like to find other employment. So I shall get someone else, I shall rent a house, and now, this place is yours."

As Julius Caesar once said, the die was cast, and Paul's second wife had left him. The house, the empty house, was his.

Paul stared into a bleak future.

* * *

Bertie-Bert and Honor Griffith set up the editing room in the basement of 1272 Redpath Crescent. Rick Kline, the company scribe, had provided such good energy during the production that Paul asked him to stay on. A quite brilliant graduate of Berkeley and apostle of the Great Piehler (as the professor became known) he'd run messages, do the shopping, and as it turned out, make cheap meals for them all.

So the little team set about editing. Paul found a kind of solace in this cohesive and creative group, all of whom liked each other, all of them focussed on getting the best film they could. On weekends, Paul saw his little son. Geneviève had for some reason turned down a book that Hal Wallis had bought for her, *True Grit,* which eventually starred John Wayne and Kim Darby. She also told Paul she had turned down Hal's offer of another costume drama, *Mary Queen of Scots.* "I've done all that. I didn't want to repeat it."

Another shock – on January 13, 1972, Auntie Hilda phoned, deeply agitated, to tell him his mother had passed away.

Paul dropped everything. Editing twelve hours a day, he hadn't been out to Mont Saint-Hilaire as much as he should. When he got there, the doctor had already issued a death certificate.

Paul travelled by train down to Shigawake to inter his mother's remains, accompanied by faithful Glenn and, oddly the next day, Geneviève and Matthew. Elton helped unload the coffin from the train onto his truck, and Rene's body was laid out in the parlour. After a gathering of friends, she was buried in the cemetery along with her husband Eric and many relatives.

Back in Montreal again, Paul saw his aunt bearing up reasonably well, sustained by several friends, so he returned to editing. So sad that his mother had died with her only son distraught, his psyche tattered and no prospects in sight. Dealing with her probate documents over the next weeks only left him even more depleted and depressed.

Journey began to come together over the autumn. The numbness and desperation that had settled in the very marrow of his bones began to lessen, though by no means disappear. He loved editing, as did the rest of them, and before spring they had a pretty good cut.

For the music, no lush strings nor choral music that had marked his earlier films. John Wyre's unusual and bizarre percussion group Nexus worked in free form and were considered by some at the top of modern music. Paul visited their studio-barn near Toronto, and decided instead of a written score like every other film, Paul should just let them improvise around themes; he'd lay in the music with Honor as required. He attended an all-day session and gave them topics to elaborate on with their clinks and dongs and bangs and biffs and clunks. For example, when Saul, the Undersky bull, came down with a mysterious illness — was this to be the end of the community? — Paul asked the group to improvise around, "there's an undefined force at the barn..."

Aware that Journey would hardly attract the crowds required for a commercial release, their only hope was Cannes. The usual committee to choose Canada's official selection was meeting at the NFB. But a huge snow storm had stopped all traffic — and the street cleaners went on strike. So when the time came to take *Journey* to the NFB, no taxi moved on the snow-clogged streets. No hope for the little green Datsun, which now replaced the junked MG.

Paul and Bertie-Bert loaded the rough-cut film, ten heavy cans of picture and magnetic sound, each thirty to forty pounds, onto Matthew's plastic swimming pool, its bottom painted with smiling dolphins. Wrapped warmly, they donned 1930s snowshoes from Shigawake and curved down the Crescent, across McGregor now snowed up and empty of cars. Holding back the plastic pool, they slithered down a steep Peel Street with its morass of cars stuck at every angle. At Bonaventure Station they caught a commuter train under the mountain to Montreal North, where they unloaded the heavy reels. Then they snowshoed across to the Film Board.

Chilled and worn, Paul and Bert were welcomed by the committee with open arms and hot mulled wine. Afterward, making their way home, they knew beyond any doubt that their snowbound odyssey would lead the committee to choose their film.

Wrong! They chose *La vrai nature de Bernadette*.

* * *

Paul had made a deal with Bob Crone to mix the film at his new Film House where he had hired Joe Grimaldi away from the National Film Board. That meant trips back and forth to Toronto.

After a long sound edit, the film finally got finished. Its distributor Astral Films set up a press conference. One of the first questions asked was: what's the next project? Paul had to admit, he had no plans; his psyche was far too battered.

The film's only hope was the Canadian Film Awards, where *Journey* might walk off with a few prizes. Paul went hopefully to Cinesphere in Ontario Place, on Oct 13th.

Again, no luck. Bill Fruet's *Wedding in White* took best film, and Gilles Carle Best Director for *La vraie nature de Bernadette*, with Gordon Pinsent taking Best Actor for *The Rowdyman*. Well, at least, Paul thought, Geneviève will win best actress, but no, Micheline Lanctôt won instead. Paul could understand all that, but was outraged that Glenn missed Best Art Direction. He had designed and made every single hand prop, every table and chair, every building, everything on site, and supervised the craftsmen. Even the reviews, mostly mystified by the film, praised its beauty. But Glenn, without a friend in Toronto was seen as an upstart genius, and some local Ontario Art Director won.

Ah well, the film got invited to the Los Angeles Film Exposition, proudly touted with tongue in cheek as "a tradition since 1971".

In the great auditorium of Grauman's Chinese Theater in early November, a goodly five hundred greeted *Journey* with more enthusiasm than heretofore. There seemed to be general agreement on its exquisite images, but no one, including the critics, could make head nor tail of it. The thing Paul remembered most was the look in his friends' eyes at the Toronto opening. No mistaking their almost pitying looks as they watched their once proud friend brought low. But Paul was happy with his achievement, and later, many audiences found this "cult" film satisfying in its beauty.

* * *

With autumn progressing and the editing crew gone, Paul was befriended by three stunning ladies: one blonde, petite Swedish Playboy centrefold, another attractive vixen, and lastly, a tall, lithe, Italian model with the deepest eyes, rich brown hair, and lots of fun. They came and went as they wanted, surrounding him at least with the aura of beauty. Being perhaps overly optimistic, he called them his muses, but they actually turned out to be harpies, tantalising but unobtainable, never once offering emotional nor physical gratification. His desperation grew.

Then, all at once, Marigold, a twenty-four-year-old Westmount socialite arrived, big-boned, with an elephant's heart, lovely warm face and inviting eyes. Paul found her sensible, down to earth, someone he could perhaps genuinely love. She seemed to need him as much as he needed her. Paul was entranced. What a long time since anyone had loved him! And allowed him to love her back.

She soon became a constant visitor, and then one night, stayed over and then, actually moved in. She offered advice, help, emotional support, they had fun together, and his feelings grew. But after a time, it became clear that she had no desire for the life of a mop-swinger. Hopeless in the kitchen, she let Paul cook, buy food, and look after her. He found that begin to pall. So he hit on an idea. "Marigold, let's fly to Germany, pick up a Volkswagen camper and, if we're careful with money, we can travel around Europe for a few months." So in January 1973, they flew off for an adventure that Paul hoped might expunge the devils of loneliness and worthlessness tormenting him.

CHAPTER TWENTY-EIGHT
1973

In January, Paul and Marigold arrived in Frankfurt, took a bus to Wiedenbruck and got there just before the Volkswagen factory closed. Excited, they climbed into their brand-new orange van, a Westphalia with its traditional pop-up top. As they drove out of the parking enclosure, they realized the shops had shut. No blankets, nothing to cook with, none of the necessities for a long camping voyage.

"Oh well," Paul sighed, "let's celebrate with a good German dinner!" So after quantities of cheap German wine in a decent restaurant, they donned layers of extra clothing, and did their best to sleep on the bare freezing bed. Midwinter here was damp and cold, worse than Canada. Not an auspicious beginning.

The next day, they bought supplies at a local hardware store and set off. After crossing Germany, they stayed a couple of days with the long-suffering Michelle de Broca in Carières-sur-Seine. Then down to the Cognac region of France where they tasted brandies in many cellars, and on to San Sebastian near the Spanish border, where they camped beside the mighty Atlantic breakers.

On they drove to Algeciras, with Gibraltar rearing up ahead, and then at last by ferry into the warmth of Morocco.

In Tangier, the lovers awoke to a Moroccan symphony: the Muezzin in their minarets calling Muslims to pray, the distant chorale of dogs led first by one, counterpointed by another and another, all to a background of asthmatic donkey brays, the coughs of a passing camel, unfamiliar birdsongs, children's laughter and, later in the desert, the yapping of fennecs, desert foxes.

They soon became accustomed to, and loved, the absolute lack of planning or preordained destinations, and the underground of campers who passed on key information: which towns were pleasant, which sites friendly, where open camping was allowed, whom to trust, what to find where. Complete within their van, they could go anywhere at any time, snooze or make love at midday or midnight, no hassles with hotel bedbugs and surly waiters — a self-contained and open life.

Every morning, something new blew in on the desert wind.

The first morning in Tangier, Paul fulfilled his one obligation and took Marigold to meet his Aunt Leo. Leo had remained with the Mater (as Paul's grandmother was known) all through the Second World War. In WWI, Hilda had served as an ambulance driver with the Scottish Women's Regiment and then, in the '20s, had left to go hitchhiking in South Africa, so brave for a lone woman. Rene had been sent to Australia to open a school of Greek dancing. Perhaps for these reasons, instead of dividing the family's possessions equally among her three surviving daughters, the Mater left everything to Leo. Forget Rene and her only grandchild starving on a disabled Veteran's pension; forget Hilda, eking out a living by teaching convent girls the elements of acting.

Leo kept everything she had inherited. Finding England too rainy and damp, she headed into the sun and settled in a roomy apartment at 25 Imm. Miramonte, bringing all the furniture from The Lions, their Essex home. When Paul and Marigold arrived, they were shocked by the drawn drapes and white sheets covering furniture like ghosts hulking in gloom. In one darkened bedroom surrounded by knick-knacks, Leo lay, drinking Spanish champagne mixed with cheap brandy.

Paul was quite unprepared for the vitriol that poured upon him and his beautiful friend. Snide remarks about his wasteful film life and this paramour flew thick and fast. Leo, unhappy and existing on one raw egg every morning, was only visited at night by a plump Arab maid, Zohra, who fussed over her and made her a bite of dinner.

Leo being a blood relative, Paul felt they should return the following day. But after that, he and Marigold were only too happy to escape this emaciated harpy with red-henna hair and suppurating ankle that kept her bedridden. When she waved them good bye, they thought they heard a mumbled, "Good riddance..."

From Tangier they motored down through Rabat, the capital, and Agadir, past endless Atlantic beaches, to a little oasis with hot springs outside Goulimine. They rested there, reading, climbing the surrounding hills for a view of the great Sahara and visiting the camel souk (market) on Saturdays when Bedouins and other "blue men of the desert" arrived with their goats, their beads and ambers and sacks of dates. The village houses, sand-coloured, some whitewashed, with little vegetable gardens and sheds for animals, were enclosed by high walls. Dogs, cats, goats, donkeys and chickens, all lived in safety at night.

Living was cheap. Twenty five cents bought five pounds of potatoes, or six pounds of tomatoes or eight oranges; meat cost a dollar a pound. With their van, they encountered real desert Bedouins, hitch-hiking. Conversations would spring up, and with that, inevitable invitations for mint tea in distant secluded desert tents. The couple soon learned to eat with their hands, observing that wives never ate with visitors and only men did the shopping. Only at weddings and fêtes could a young man spot a future wife and so acquire, as Marigold pointed out, a free slave for life.

After getting down to the southern tip of Morocco at Tan-tan Plage (beach) where they were chased by beach bees and nuzzled by donkeys, they came north to Marrakesh for the *Fête des Thrones*, March 3rd, the day Hassan II had ascended the throne in 1961. In the great square, Jemaa el Fna, they mingled with snake charmers, fire-eaters, tumblers, singers, dancers, scorpion-eaters, boxers, story-tellers. This Square of the Dead had been named after those condemned by the king whose heads he'd struck off and stuck on pikes to stare down at the crowds.

In the medina (old city) with its labyrinthine alleyways, they passed darkened rooms where little boys and girls sewed busily, some grouped around candles, hammering away at bronze trays, stitching jellabas, or pounding at plywood cabinets. School was supposedly compulsory until age thirteen, but local school inspectors hardly ever penetrated here.

One day while driving off the beaten path, they came upon an improvised barrier blocking the rutted track. A group of armed and fierce-looking Berbers held up their hands. With no way to turn around, Paul quickly reversed. The men started running towards them.

Marigold, panicked. "What'll we do? They'll pull us out... I'm going to be raped!"

Thinking fast, Paul got fearlessly out of the van, put on a broad smile and greeted them warmly in French: "I'm happy to meet you... How are you? What's happening? We are Canadians. We want to help." In French he told them that he and "his wife" loved their beautiful country. It seemed to work. Smiles appeared and they explained that their government was the problem.

This motley bunch, trying ineffectually to confront the savage might of Hassan II's secret police, brought them behind some bushes. Uh-oh! What now?

There, buried in a pit in the sand, *meschoui,* slow roasting lamb, lay cooking in leaves. Paul ran to get some wine from the van, and they all tore at the meat with scalded fingers and passed the bottles around in spite of Muslim inhibitions.

But the next encounter with danger did not end quite as happily.

After the Gorge of Dadès with its breathtaking trails twisting up and down sheer sides of the snow-covered Atlas Mountains, against all advice, they drove north and across the Rif Mountains towards the only border crossing into Algeria.

The French occupying Morocco had never been able to subdue the Rif tribes, known for their savagery. Cars with hoods up would beckon drivers to stop and help the supposedly stranded group. Earlier at a campsite, Paul had been told these decoys were offering hashish at a low rate. A few miles beyond, *les flics* (police) would search the van and arrest the hapless tourist. The offenders would then have to pay *baksheesh* to get released, which the police split with the decoys.

One evening, they pulled off onto a level area on the hillside, put up the slanting roof, pulled the curtains around, and cooked supper. As they were getting ready for bed, voices approached. They froze. Men! Talking quietly, laughing. Marigold was even more afraid; something told her they were up to no good.

The men began to bang on the van. Paul and Marigold exchanged whispers — what should they do?

The van began to rock as the devils tried to tip it. Paul stood ready to drop the roof and signalled Marigold to start the motor. With roof down, she dropped the front curtain and gunned the van over rough rocks to the main road, where they lost their pursuers and sped to the next village.

At a police station, Paul asked the sleepy police sergeant in his best French if they might stay the night? Soon the Caïd, head man of the village, paid a visit. He welcomed them most courteously and apologized: the young men had only been having fun. Nonetheless, he promised that the next morning, if they came to the main square, they would witness every village teenager thrashed, as a lesson not to frighten tourists, Morocco's most important trade.

Needless to say, Paul and Marigold wanted no part of that, and hightailed it for a very different atmosphere: Algeria and socialism.

What a contrast. No family compounds, everything built out of cement blocks from Russian factories. True, electric lights lit villages; true, no starving children appeared in the desert to snatch loaves of bread. But everywhere, bleak, sullen looks. Next Tunisia, and the island of Djerba, full of Roman remains that reminded him of Shelley's *Ozymandias.* On to the flat *schotts,* dried salt lakes, and then to the strange cave dwellings. Small clean rooms had been dug into the sides of deep, round, flat-bottomed holes, and made comfortable with tapestries and rugs. With only one narrow staircase down steep walls, the cave-dwellers were safe from wild animals or other marauders.

With their money running out, they took the ferry over to Sicily, then up through Italy and across into Austria, where they stopped for a few days with Harry Boyd, Paul's hockey friend. Finally, after six months of travel, they left the van in a garage near Orly Airport and flew back to Montreal.

Paul had found life with Marigold reviving. She was strong willed and had a great sense of herself. Their nights were just glorious. He'd been hoping and providing chances for her to share some of the housekeeping. But she was not cut out for a life of domesticity. What about the future? Could he really write scripts, go through shooting, editing, and all the time cook as well, and do every household chore?

* * *

With no money left, the sooner Paul got another project, the sooner he'd get the wherewithal to live. Marigold just could not stifle her antipathy to anything domestic — cooking, washing up, doing laundry, keeping up the house, much as she wanted to. So in the end, she decided to go off and pursue a career in the fields of film and music; she had a lovely voice. The couple separated in yet another poignant farewell: they had each loved in their own way.

Once again, Paul was alone in his castle-like home.

Later, in November of 1973, Graeme Gibson would gather a dozen authors to protest Ryerson Press being sold to an American company, McGraw Hill. It turned out to be the nascent Writers Union of Canada, which soon drew in Alice Munro, Margaret Atwood, Farley Mowat, and Paul's friend Pierre Berton. Margaret Laurence, living in the UK, became Honorary Chair. But Paul was no longer interested in writing — novels at least. He was on the track of his next screenplay.

The new "vibes circling the globe" at that time, Psi Phenomena and New Age attitudes were being touted in a wave of books: *The Secret Life of Plants, The Secrets of the Great Pyramid,* and Lyall Watson's *Supernature.* The glimmerings of an idea began to take shape.

The winter solstice, the ancients believed, was the time of maximum conflict between the powers of light and of darkness. A clue. While in England researching this next film, Paul and Glenn became intrigued by so-called ley lines, dead straight paths along which the ancients must have aligned their impossibly straight grid of ancient centres, miles apart: Salisbury, Stonehenge, and so on, all impossible without the ancients tapping into mysterious sources of energy. So why, they figured, would not these ley or energy lines cover the entire globe? Put a stone age monument where all the ley lines converged, and you'd have an epicentre capable of producing astonishing energy.

One physically bulky character in G.K. Chesterton's *The Man Who Was Thursday* suggested to Paul a "Gabriel Pentecost". Being immensely rich, he could feed into his enormous computer centre (a gigantic room filled with monster machines) the coordinates of the still unexplained monuments: Tikal, Machu Picchu, Easter Island, and thereby locate the earth's energy lines. Then the computers would find one central point where they all intersected. Of course, because of his latent love for Morocco, he wanted that point to be on a peak in the High Atlas.

Paul and Glenn travelled to Los Angeles, having heard about some new computer complex. They managed an entry into a highly secret area to witness a giant computer, as big as a truck, which could, from just scientific formulae, draw a three-dimensional-looking egg. Amazing! What a scientific advance!

He kept constantly revising his script, hardly aware he was still somewhat unbalanced. He believed the film's message would somehow change the world's consciousness. Why not indeed finally fuse mind and matter, spirit and the material world?

Back and forth he went between capitals in search of finance. In London, he met John Heyman, at his World Film Services headquarters and even got to see Barry Spikings and Michael Deeley at British Lion Films. He offered *Solstice* to the last of the great old British moguls, Nat Cohen; in Rome, to Italian producers Alberto Grimaldi and Carlo Ponti, and in Munich to Bavaria Films and Constantin. All frantic, rushed, trip after trip, hoping against hope the travel would somehow put him back where he once was, a bona fide film-maker.

Joe Schoenfeld, head of the William Morris motion picture department, took him to meet David Begelman, head of Columbia Pictures and former boss of Stevie Phillips. But David only said, "Paul, you've put so much together, let's just forget the picture and shoot the deal!"

Charles Aznavour, the great *chansonnier*, had impressed Paul in Truffaut's *Tirez sur le pianiste.* He flew to St Tropez and spent time with Charles, a gracious host, who took Paul to his favourite nightspot. In Paris, for the part of JoJo Paul met Maria Schneider who had achieved momentary fame opposite Marlon Brando in Bertolucci's film *Last Tango in Paris.* She too agreed. In New York he met Bergman's hero, Max Von Sydow for the magician. For the young stonecutter, Paul asked the newly emerging Beau Bridges, the son of Lloyd and brother of Jeff.

For his greatest creation, Gabriel Pentecost, Paul wanted Orson Welles.

He first wrote to him when Orson was staying with Mrs. John Houston. Next, he chased Orson to the little French village of Orvilliers, where his Yugoslav girl-friend, Oja Kodar, owned a house. Paul went to stay with Philippe de Broca nearby, drove to Orvilliers, parked outside the isolated house where Orson was shooting and gave his letter in at the door to the first AD. Paul doubted the great man would emerge, and in fact he didn't, but the letter and script got to him.

Keeping up the chase, Paul finally did meet Orson in his make-up trailer in Los Angeles, shooting a commercial for some Japanese company. He pinned Orson down, or so he thought. If he were to play Pentecost, though, Orson insisted on Oja playing Claire. He set up a screening of his *The Other Side of the Wind*, in which Oja had acted, with dinner beforehand. Secretive as always, the great man rang in the morning to say where they should meet. When Paul got there, the maitre d' handed him a message where to go next. Paul went there and found, instead of Orson, the dark-haired Oja who said Orson would join them later, but he never did. After a pleasant dinner, some canny instinct told Paul that he would shoot most of the film with Oja and then? Orson just wouldn't turn up. So in the end, all that fell apart.

* * *

One evening at dinner on Redpath Crescent, Donald Johnston asked him, "What do you think of this?" They had discussed Trudeau being re-elected for the third time, with a majority government. "The Income Tax Act provides for capital cost allowances (depreciation) that can shelter income for wealthy individuals, and even corporations. Our firm has been using it for aircraft."

"Sounds interesting, I guess. But so what?" Paul began to clear the dishes.

"Well..." Donald handed him their plates, "I've been thinking..." Paul sensed a revelation coming, "we might be able to offer the same arrangement with film." Paul's eyes widened. "Investors could buy the rights in and to a motion picture — providing its copyright was owned by a Canadian. Depreciation on films is really high — sixty per cent. Properly structured, it could be an attractive investment for some wealthy individual."

Paul was startled. "That might channel terrific amounts of money into our industry. So you'd talk to John Turner, the Minister of Finance? I knew him at Oxford." Paul paused in the arched doorway. "Remember his sister?"

"Brenda? Of course. We're very good friends." Donald gave a sideways glance at Heather. Had he spoken too quickly?

"She was a killer at McGill," Paul remembered.

"Let's hope the government allows it." Donald looked pleased with himself, and Heather smiled. She was so sweet, gracious, a perfect wife for this rapidly rising lawyer, and she even hailed from Nova Scotia.

"Donald, every film-maker will bless you."

Thus began the era of tax shelter films, invented solely by Maitre Johnston. But with no immediate impact upon *Solstice*.

Then Paul's agent, Joe Shoenfeld, retired. Another blow. His replacement was not excited about *Solstice*, nor indeed its director-writer.

Dead end after dead end.

PART THREE — JOAN

CHAPTER TWENTY-NINE
1975-76

Meanwhile, on many jaunts to Los Angeles to find distribution, Paul had been in the habit of visiting Geneviève in Malibu to see his son, now six years old. The couple had been granted a divorce decree nisi on June 10th, 1975, but continued to be friends, of a sort.

At the end of August 1975, Geneviève was carrying on with Cary, a handsome, well-built young surfer of nineteen. He was now off to study in Italy so his best friend Trey was giving him a going-away party. "You gotta come, Dad," a precocious Matthew said, "lotsa chicks there for you."

With the hot sun shining as it always does in Malibu, Matthew took his daddy by the hand and led him down the beach and up onto a bulkhead. Paul stared. The patio was filled with beautiful teens, lusty young surfers mingling with girls in bikinis. What delight!

Paul, at forty-five, was ignored, so he threaded through into the house. Such a comfortable home! Attracted by aromas, he headed for the kitchen and saw, stirring a huge pot of spaghetti, a small, athletic woman, Trey's mother, Joan, A former model and surfer with short auburn hair and big brown eyes full of wisdom, she easily matched any beauty in her patio.

Well trained in giving parties, Paul pitched in to help. "Where is your husband this fine day? Shouldn't he be doing this, too?"

Joan hesitated. "He died in an accident on the highway six years ago."

"Oh, how awful!"

"I've been working in my darkroom all summer..." — why Paul had not seen her on his beach walks. "But Trey persuaded me to get out and give Cary a party."

"You're a photographer?"

She nodded. "I'm helping our local newspaper, the *Surfside News*. Meeting deadlines helps me learn more about photography. But what are you doing here?"

"Right now, just trying to get another film on. I used to be a poet at Oxford, but got sidetracked into doing a bit of directing on television, and then sidetracked even more by making motion pictures. I'm Matthew's daddy."

"And who is Matthew?"

"That little six-year-old out in the patio. His mother... well, she is... with the surfer you're giving this party for."

Joan looked at him with understanding eyes. "Your ex-wife? Carrying on with Trey's friend Cary?"

Paul nodded. "A lot of fun..."

She gave the hint of a smile. So she did grasp his torment. "And what about your wife? Doesn't she mind?"

"I don't have a wife. Or even a girlfriend." He decided to milk it a bit. "You see, I'm a failed filmmaker, a failed writer, and a failed producer."

"All three?" She grinned. "Good for you."

Paul stayed in Los Angeles with his friend Douglas Campbell until after Labour Day. So once again, Matthew took him to the annual children's party Joan was organizing on the beach. By the bonfires blazing in front of her house, children were feasting on hamburgers, hot dogs, and spicy Mexican food. Paul came to sit with his son. A little later Joan joined them.

"Don't tell me you did all this?"

"Oh no." She gestured to her teahouse full of mothers and housekeepers. "But I usually organize this Labour Day party. Ever since my kids were little."

"Cary's friend Trey, is he your eldest?"

"Yes. Tracy over there..."

"That pretty girl?"

"She's eighteen and starting university next month. Then comes Timmy, the blond surfer, such a young devil, and that one with dark hair, he's Chris, sort of a genius, I think, at thirteen."

"Four children? Raising them all by yourself? Amazing! Geneviève split with my son when he was about two. Our divorce came through last July. But I still visit him here, of course."

Joan nodded, her eyes reflecting her concern. She knew how much it probably hurt. "I send the boys to boarding school. With all the drugs in Malibu, raising kids can often be a nightmare."

They spent the evening chatting over the bonfires. Then he walked slowly back to his bedroom at Geneviève's with its thin walls next to the master bedroom, where his ex-wife was giving a rather boisterous farewell to her surfer.

* * *

In his usual frantic fashion, Paul rushed off to Europe again, stitching together co-productions, losing them, finding actors, losing them too, and finally returned to Los Angeles to see Matt and possibly put together what he thought might be the final financing. Sam Arkov, who ran the famous AIP, purveyor of B movies, had a wife from Winnipeg, and was interested. Also a sleazy lawyer from Cleveland. So doors were opening.

On Hallowe'en in the Colony, Paul took his son trick-or-treating. When they got to Joan's, she answered the door. Paul looked in and frowned. "Where is everybody?"

"Everybody? I'm alone." She paused. "Disappointed?"

"Of course not. But I've only ever seen you in a crowd."

Joan deposited some candy in Matthew's little sack, and went to close the door.

"Wait a minute! Er... would it be all right if I came back after Matthew's in bed? Just for a quick drink?"

After a pause she said, "I suppose so," and shut the door.

Later, Paul walked from #97 down to Joan's at #54, and was invited in. They sat in comfy chairs on opposite sides of the fireplace. Joan had poured herself more white wine and made Paul a stiff gin and tonic.

Paul told Joan how his two friends, Michel Brault and Robin Spry, had won some Canadian Film Awards three weeks before with *Les Ordres*, and *The October Crisis*, both about the War Measures Act. He told his own story of the trade commissioner's kidnapping on Redpath Crescent.

"What film are you trying to get made?"

He thought for a moment, and began to tell her. And then an idea grew in his mind.

* * *

Christmas approached, but now Paul dreaded the season. Dutifully, he flew from Montreal to Los Angeles to be with Matthew. He ate Geneviève's celebration dinner with their son on Christmas Eve, a French Canadian tradition. So Christmas day, Paul was free to spend with Joan and her family. All autumn he had longed to see her. In Paris when searching for finance, he would hold on to any five-franc piece and at the one public telephone on the Champs Elysées that allowed long distance, he'd talk to her for three precious minutes. These calls sustained him while he hustled here and there, arranging meetings, giving out scripts, all in abject frenzy.

A family Christmas with Joan and her children was a delight he had not experienced for a long time. But that night he had to fly to New York, where he would pick up the Royal Air Maroc flight to Marrakesh and meet Glenn, who had spent the autumn in Morocco searching for and preparing locations. As Joan drove Paul to the airport, he got up the courage to ask her, "With everything coming together, I'm going to make a recce trip with my production manager and designer in March to survey locations. It would be great to have a photographer along. Would you like to fly over?"

Joan hesitated.

"I'll send you the ticket," he said hurriedly. "It would cost you nothing. Only two or three weeks," he went on. "Have you ever been to Morocco? You'd love it. I sure do."

Joan took time to respond. "No, it's too complicated. I have four children…"

"I knew you wouldn't answer right away, but could you at least think about it?"

"Of course. But I doubt if I'll manage it."

Such a slim possibility but it sustained Paul through the next month, until he heard that, yes, she would come!

That winter Paul had gotten an advance grant from the CFDC. In March, his new assistant, Stewart Harding, arranged tickets: Ann Pritchard flew in from Paris where she had been staying with Donald and Francine Sutherland; Peter Samuelson, a nephew of the *7Up* cameraman and now a production manager, arrived from London, and Moshe Safdie, wildly busy, had nonetheless agreed to come and help Glenn design the stone-age monument, the Mahal Sokhour, to be built on some Atlas peak.

The little Marrakesh airport was thronged with Moroccans as Paul waited for Joan's flight from New York. Ten minutes before the flight arrived, didn't the generators fail? The whole airport was plunged into darkness.

Paul's anticipation had built all through the winter and had now reached fever pitch. But the Immigration officials would allow no one through — without a light, they could not look into carry-on baggage. Paul was beside himself.

Suddenly, he saw a flashlight. The official motioned the person forward. Paul stared. Joan! The only one with a flashlight in her purse.

Paul cried out, "Joan. I'm here. Come right through!"

But the Immigration Official asked her in halting English to use her flashlight until everyone cleared.

Joan could never put herself first. She had to help. So she held her flashlight while every one of the forty passengers had their cases examined. Paul had to wait. Please God, Paul prayed, don't let the flashlight go out before she gets through.

Happily, it did not, and Joan came forward into his arms. They hugged, and dashed off to meet the others for a glorious never to be forgotten evening.

* * *

At Oukaimeden, a new ski resort, the highest point in the Atlas that could be reached from Marrakech, they surveyed surrounding peaks with Moshe and picked one that had a flat area. Then Moshe flew off to design buildings in Iran, as well as in Jerusalem,

Frobisher Bay, all over.

Paul crammed all five of them into a Renault Cinq, the smallest (and cheapest) of cars, and they climbed the twisting road into the High Atlas, crossed the Tizi n'Tichka Pass, and turned left down a rutted track to Telouet, the empty decaying palace of the *Glaoui*, perfect for Glenn to work his magic and for Anne to design the furnishings. This renowned and evil Pascha of the Atlas, immortalized in Gavin Lambert's *Lords of the Atlas,* had (viciously) ruled the High Atlas and all the South. They went south to Ourzazate, an impoverished desert village with one wide main street, where Peter decided to set the base of *Solstice* operations.

From there they drove up the Dadès Gorge along a dry river bed with now its shallow stream running, so Peter Samuelson had to roll up his trousers and slosh ahead of the car to check for submerged boulders. They then snaked off it up a winding roadway for which Paul had written a frightening car chase.

At the top as the sun set, they turned back. But Glenn exclaimed, "What's that?"

Paul got out his binoculars. "A wall of water!" Two or three feet high, it would smash any car to smithereens. Down it came, plunging along the narrow gorge.

They jumped into the car and raced down, Anne crying, "It's coming, it's coming!"

Indeed, it was coming! Once it struck their little car, they'd be drowned, crushed, killed. Gunning the motor, headlights blazing, Glenn raced ahead of the water. But the flood kept coming. The car, unable to go fast over the rock-strewn riverbed, lost ground. With the women looking anxiously out the back window, Paul offered encouragement. "Don't worry, we'll make it!"

They charged on, the torrent coming ever closer.

"What an expedition!" Paul exulted. "Don't you love it! Excitement, excitement!"

The other four, especially Glenn gripping the steering wheel with whitened fingers, were not quite so enthralled...

The wall of water came closer and closer.

"Hurry, hurry!" Anne screamed.

"I'm trying I'm trying," Glenn gasped.

"He's doing fine!" Paul encouraged.

Suddenly the headlights caught a track sweeping up the bank. Glenn swerved and tore up just in time! The roaring flood swept past. The car stopped. Shivering and shaking, they got out to watch the boulders rumble past.

"No one warned us!" Glenn complained.

"How could they know?" Paul countered.

"I could do without this excitement," a white-faced Peter Samuelson said.

* * *

On the flight back to New York, Paul sat beside Joan. At last he had found what his heart had been seeking for almost half a century. But how to make it work? He screwed up his courage. "Joan, when we get to New York, why not, instead of catching that flight to Los Angeles, fly with me up to Montreal? I can show you where I live."

"Oh no, I could never do that; my children are expecting me. Thanks all the same."

"But at the airport, can't you at least call Bonnie?" Cary O'Neal's sister, only a couple of years older than the children, had been baby-sitting. After landing, Joan did call from a pay phone. Paul stood close by, watching anxiously.

"Bonnie! How's it all going?" She listened. "Oh really? Well, Paul has invited me to see his house in Montreal. I know the kids want me back right away. So I don't think I should go."

She listened and her eyes widened. "What?"

She turned. "She'll ask them. They seem to be having fun."

They both waited, Paul on tenterhooks. And then the answer came.

Joan turned to Paul. "They want me to stay away as long as possible..." She shook her head and smiled as if to say, "Wouldn't you know!"

* * *

As they taxied up Redpath Crescent, Paul could see Joan was impressed by this location. They entered the house with its ample garden. Joan checked the kitchen that Moshe had redesigned with a brick fireplace to warm them when they had breakfast together. The lush dining room was centred by a fine oak Elizabethan table, which Paul had bought from the old Van Horne mansion. They went up the curved staircase with its white plastered arches into a cosy den and then out into the sunroom with all the plants. Then up to the master bedroom with its stunning view over Montreal. Oh yes, a comfortable place, in spite of its five floors.

They spent a week together, Paul showing her his Montreal haunts and walking with her up the mountain road. Glenn was relieved to see his friend relaxed and seemingly happy.

When the time came for Joan to go, on the way to the airport, Paul popped the question he'd been dying to ask ever since Marrakesh. "Joan, what would you think about us... well... marrying? I mean, at the end of the summer?"

Joan took some time thinking it over, but later, the answer turned out to be yes. And so, on September 11, 1976, in the teahouse of Joan's patio, Paul and Joan were joined in holy matrimony.

CHAPTER THIRTY

The couple returned to Morocco, where Joan took some beautiful photographs. They loved the country: its sand-brown buildings made from the very earth around them, the friendly welcoming Berbers, the indigenous inhabitants before the Arab invasions of the seventh century. They'd rented a car and driven all over, working as a team. While Joan photographed, Paul would take Polaroids and hand them to the children, diverting them so that Joan could take pictures unnoticed by crowds that usually followed.

He was always amazed at how his wife blended into the landscape. She was able somehow to make herself invisible. Nobody noticed her — a trick he hadn't learned for himself! She used mostly a silent Leica and later would show Paul the proof sheets, printed in her darkroom from negatives she had developed herself, a hands-on photographer. She would then print her own proof sheets and mark them with a wax pencil; from these, she made 8x10 glossies, the forerunners of her 9x12 gelatin silver prints sold in solo exhibitions across North America and even in

Egypt. She eventually made a book, published by St. Anne's Press.

* * *

"There's a phone message from your aunt's nursing home."

Paul turned to Joan. "Oh?"

"Yes." Joan dropped her eyes, and paused. "Auntie Hilda... "

Paul sat up. He knew she hadn't been well, but had not expected this.

"She'll be cremated, and they'll hold her ashes." She paused again. "I'm sorry."

Back in Montreal for the winter after a summer in Malibu, the couple headed to the Gaspe Coast in Paul's little blue Riley with auntie's ashes.

"I've been hearing so much about your Shigawake home," Joan said as they drove down the wide boring highway toward Quebec City. "I can't wait to see it. I don't know why we've waited so long."

"I guess we've been busy. I can't wait to show it to you." But how would Joan take it? The visit filled him with trepidation. All his childhood, his growing up, was melded into the walls of the Old Homestead. What if she hated it? What would he do then? That question lingered throughout the journey.

Beyond Quebec, as they drove along the St. Lawrence and past Bic with its unusual hills, Joan remarked, "I'm trying to imagine what your old family home will be like." She had taken over the driving.

"It's been there a long time." He grinned. "Big contrast to the shark-infested world of film financing... Mother brought me down from Iron Hill when father went into hospital. I was just a baby."

Joan pulled out to pass a truck. "You never really talked about him. It must have been a difficult childhood, I mean without a father."

"Are you kidding? It was wonderful. I lived with my mother and aunt, and no father came back after work to give me a good hiding, as other dads did. I loved not having a father."

Joan took her eyes off the road to look at him. "Really?" She seemed puzzled.

"Really. To me, it was normal. Better without one, than having to face a disciplinarian every evening."

Joan shook her head. "And all this time, I'd been thinking, poor Paul growing up without a father..."

"No reason to think that. I was fine."

"Did you know how sick he was?"

"He wasn't 'sick'. He had shell-shock."

"Did you know what that was?"

"No, of course not. All I knew was he was in hospital. Caused by the war. Mother went to visit him on the train every Saturday. She'd say he was fine."

"So you never discussed it?"

"No. Why? He was well looked after presumably. Nobody talked about it."

They drove on in silence for a bit. Then Joan said, "I wonder how your mother must have felt."

"Fine, I presume."

"But seeing her husband every weekend..."

"Well, I thought that's what mothers did, visit their husbands on Saturdays if they were in hospital. But she never told me how she felt. We never discussed it."

"Obviously a brave woman."

Paul looked across at Joan and frowned. "Why so brave? What else would she do? Surely not leave him there and never see him."

"Well, helping you see that everything was normal. When it clearly wasn't."

"Who's to say it wasn't? Maybe it wouldn't be for you, because you had a father. It was quite normal for me."

"Are you sure?"

"Well... Okay, I guess when I was in therapy, back when I was with Angela, I do kind of remember spending a lot of time on that, although I was really there to see how to make things work with my wife." He paused. "I suppose I did cry, a bit. But," he went on sharply, "not because of my own childhood. Because I realized how awful his life must have been in that darned hospital. No family. No little son..." His eyes misted over. "Poor guy, I know what I went through when Matthew was taken away from me. Just like him, actually," he realized. "So much worse for him, for sure ..." He sighed. "But this is now, it's over, done: I've sorrowed for him; I've prayed for his soul. You see, in those days no one knew what to do with shell shock, PTSD, as they're starting to call it. All I can say now is I've realized how lucky I am to be Canadian, not having to volunteer for wars, as my father and Uncle Jack did."

And that seemed to put the matter to rest, at least in Joan's mind.

As they were about to pull in at the Old Homestead, Joan had a good view of the house with the maple trees bare of leaves. "I had no idea it was so large!"

"First, let's go to the churchyard, where Auntie will be put down..."

The little cemetery lay behind St Paul's Church, a pretty white-washed wooden building with its red roof and tall belltower. Paul pointed out the white tombstone of his grandparents, and beside it, a small grey marker for his father and Uncle Earle. Being a warm spring day, icicles dripped from the roof and some heaps of snow were melting. Joan walked around the frozen graveyard, looking at the many other Alford tombstones. Then they drove back to the Old Homestead.

"Ted must be out working, so it's just us. Leave the bags, I want to show you around." Paul was excited, but apprehensive.

As customary on the Gaspe, they entered through the back kitchen. Oh boy, thought, Paul, she's not going to like this! Cousin Ted was a bachelor and unlikely to keep the kitchen tidy.

Joan took in the mess and thankfully, went quickly through to the old dining room. "This is original," Paul said proudly, waving his arms, "built a couple of hundred years ago. Against that back wall they had a stone fireplace, but when stoves came in around the middle of the last century, they got one to cook on, front of those steep stairs."

The room had yellowing cupboards along the side wall, blue patterned wallpaper many years old, and a front door that looked out onto the bay. The ceiling was crossed by spindly but strong beams. "Ted's parents opened up the ceiling to expose them; they've been here for a couple of hundred years."

They went through the living room with its new stone fireplace and into the parlour. "This is where I shot the opening scene in *Isabel,* the mother in a casket. When I was young, this was only used by clergymen coming for tea, and for weddings and funerals. Every one of the Alfords was laid out in this room. Otherwise, they never used it."

"Is this part of the original house?"

"No, Ted lifted wallpaper in one corner and found under it newspapers glued to the wall, dated 1886. I guess that's when they added this wing for their growing family."

"1886?" Joan reacted. "Before Los Angeles was really settled. My grandmother's farm in Hollywood was still an orchard then."

"Yep, long, long after the original house was built. When I came back from Oxford, I tried to write a novel here." They went upstairs and Paul showed her the tiny bedrooms. "My grandparents had ten children, you know." They passed through into the large original bedroom above the dining room. Its slanted ceilings followed the contours of the roof. Paul told Joan proudly, "Old Momma and Old Poppa's room. My grandfather was actually born in that bed, I think in the mid 1800s. He died in that bed too, and so did my grandmother. There is where she had all her children, my father being the last." He sat on it. "So, what do you think?"

"I love it all. I'd enjoy fixing it up. When we come for longer..."

Paul's heart leapt. So she might come back with him. Good news.

"Paul, this house has such history." Paul could only nod. "You should..."

"— Make a film about it?" An idea began to grow in his mind. "Or Joan... wouldn't it make a great idea for a novel, too, maybe?"

"You've always wanted to write, you said."

"Yes yes, a novel. Maybe even a whole series of them. What an idea!"

Joan smiled.

AFTERWORD

J ust as Jack Alford, the Pilgrim, was patterned after Col. the Ven. John Almond and Eric Alford, the Gunner, was patterned after my father, Rev. Eric Almond, so this book about Paul Alford is patterned after me. Some may quibble with the form I have chosen, written as it is in continuation of The Alford Saga. I can only say that the other seven books have also been about real characters and based upon real facts, as has this.

My first wife, Angela, died in 2004, but Geneviève and I still go for monthly walks. My lovely wife of forty years, Joan, having given up photography, tends our gardens with fierce dedication. Stephanie, full of *joie de vivre* and energy, grows a fine market garden near Victoria, BC. Marigold and I have lost touch, such a shame, I feel. My son, mentioned herein as a baby, continues to astound me with his energy as he teaches under-achieving students in the LA school district, although, having been raised in Malibu by his mother, he will not be returning to the Gaspe, so The Alford Saga well and truly ends with this book.

In the years after this book ends, I never did get Solstice on but

I continued to make films until the stress brought on by financing the last one in 1990 caused open-heart surgery. That meant I could return to my first love, writing. After spending time at UCLA Extension learning about the novel form (so different from screenplays) I began to write this saga in the Old Homestead in Shigawake. Now, after these eight books with their attendant launches and speaking tours, I am looking forward to a comfortable retirement with Joan in our beach home on the shores of the Pacific, watching our many children and grandchildren grow and flourish, but still returning to my Old Homestead on the Gaspe Coast.

ACKNOWLEDGEMENTS BOOK EIGHT

My mother, to whom I wrote almost every week throughout the 50s and 60s, kept all my letters and thus handed me the means to describe events in such detail. Ann Goddard, the greatest archivist Library and Archives Canada ever had, collected and preserved them, as well as other documents from earlier Almonds. Soon afterwards, she resigned, disheartened by the way in which our once great national repository was being destroyed.

At the CBC archives, now also disbanded by Government cuts, Russ McMillen of film and Brenda Carroll and Janet Muise of photos, provided much information. I hope readers noted that the entire complement of the CBC's Drama Department, only about two dozen of us, turned out two and a half hours of drama a week. Now, with its vast bureaucracy, the CBC does not turn out any.

I am lucky to still have friends among the dancers: that priceless ballerina turned film-maker Veronica Tennant, the sleek and beautiful Myrna Aaron, a tremendous help in all aspects, attractive Colleen Kenny, another charter member of the National Ballet just recently deceased, and the incomparable Karen Kain, now its Director. Choreographer Grant Strate has also been a great help, as has Sally Brayley (now Bliss), Trustee of the Anthony Tudor Ballet Trust, and Adrienne Nevile at the National Ballet Archives. Dance Collections Danse, headed by Miriam Adams and Amy Bowring helped me, as did my step-daughter, Stephanie Leigh, once a National Ballet dancer herself. Writing this, I was again amazed at those exhausting one night stands all over America and Canada. I also deliberately included the lists of plays I saw in New York City to contrast the waste land that Broadway has become.

For the excerpts on Journey, I want to thank Rick Kline, now a major acting coach in Los Angeles. Prof. Paul Piehler, who lives now with Maj-Britt in the warmth of Florida, continues to propagate ideas with his Atlantis Educational Initiatives. I also thank Bert Tougas and Honor Griffiths for their writings in the appendix. Donald Johnston, a friend for fifty years, helped with the passage on the capital cost allowance. Odd that of all the children I chose in 7Up, only one has kept in touch — "Taxi Tony" Walker, loyal throughout the years. In 2011, British critics named it finest documentary of all time.

I want to thank the many readers who went over various drafts, especially Gloria Varley, herself a consummate writer, and John Morrell, both friends for sixty years. Had I written about the last decades of the century, I would have extolled another genius as brilliant as the great Rudi Dorn: Yurij Luhovy, who edited most of my films. He gave my novel the same attention as his prize-winning documentaries on the Ukraine. Rexx King, from my original Writers' Group, proved helpful, too. Tom Farqhuarson, cameraman extraordinaire and his wife Sarah, and also Jim Jones, both of whom worked in CBC's Design department, corrected early facts. Eleanor Fazan, O.B.E., whose book "Fiz" details her enormous career, checked my facts on Stanley Myers and Kenya, and my son Chris checked for misprints and inconsistencies. And I would be remiss without thanking Lynda and Harry Boyd for their hospitality in Toronto over all eight books.

The later drafts were read by Oren Safdie, a playwright of no small distinction, Anne Tait, a film producer and former script assistant, and finally, Shannon Wray, a professional editor and writer herself. Cousin Ted Wright continues to be a stalwart supporter and helped prepare the index. My good friend, himself a brilliant novelist, David Stansfield, did a final consummate editing, and also worked on the index.

I should acknowledge the contribution of McArthur & Co, my first publisher that shut its doors in 2013. Kim McArthur, though often without funds, managed to publish books one to four. Mark Rosin, my excellent advisor and literary executor, kept that relationship on track, and even my more recent dealings. But I doff my hat to my present wonderful team at Red Deer Press.

APPENDICES

Journey Days by Bert Tougas

Stories: I have stories. Stories of every rank and kind. What do you want? Adventure, love, near death experiences, film education, jealousy, conspiracy etc... All the things that went into the most unbelievable experience of a lifetime. That's what "Journey" was to all of us.

In the summer of 1971 I had just graduated college at Loyola with a Bachelor of Arts degree in Communications. It was the best summer of my life.

A friend, Charles Braive, informed me that a feature film was about to be shot in Quebec and that they were looking for "Gofers", today's production assistants, for the preproduction portion in Montreal. He asked if I had a car and I said I did. Well, I didn't. But my retired father certainly did and I cajoled him into lending it to me for the remaining two weeks of prep. It was a nice car. So nice that besides my day-to-day duties as gofer, I kind of became Geneviève Bujold's unofficial chauffeur. So here I was, twenty-one years old, driving around the most beautiful woman in the world, working for the hottest director in town, and actually employed in the film business in my home town. Not bad for a kid from Verdun.

My last duty in "prep" was to pick up a generator from the equipment rental house and drive it up to Tadoussac, where filming on "Journey" was to begin in a week. The plan was to drop off the "gennie", stay overnight and take the bus back to Montreal the next day. A room had been booked for me at the Hotel George and early the next morning I drove out to the location to drop off my load. As I was waiting for a lift back to town I was in awe of all the frantic activity going on around me. I noticed someone signaling me out of the corner of my eye. It was Anne Pritchard, Montreal's top costume designer, with her sleeves rolled up and arms purple up to the shoulders. "Qu'est que tu fait là!"

"I'm going back to Montreal.

"But I only have two days to get all these costumes dyed. How about giving me a hand?"

So that's how the best summer of my life and my career in the film business started. After working with Anne for two days and then three days with Glenn Bydwell, the production designer, who had a loft to finish in the main squared-timbered house which was up first in the shooting schedule, I asked the production manager if I was on the movie or not. I was wearing the same jean shirt and jeans I had come up with thinking I was only there overnight — washing my socks and underwear in the the sink in my room every night. I was in, $75 bucks a week but I had to pay for my room. Deal! (We went on strike later on and our accommodation was picked up). My parents shipped me up some clothes and I was all set.

In those days everybody did everything. I went from production assistant (gofer) to 4th or 5th AD. At night I helped out in the editing room befriending Honor Griffith, who was one of the best in the business. After we started filming I was one of the drivers who dropped off the negative at the airport and picked up the dailies and any actors or equipment that came in on the flight from Montreal. It was a brutal drive along a dirt road and after putting in a 15hr day, we had all we could do to stay awake. John Mckay, a close friend and fellow gofer, flipped his Chevelle one night on the way back, claiming he swerved to get out of the way of a giant rabbit. No one doubted him.

There are dozens of stories that came out of that summer. Here's one of my favorites. Paul was known for his passion for authenticity. All costumes, sets, props and the like had to be the real deal. No half measures. We had a scene to shoot that involved the birthing of a calf. We had set up three cameras but the cow wasn't ready. Over the next week this happened three times. On the fourth attempt, the script supervisor, Monique Champagne, had taken ill (a hangover?) and had to go back to her hotel. I was talked into taking her place and thus followed possibly the worst continuity reports ever penned in the industry.

When the world famous Director of Photography, Jean Boffety, had to leave a few days early, Paul Vanderlinden who was the first AC (Assistant Cameraman) took over and Al Smith became his focus puller. They had let me practice 'dry' magazine loads during the summer and now were allowing me to do it for real. I don't think I'd ever been that scared in my life. I went on to make a career as a Cinematographer, which I'm still practising.

Up to now these have all been stories about me but it was the experience of meeting all these incredible people that made it so unbelievable. On a rare day off we all gathered on a foggy afternoon at Greg Adams cabin right on the beach in the bay of Tadousaac to sing his Ferryboat Song, written there. It became a hit in Canada and propelled Greg to a life-long career as a song-writer.

Bert Tougas became one of Canada's foremost cameramen. When he joined us, he was a tall, stringy lad with a winning personality whom everyone loved. Over the years (he is now in his sixties) he has worked in the camera Department of over a hundred movies and series, been the DP (Director of Photography) of approximately 35 movies and 110 episodes of Television. (PA)

Honor Griffiths, the Editor

Who could forget the night of a raging snow storm that shut down the city, when Paul and Bert (whose jaw dropped at the very idea) donned snowshoes to trek to the Film Board — an expedition that would have been far beyond the realm of likelihood for another soul to even contemplate. For Paul, it was not only an achievable goal, but an exciting adventure. I was, that evening, left warmed by the upstairs fireplace with an unfinished bottle of equally warming red wine, and very content that a third set of snow shoes did not exist.

Perhaps we should reconvene at the original location, including the red wine in my goblet and the logs burning in the fireplace. The blinding snowstorm will simply have to be imagined.

However, it was most certainly referred to as the storm of the century. I remember the snow being 10 or 12 feet deep and the temperature hovering at minus 30 – making it far too dangerous to harness the sled dogs. We said our tearful farewells – there was little hope that you two would survive the journey. I braced myself with more wine and tried to maintain my balance and appear strong. Bert kept muttering something about insanity but his words were drowned out by the howling winds. Unlike many others, I believe the whip in Paul's hand was used only sparingly to urge Bert to greater speed but those details have never been revealed. It was, however, most regrettable that Bert lost his manhood due to severe frostbite.

PS: TO PAUL.

Paul, no eyes sparkled like yours did (mine sometimes bloodshot due to Bert forcing (?) me on pub tours). I can still so clearly see your face lit up with an excitement that would leave me wondering whether I was about to be posed a baffling question, or if you were going to unveil an extraordinary surprise that you could not wait another second to share. Your eyes twinkled with a child-like Christmas morning glee, your optimism and determination were contagious, and there was never the least possibility allowed for disappointment or defeat.

I am grateful for the life lessons that you never preached, but rather were learned by being witness to how you lived so generously, loved so truthfully and inspired all.

Honor Griffith writes:

Camp Journey, with our mentor Paul at the helm, flipped my perspectives and clarified future roads that could never have been imagined, nor realized, otherwise.Two children put an end to those gruelling hours in the film world. Once they were old enough, I formed my own company renovating and redeveloping rental and condominium housing. After 25 years, I sold the company and moved to my heaven on earth home in the beautifully isolated wooded hills of Northumberland County, where nature gently, quietly and very wisely determines the rules. I have, in many ways, happily travelled the Journey back to the days of Tadoussac.

POEMS

MONT ST. HILAIRE
(for Angela)

Muffled angelus through this white town
Sounds the hour of sunset down —
The moon slides slowly out to print the trees
On their books of snow.
                              Orchards
Of silence, sad silent orchestras
Of branch and bole. (Ripe apples sang
My fall away but now they oaken lie
Cellared for some other Adam.) Mute
Are the tongues of wood, the lilting
Tongues those bells of apples tolled in a branching sky
Long since gone by.
            We snowshoed that Sunday, striding
            The tree lanes down; and you laughed
            To tears my fall, your white mittens
            Tiny as mice in your sleighing coat.
            Why aren't there symphonies, you asked,
            For me to dance? Your thoughts
            Crowding the wings to pirouette their joy

For my mind's yearning audience.

But now the apples lurk
In frozen sap; the symphonies are scores
On sheeted snow. Silent our sins
Were unplucked and unknown are festivals
Of fruit and kisses. White as earliest Eve
And orchard snow you dance to other lustres
Than my moon. The choral blossoms throb in roots of ice.

Paul Almond February 1954

THE SOLDIER

If I should die, think only this of me:
That there's some corner of a foreign field
That is for ever England. There shall be
In that rich earth a richer dust concealed;
A dust whom England bore, shaped, made aware,
Gave, once, her flowers to love, her ways to roam,
A body of England's, breathing English air,
Washed by the rivers, blest by suns of home

Rupert Brooke

INDEX A-Z

February 4, 2015

* CMofNB (Charter member of Nation Ballet)
* DbyP (Discovered by Paul)

Aaron, Myrna (b.1935) CMofNB, went on to dance and act abroad, then became a psychologist. *19, 40, 170, 82, 83,116, 170*

Allan, Andrew (1907–1974), head of CBC Radio Drama from 1943 to 1955; later first Artistic Director of the Shaw Festival (1963–1965) and prolific freelance writer and commentator. *178*

Allen, Rita Greer (1918-2010) broadcaster, writer and sculptor. *181, 229, 236*

Allen, Robert (1917-2005) Supervising Producer of *CBC Folio,* then *Festival,* CBC's flagship (90 minute) program of drama, opera and ballet until retirement in *1990. Pt1. passim*

Anouilh, Jean (1910-1987) one of France's most prolific playwrights after World War II.*174, 212, 214, 232*

Appleby, George brilliant film and commercials editor in 50s & 60s. *238, 247*

Apted, Michael CMG (b.1941) prolific British film director, president of the Directors Guild of America. *201-203*

Ashton, Sir Frederick (1904-1988) principal choreographer and director of England's Royal Ballet, which includes about 30 of his ballets. *197*

Auden, W. H. (1907-1973) Anglo-American poet, regarded by many as one of the greatest writers of the 20th century. *28-30*

Aznavour, Charles (b. 1924) French Armenian singer, songwriter, actor, public activist and diplomat, arguably the most famous Armenian of his time. *300*

Balchin, Nigel (1908-1970) English novelist and screenwriter. *90*

Ballantyne, Michael (b. 1931) poet, journalist, editor & translator.*8*

Barry, Ivor (1919-2006) Welsh film and television actor. *171*

Barry, Michael (1910 –1988) TV Producer and head of BBC Drama (1952-61). *156, 158-159*

Bates, Alan CBE (1934 – 2003) English actor in motion pictures and theatre. *229*

Bell, Marilyn (b.1937) swam Lake Ontario and later the English Channel and Strait of Juan de Fuca. *46-47*

Belmondo, Jean-Paul (b.1933) French actor of the New Wave (1960s) whose breakthrough role was in Jean-Luc Godard's *Breathless* (1960). *231*

Berg, Alban (1885-1935) Austrian composer, member of the Second Viennese School with Schoenberg and Webern. *167*

Bernstein, Sydney (1899-1993) media baron who founded Granada Television, one of the original four ITA franchisees, and one of the most successful British production companies in history. *177, 179, 200-202*

Betjeman, John (1906-1984) KBE and CBE. Poet Laureate and lifelong defender of Victorian architecture. *152*

Blackman, Honor (b.1925) English actress, known for her role in *The Avengers* (1962–64), and Bond girl Pussy Galore in *Goldfinger* (1964). *199, 224*

Blake, Katharine (1921– 991) leading actress on CB and then in the UK. *67, 103, 129, 199*

Bluhdorn, Charles (1926-1983) acquired a small auto parts company that eventually grew into Gulf+Western Industries, under whose ownership Paramount went to number 1 in box office with such hits as *The Godfather* and *Chinatown*. *234, 239*

Boffety, Jean (1925-1988) brilliant New Wave cinematographer. *251*

Bonniwell, Charles producer a/c on *Act of the Heart,* later assistant director in Hollywood *254*

Borduas, Paul-Emile (1905-1960) Québec painter born in Saint-Hilaire. *25*

Bourassa, Robert (1933-1996) served roughly 15 years as Provincial Premier. *261*

Boyd, Harry (b.1927) professional hockey player and history teacher. *8, 47, 123-125*

Braithwaite Dennis columnist for the *Globe and Mail* and the *Toronto Star* in the sixties and seventies. *155*

Brault, Michel (1928-2013) Canadian cinematographer and leading film director. *213, 215, 307*

Brayley, Sally (bliss) (b.1937) dancer with Nat Ballet and many others, Trustee of the Antony Tudor Ballet Trust170

Bridges, Beau (b.1941) American actor, recipient of many awards. *300*

Brittain, Vera (1893-1970) British writer and pacifist, author of best-selling 1933 memoir *Testament of Youth. 13*

Britten, Benjamin (1913-1976) English composer, conductor and pianist, central figure of 20th-century British classical music, best-known works: *Peter Grimes* (1945), *War Requiem* (1962) and *The Young Person's Guide to the Orchestra* (1945). *10*

Bujold, Genevieve (b.1942) DbyP, went on to star in over 65 films. *Pt II. Passim*

Burton, Richard (1925-1984) Welsh stage

and cinema actor talent, nominated seven times for an Academy Award, one of the highest-paid actors in the world. *151, 255*

Bydwell, Glenn (b.1948) award winning production designer, commercial director, photographer and architect. *263, 275*

Caldwell, Zoe OBE (b.1933) DbyP Australian, after CBC went on to win Tony Award four times. *182-183, 185-186*

Campbell, Norman (1924-2004) CBC Producer, adapting ballet for television, two Emmy awards, and wrote *Anne of Green Gables. 167*

Carle, Gilles O.C., GOQ, (1928-2009) director, screenwriter and painter. *247, 289*

Carter, Peter (1933-1982) assistant director on many Canadian TV series and director of *The Rowdy Man* and other movies. *164-165, 235-237, 251, 272-273*

Catlin, Shirley (Baroness Williams) (b.1930) founded the Social Democratic Party (SDP) in 1981 leader of the Liberal Democrats in the House of Lords, Professor Emerita of Electoral Politics at Harvard University. *13*

Chilcott, Barbara (b.1923) a founder of the Crest Theatre, made her West End debut in June 1949 then established herself as one of Canada's leading actors. *42, 92*

Champlin, Charles (1926–2014) dean of film critics in Los Angeles. *251*

Clark, Susan (b.1946) DbyP, went on to become a Hollywood star.

Clayton, Jack (1921-1995) British film director, of international prominence, won Oscar with *Room at the Top. 162*

Clurman, Harold (1901-1980) American theatre director and influential drama critic, a founder of the Group Theatre Author of seven theatre books. *175*

Cochrane, Elspeth (1919-2015) one of the most successful and respected theatrical agents, her career spanned over half a century. Assisted in setting up the Stratford Festival Theatre. *179, 182, 228*

Coghill, Neville (1899-1980) fellow of Exeter College, Oxford, with a bust in the college, a noted director and an associate of "The Inklings." *53-54*

Cohen, Leonard CC. COG, (b.1934) singer-songwriter, musician, poet, and novelist. *31, 271*

Connery, Sean (b.1930) Scottish actor with many awards, often called "The Greatest Living Scot." *182, 185*

Conway, Susan (b.1952) actress. *198*

Craig, Michael (b.1928) JA Rank star and stage actor and writer. *176*

Crainford, Leonard Head of Design for CBC. *225*

Crawley, Budge (1911-1987) director and photographer of many notable documentaries, founded Crawley Films in 1946 which made innumerable films, winning Canadian and international awards. *162-163, 166, 228, 232-233*

Crist, Judith (1922-2002) American film critic and academic, appeared on *Today* show from 1964 to 1973 and author of various books. *246*

Cross, James (CMG) (b.1921) former British diplomat kidnapped by Front de libération du Québec (FLQ) and Under-Secretary in Department of Trade and Industry. *260-261*

Crutchley, Rosalie (1920-1997) English actress, stage début in 1932 later on TV and screen. *157*

Daley, James (1918-1978) fine theater, film and television actor. *207*

Davies, Sarah Welsh actress, performed in Canada in the 1950s and later in the UK. *98, 155*

Davis, Donald (1928-1998) Canadian actor and main founder of the Crest Theatre in Toronto. *42-43*

Day Lewis, Cecil (1904-1972) CBE, Poet Laureate from 1968 until 1972. Father of Daniel. *151*

de Broca, Michelle film producer from 1966 for 40 years. *229-230, 292*

de Broca, Philippe (1933-2004) directed 30 commercially successful feature films. *229-231, 300*

de Valois, Ninette (1898-2001) danced Serge Diaghilev's *Ballets Russes*, later established The Royal Ballet, widely regarded as the "godmother" of English ballet. *22, 39*

Dee, Ruby (1922-2014) award-winning actress, poet, playwright, screenwriter, journalist and activist. *222*

Desruelles, Michel makeup artist on *Isabel*. *236*

Dodds, Noel (1932-2012) superb film editor with CBC and later on a director, writer, and filmmaker. *191, 198, 206, 240*

Donat, Peter (b.1928) Canadian-American actor with many roles on American television. *125*

Dorn, Rudi (1926-2011) Canada's finest television drama designer of the 50s and 60s, worked on many masterpieces in the Golden Age of Canadian Television Drama. *Pt. I. passim*

Douet, Johnny Quebecois grip on many films. *253*

Doyon, Jean (b.1934) Québec actor. *216, 232*

Drapeau, Jean (1916-1999) Mayor of Montreal mostly 1954 to 1986, responsible for Montreal Metro system, Place des Arts concert hall, and conceiving Expo 67, etc. *258*

Dudek, Louis (1918-2001) Important Montreal poet and McGill Prof. *16*

Dufaux, Georges (1927-2008) Director of Photography *235, 247, 251*

Duncan, Chester (1913-2002) Manitoban pianist, composer, Professor of English, and radio, television, book and cinema critic. *155*

Duncan, Ronald (1914-1982) Poet, dramatist, journalist, man of letters *8-9, 50, 92, 190*

Elliott, Denholm (1922-1992) English film, television and theatre actor with more than 120 film and television credits. *149*

Endersby, Ralph (b.1950) actor and producer, began on *The Forest Rangers,* adding writing and directing later. *198*

Espie, Tom PhD playwright, bureaucrat in Canadian Federal services. *12-14, 156*

Evans, Lewis (1911-1988) English teacher for four decades at BCS. *262*

Evans, Maurice (1901-1989) English actor noted for Shakespearean characters. *130*

Farquharson, Tom (b.1934) in PA's view, the finest live TV cameraman ever. *170, 227-228*

Ferry, Vic technical producer in 50s and 60s, especially on Festival, *226-227*

Ffrancon-Davies, Gwen (1891-1992) actress and centenarian: stage debut in 1911, and final appearance in a teleplay at 100. *157*

Flannery, Seamus production designer on films and live TV in UK, US and CBC. *177*

Fonda, Jane (b.1937) actress, writer, political activist, a two-time Academy Award winner. *272*

Fonteyn, Margot DBE (1919-1991) widely regarded as one of the greatest classical ballet dancers of all time, appointed Prima Ballerina Assoluta of The Royal Ballet by Queen Elizabeth II. *38, 197*

Forman, Milos (b.1932) Czech film director with many awards, screenwriter, actor, and professor, came to North America in 1968. *231*

Foster, Jill actress with many roles for CBC and U.S. networks in 50s & 60s. *98, 128, 165*

Fournier, Claude (b.1931) film director, screenwriter, editor and cinematographer. One of the forerunners of the Cinema of Quebec. Founded Rose Films. *247, 251*

Franca, Celia (1921-2007) founder in 1951 of The National Ballet of Canada and its artistic director for 24 years. *39, 82-83, 164*

Francks, Don (b.1932) actor, vocalist and jazz musician. *163*

Freedman, Harry (1922-2005) Polish Canadian composer, English hornist, music educator, and composer in residence at the Toronto Symphony. *250, 254*

Freedman, Lewis (1926-1992) television producer and program executive for CBS and PBS, with 45-year career that won many Emmy and Peabody Awards. *97*

Freeland, Brian (b.1925) head of Religious programs for CBC, now Assistant Priest (at 90) at St Thomas's Anglican Church. *90, 123, 137, 188, 236*

French, Hugh (1910-1976) top British agent in Hollywood, with clients Richard Burton, James Mason, Marilyn Monroe, Yves Montand, Jane Fonda, Terence Rattigan Nigel Balchin, Christopher Isherwood, Margaret Leighton, Patrick Macnee (and PA). *148, 160-161*

French, Robin (b.1936) former agent, V.P. for Domestic Production Paramount. *148, 160-162*

Gander, Mogens freelance cameraman worked for CBC in 60s and 70s. *206*

Garnett, Gale (b.1942) New Zealand-born Canadian singer, actress and writer. *275, 294*

Gault, Hamilton (1882-1958) Brigadier-General The Rt. Hon. M.P., D.S.O., raised at his own expense Princess Patricia's Canadian Light Infantry, vigilantly defended Mont Saint-Hilaire from expropriation by mining interests and bequeathed it to

McGill University. *25*

Gibson, Luke (b.1946) singer guitarist and songwriter, also member of Luke and the Apostles. *272, 275, 280*

Godin, Gerald (1938-1994) Quebec poet and politician. *261*

Goldoni, Lelia (b.1936) prolific American actress, known for John Cassavetes's *Shadows* (1959). *199*

Goulet, Robert (1933-2007) American singer and actor of French Canadian ancestry. *164*

Greenberg, Harold OC, CQ (1930-1996) hugely important film producer and entrepreneur, founder of Astral companies. *237, 273*

Greene, David (1921-2003) British television and film director, mainstay of CBC Drama Department later the US and the UK. *56-59, 67, 91, 129, 149*

Greene, Eileen graduated from Edinburgh University, joined CBC as a script assistant, later married David Greene, moved to the UK in the 60s. *149*

Gregory, Dick (b.1932) American comedian, civil rights activist, social critic, writer and entrepreneur. *222*

Griffith, Honor (b.1946) film editor and property manager. *286*

Grimaldi, Joe finest mixer of films in Canada for many years. *240, 289*

Groulx, Georges (1922-1997) French Canadian actor and comedian. *16, 218*

Guthrie, Tyrone (1900-1971) director, founder of the Stratford Festival and the Guthrie Theater in Minneapolis. *23, 26*

Harris, Rosemary (b.1927) English actress. Four-time Drama Desk Award winner and nine-time Tony Award nominee, Emmy and Golden Globe award winner. *141, 164*

Harrison, Joan (1907-1994) English film producer, *Alfred Hitchcock Presents* and screenwriter, *Jamaica Inn, Rebecca, Suspicion*. *148, 149*

Harron, Donald (1924-2015) Canadian comedian, actor, director, journalist, author, playwright and composer. *147, 186*

Harwood, Vanessa (b.1947) prima ballerina,choreographer, artistic director, teacher, actor, retired from the National Ballet in 1987. *167*

Hayes, Elton (b.1929) dairy farmer, horse breeder, and sometime actor. *269, 273*

Heneghan, Maureen costume designer, worked for the BBC and for the CBC. *157*

Henry, Martha (Buhs) DbyP (b.1938) stage, film, and television actress, best known for Stratford Festival. *176, 182, 187, 207*

Heroux, Denis OC (b.1940) film director and producer, co-founder of Alliance Entertainment. *247*

Hewitt, Tim (1928-2004) provocative television journalist and creator of *World In Action*. *200*

Hitchcock, Alfred (1899-1980) English film director and producer, who moved to Hollywood in 1939. *148-149, 166*

Hodgson, Emma casting director for Radio Canada in Montreal. *212-213*

Hofsess, John fine film critic for *Macleans* etc. *259*

Homolka, Oscar (1898-1978) Austrian film and theatre actor. *166*

Houghton, Norris (1909-2001) renowned theatre visionary and major force in creating the "off-Broadway" movement also a distinguished scholar and teacher, and prolific author. *33, 84*

Howells, Dave sound engineer the NFB and on many films. *251*

Hutt, William CC OOnt MM (1920-2007) distinguished Canadian actor of stage, television and film. *186*

Hyland, Frances OC (1927-2004) well-known Canadian theatre, film and TV actress, who began in the West End opposite John Gielgud.*75, 77, 168, 182*

Iseler, Elmer OC (1927-1998) conductor of the Toronto Mendelssohn Choir and founder of the Festival Singers of Canada and the Elmer Iseler Singers. *251*

Isherwood, Christopher (1904-1986) important English novelist. *32*

Israel, Charles (1920-1999) US born Canadian novelist, scriptwriter and columnist. *90, 207, 228*

Ivings, Jacqueline CMofNB soloist with National Ballet. *170, 185*

Jago, Syme actress, began in *The Forest Rangers (1963)*. *198*

Jarrott, Charles (1927-2001) British film and television director who began at the CBC. *255*

Johns, Cec technical producer for CBC Drama Department. *105*

Julien, Pauline CQ (1928-1998) singer, songwriter, actress, feminist activist and Quebec sovereigntist. *261*

Jutra, Claude (1930-1986) film director, actor, and writer. The Prix Jutra was named in his honor. *215, 255*

Kain, Karen CC (b.1951) prima ballerina, former President of Canada Council, Artistic Director of the National Ballet of Canada. *167*

Kaplan, Hank (1926-2005) CBC Drama director and later in London and New York. *70-71, 131, 199, 233*

Katz, Joel producer and sometime executive at Universal Pictures. *252-253*

Kenny, Colleen (1933-2014) CMofNB, soloist and then a nurse. *19, 82, 116, 170*

Kline, Rick (b.1948) foremost Hollywood TV acting teacher. *274, 286*

Knapp, Budd (1925?-1982) important actor with CBC. *198*

Kotcheff, Ted (b.1931) film and television director, who began at CBC. *129-131, 224, 232*

Kozlik, Paul DbyP went on to found a theatre in Los Angeles. *226*

Kraemer, Franz (1914-1999) CBC Festival music producer. *167*

Kyasht, Lydia (1885-1959) dancer and teacher. *38*

Lalonde, Donat gardener on Redpath Crescent. *260-261*

Lamberts, Heath OC (1941-2005) DbyP, went on to star in the Shaw Festival and Stratford, and on Broadway. *187*

Lang, Jennings (1915-1996) film producer, screenwriter and Universal Executive. *256-257*

Langbord, Eva (1910-1999) casting director at CBC and former Broadway actress. *50-52, 56, 212-213*

Langham, Michael (1919-2011) actor and director, Artistic Director at Stratford (1956-1967) and director of the Juilliard School, *224*

Laporte, Pierre (1921-1970) lawyer, journalist and Deputy Premier and Minister of Labour of Quebec. *261*

Layton, Irving (1912-2006) wild and widely known poet. *30-31*

Leacock, Stephen (1869-1944) political scientist, writer, and humourist. At one time the most widely read English-speaking author in the world. *243*

Learned, Michael (b.1939) actress, won record four Primetime Emmy Awards. *228*

Leblanc, Diane (b.1943) DbyP, went on to become important theatre director. *183*

Leduc, Ozias (1864-1955) painter, born in Saint-Hilaire. *25*

Lehmann, John (1907-1987) poet, man of letters, distinguished editor, founded *New Writing* and *The London Magazine*. *29*

Leigh, Angela (1926-2004) CMofNB, principal dancer, and artist and designer.passim

Leigh, Stephanie (b.1949) dancer, market gardener and fitness guru. *Pt. I passim*

Leighton, Margaret (1922-1976) foremost theatre star in the West End for many years.*149*

Lesley, Carole (1935-1974) actress and "blonde bombshell." *177*

Leyrac, Monique OC, CQ (b.1928) Québec singer and actress. *250, 255*

Linzee, Lewis editor with Granada TV. *203*

Lloyd, Norman (b.1914) actor, producer, director (roughly eight decades) and Associate Producer on *Alfred Hitchcock Presents*. *148, 149, 151*

Lowenstein, Oscar London Theatre impresario. *10*

Mackie, Philip (1918-1985) British film and television screenwriter. *204*

Maclean, Ross (1925-1987) important CBC TV producer. *198, 206*

Macnee, Patrick (b.1922) actor, began in UK then CBC, later US & UK, especially known as John Steed in *The Avengers*. *42, 67-69 160*

MacNeice, Louis CBE (1907–1963) Irish poet and playwright. *152*

Maddox, Diana (b.1926) Welsh actress and writer, began on CBC Television in the 50s and 60s. *155*

Malle, Louis (1932-1995) French film director, screenwriter, and producer, both

French and English language films. *231, 250*

Markle, Fletcher (1921-1991) Canadian actor, screenwriter, television producer and director. *206*

Marleau, Louise (b.1944) distinguished Quebec actress. *213*

Maxwell, Roberta (b.1942) DbyP, went on to star on Broadway and West End. *178*

McCallum, Neil (1929-1976) British-Canadian actor. *85, 106, 209*

McDougall, Gordon Scottish Australian-based theatre actor and director and television actor. *201, 203*

McKeehan, Gary actor, and member of Perth County Conspiracy. *275*

McLaren, Norman (1914-1987) award-winning animator and film director in NFB, pioneer in animation and filmmaking. *198*

Michell, Keith (b.1929) Australian television and film star. *177*

Millington, Olwyn script assistant. *74-75*

Minnelli, Liza (b.1946) actress, singer and dancer, daughter Judy Garland and Vincente Minnelli. *233, 239*

Mitchell, Jim A.C.E. (b.1929) prolific film editor and later professor. *255*

Molson, John (1896-1977) brewery owner and philanthropist. *219*

Montand, Yves (1921-1991) major French acting and singing star, born in Italy. *221, 223*

Moreau, Jeanne (b.1928) award-winning

French actress, screenwriter and director. *231, 250*

Myers, Stanley (1930-1993) British film composer (60 plus films) who wrote "Cavatina." *12-13, 113, 180*

Narizzano, Silvio (1927-2011) film and television director. Began at CBC, emigrated to the UK, best known for *Georgy Girl* (1966). *70, 131, 199, 232*

Nesbitt, Cathleen (1888-1982) British actress of stage, film and television. *209*

Nichol, Donna film editor. *255*

Oliphant, Betty (1918-2004) ballet mistress for the National Ballet of Canada and founded the National Ballet School of Canada in 1959. *114, 167*

Owen, Don (b.1935) film director, writer and producer, subject of a retrospective at the 2005. *247-248*

Page, P.K, CC OBC FRSC (1916-2010) poet, novelist, scriptwriter, playwright, essayist, journalist, librettist, teacher and artist. *31*

Parkes, Gerard (1924-2014) award-winning Irish Canadian actor. *235, 247*

Pecetto, Mme. nanny for Matthew Almond. *Pt. II passim*

Pelletier, Gilles OC (b.1925) award-winning French Canadian actor. *163*

Perrault, Pierre (1927-1999) Québécois documentary film director (20 films). *215*

Phillips, Stevie (Stephanie) New York agent. *233, 239, 300*

Piehler, Paul (b.1929) world authority on

allegory. *262, 281, 287*

Pinsent, Gordon CC FRSC (b.1930) television, theatre and film actor. *198, 273, 289*

Pinter, Harold (1930-2008) Nobel Prize-winning English playwright, screenwriter, director and actor. *178-179, 180, 188, 205*

Porteous, Timothy CM (b.1933) Canadian administrator headed Canada Council and the Ontario College of Art and Design. *252*

Poulton, Ron TV critic for *Toronto Telegram* and News Director at CFTO-TV in the 50s. *155*

Pritchard, Anne DbyP, went on to become award-winning production and costume designer, *Act of the Heart, Journey. 251, 258*

Prizak, Mario (1922-2012) director on CBC festival. *167, 181*

Rain, Douglas (b.1928) important actor on stage and TV. *Pt. I passim*

Redford, Robert (b.1936) actor, director, producer, environmentalist, philanthropist, and founder of the Sundance Film Festival. TIME called him one of the "Most Influential People in the World." *233, 239-240, 249-250*

Reed, Oliver (1938-1999) British actor. *271-272*

Reid, Kate OC (1930-1993) long and varied career on film, television and stage in both Canada and the United States. *168, 176*

Resnais, Alain (1922-2014) award-winning French film director. *221, 223, 231, 251*

Rhodes, Donnelly (b.1937) DbyP went on

to play in Stratford and in many films. *187*

Richardson, Tony (1928-1991) theatre and film director and producer (five decades). *50, 113, 232*

Robins, Toby (1931-1986) beautiful actress of film, stage and television. *89, 132-133, 222*

Safdie, Moshe (b.1938) Israeli/Canadian/American architect, urban designer, educator, and author, created Habitat *67.268, 309*

Safdie, Nina wife of Roch Carrier, close friend of PA. *268*

Samuels, Maxine (1922-2001) producer, began *The Forest Rangers* (1963) and *Seaway* (1965). *198*

Samuelson, David (b.1924) fine cameraman and entrepreneur. 201

Sarrazin, Michael (1940-2011) DbyP went on to star in Hollywood films. *218*

Savard, Emile fine craftsman in Tadoussac Quebec. *269*

Schaefer, George (1920-1997)] distinguished director of television and Broadway theatre from the 1950s to the 1990s. *239*

Schneider, Maria (1952-2011) French actress known for important English roles. *300*

Scott, F.R. (1899-1985) Canadian poet, intellectual and constitutional expert, helped found the CCF, won two G-Gs. *30*

Shatner, William (b.1931) actor, writer, director, and comedian. Won two Emmys and a Golden Globe. *27, 174*

Shebib, Don (b.1938) film director, writer, producer and editor. *259*

Shoenfeld, Joe (1907-1988) head of William Morris Agency Film Dept. *302*

Smith, Lois (1916-2000) important PR person with clients such top stars as Marilyn Monroe, Robert Redford, Martin Scorsese, Rosie O'Donnell, and Meryl Streep. *20-21, 40, 140, 246*

Smith, Maggie CH, DBE (b.1934) DbyP went on to substantial career in theatre and movies. *69*

Soloviov, Nikolai (1910-c.1980) production designer for CBC after *Alexander Nevsky* 1938 with Eisenstein. *55, 95, 225*

Somers, Harry (1925-1999) influential and innovative contemporary Canadian composer, founding member of the Canadian League of Composers (CLC). *198*

Spence-Thomas, Patrick (1933-2008) sound engineer on films. *278-279*

Spencer, Michael director, creator of the CFDC/Telefilm Canada. *238-239, 252, 273*

Spender, Stephen (1909-1995) KBE, CBE. Seventeenth Poet Laureate & Consultant in Poetry to the U.S. Library of Congress. *152*

Spry, Robin (1939-2005) filmmaker of documentaries and television producer. *307*

Sterke, Jeanette (b.1934) DbyP Czech-English actress with long career in UK. *177*

Stevens, Robert (1920-1989) film and television director. *149*

Strange, Marc (1942-2012) DbyP went on to star in *The Beachcombers* and a folk singer, songwriter, poet, TV director and successful mystery writer. *235*

Strate, Grant (1927) CMofNB, professor emeritus, dancer, choreographer of 50 ballets guest teacher at the Juilliard School founder of Canada's first degree program in dance at York (1970) and director of Simon Fraser's Centre for the Arts (1980-89) *20, 63, 125, 185*

Sutherland, Donald (b.1935) Canadian actor whose film career spans fifty years. *199, 250, 254, 308*

Tassé, Francois (b.1938) Québécois actor. *232, 255*

Taylor, Elizabeth DBE (1932-2011) one of the great screen actresses of Hollywood's Golden Age. *255*

Tennant, Veronica CC, FRSC (b.1946) prima ballerina and film producer and director. *167*

Thomas, Caitlin (1913-1994), wife of Dylan Thomas, wrote *Leftover Life to Kill* 152

Thomas, Dylan (1914-1953) Welsh poet and writer, author of *Under Milk Wood.* *5, 33, 155, 178, 229*

Thomas, Powys (1926-1977) Welsh actor of CBC roles, co-founded Canada's prestigious National Theatre School *123, 155, 171, 187*

Till, Eric (b.1929) English film and television director. *168, 181, 226*

Tougas, Bert (b.1950) important director of photography. *285-286, 288*

Trudeau, Pierre (1919-2000) one of the

greatest Canadian Prime Ministers. *285-286, 288*

Tundo, Matt assistant camera on *The Dark Did Not Conquer*, then cameraman with many credits. *188*

Turner, John (b.1929) lawyer and politician, 17th Prime Minister of Canada. *301*
Vernon, John (1932-2005) Canadian actor with a career in Hollywood. *272, 275, 278, 280*

Vigneault, Gilles GOQ (b.1928) poet, publisher and singer-songwriter: "Mon pays" and "Les gens de mon pays." *254*

Von Sydow, Max (b.1929) actor, *Commandeur des Arts et des Lettres* and *Chevalier de la Légion d'honneur. 300*

Walker, Tony (b.1956) DbyP known for his work on the Up series. *201*

Wallis, Hal (1898-1986) film producer: *Casablanca* (1942), connected with Paramount Pictures. *251*

Wasserman, Lew (1913-2002) talent agent and studio executive, head of Universal Pictures. *257*

Waxman, Al (1935-2001) Canadian actor and director of over 1,000 productions on radio, television, film, and stage. *235*

Webb, Phyllis (b.1927) poet and radio broadcaster, writer of stature in Canadian letters. *31*

Webster, Hugh actor, many roles on CBC. *171*

Welles, Orson (1915-1985) consistently ranked as one of the all-time greatest film makers. *300-301*

Weyman, Ron (1915-2007) producer, author, and director NFB and CBC, 1954-80. *117, 229*

White, Leonard (b.1916) producer and director, London's Armchair Theatre, *The Avengers* and Armchair Mystery Theatre. *222*

Winchester, Jesse (1944-2014) American musician and songwriter opposed to the Vietnam War. *271-272*

Winsten, Archer (1905-1997) movie reviewer at *The Post*, called dean of critics. *246*

Wright, Teresa (1918-2005) American actress. Two Academy Awards and three Emmy nominations. *207, 228*

Wyre, John (1941-2006) percussionist, composer, and music educator. *288*

Dane, (Zahab) Lawrence (b.1937) character actor and film producer. *163*

Zuperko, Stephanie artist and psychologist. *31-33, 36*

Paul Almond in 1963, on whom Paul Alford is based

Paul Almond began his career producing and directing over 120 television dramas for the CBC in Canada, the BBC, ABC and Granada TV in England (where he created the landmark documentary *7Up*) and many other networks in the United States. His numerous awards include 12 Genies (Canadian Academy Awards) including Best Feature Director and Best TV Director, a Hollywood Golden Globe Nomination for Best Foreign Picture and another by his peers in the DGA as Best Feature Director. He has written or adapted a dozen plays for television and five screenplays for motion pictures, as well as having made pictures for such major studios as Paramount, Universal and MGM. His trilogy starring Genevieve Bujold, *Isabel*, *Act of the Heart*, and *Journey*, is considered part of the Canadian film canon. A retrospective of his films toured Canada in 2000-2001.

Paul Almond was recently appointed to his country's highest honour, the Order of Canada, and received a Lifetime Achievement Award from the Directors Guild of Canada. In 1990 he turned to full-time writing, and recently began publishing novels in The Alford Saga, romantic adventures from 1800-2000.